The Orphan

a novel

JAMES LLOYD

Pedestal Key Publishing
13250 Keylime Boulevard
West Palm Beach, FL 33412

Book design by Maureen Cutajar
www.gopublished.com

ISBN: 979-8-9860003-0-5 (paperback)

❧ Prologue ☙

"I'M COMING. HOLD ON!" He shouted at the aging but colorful transit bus as though the driver could actually hear him from so far away. Its busy collection of billboards seemed to be tattooed over every square inch of its skin. The driver wheeled sharply into the bus stop next to an empty bus shelter, needing to wait a while on his next passenger. He was running at full speed before his shoes, slick with layers of mud from a nearby puddle, caused him to skid on the dampened pavement before coming to a stop. The doors from the bus swung open sharply with a familiar rattle. Their decorative glass inserts almost cracking from the turbulence. He kicked the excess mud from his shoes, wiped them on the grass, and then moved quickly onto the first step with barely enough free digits to grip the safety rail. His other foot was still firmly planted on the pavement until he suddenly switched baggage from one hand to completely free the other, pulling himself up onto the platform. Vick, the driver, stared impatiently and gunned the engine, obviously irritated as to why this particular passenger keeps running late, and holding him up; his tone confirmed it. "This is the 4th day in a row Omar. You going for the record tomorrow?"

He looked at Omar with chastising eyes that pleaded his intolerance for it. Omar recoiled with a little hostility of his own—"Just drive the bus man!"

Vick glared at him through his rear view mirror while Omar was getting ready to take his seat. He and Omar had at least been civil with one another. They had chatted more as time went by. Swapping stories about their exploits, as guys do sometimes, but unable to boast of any real conquests. That exchange was just another familiar wrinkle that would eventually work itself out. The bus wheeled out of the bus stop in a hurry. Vick seemed less concerned about the comfort of his passengers from the way he plowed through the pot holes in the road. A sure sign he was at least venting a little. Some of the passengers were tickled from being tossed around so much. It must have seemed almost like a theme park ride to some of them. Omar wasn't among them though. He clutched his satchel tightly, and kept the other bag close to his body as if guarding with his life, the only things he really owned. He wore a blank stare while his eyes stayed fixed on the outside. It was a look that announced he was being transported to another place for the moment, and the other passengers need not bother invading his space. He then sat crouched a little, stroking his new beard several times but not really conscious of it. Rupert, another regular rider sitting across from him, decided to take the plunge and asked, "Are you o.k. Omar?"

Omar replied, "What? I'm sorry I didn't hear you."

"I just asked if you were ok. You seem to be somewhere else."

"Oh, yeah—I'm ok. Just things on my mind I guess. Don't let it bother you." Before Omar could return to nursing his woes, Rupert decided to try and strike up a conversation, again. It would be just another attempt out of many that previously failed.

"What did you think about those U.S. track & field teams in the Olympics? They looked like the best we've had in a while. A lot of endorsements should come from that group don't you think?"

"I'm sorry. I'm—I didn't really follow the games this summer." He hung his head, stroking his beard more vigorously now and staring at the floor as if he was looking for loose change.

Rupert asked, "Wasn't that your sport in school? The 100 meters right?"

"Yeah, that's right."

"You said they called you meteor man wasn't it? I'd hear you and Vick talk about it sometimes."

"That was a long time ago man." He folded his arms and turned away from him.

"What happened? You just lost interest?" Rupert was trying to at least scale the wall of indifference Omar had erected for himself, but it was to no avail.

Omar replied, "Look, I'd rather not talk about it, ok?" He turned to Rupert and said sharply, "It's history, Ok!"

Rupert turned in his seat with eyes forward and silent for the remainder of the trip; wondering what he had done to draw what seemed like enemy fire, when he was only trying to be friendly. He couldn't really understand why Omar avoided having conversations with him, but seemed to open up with Vick most of the time. Rupert is a software specialist, with his own business, who was riding the bus temporarily while he shopped for another car. He was in the process of searching for bigger office space, when he decided to suspend the search until his transportation situation was settled. He loaned his car to his sister who suddenly lost hers in a fire about a month before, and decided her need was greater than his at the moment. He was in his mid-thirties. Well groomed, tactful, and courteous which shouldn't have branded him a 'pariah', but in Omar's world of miscues, miss-hits, and lost opportunities, he might as well have been. He reminded Omar of what he could have been, and the 'slings and arrows' from his misfortunes were the proverbial thorns in his flesh that gouged even deeper when he compared his life with someone like Rupert's. So, his solution was to avoid the contact altogether, pretending to insulate himself from the sting of failure. Trying not to own the shame that seemed to hang around him like traces of a pungent odor. Another rider named Micki, was sitting behind him. They always seemed to end up close to each other on the bus. She leaned forward and carefully placed her slender, well-manicured fingers on top of the seat backrest; then gently rested her chin on top of them so as not to disturb her handiwork. As usual, she came calling once she got a glimpse of Omar's newspaper.

"Are you done reading the Society page Omar?"

"Micki, you're like clockwork. Can't you pull that up on your I-Phone?" He pulled the three page section and handed it to her.

She said, "Thank you, sir", in an adolescent tone of voice. "Anyway, my phone's on lockdown right now."

"You mean your bill's past due"—His tone was unapologetic—"What do you see in that stuff anyway?" She playfully shoved him in his back. Everyone else was still quiet and unaware of what was going on between the two of them, but Micki felt she and Omar had a pretty good rapport with one another.

"It's not 'stuff' Mr. Duncan. One day you're gonna see my picture on that page with me showcasing my own salons, and my own charity work too."

"Yeah, right."

"Don't hate. You've heard that phrase, 'Plan the work, and then work the plan'; well that's exactly what I'm doing."

Vick slowed for his turn onto Wisconsin Street on the way to his first stop. It had started to rain pretty heavy again and Omar remembered he didn't think to bring his umbrella. When the bus pulled into the bus stop, two new passengers exchanged places with Rupert and Micki. They happened to work in the same plaza and were getting off. Micki threw up her hand to say goodbye to the other passengers. "Have a great day everybody! "

Rupert waved goodbye as well, but irritated over Omar's abrasiveness. Everyone seemed to return the courtesy, except Omar. Rupert exited first, taking Micki by the hand, like the gentleman that he always was, making sure she didn't lose her footing. Both of their umbrellas opening almost at the same time before leaving the bus shelter. Omar watched with amusement as they walked hurriedly in opposite directions. The rain beating down, and the water falling harmlessly to the ground around them. The envelope of protection doing what it was designed to do. He thought to himself sarcastically, 'I guess they just couldn't run the risk of melting in front of their fans; Amazing'. Then shaking his head in what seemed to be obvious contempt he thought, 'What's the big deal over a little rain anyway?' For something that seemed so mundane, was also quite telling in Omar's case. Things like that he always seemed to take for granted. It was the little things, and attention to details that just didn't seem to be part of his DNA— *Or could it be that something, or someone, had robbed him of the will to embrace it?*

He sat back in his seat when the bus pulled out again. He then had a few more minutes to think about Rupert's decision to put his expansion on hold after willingly giving up his car to help his sister. Then there was Micki's dream of opening her own chain of salons, while establishing her charitable work. Their paths were quite different, but they shared one common thread; they were both focused and fully committed to whatever they were trying to accomplish. His stop was next but the rain hadn't let up any. When Vick pulled into the bus stop, he saw Omar already standing and only a few steps from him. He turned toward the door, watching Omar from the corner of his eyes and said, "You have a good one Mr. Duncan."

Omar responded, "Likewise," after managing only a hint of a smile. He stood at the door for a moment with his paper over his head, thinking how best to negotiate his trip through the heavy rain. He then stepped off making his way to the nearest building with a covered entry, but not before getting soaked first. He stood there for a moment, wanting desperately to wring the water from his shirt and trousers in the worst way as they clung to his skin like spandex. He watched the bus slowly pull away, thinking about how much longer he'd have to continue riding that bus before he's allowed to drive again. As the rain began to fall even harder, he still had to walk another block and a half to get to his office building. He sighed, reluctantly yielding to his predicament, as it played like scratches on an LP over and over in his mind. Then, with a look of despair he mumbled, "It's the story of my life."

Chapter 1

LATE SUMMER SEEMED MORE arid in recent years, for the Midwest part of Florida anyway, with the exception of the downpour that occurred the morning of October fourth. Rainfall had become more scarce with no large bodies of water nearby to cool the earth, and the atmosphere, that seemed scorched from the record temperatures. The St. Johns River was too far east, Lake Okeechobee too far south, and Tampa Bay too far west for either of them to matter, in helping relieve the distress over the record heat. Sumter County was already getting into high gear for its Cabbage Patch Festival though, despite the stingy rainfall which threatened the citrus crop. Thanks to innovative irrigation and nutrition supply methods developed by a relative newcomer to the corporate community, the show would still go on. The festival took place just before Halloween, and in the town of Mumford both were in the same class as Christmas or New Year's Eve. Visitors from all over the agriculture universe anyway, including corporate vendors from Florida, Georgia, and even parts of the Carolinas, converged on the area for the week-long festival. It was an elaborate show about agriculture science. Any and every type of plant that would grow in the southern hemisphere, from produce to ornamental trees, shrubs, and groundcover, were featured at the festival. The 'Science and Technology' displays for farming and landscaping would include Omar's employer, Earth Burst Industries, for the first time. Their new system of water recovery to enhance irrigation and delivery of nutrients to plants would include demonstrations of a working model of the system to corporate sponsors, farmers, and nurseries. It was also Omar's rookie appearance as liaison, to three other companies being targeted for their sponsorship. It would be Omar's job to help them determine the size of the check they would be writing. He was hand- picked for the job primarily because of what was in his resume. He was a communications major in college almost two decades ago and honed his skills as a professional at the school's own radio station, covering school news and human interest stories. Omar knew the drill all too well and was pretty comfortable with his ability to sell himself, and the company's interests. The company's liaison needed to be well-spoken and personable, and every year a select group of employees would be chosen from several companies to court area industries for their sponsorship. His supervisor, Clarence Colter, had him pegged from the start, but Omar continuously resisted the idea. For him, it might as well have been a walk to the gallows, before Clarence made him an offer he couldn't refuse.

Clarence Colter is the Supervisor for Omar's unit; Part of the 'product development group' at Earth Burst Industries. He's only been with the company for 18 months but recently graduated from the University in the area with his Bachelor's degree, and will start the Master's program soon. He's only 30 years of age, but is married and has a three year old son with a baby on the way. He and his wife recently purchased their first home in an older middle-class neighborhood in the outskirts of the city, and is excited about being near the neighborhood he intends to serve. He's also a man of faith, who's decided not to compromise on his values because of personalities and circumstances that seem to challenge him at every turn. He even sees Omar's opinions about his own so-called 'detractors' as nothing more than an inconvenient Pre-occupation; especially the imaginary ones, that only seem to sap his ambition.

The gentleman in Omar, what little there was, didn't want to seem ungrateful over Clarence's decision of getting the company to agree to cover the cost of his tuition. He chose to pursue a Specialist Degree in Earth Sciences, but seemed lukewarm about it. As usual, he fitted himself for blinders once again when it came down to appreciating the long view of things. He couldn't quite erase his suspicions over the company's expectations of immediate returns on their investment, and dreaded the idea of becoming its pawn. Clarence, however, didn't have one shred of cynicism about it.

"What is it with you and this 'fox in the hen house' mentality when it comes to me? It seems my name is the only one on this short list you've been chasing since sponsorship for this festival has been coming up."

"Look, I know I'm not wrong about you on this. It's too bad I had to bribe you to agree to it though."

He then smiled, but continued with the housekeeping he was in the middle of when he called Omar into his office to discuss it further. Omar sat there motionless, suddenly reminiscing about the days he would be called into the Principal's office after getting busted for smoking in the little boys' room when he was in middle school. He almost felt like he was giving up a piece of himself for this 'chore'. Clarence continued to talk to him, but not glancing his way as he closed out routines on his desktop. He reached over to close the door to his office completely: the latch making a distinctive clacking sound. It was sharp and crisp, which reminded Omar of the first night of a two week stay inside the county lockup for DUI. Remembering the sounds of the doors closing behind him as he was shuttled through layers of security from one area to the next in the 8-story behemoth of a public service building. It was massive, and every bit of the county's business probably took place there. There was so much about his life that had been taken for granted up to that point; the freedom to roam whenever, and wherever he wanted, a comfortable queen sized bed to sleep in every night, exclusive rights to his own T.V. set, semi-gourmet meals every now and then, and a trio of loose fitting bright orange jumpsuits conspicuously absent from his wardrobe, that weren't really meant to make a fashion statement. They would be inconveniently sacrificed by his misfortune that night. It was his first arrest but second citation in the previous four months with an alcohol level registering twice the legal limit. It was the weekend his license was suspended.

"Omar—Omar!"

Omar replied, "Yeah, Cee Cee." He snapped back from what seemed like suspended animation, pretending to give Clarence his undivided attention.

"You're not gonna trail off like that when it's time to speak with those sponsors are you?"

Omar leaned up from the back of the chair then raised his right hand in a sarcastic gesture.

He then said, "Scouts honor, I promise."

"I hope you mean that, because how well you sell the importance of it will play a big part in deciding whether the festival will be back again. I don't think I have to tell you what it really means to this town's economy in the long run."

He offered Omar a bottle of water and trail mix from his stash.

"Thanks for the water, but I'll pass on the mix." Omar thought to himself, 'I guess we all have our fetishes', while he opened his bottle of water; watching Clarence pop the trail mix in his mouth several times before he started speaking again…

"I know you think the company should have selected someone else with as much dodge-ball as you played with me about it, but my instincts haven't failed me yet."

Clarence leaned forward in his chair, resting his elbows on his desk. His chin propped on hands that were clasped together like a vice. Omar was a little uncomfortable, not really knowing what to make of Clarence's fixation on him…

"I'm aware of your bout with the law, and the fact that your license was suspended, but I'm o.k. with that. And just so you know, it didn't affect my decision one way or the other. We can get around that."

Omar adjusted his posture if only to let Clarence know he was still alert. He was as still as a mannequin until then; listening to Clarence try to erase any reservations he thought he may have had about him.

Clarence continued—"Evelyn will work with you on prepping for it. I've also asked her to serve as your chaperon to and from the venues."

Omar said excitedly, "Chaperon?"

"Well, somebody's got to drive you!"

Omar pinched his lips together, pressing his palms hard against the sides of the leather chair; regretting the assignment even more now.

"Thanks a lot," He replied with knitted eyebrows.

"Look, it's not a dig at your situation, but I'm just trying to make it easier for you to succeed at this. Aren't you and Evelyn friendly?"

Omar nodded in agreement with a more serene expression this time. "Yeah, yeah we're ok. She's good people."

"Well, I've gotta tell you, she didn't exactly look at this as a chore when I approached her about it. She almost breathed a sigh of relief. I guess you must have discussed it with her after I asked you to think about it."

"Yeah, we talked about it a little."

"She seems to care for you, on a platonic level I mean."

Omar rolled his eyes with a hint of smile. He then said, "Oh, I'm sure that's what you meant Cee Cee,"

"Well I didn't mean to sound flip. The way she talks about you just gave me that impression." Clarence started setting up his coffee pot for his mid-morning cup.

He then said, "You know the idea of you two that way, probably wouldn't be that much of a stretch these days. Who knows, she could turn out to be your soul mate."

He started to grin as he waited patiently on the coffee pot to finish brewing.

Omar recoiled, "Oh really? She's almost old enough to be my mother."

"Look, I'm just kidding. What I really mean is, she's probably the best person to ride shotgun for you on this. She's easy going, organized, and respects what we're trying to do here."

The coffee pot was noisy and steaming, and just about done brewing. Clarence poured himself a cup as the last drops were falling into the decanter. "You want a cup?"

"No thanks; had my limit for today already."

Clarence started to sit again, brushing his hand over his tie as if making sure it fell squarely over the buttons to his shirt. Omar felt that it was probably just another one of his reflexes that was as common as blinking his eyes. It seemed every square inch of space in his office was always without blemish too, but not to the point where you'd feel funny about taking a seat in it. He was neat, and well organized, but it still somehow made Omar feel a little uncomfortable. Clarence pulled three folders from his desk drawer and handed them to him.

"These are the prospects we're targeting this year", taking a few sips from his company monogrammed coffee cup—"You're probably familiar with at least one of them. I believe you worked for Dillon at one time didn't you? "

"Yeah, I did, a while back."

"I remember seeing it in your file; sounds like not much love lost there, huh?"

"It wasn't exactly an amicable parting of the ways, if you get my drift." Omar stared at the folder with the 'Dillon Industries' Logo on the inside flap. He rifled through it as his enthusiasm registered at almost zero; His blank stare indicative of the animus invading his spirit suddenly, and Clarence sensed it.

He asked, "Want to talk about it?"

"I don't think it'll do any good."

"Well, I don't want you to think I've handed you an elephant. Anyway, maybe I can be your point man on this one to see if anybody knows you, or your history. It's been a while since you were there, and there might not be traces of any bad blood, if that's what you're worried about."

Omar said, "Well, I can see you're the eternal optimist."

"Why do you say that? "

"You always manage to see the light at the end of the tunnel, no matter how long you've been in the dark."

"And what's so wrong with that? You have to hope your situation will get better at some point, no matter how bleak it seems. It's called Faith, Omar."

"Yeah, right."

"Listen, you're not in this alone. I know sometimes it takes longer to get rid of certain baggage that seems to have weighed you down emotionally, but it's about trusting and believing in the power that's already within you to shake it, and put your energy into other things."

Omar listened intently as Clarence continued; crossing his legs and leaning back in his chair which meant he was getting ready for 'lecture mode'. Omar anticipated it. Bracing his right cheek with his index finger before letting go of a deep sigh..

"When I was twelve, I had a humongous crush on this girl at my school named Deloris Poole. Man, she was a goddess, at least to me anyway. She wore her hair in braids with these mile long plats in the back that were curled at the ends. She had this—this doll like face, and hazel eyes with a little pug nose and pouty lips. Well, we just called them big lips back then. Some of the so-called 'A-Listers' thought she was geeky because she was smart too, and they wouldn't be caught dead inviting her into their Circle. But I could see well beyond all of that 'geekiness' and decided to judge for myself."

Omar started to become restless. Wishing the moral of the story would come much sooner than later. Clarence continued…

"None of my friends even knew how I felt about her. I guess I really didn't think there was a threat of anybody getting to her besides me, so I took forever to get up enough courage to approach her."

Omar couldn't resist playing devil's advocate while Clarence told his story.

He asked, "Was that delay also about avoiding the embarrassment of having been seen talking to her? "

"Oh no, not at all. It was never something I needed to be cynical about. My mind was made up. When I did decide to approach her one day between classes, she seemed shocked that I would even be interested in her. I could tell it was awkward for her because she was shy and a little withdrawn, well with guys anyway. When I finally asked if she would meet me after school in front of the auditorium so we could talk more, she acted like a cornered house cat who needed to escape in the worst way. I asked what was wrong, and she settled down enough to reveal her worst fear to me."

Clarence stopped talking and turned to see the bustle already going on inside the office through the other side of the large glass partition. It was a curious pause as he also took another sip of his coffee, as if savoring it for as long as he could, or maybe to mask a deep seated emotion that all of a sudden wrestled its way to the surface.

Omar decided he would interrupt his 'meditation' with another question—He asked, "So, what was her worst fear?"

Clarence turned back, facing him again, with a somber expression..

"She didn't want to feel rejected," he replied. "She told me some upper-classmen had played a cruel joke on her just before the end of the previous term. Afterward, she felt she would always be labeled an outsider, with nobody ever being interested in getting to know her, for who she really was."

He shook his head as if disgusted over the emotional scars it must have left her with.

"It's a pity isn't it?" He then smiled a little and continued; "We sometimes judge people on what we think we're seeing, but without any real evidence. You would think we'd owe it to that person to at least try and get to know them before allowing our opinions to be etched in stone."

Omar was more curious now as Clarence swiveled to his right with pinched lips. Looking past the mid-morning commotion on the other side of the partition. Omar wondered why he would hang on to something that happened so long ago, conveniently ignoring preoccupations with his own history.

He then said to Omar, "I guess you're wondering why I'm telling you this."

"The thought had crossed my mind, yeah."

"Me and that girl, became good friends after I helped her erase her inhibitions. I reminded her of her attributes, physical and otherwise, that compared her to the swan she really was. That was all she needed to hear. Someone to say in a nutshell, that she really mattered. The way she looked, her intelligence, her quietness and easy going nature. It all mattered in the grand scheme of things and there was nothing she needed to apologize for or feel uneasy about. She started to trust her own instincts more and in time, understood that not everybody would be her friend but once she decided to open up, real friends would find her."

Clarence put his cup down, and exhaled heavily, then leaned forward and looked Omar in the eyes.

He then said, "You don't get off that easily Duncan." Shaking his head from side to side. "Running from your troubles is too easy. It dupes you into thinking you don't have to worry about facing them, but you might as well try and outrun your own shadow. It's what they become eventually you know, if you let them."

Omar became visibly impatient, almost interrupting Clarence. "And the moral of the story is—", he asked.

"Don't let them define who you are," Clarence replied. "You do have some say so in the course your life takes you know. Try not to let situations or your past decide that for you; like Deloris finally did."

"So, whatever happened to your, friend? "

Before Clarence could answer, there was a knock on his door. He yelled, "Come!"

The door opened slowly and a well-dressed and attractive woman stepped in, who looked to just be leaving middle-aged behind her. It was Evelyn Beacham, Omar's friend, and chaperon. She flashed a broad smile at both of them…

"Good morning gentlemen."

"Good morning Evelyn. You're just in time." Clarence had the look of the cat that just swallowed the canary since her appearance was a surprise to Omar, in more ways than one. He wanted to make sure he made it easier for Omar to accept the assignment with little or no resistance if Evelyn was in the room. His instincts didn't betray him.

Omar seemed glad to see her.

He said, "Hi, Ev, welcome to the party."

She moved closer to him; playfully bumping her shoulder against him slightly.

"I guess we'll be the dynamic duo for a minute, huh?"

Omar looked at Clarence with an expression that meant the jury was still out on whether he was completely on-board now. Getting Evelyn involved made him feel a little insecure, but his reservations were short-lived after taking a moment to think about how much help she really could be to him. Her infectious smile seemed to seal the deal.

Clarence said, "Well Omar?"

Omar smiled himself, then turned to Evelyn again. "Yeah, the Dynamic Duo it is."

Evelyn Beacham is a friend and co-worker of Omar's for the six years he's been with the company. She's in her mid-fifties and looking forward to retirement in about 6 or 7 years, and the two of them are in the same Unit. They share similar interests and find it easy to relate to one another, but even she outpaces him when it comes to her ambition

Evelyn took a seat next to Omar. Pushing her freshly curled locks away from her eyes. She crossed her legs with her pen and pad in hand.

Omar said, "I like your new hair", while looking curiously at it. Pinching some of it between his fingers as if needing to satisfy some nervous reflex.

Clarence then said, "It looks good on you Evelyn."

'Thank you; both of you." She cut her eyes at Omar, who had quickly moved his fingers away. She then asked, 'Trying to see if it's real or not?"

"Oh, no. I'm sorry Ev. It's just that, it's a different look for you that's all. It really makes you look—"

She interrupted, "Like I've got attitude?"

"Well, what I was going to say was, it makes you look more, in vogue."

He and Clarence both smiled at her, waiting for a comeback.

She then said, "Well, I'll take that too", as she smiled back at them while pinching her skirt tail to cover her knees. She was still very modest in some ways.

Clarence said, "I was just getting ready to go over the itinerary for the sponsors with Omar."

Clarence took a 2nd folder from his drawer and handed it to Evelyn. She opened it carefully and spotted the index page. She homed in like radar on one company's annual revenue page then asked, "What's our target?"

Omar was impressed with her eagerness, from the look he gave Clarence. Clarence also knew then that pairing the two of them was the right call…

"That's what I'm talking about. I knew my instincts were right about you. Just being inquisitive about that alone, without me having to go on a 'fishing expedition' tells me you don't really treat this assignment as a chore; that you're conscientious about what we're trying to do with it. Honestly, I can't think of a pair more suited for this than you two."

Omar sat motionless with a fixed stare. Not sure whether Clarence's 'stroking' of them bothered him more, or the possibility that he was almost being upstaged by Evelyn's assertiveness. Then again, she was just being who she is. Always in high gear when it came to her work. He never knew of a time when she had anything negative to say about her current job or her co-workers. Omar respected her commitment to simply do what was necessary and natural for her by giving her best to everything she touched. Her previous attempts at a promotion hadn't paid any dividends yet, but she was patient. If it happened it would be, by her own admission, her swan song. She twisted her mouth to one side a little in an attempt at a smile. Trying to digest what at first seemed like Clarence's patronizing of her allowed her to think better of it.

She then said, "Well, thanks Ce Ce. I'll just keep doing what I can to help the team."

"If I was a betting man, I'd put my money on you two, leaving the rest of them in the dust."

"Well don't count your biddies before they hatch," Omar said. "We wouldn't want to disappoint you."

Evelyn chimed in, "Who says we might disappoint him? We've got this." She then raised her head with a coquettish smile.

Clarence replied, "Evelyn, I like your style."

Omar's feelings about Evelyn possibly stealing some of his thunder loomed even larger now. She seemed to be getting all the good press the moment she stepped into the room.

"You paying attention Omar?", Clarence asked.

"Alright, go ahead and rub it in Cee Cee."

Omar was noticeably a little agitated. "I'm not tone deaf you know. I get how important this is to you, and I will be committed to its success, even though it may have to grow on me."

Clarence ignored Omar's ambivalence, and his resentful glare for the moment.

He then said, "There's a tutorial I'd like the two of you to watch before we hit the ground with this. It'll give you some ideas on what to expect at the event venues; itineraries, a list of lead reps for the sponsors along with their contact information, and what our target should be for each of their contributions. I'll email the link to you so you can download it. It's only 10 minutes long, so as long as you've set aside some time to watch it before our staff meeting on Thursday would be fine. You can let me know then what you think about it, and if you have any questions or concerns."

Evelyn seemed really excited over the chance to do something new and challenging.

"It's probably the closest I'll ever get to a promotion again at my age." She replied. She smiled at Clarence with a confident expression. Her hand still positioned to take notes, but with an uncharacteristic nervous twitch. She was really hoping deep down, that this assignment wouldn't be just another zero-sum game for her.

Clarence said, "Well, I've got my leadership meeting with the brass so I'd better button up a few things first, but I want you two to really put your heads together on this, ok? Let me know if you've got any ideas on how to spice up the presentations."

Clarence gave them a look that meant he really would be expecting something that showed they belonged at the top of the heap.

Omar and Evelyn both stood up, and Omar was about to speak when Evelyn beat him to it.

"We won't let you down Cee Cee."

Clarence smiled, then looked at Omar, watching him just shake his head in agreement…

"Good, that's good to know. I know you'll make us proud. Well, I guess I'll speak to you about it again by Thursday if not sooner, ok?"

Omar reached for the door letting Evelyn out first, but allowing the door to almost slam shut. Evelyn turned back toward him afterward. Obviously pleased to be a part of something that would have her brand on it, and the opportunity to work one-on-one with Omar was a bonus.

Omar, however, was at the opposite end of the emotional spectrum and noticeably irritated. "Look, let's set some ground rules Evelyn. Understand that I'm the lead on this assignment and I don't really need you to speak for me when asked about it, ok?"

"Well, what did I say that made it sound like I was getting ahead of you?"

"Well, statements like, 'who says we might disappoint him', 'we got this', and, 'we won't let you down Cee Cee'. We've never done this before and who knows what kinds of problems we might run into, or who might be lurking around some corner to mess it all up for us." He turned away from her with the look of a blank canvas.

Evelyn said, "I wasn't trying to oversell it or upstage you, if that concerns you. I just wanted to convey to him that he really did have the best team for the job." They continued walking slowly toward their desks, then she stopped just short of her own with her back against the wall and proceeded to lecture him..

"You know, in my 54 years I've learned to look at the glass as half full rather than half empty." She said. "Not being so concerned about how I might lose what's left in it, but how I might find the thing to finish filling it up." She stared at him for a moment. It seemed to intimidate him a little because he hadn't seen that side of her.

She continued, "When I used to focus on who, or what, might interfere with what I was trying to get done, I was only robbing myself of time and energy I needed to spend on my own efforts. That's the surest way to lose what's left in that glass, if I let the forces working against me just take it away without a fight. It's the same as me just tipping it over and letting what's in it spill all over the place. I have to be even more committed to keeping it filled, as that thing working against me is about trying to make sure I lose it. I owe that to myself. Anyway, it lets me sleep better at night." She playfully shoved him in his side again and smiled.

He smiled back this time, while she continued—"I don't mean to sound preachy, but it's just the way I look at life and it just so happens to pay dividends, eventually."

They both looked at each other and started to laugh a little about each of their situations. Evelyn, thinking about the number of times she had posted for jobs within the company but only being interviewed once, and passed over. In Omar's case it was the number of times he was encouraged to post but just didn't bother; mostly because of the fear of failing.

She then said, "I'll tell you what, I will make sure our sponsors understand that you're the lead and I'm, well I'll be your 'right hand man', or something like that; not quite Captain America and Wonder Woman, but close, Ok?"

Omar said, "Alright, it's a bet." Omar always did appreciate Evelyn's sense of humor, and how she had the uncanny ability to just let most things roll off of her back with little or no fanfare afterwards. Her ability to put things in perspective was something she was still showing him how to do. He began to appreciate even more how she really did have his back, as a friend.

She said, "Well, I'd better go earn my keep", as she dropped her note pad and pen on her desk. "Maybe I'll see you in the lounge later and we can pick up where we left off with those investment opportunities I was telling you about."

He said, "Yeah—that sounds good. Usual time?"

"Uh huh. You know you've got the chops to be a really good agent, maybe even a broker; ever thought about it?"

"Not even."

"Why not? You'd be convincing enough with that ready for prime time voice of yours."

She gave him a serious stare, then suddenly laughed.

"You're blushing. I'd better stop before I create a scene."

A real scene was unfolding as Omar was getting ready to take his seat. Some of the staff stood up suddenly, mostly females. They were looking in the direction of the breezeway, as their whispers almost reached a low hum there was so much of it. Nadine, the department 'comedian', also stood and called Evelyn on the phone right away…

"Looks like fresh meat is headed our way"

Evelyn stood slowly, as if maybe expecting to see another prospective suitor. She then sighed and said, "He's a baby! How do you know he's a new employee?"

"Just a wild guess. Chris is always by herself when she's showing the place to new blood. If it was more than that, some of the brass would probably be along for the ride too."

Evelyn replied, "Yeah, you're probably right. Boy, he's tall."

Nadine then said, "He reminds me of that Czech guy that used to play for the Sentinels, only darker. You know, the one with all those syllables in his name."

Evelyn responded in a frustrated tone, "Nadine, I have no idea who you're talking about." Nadine said, "Never mind." She paused, then started to twist from side to side a little. Almost like a middle-schooler experiencing her first crush.

She then said, "Well, he 'ain't' no Denzel, but he'll do nicely."

Evelyn said, "Well, you might as well turn yourself in to the authorities right now for thinking that way. He looks so young!" Then they both started to laugh.

Omar was only two cubicles over, but might as well have had his head buried in two feet of sand. He had started researching the curriculum for the Specialist Degree the Company would be paying for, and had closed himself off from everything else around him.

Theo Biggs, another co-worker and Omar's protégé, interrupted. "Omar—Omar!"

Omar rapped his fingers on the edge of his keyboard in frustration. "Yeah, Theo, what is it?" "Come look at this guy. He's gotta be a baller."

Omar stood slowly. His eyes stretching curiously at the young man. They didn't blink either, as if he was stuck in some catatonic state, and stroking his beard again. It had become habit forming and would rear its head whenever he found himself imbedded in some great mystery or revelation about something, or someone. His mind usually transported him to surprise destinations whenever it happened, and the annoying syndrome had unfortunately re-claimed another memory. His tattered self-confidence was overcome once again, by the stigma of regret. The tug of war between his desire to re-construct his image, and those triggers that sounded the alarm stopping him dead in his tracks had proven to be relentless; like the sudden and dramatic dying of the wind against the sails of a ship whose course had otherwise been true, only to be set adrift inside the endless expanse of the sea; wishing it would be spared from its tumultuous nature. His survival instincts unfortunately, seemed less and less reliable each time it happened. Clarence came up from behind him, still putting on his jacket for the meeting. Everyone got a little quieter as the H.R. Rep. and the young man approached Omar's section.

"You almost missed me Chris," Clarence said. "I expected you earlier. I was just on my way to a meeting."

"Oh, well I guess I was just in time then. I'd like you to meet Blake Bristol. He's one of our new I.T. Techs. His mother and I happened to be college roommates."

Clarence and Blake shook Hands.

Clarence then said, "Looks like you're just in time for the new P.C. upgrades we're supposed to be getting."

Blake said, "That's what they tell me."

Clarence asked, "So, where's your home?"

"I was born here, and lived here until I was six then sort of back and forth between here and Savannah after that."

"Oh, a native son. I guess a lot about this place is still pretty familiar then."

"Somewhat", Blake responded. Shaking his head in agreement. "I still have family here." Clarence asked, "You play ball?"

"I know my way around the court pretty well. I was first All-American at Rutherford High in Savannah. Had a few high profile S.E.C. Recruiters check me out during my second term at Savannah State."

Omar got wind of their conversation and said under his breath, 'Show off '…

Clarence said, "Well, in that case maybe we can hit the hardwood together at some point to see what you've got, if you're game."

"Oh, that works for me. Just say the word."

"Ok, it's a bet." Clarence then said, "Good meeting you, and welcome to the family."

Clarence then said, "Chris, I'll see you later—gotta get to my meeting."

Chris had moved only three cubicles from Omar, almost in front of Nadine's desk. Nadine walked a few paces to face Blake directly, looking straight up at him in an exaggerated posture. He looked down at her with a curious look as though he knew the punch line was on its way.

Then she asked, "How's the weather up there?"

He smiled, then replied, "It's a little frosty in the mornings but other than that, it's ok."

She grabbed him by the hand then said, "I'm Nadine, and these are my loyal subjects."

She pointed toward her co-workers. They all laughed having gotten used to her antics.

She then said, "You're gonna work out just fine." He smiled at her again.

Chris then said, "You'll get used to Nadine. She'd like you to believe this place can't function without her."

Nadine blurted out, "Well it can't!"

"Stop it Nadine," Chris replied. "You're gonna corrupt him even before he gets started." Everyone within earshot started to laugh, even Nadine who had gotten used to laughing at herself. Her credibility fell somewhere between 'class clown' and everybody's 'confidant', and she wore it like a badge of honor. The laughs to her were like a shot of good booze. It was the perfect sedative that let her forget her nagging troubles and trade them for a little celebrity, at least for a while. Omar stayed inside the jocularity for different reasons though. He had trailed off, deeper this time. The laughs seemed to be non-stop. He cupped his hands over his ears trying to muffle the sound, but the assault on his senses intensified, as if it had suddenly transformed into physical pain; like daggers gouging into his flesh; driving deeper and deeper, leaving him writhing in agony.

THAT BULLY JUST NEVER stopped laughing at him. He dreaded taking that route home anyway, because he didn't want to see him again, not today. He compared it with having to tread a big metal vat of toxic waste when he confronted him; the odor never failed at stifling his attempts to breathe. It left him disoriented while he desperately searched for an escape, but instead was greeted only by the dull and endless pigment of rusting metal. He seemed to stalk him, and for the bully, it was wishing he'd see Omar for another 'beat down' that he knew was undeserved, but was compelled to carry out anyway. It was always convenient, and met with little or no resistance so, he felt somehow justified in his condemnation of him. His name was Deon, and no matter the degree of protests from his nine year old adversary, it seemed to add more fuel to an already raging fire for Deon. Omar was late leaving detention at school, and got stuck with having to take that way home again. He felt he had no choice, but he needed to get the timing right from now on, detention or not, so he wouldn't be greeted by this guy's fist day after day. Getting distracted and losing track of time was a common occurrence for a kid his age, but he was hard pressed to master it, or else expect to keep rehearsing the same script day after day, after day…

"Hey, 'match sticks'—I'm talking to you!", Deon said.

He laughed almost hysterically as if his taunting was praise worthy. Omar suddenly stopped in his tracks. Deon's voice could be compared to the sound of roaring lions, and Omar never got used to it knowing what awaited him. Each time he did it, seemed more ferocious than the last. As he turned toward the direction of Deon's voice he felt a stout punch, then shove to his shoulder. He dropped his book bag then grabbed his arm. Holding it firmly. Almost massaging it until the next assault. He shoved him again with both hands this time; three times in succession. Omar almost coiled, clinching his fist as if he was ready to retaliate. He had stumbled from the last shove, dropping to one knee, then the other. Crouching over his book bag and losing one shoe from the tumble. Breathing heavily, he looked up at Deon, who stood over him like the giant he imagined in some of his nightmares. Rationalizing once again that he might as well have been in enemy territory with no formidable weapons. He wasn't going to try and kid himself. Deon could probably clean his clock with one good sucker punch if he tried to fight back. He then looked down at the ground; anywhere except having to look deeper into Deon's pitch black eyes.

He relaxed his fist, picked up his bag, then shouted, "Why don't you let me alone! "

"Because!"

Omar replied, "Because what?"

"Because, you're a 'dweeb'; and dweebs don't get no respect from me you understand?"

Omar ignored his logic, as though Deon expected him to understand it. All of a sudden Deon stared at him mysteriously, as if he was attempting to reconcile his own reasoning for the hostility, then walked away slowly while looking back at him. He began to knock his fists together, then trotted in the opposite direction. Omar bent over; both knees still on the ground, and quaking from the wake of Deon's fury. It was a struggle for him to start breathing normally again until the fear almost seemed merciful, by letting go of him suddenly.

"Dee!, Dee!" A voice yelled from a distance away. The unmistakable rattle of metal finders to someone's bike was getting closer as Omar turned slowly toward the noise. The braking of its tires caused the bike to hook a little, just barely missing Omar.

The boy asked, "Hey man, you o.k.?"

Omar replied, "Yeah, yeah, I'm alright."

It was Omar's best friend, Breeland. He laid his bike down and kneeled in front of him.

"What happened?"

Omar was still on his knees. Breeland looked him up and down. Omar couldn't look him in the eye just yet, which was a dead giveaway for Breeland.

He asked, "Ran into Deon again didn't you?"

"How'd you guess?"

"Well, it 'aint' that hard. You always come this way when you're coming home late from school, and besides, this is where he and his buddies like to roam. Did he hurt you?"

"No, just the usual stuff. Shoving, a punch or two, you know."

"Man, you talk about it like you're serving yourself up for lunch to this bum."

Breeland decided to inject some humor in the situation by teasing Omar about it. He grabbed him by the shoulders..

"And will it be the usual today sir? A double-stacked knuckle sandwich, and 'heel to butt cheek' pudding with a little bloody nose topping?. Yes sir, right away sir."

He tried speaking in a different accent for his role play. The accent wasn't recognizable, but it must have worked. All of a sudden Omar let go of a deep sigh, as if real relief had finally come. Then they both started to laugh out loud as he stood up, grabbed his bag, and they started walking. Breeland pushed his bike alongside while Omar began to spill his confessional…

"I don't know why I can't just cold-cock this guy 'Bree' once and for all." It's like if I do decide to fight back, I might not live to talk about it."

Breeland said, "He 'aint' the guy you think he is."

"What do you mean?"

Before he could respond, the roar of thunder could be heard in the distance. No sooner had they noticed the darkening clouds there was more thunder; louder this time, then it started to rain. They picked up their pace and found shelter under the covered island of a gas station about 40 yards away. As the rain got heavier, Omar asked him again..

"What did you mean, he's not the guy I think he is?"

THE SOUND OF THE rain outside the plate glass panel was really heavy now. It sounded almost like hale; enough to bring him back to reality. Omar stood in front of it as if it had become his sanctuary. He noticed prompts to check messages on his cell that he had missed, and found another message from his uncle Seth, wanting to talk, again. He decided to also ignore it, yielding once again to the deep seated animosity toward him. He felt he was more likely to grow ten inches taller than to revive the feelings he once had for him, at least not any time soon. He just couldn't see it because of what went down between them.

"Omar, Omar!"

Omar responded, "Oh, hey Chris. How is it?"

She gave him a curious look first. "You're not checking out on me are you?"

"What do you mean?"

"You were sort of like, not here for a moment. Day dreaming?"

"Oh, I'm sorry. I was distracted just for a minute." He approached her and Blake with the typical courteous body language, but really haunted a little by Blake's appearance. Chris introduced him to Omar, and to Theo who was close by.

Chris said, "I'd like you to meet our new IT technician, Blake Bristol. He'll be helping set up the new upgrades to the computer system we've got slated for your department and a few others in about a week."

They shook hands, but Omar reacted as though he had just gotten burned, withdrawing his hand suddenly.

"I'm sorry. Would you believe I just got a shock?" (But he exaggerated) "My hands must really be dry."

Blake said slowly, "It's ok. I've been told I'm electric, but I didn't think it was literal."

They all laughed a little, except Omar. It was a little spooky to him. This guy could easily be an older version of that bully from his childhood, Deon, with his six feet-plus frame peering over the heads of everyone else, and a cockiness to go along with it. It was also curious that he had the same last name as his Uncle Seth, which was more than likely just coincidental, but seemed to give him more justification for feeling the way he did…

"Hi, I'm Theo Biggs. Good to meet you. So, I know you must play ball, right?"

"I guess with this height it would seem almost sacrilegious if I didn't, huh? Yeah, I play."

Theo held on to his stoic expression while everybody else laughed about it.

Omar wasn't exactly subtle about his indifference toward Blake. Theo seemed to have finished what seemed like more stroking of Blake's ego, in Omar's opinion.

He then said abruptly, "I'll see you around", then stepped back toward his desk.

Blake shrugged his shoulders slightly, dismissing Omar's reaction, and so did everyone else. Theo continued to converse with Blake, and Chris, while Omar returned to his cubicle briefly. It was as if he couldn't quite decide on what he should do next. Blake's presence bothered him more than it should have, so he parked himself in front of that large glass panel again, letting the sound of the rain almost sedate him; sifting through muddled emotions that only provided more questions than answers.

Chapter 2

"Hey mister."

Omar decided to finally come up for air from having sat at his desk for almost two hours with hardly a stir. He raised his head to see Evelyn standing in front of him with her hands on her hips.

"Oh, hey Ev." He looked at his watch. "That time already?"

Evelyn said, "Clock's running."

They began to weave their way through the crowd from the mid-morning rush to get to the break areas only about 30 yards away, but it seemed like an eternity getting there. Trying to converse during the trip really wasn't that important. It would have been frustrated anyway by the number of times they probably would have been separated until they reached their destination. Bringing their own snacks and soft drinks was a must too, if they were going to avoid squandering the 20 minutes they did have, from standing in line at snack machines.

She then asked, "Did you take a look at Clarence's tutorial yet?"

"I did, and we've got a little work in front of us."

Evelyn said, "It seemed pretty straight forward to me. Of course the salesmanship all belongs to you, but I've already been thinking about how we can set our presentation apart from everybody else, assuming they follow what's in the tutorial to the letter."

He smiled at her, sipping on his Fruitopia and said, "That doesn't surprise me."

"You want to hear about them?"

"You can tell me later. I've got a few questions for Clarence first. I wouldn't want us to get ahead of ourselves."

Evelyn thought it curious that he didn't want to hear her ideas at that moment. It couldn't have hurt. She was left thinking Omar wasn't really interested in seeing any original thinking from her, but as usual, gave him the benefit of the doubt.

She asked, "What kind of questions did you have for him about it?"

"Oh, what other kinds of incentives we may be able to offer them, depending on the size of their pledges; Like advertising space on the company's blog, you know; things like that."

"That's good—That's good. I just hope he doesn't treat it like it's an albatross around the company's neck."

"Now why would he do that? You've got to give them a good enough incentive."

Omar recoiled; a little annoyed over Evelyn's response.

"Hey, I'm on your side," She replied, "But you know Clarence. If he's faced with having to make a decision that seems too far above his pay grade, his first impulse is to resist it."

"So you're saying it's probably not a good idea?"

"No, I'm not saying that at all. It's just that you should be ready for a possible push back that's all. It still shouldn't keep us from thinking outside the box you know."

Omar got quiet. He propped his chin on his thumbs and began flicking them against his beard, and staring into space. Evelyn stared curiously at him for a moment. Thinking how best to push through the turbulence she thought she had created. His obvious sensitivity caught her by surprise. She felt it would probably be about as useful to their assignment as a barbell around the ankles for someone who's trying to tread water. It didn't look good on him and would most likely create more friction than she'd like to deal with. She respected him, but felt he let certain things impair his judgement, that really shouldn't. She decided she'd need to try and nip his predilection in the bud, or else stand by and watch their partnership slowly disintegrate.

She asked, "Omar, you still with me?"

She sighed, then began wringing her hands. He glanced her way slightly.

"I'm sorry if I struck a nerve, but I need you to know that what I said wasn't meant to be a knock against you."

He gave her a look as if he was begging to be rescued from something, then barely managed a smile.

He said, "I'm sorry. I guess I'm a little thin-skinned at times. I know that you'll have my back, and I appreciate it."

She breathed a sigh of relief, then brushed the curls away from her eyes and said, "I tell you what, why don't we switch gears? I checked out this mutual fund I told you about before, and it looks like a solid performer. The percentage of stocks in your portfolio should create a nice balance for you, since you've got some years before you retire."

She expected he'd be more engaging about the subject but drew blanks trying to gauge his enthusiasm.

The mystery was short lived when he said, "You don't really want to talk about that do you? Why don't you just tell me about those ideas you said you have for the assignment anyway."

He was intuitive enough to know that the invitation for her to strut her 'creative stuff' was what she really wanted, and needed. She wasted no time obliging him either.

Speaking slowly, but still a little cautious, she said, "Ok, if you say so. You sure you wanna hear about them?"

"Yeah, I'm sure," he said with a smile that she didn't have to pry from him for once.

"Well for one thing, I thought rather than 'stills' with an over-head projector for the graphics, we could produce our own short video with live actors. You know, company employees mostly, to set up the outline for the benefits of the new recovery system. I know what you're going to say about the corporate video that's already out there, but ours would be much shorter and more public relations oriented."

She stretched her eyes at him and stopped talking. Waiting for a nod of approval. He was hesitant to respond, not knowing whether he should object, or not. It seemed a little ambitious for their purposes but he didn't have the heart to shoot it down.

So he decided to play it safe and asked, "And how do we do that?"

She said, "I've got a nephew who's itching to get his feet wet. He's an Art Institute graduate who majored in multi-media production. Besides, filming is also his hobby so he'll probably do it for next to nothing just to get the exposure."

"I like it—I like it a lot, but before we give Clarence anything specific why don't you approach your nephew about it to see if he's on board. You know, how long it might be, time he'll need to produce it; things like that."

"Ok, I'm on it," she replied.

"We'll probably need a script to show him soon so we'll have to get to work on that too. We've got to also find actors, but I'll leave the talent search up to you; you up to it?"

"Am I? You and me are gonna make the front page of the Quarterly for this one."

She started to laugh a little as she tilted her head back with an air of confidence, noticeably pleased with Omar's acceptance of her idea. It didn't quite quench her thirst the way a promotion would, but it would certainly wet her appetite for more of it. She tossed what was left of her chips in the trash, then glanced at the clock on the adjacent wall..

She then said somberly, "It's that time."

The bell must have tolled at the same time for everyone else too. It looked like a cattle call as people vacated the area in a hurry.

"I'll call my nephew later today to try and get a feel for whether it's something he feels he can really handle."

He said, "Yeah, might as well cover our bases. You know, I'd hate for him to think we're exploiting him."

Omar's body language didn't really give her an indication he was joking, or not.

She then said, "I wouldn't be concerned about that. Anyway, I'm his favorite Aunt; so he tells me." Then she started to laugh. Omar knew Evelyn was on an emotional high she was in no hurry to come down from. He knew her circumstances well enough to know it was a real privilege for her to do this project because of how she must have been pigeon-holed professionally since her arrival there. She had complained about not being challenged enough during their conversations. How there must have been some reason that escaped her, to be denied all but one interview for the jobs she had posted for. She needed reason to celebrate for once the opportunity of being a part of something as important as this. He knew he needed to be on board for her sake, but in the back of his mind was that still small voice that kept trying to convince him it was too flamboyant of an idea for what they were doing. It left him feeling uneasy, especially knowing Dillon Industries was in his past. As they were heading back to their department, he noticed Theo and Blake at the other end of the floor. The scene was a little unsettling and he forgot for a moment that Evelyn was with him. Theo treats him like a mentor, but Omar recalls how he avoids his 'big brotherly' overtures most of the time.

Omar told Evelyn, "I'm gonna stop here for a minute Ev—I'll just see you inside."

"Ok, have fun"

He leaned over the parapet wall overlooking the atrium below and stared at them for a moment; appreciating how predictable the exchange between them must be, for young men their ages. Wishing he was better at navigating the myriad of discoveries new acquaintances seem to provide, but doing it without any awkward missteps. He could only sense that Theo was probably more adept at it than he was. He sighed heavily. A blank stare washed across his face suddenly like a tidal wave, as if trying to restrain the memory of every regrettable thing he had ever done in his life. Hoping desperately that his universe would somehow, miraculously become trouble free. He started to stroke his beard again; thinking how he didn't want to disappoint Evelyn by making her aware of his real ambivalence over her idea, but also unable to pin point the real source of what he was feeling. She had become a trusted friend in recent months, who conveniently managed to sidestep the effects of his ancient stigmas that continued to haunt him. He leaned against a nearby column; His surroundings reduced to a blank canvas, as if a switch was turned on suddenly arresting his posture, and his consciousness. Allowing it to place him once again inside a dubious past, that demanded its time and space. The relentless assault on his psyche having to submit once again to what seemed like house arrest for the moment. It was darkness descending over his feeble, but muted cries for help.

"COME ON DUNCAN, COME ON! Pick those feet up. You 'ain't' got all day you know."

His physical education coach was a real task master with everybody. A 40 something year old ex-marine who was in better shape than guys half his age. He was more impatient with this troop of 12 year olds though. He must have felt they should be like supermen from the moment they escaped the womb. He was especially hard on Omar, who seemed to always be close to last place when they had to run. Omar made it to the finish line in the 40 yard dash, but put both hands on his knees to keep from tipping over while trying to catch his breath. The sprints always took a lot out of him. He thought after a while it was God's punishment for some mischief he had done, but couldn't name. He looked like a 90 year old who needed a tool to help get himself upright again. Some of the other boys seemed to get in line to tease him. Two of them poked him in his side as he stayed in that position to catch his breath. They'd say 'old wash woman. Why don't you just walk it?' Then they would laugh hysterically. He didn't have a comeback, since he really would have been o.k. with walking it.

Coach yelled, "Alright everybody, let's huddle!"

Coach noticed Omar with his hands on his hips then, and presumably on the downside of his recovery.

He yelled, "You too Duncan. Come on over here!"

Omar wiped his hand across his brow and started walking slowly toward the rest of the boys. Breeland was in the class too but left him alone while he was in the middle of his recovery. It was Breeland's favorite class, even the running, but Omar could take it or leave it.

Coach said, "A few of you need to improve your times in the 'forty'. If you're over 12 seconds it means you're marginal, but it doesn't mean you'll flunk the class. You can do things to improve your performance. Also if you're stronger in another segment it'll boost your overall grade."

A few of them started to mumble. Coach shouted, "No talking while I'm talking please!"

It got so quiet he might as well have been speaking to a group of mannequins, except for the barely audible breathing from Omar, who hadn't quite made it back from 'death valley'.

Coach then said, "I'll post your times on the bulletin board in the locker room after each run, and use the best time to calculate your overall grade at the end of the term, ok? Now, I've got footballs and basketballs for the free quarter. Pick your 5 man teams and have fun. I'll call you in, about fifteen minutes from now."

He turned to face Omar after braking the huddle and said, "Duncan!"

"Yes sir?"

"Let's talk for a minute." Omar felt having to talk to him in that instance couldn't be a good thing. He knew that running was his 'bugaboo' but felt there wasn't much he could do about it. He felt he just wasn't built for it. He at least hoped the infraction wasn't so bad that his folks needed to know about it.

Coach beckoned to him, "Let's talk over here. This won't take long."

When they sat down on one of the benches nearby, the coach's countenance seemed to morph into a father-like figure suddenly. Omar needed to feel less intimidated by him to completely relax. He couldn't put his finger on it, but it was obvious coach switched gears when he needed to do a one-on-one with them.

"You think I'm hard on you don't you?"

Omar just stared into space for a moment before trying to figure out how to answer him.

"It's ok. You don't have to answer. Your body language just did. I don't usually care much if these kids break records out here or not when they're running. Most of them bring a 'sand lot mentality' to the field anyway. As long as they're heroes in the eyes of their friends and the little girls that hang around them they don't care much beyond that, but you're different. I see something in you that I think you even miss, and that is your technique when you run. How do you feel about running, in general?"

"I just wished I was better at it."

He confided in coach for the first time since laying eyes on him and it felt pretty cool.

"I guess I'm just too skinny."

"You sure there's nothing else? Because for a kid your size you seem to run out of breath easily."

Omar swallowed several times. Not sure whether he should uncork a secret that wasn't really meant for public scrutiny. Then on the other hand, he felt the coach had already started to make the swing from 'cold blooded' to 'confidant', so he opened up.

"Well, my parents say I was born with one lung smaller than the other."

He looked away again; ashamed of the admission. Coach didn't interrupt, feeling he had more he wanted to say about it.

He hung his head as if it was the confession of some death row inmate who would not realize the promise of a reprieve.

"They said my doctors told them I should outgrow it, but not yet I guess."

"I'm sorry, I didn't know."

Coach looked away, noticeably depressed a little from the news.

"Look, I was a kid once, and—,"

Coach noticed Omar smiling a little as though he felt he might have skipped that stage. Coach even started to grin a little.

"I know, I know that's hard to believe, but 'Robo Coach' does have a mom, and a past, not unlike yours."

Omar said, "You know about that name the kids have for you?"

"I know everything Duncan", then laughed, and so did Omar.

"I'm gonna work with you on your technique and stamina. The good Lord will do the rest."

He then stood up, patting Omar on his head.

"I'll tell you more about what I have planned soon, but for now I'm gonna replace the forty yard dash with something else for you, ok?"

"Yes sir."

He handed him one of the basketballs.

"Here, why don't you practice your jumper with Kevin. You've only got about 7 or 8 more minutes left. I'll see you in a little bit."

Omar started toward the courts while dribbling the basketball. Breeland raced beside him as he started to trot.

"Hey, you in any trouble?"

"Nope." He stopped dribbling, tucked the ball under his arm and said, "You know, coach 'ain't' such a bad guy after all."

Breeland stretched his eyes and said, "Says who?"

"I think he wants to teach me how to run."

Breeland got the basketball from him and took a couple of shots, missing them both. Omar had the ball now with Breeland defending. What Omar lacked in stamina he made up for with his quickness. He dribbled to his right, then switched hands. He drove, then spun in the opposite direction for an uncontested layup.

Breeland high-fived him. "Good move."

The two of them traded shots, along with Kevin, for a few minutes, until Breeland asked while getting ready for a free throw, "So how is he gonna teach you how to run?"

Before Omar could respond they heard the coach's whistle for them to come in.

"I'm not sure what he means but he says he can, and said he'll tell me more about it later."

The rest of the class raced by the two of them to claim bragging rights for who's first to the doors of the gymnasium, for that day anyway. After getting showers and having changed, Omar checked his time in the '40' on the board. Breeland was next to him. Omar shook his Head; disappointed in the time he had posted. He thought to himself, 'How does coach intend to help me improve on that?' Breeland knew his friend was already punishing himself over his run time, and decided to say nothing as they headed to the next class.

"See you in the next hour, Bree."

"Later man."

They walked to opposite ends of the 2nd story corridor for their next class. Omar was always a little early for this class. It was Business English, his best subject. It was the one bright spot within his otherwise timid and myopic existence. He took a seat one row from the front of the class as usual. It was more strategic than random. He was making sure he wouldn't be bothered with classmates needing answers to pop quizzes the teacher sometimes sprung on them. There was a better chance they'd let him alone if she had a clear view of him, and what went on around him. His heart throb, Priscilla Eagan, decided to sit next to him just before the teacher walked in. She also flirted with him a little but Omar couldn't really tell if she was for real, or just wanted to be entertained by his reactions. It was too complex for him to try and process all at once. He only lived in the moment and as far as he was concerned, if Priscilla wanted him to get down on all fours and bark like a dog he might be inclined to do it, just to prove he was worthy of her affection.

"Hi, Omar."

"Hi, Priscilla. You look nice today."

He avoided her gaze for fear of doing, or saying something goofy, but the teacher, Mrs. Dowdy, rescued him, almost that is. She sprung a pop quiz on them from what they had discussed the day before.

"Anyone want to volunteer?"

No one spoke up. Omar was still clinging to the fantasies Priscilla's flirting left him with When Mrs. Dowdy interrupted..

"Well, I guess I'll have to draft somebody. Omar, do you want to take a shot at it?"

"Mam?"

"Are you even listening to me?"

Most of the class snickered, as all eyes were on Omar.

"I'm sorry. Could you repeat the question?"

He glanced at Priscilla, who had a confused look on her face; surprised Omar didn't just blurt it out.

"I know you know this. What is the correct expression for the plural of mother-in-law?"

"It's ahhh—it's mothers-in-law, mam."

"And what's the rule that applies here?"

He was a little more confident once reality set in, knowing his prospects with Priscilla had the same effect as watching a celebrity on T.V. for an hour or two, then having to turn the set off afterward, only to stare at a blank screen.

He said, "The rule is that the plural is always attached to the noun, not the modifier."

Mrs. Dowdy said, "Very good."

She didn't bother him for the remainder of the hour, but when it was over she asked him to stay for a minute.

She asked, "Is everything o.k. with you? You seemed distracted today when I called on you. I wasn't trying to embarrass you, or put you on the spot." She smiled then said, "You're my 'go to guy' when everybody else seems to struggle."

He looked away, then said, "Nothing's wrong Mrs. Dowdy", but his expression told a different story.

"Look, if there's something you want to share it's ok, you know."

"It's all good mam. I'm gonna get to my next class now."

"Alright Omar. See you tomorrow."

He rushed out of class as though he was being chased by some predator. Breeland met him at the door. They had Social Studies together and only needed to report to class before heading for the library to start an assignment together.

"Did you see your precious Priscilla today?" Then he started snickering.

"Cut it out will ya?"

"Well, I'm not the one who wants to elope with her."

"It's not like that anyway. She's just, she's nice that's all. She talks to me. Not like the other girls."

"I'm gonna see if I can find us a couple of terminals so we can get started."

"Ok. I'm going to the head. Be back in a minute."

Omar found himself on the other side of the floor later, searching for books to use on their class project, but found nothing that peaked his interest, except a body building magazine in the periodicals section. He really wasn't into magazines, but wondered if strength training was also something coach had in mind for him. He picked it up and thumbed through the first few pages, thinking there was nothing more hideous than having a body that looked like a bunch of stacked melons; not for someone his age anyway. He thumbed through one magazine, then another, and another, as if trying to find an image that would suit his less potent impression of physical conditioning. Suddenly his trip was cut short by a strong tug on his shoulder. It was Clarence.

"HEY MAN. YOU BEEN in an altered state or something? I've been trying to get your attention for a while now. You ok?"

"Yeah, Yeah Cee Cee I'm alright."

He looked straight ahead, and had a bewildered look on his face, then asked, "How long—?"

He was in mid-sentence before Clarence interrupted.

"Just a few minutes. I didn't want to keep raising my voice across the floor so I decided to come out here and get you." You and Evelyn watch that tutorial?"

"Yes, we did and we've already been knocking some ideas around about maybe changing our approach."

"Good. Then you'll have something you can share with me after the meeting today?"

"Sure. We can do that. Nothing nailed down yet. Just brain storming."

"I understand. It's all I'd expect at this point anyway."

They walked back to the department together to prep for the afternoon meeting, but Omar decided to square things with Evelyn first before re-opening his desk top. He knew his sudden detour after their break caught her off guard. He needed to clean things up with her; not give her enthusiasm for their assignment a reason to grow cold because his seemed to be nothing short of anemic, but Theo intercepted him before he made it through the breezeway on the way to her desk.

"Omar, how is it?"

"Hey Theo, how's it going?"

"I'm good. Still trying to get through that Humanities, though—Man, that's a tough subject."

"I thought you were doing better with that since we last talked about it?"

"Yeah, I thought I was too, but writing those essays to try and tie the history and the art together is what kills me."

He all of a sudden had a bewildered expression, feeling he might not survive the course. Omar stopped walking and grabbed Theo's forearm.

"Did you try the study schedule I recommended to you?"

"I've gotta admit, I got a little lazy with it."

"Look, I was intimidated by that subject too at first, but my wanting to succeed in it was even greater. So, I figured out a way to give myself the best chance at doing that. I knew I had to work harder than some, but I did what was necessary and it paid off."

"Three hours a day devoted to one subject? Still sounds like prison."

"It won't seem that way once you see your grades improve, but don't give up on yourself. It's the same as deciding to jump ship to take your chances swimming with the sharks. You might think your trip is a little slow while inside the boat, but you can be certain you'll get there in one piece, literally; know what I mean?"

"You're right. It's time I regrouped."

They started walking again, but he thought for a moment how hypocritical it was for him to give such poignant advice to someone like Theo, but be unwilling to follow the same advice himself. He tried to waive it off as a condition totally unrelated to what he was experiencing by thinking of it as 'youthful indiscretion' that needed the guidance of an elder statesman, but there really wasn't any difference. His problem, and Theo's problem, were both kept alive through fear. ..

Theo asked, "Hey Omar, I was talking to that new IT tech., Blake, a little while ago, and we might be at the courts this weekend for some hoops. You interested?"

"I'm not sure if I can. Evelyn and I have the sponsorship gig this year for the festival and I may be doing some work on that this weekend. Speaking of which, I've gotta see her now so, I'll talk to you later?"

"Ok, later."

Omar was actually relieved he was ending the chat with Theo. He felt eventually the subject of Blake might be at the center of their discussion, which he would have resisted. He knew deep down it wasn't altogether fair that Blake already had the distinction, in his mind, of only parading as a nice guy but in reality would become his nemesis. He was overthinking this one almost to the point of hysteria. Seeing Evelyn's smiling face was the shot he needed at that moment to arrest whatever reservations he may have had about Blake.

Evelyn asked jokingly, "Just decided to dump me, huh?"

"Sorry about that Evelyn. I had just remembered I needed to deal with a real personal issue, and frankly, I needed the space to think clearly."

"I get it. Can't afford to be seen with this old hag for too many minutes at a time."

She looked sad for a moment, but then the wide grin returned.

"I'm just kidding you Omar…It's no big deal."

He smiled and said, "I wished I had your sense of humor."

"You probably already do. It's just that it's most likely buried under tons of emotional rubble."

He looked at her and shook his head with a half-smile. She returned the gesture, then began rapping her pen on the desk; a signal she was ready to change the subject.

He said, "I spoke with Clarence a little while ago out there. I told him we looked at the tutorial and were already putting our heads together on some different ideas—Said he'd like to hear about them even though we don't have anything concrete."

"Well, I guess we're getting closer to zero hour by the minute. What's your gut feeling? You think he'll like what we want to do?"

"Hard to say. He said it himself. He wanted to be blown away by whatever we did; anything but the status quo." Evelyn's body language indicated she was getting into high gear again just talking about it.

Omar said, "If he's not receptive then we'll have to move to Plan-B, whatever that might be. Anyway, it's not like it's a job."

Evelyn's tone became serious. "Well, it is for me." She dropped her head a little then looked him in the eye. "This is the closest thing to a new job I've seen in a while, and frankly at this point in my life it's not so much about the money, but the challenge. Just the satisfaction of knowing I made an impression; making a difference for a change, you know what I mean?"

She had a desperate look in her eyes that seemed to beg for his understanding about it.

"I know exactly what you mean, and if he resists, I guess we'll just have to make a believer out of him."

For the first time since he had known Evelyn, he had a crystal clear view of her motivations and how drastically different they were from his own.

He said in a somber tone, "I'll see you at the meeting"—then returned to his cubicle.

Chapter 3

CLARENCE'S HOME SEEMED TO be the new jewel on his block since they moved in. He and Melanie went overboard with their upgrades. It was the surest way to build equity from the day they moved in, even if their stay was temporary. Clarence is thoughtful that way. He is the type of husband and father who knows the importance of planning ahead for any unusual twists in his circumstances that could otherwise leave him in a 'pickle'. It is the strength of his character that always makes him seem larger than life. For everyone that knows him, it means having faith that in situations where his metal is really tested, he would never choose to flaunt an unflattering version of himself that might give them pause. He prefers to try and be a friend, even to those who aren't so friendly by nature, which makes it easy for others to like and respect him. It isn't a particular chore for him, but simply proof of what he is made of, what he is led to do, and who he is led by.

Melanie usually busied herself preparing dinner for the three of them, even though she was still working full time and halfway through her pregnancy. The physical toll on her was not quite evident yet. Besides, Clarence's culinary skills left much to be desired still. It was never anything she pressed him about, but he'd need to learn soon enough as time passed. Their three year old, Nathan, was busy playing with the new toy he got from the day care earlier that day when he heard the gate open. It was his que, like clockwork, to drop everything and meet his dad at the door…

"Daddy's home!" He yelled as he dropped the toy and ran to the door, trying desperately to turn the knob to open it not realizing it needed unlocking first. Melanie moved him aside casually as she brushed the sheer panel over the glass insert to one side, wearing a broad smile. She unlocked the door while Nathan bounced up and down in anticipation of meeting his father. Clarence had placed his jacket over his shoulder and was loosening his tie as he slowly headed toward the door. He looked somewhat spent, but suddenly came alive when he saw Nathan racing toward him with arms outstretched and a wide grin. Clarence dropped his briefcase onto the walkway and stooped slightly to pick him up for the ride on his shoulders.

"Hey big guy. How'd it go today?"

"Fine daddy. Daddy, I—I learned a new rhyme today."

"You did? You wanna sing it for me?"

"Ok" Nathan really looked forward to each day around that time. There was always some kind of prize for him whenever Clarence made it home. Clarence balanced him on his shoulders with one hand while picking up his briefcase with the other. He slowed his pace while making his way to the door. Melanie waited patiently with the door propped open slightly.

"Incy wincy spider climbed up the water spout.
Down came the rain and washed poor Incy out .
Out came—Out came the sunshine and dried up all the rain,
So Incy wincy spider climbed up the spout again.

"He started to grin, pressing his palms against the side of Clarence's head.

"That's awesome big guy."

"I'm not finished daddy!"

"Oops—Daddy's sorry." Nathan started to grin again then continued singing the rhyme.

> "Incy wincy spider climbed up on my chair.
> He climbed up my arm and then hid in my hair.
> He tickled my—He tickled my leg and; and he—"

Clarence could hear him sighing not being able to recall the rest of the rhyme.

"You o.k. up there big guy? Wanna get down now?"

Nathan said softly, "Yes sir."

He dropped his case then reached up,

"Ready?" Clarence wrapped his hands around Nathan's fore-arms, lowering him gently to the ground, removing the jacket from his shoulder afterward. He held Nathan by his waist while kneeling in front of him, with a compassionate look in his eye. He then pulled two lollipops from his jacket pocket.

"Your prize sir."

Nathan hung his head, fretfully stroking his bottom lip with one finger.

He then said, "But I forgot the rest."

Clarence put both hands against his cheeks, smiled, and said, "Those are for having the courage to try."

"Thank you daddy", then gave Clarence a big hug around his neck before stepping back behind his mother.

Melanie then said, "Hi, handsome."

"Hello pretty lady" He kissed her on the lips, then patted her swollen stomach. "How are my girls today?"

"Oh, they're fine. She's been a little restless though."

Clarence said, "Can't wait to make her debut no doubt."

He put his jacket across the back of the couch at the edge of the living room, then kneeled in front of Melanie kissing her stomach twice. Staring at it curiously and rubbing it gently.

"Hello little princess."

Melanie ran her fingers through his bushy hair while he put his ear to her stomach, desperate to feel some movement from the little miracle growing inside of her.

"She's decided to take a nap I guess." He raised up and kissed her on the forehead.

She then whispered, "I'll let you know when she wakes up."

She brushed her delicate hands against his cheeks. Wishing that his disappointment would be short-lived, then walked back to the kitchen to finish preparing dinner. Clarence watched her as she walked away. Remembering how their romance started as more of a 'slow burn'. Something that seemed about as likely as an elephant sprouting wings at first, but then he had grown too, and Melanie truly blossomed in more ways than he could have imagined in the beginning. Remembering the effect she had on him even when they were in middle school, when her alluring eyes captivated him. Then a heart swelling with compassion, in time, had claimed his own soon after the first real glimpse into his manhood. She seemed to fill every space inside his dreams, and proved to be the long awaited answer to his prayers. She is a virtuous woman; always gentle in her spirit, guarded in her speech, and thoughtful in her relationships. She had become his flower in full bloom.

He decided to spend time with Nathan before he did anything else, and sat on the floor beside him in the the family room…

"Look what I got from school today daddy?"

"Oh, a new friend." Clarence looked at it closely. "It's Roger Rabbit."

"How did you know his name already?"

"Oh, him and me, we go way back. He's a big T.V. star you know."

He took the toy out of Nathan's hands, then held it up to his face and asked in a more serious tone—

"Are you still a movie star Roger Rabbit?"

Speaking now in an animated high pitched voice, he held the stuffed toy close to his face and said, "You'd better believe it, and me and my buddy Nathan are gonna have some big fun together."

Nathan started to grin, reaching for the toy.

"I know that's you daddy." He kept reaching for the toy but Clarence kept moving it around each time Nathan would reach for it. Still speaking in the animated voice.

"I'll bet you can't catch me. Catch me if you can."

It tickled Nathan to no end, and he couldn't stop grinning. It was a fun time for him; bonding with his father. He stood to his feet suddenly thinking he'd have a better chance at taking it from him.

Clarence then said, in the animated voice, "Ok, you win. I give up."

Nathan clutched the toy tightly then started rubbing it in Clarence's face. Clarence fell over, lying on the floor and laughing. Nathan began to roughhouse with him a little. Then the tickling started. Nathan liked the tickling, and so did Clarence. The fun they'd have together left little room for the intrusion of parental correctness, except when Melanie stepped into the room.

"Ok you two, dinner's almost ready."

"You heard the lady of the house big shot. He got to his knees, then patted Nathan on the head. "Daddy's gonna get his shower now."

The aromas from Melanie's cooking always caused Clarence to suddenly shift into high gear. It was irresistible, and she just kept getting better at it as time passed by. He understood the challenge of being a working mom and homemaker was no easy feat, but she made it seem so effortless. It was proof enough for Clarence that their future together was far from accidental. As certain as her transformation was from 'little girl' to 'his goddess', she tried to reassure him often enough, that for every new thing they would face together, she would trust him unconditionally; staking her love and devotion on keeping a smile on his face, as well as contentment in his heart.

She asked, "How was your day today sweetheart?"

"Oh, nothing earth shattering. Got bogged down with trying to familiarize myself with some of the new templates for the P.C. upgrades."

He blessed the table, then took portions from the few bowls that were there. It was spaghetti and meatballs. One of his favorites.

"Umm, smells good."

"How about your day? You're not trying to do too much are you?"

"No. Gordon has suspended my field assignments already. You'd think it was his baby I'm having with the way he fusses over me."

"He's just being cautious."

She started fixing a small portion for Nathan when she said, "I know."

Clarence asked, "How was your day at school today big guy? Anything exciting happen?" Nathan felt as tall as Clarence sitting in his high chair. In his mind, they could talk like men then…

"The teacher showed us pictures on the wall of heroes. She said they were—, some of our greatest heroes."

"She did, well that's great. You remember any of their names?"

He paused then said, "I told her, my daddy was my biggest hero."

Nathan kept twirling his spaghetti with his spoon as if it was a new play thing, while staring at his plate. Melanie stopped dishing her food, then cupped her hands placing them under her chin with a satisfied expression. Grateful that the bond between father and son seemed unshakeable.

Clarence looked at him then said, "That's funny, because I feel the same way about you", then poked him in the stomach a few times.

Nathan started to grin, then put the first spoonful of spaghetti in his mouth. Melanie grabbed her stomach suddenly.

"Oh boy. She's really active now."

Clarence jumped up, "Really? Let's see."

He rushed to her side and gently placed his hand over her stomach. "Ahhh, Hah!" he said excitedly. "She's dancing."

He then put his ear against it, but the baby had settled down already. Nathan looked on curiously, wondering what all the commotion was about. Clarence kissed Melanie on the lips, and said, "Thanks for the sneak peek."

When he sat back down she asked, "How are plans for the festival coming; with the sponsors I mean?"

"Oh, I've picked my team. I think I've given them a good start but, I'm a little curious about my pick for lead."

"Why, who is it?"

"Omar Duncan. You met him once, or twice maybe."

"I think I remember him; slender, fortyish? Has the radio voice?"

"Yeah, that sounds like him."

"So, what's the problem?"

"His self-confidence. The guy is talented, but he's not convinced that he is. Something went down in his past that's shaken him but he won't talk about it."

"Umm, that's not good."

"Tell me about it. I believe I know the 'who' but not the 'why.'"

"Meaning?"

"One of the sponsors I assigned them to is a former employer of his; Dillon Industries." Clarence sighed, then put his fork down. "He got a little defensive when I offered to do some checking with them before he and Evelyn set up their meeting with them. Thinking maybe I could find out if there was any one still on staff that had a bone to pick with him."

"You must really be impressed with him to go to that extent."

"He's a natural; Great presentation skills. I know he's the one, but that one thing is blocking his potential. The other half of the team has just the opposite outlook. Evelyn has a great attitude. You know, as long as she's been there she hasn't been promoted yet, for whatever reason. Not that she hasn't tried either, but she runs on one speed, overdrive. She never complains; always upbeat. I'm gonna see what I can do to change things for her too."

"You know baby, if you're that concerned about Omar maybe you should do the advance work anyway. Who says he has to know about it?"

"I don't know if I should."

"Look, as long as I've been an investigator for C.P.S., I know I have to have a sixth sense about some things and just follow my instincts. What you do know, is that if this festival is going to succeed the sponsorship is critical. So, trust yourself and follow those instincts again, like you did when you picked him as your Lead."

"You know, you're right."

"Like I said, he doesn't have to know about your snooping around."

They both laughed. "You make it sound sinister."

Nathan had become restless trying to free himself from his chair.

"Mommy can I get down now?" She noticed he had eaten most of his dinner, then got up to let him down.

She then said to Clarence, "Don't run the risk of it becoming a problem if you've left some stone unturned that could bury you in the end."

She took the bib from around Nathan's neck and told him to go wash his hands.

Bath time was also play time for Nathan. He seemed to want his entourage around him then too for the nightly ritual; Kermit the frog, Buzz Light Year, Sponge Bob, Humpty, Spider Man, and Mini Me. All present and accounted for. Melanie set up his bath for him while he situated his playmates facing away from the tub. He introduced Roger Rabbit to them and insisted they be nice to him. Melanie smiled, thinking they may have a future diplomat on their hands, who also wasn't lost on the need to show a little modesty. After putting Nathan and his friends to bed, Clarence and Natalie looked forward to their alone time together. They were also best friends and even after unplugging from their careers, were each other's lens that brought their world into sharper, more intimate focus. They were young, and sought a deeper understanding as parents, but appreciated the joy it brings that is also too often unsung. The anguish they each felt over the condition of the nation ran deep, and what seemed a foreshadowing of the 'death of charity' inside a world their children will most likely inherit. Natalie's fatigue forced a deep sigh; finally able to lay her head in Clarence's lap. It was her favorite posture after a trying day. He was her strong tower, but whose heart was made more malleable by the sweet sound of her voice, and the titillating aroma of cocoa butter over her silky smooth skin. Her arms lay loosely against his lap as he massaged them gently with one hand, while caressing her well rounded buttocks with the other. She turned her face toward his with a flirtatious smile. He gently stroked her slightly matted hair for a moment, then their lips met in a long and passionate kiss before she suddenly moved his hand to her stomach.

He smiled and said, "She's on the move again. Maybe she's restless thinking we're about to get into a little mischief."

They smiled at each other, then thought it best to delay the passion for another time. After all, circumstances for it were not exactly ideal. They decided instead on refereeing the political side shows, courtesy of their favorite T.V. talk forums. Actually, it was more comic relief than anything else. Time seemed fleeting that night. They had their fill of the pundits' partisan rants, with real news mixed in sparingly, and decided to retreat to a little nostalgia. Clarence always ended up there to settle things down. Natalie also didn't mind. It was a safe destination before bedtime. Natalie had nodded out on the movie they were watching after the first hour when Clarence's cell phone Rang. It was Omar…

"Hey man, what's going on?"

"I—I need a favor."

"Ok, name it."

Omar was ashamed to admit his problem. He kept breathing heavy, looking for the right opening. He had stopped at the bar not far from work at the end of his shift, and had a few too many.

"Omar—Omar, what's wrong?"

"I'm at Dooley's, on Richmond. You know; not far from work."

Clarence raised Natalie's body up gently, turned the T.V. off, and then moved to the living room to talk.

"You've been there since after work?"

"Not exactly."

He was breathing heavy and sighing in between. Clarence could tell he had been drinking, and was disappointed. He had broken his sobriety, which he swore he would never do.

"I was at the book store for a while at first."

There was silence for a moment. "How much have you had to drink Omar?"

He paused, then said, "A few beers. Well, maybe a couple of Hennessey too, but it's not like I'm not in control of myself. Look, I just didn't know who else I could call. I didn't really trust trying to catch the last bus home. Look, I'm sorry to bug you so late. Don't worry about it. I'll manage."

Clarence said abruptly, "'Wait! Wait."

He checked the time. It was almost 8:45pm. "I'll be there in about 20 minutes. Just stay put."

"Thanks Cee Cee."

"Yeah, ok."

He told Melanie where he was going and he'd be back in about an hour.

He kissed her and said, "I'll understand if you're already in bed, but he's in trouble, and needs a little help."

When he got to Dooley's and parked out front, he was opening his door to go inside when he noticed Omar coming out to meet him. He didn't notice him wobbling, which gave him the impression the drinking wasn't about trying to drown his troubles altogether, but just to escape them for a while.

"Hey Boss. I appreciate the lift", and got into the car right away.

"You live at the same apartment complex, right?"

"Yeah, you know the place."

Omar could see the disillusionment in Clarence's expression. He looked straight ahead and said nothing almost 10 minutes into their trip.

"How's your wife and kid?"

"They're good."

"So, when are you guys expecting your second one?"

"She's a little over halfway through. Hopefully sometime in February."

Clarence's voice seemed mechanical. His eyes also gave no indication he was ready to be conversational all of a sudden.

"You picked any names yet?"

Clarence turned to him finally and said, "Look, I'm not much for small talk right now when you know we should be talking about something else."

He finally showed some signs of life but Omar knew he owed him an explanation and he might as well not delay the inevitable. The fact that he felt comfortable calling Clarence for help without thinking twice about it let him know he would probably be more concerned about his welfare than the amount of gas he would have burned for the trip.

"Why did you break your sobriety? It's the only way you're gonna help make things right again you know. And don't think your counselor at AA, or anybody else for that matter, is gonna pat you on the back for it."

"I know; I know but, I was alone and I didn't think one or two would hurt, ok? I mean, it's not like I'm some lush. Anyway, my life ain't perfect like yours Cee Cee."

He brushed his hair back and started stroking his beard again, letting his agitation run its course. He then hung his head and said, "I'm sorry—I'm sorry, I shouldn't have said that."

The frustration in his voice was more about how he was punishing himself than from Clarence's brow beating him. Clarence took a deep breath, disposing of his own emotional residue, as he parked in front of Omar's apartment building.

"Why don't you go sleep it off and I'll see you in the morning. I will see you in the morning, won't I?"

He stared at him with the blandest expression plastered across his face.

Omar responded, "Yeah, sure. Why wouldn't you?"

Clarence decided to wait until he made it safely inside before he drove off. Omar had disguised his intoxication pretty well before they left Dooley's because it was more noticeable the moment he stepped out of the car. It's as if he had decided there was no need to stay inside the charade any longer. Besides, Clarence had already judged him and found him 'guilty as charged'. He threw his keys on the cocktail table on the way to his suite, and slung his bags on the floor, watching them slide just inside the doorway. His frustration drove what little was left of his sensibilities into hiding. He found himself wallowing in his disappointment as he headed toward the bedroom. He didn't notice his bags on the floor, and almost tripped, but caught the edge of the door frame to steady himself. He leaned against it, breathing heavily. Fear had suddenly gripped him because of the break with his sobriety. He knew it was an act of betrayal to his counselor, his family, his associates, and especially to himself. He was stuck in what seemed suspended animation for a while trying to pin point the reason he succumbed in a moment of weakness. The ransacking of his self-confidence through the years had left so much rubble that he didn't really know where to begin to try and repair the damage. He glanced at his watch while still leaning against the doorframe. It was 9:25pm. He forgot about the time just as quickly when he kicked off his shoes and unbuttoned his shirt, only to stop suddenly as his mind churned scenes of an alabaster shroud with lots of hands underneath, pushing frantically against it, needing to escape. He detached quickly, to then search his heart for the thing that led him to sobriety in the first place, but it was nowhere to be found. It was the loneliest feeling he had ever felt in his life. He noticed the full length mirror in the corner of his eye a few feet away and decided to step in front of it for a little self-recrimination. The subdued light was perfect cover thinking it would be less panful if his image was not so vivid. He was obviously optimistic about being not so 'self-aware' in that instance, but as he stood there rehearsing in his mind what he would say to a reflection of himself, it appeared.

He was understandably startled at first; shaking his head from side to side repeatedly in disbelief, then wiping his eyes only to see what looked to be a vapor in the form of a man. It had no features that were distinguishable. Moving with fluid motion it remained within the sharp confines of its likeness. Omar could not take his eyes from it as it stood a little behind him and to one side. A loud hissing sound suddenly enveloped the room, and ended after a few moments, then it spoke. Its voice was deep but pleasant and non-threatening; as in the manner a father might address his son.

"OMAR, I SEE THAT you are still haunted by your troubles."

The voice seemed to fill the room but Omar kept his eyes on the image. He remained rigid and started to tremble; making fists in a defensive posture, but feeling there really was no defense to mount against it. He relaxed a little, then spoke to it.

"Who—, are you?"

"Just look at me as an agent of, The Comforter; Your conscious by any other name. It paused briefly—"I've been abandoned because of years of neglect; neglect by you, Omar."

Its tone seemed bleak and foreboding. Omar thought to himself, 'Am I really doing this; talking to a spirit? This can't be real.'...

"Oh Yes, you are talking to me and I'm as real as everything else your eyes have seen."

"But, I wasn't speaking."

"True, but I'm still aware of every thought that crosses your mind, even while trapped inside this, prism."

"This isn't possible."

He then backed away from the mirror a little and turned away from it, but it wasn't in front of him anymore. Then the voice said, "Hear I am, right where you found me."

Omar turned to face the mirror again. He stepped closer and there it was.

"What do you want from me?"

"I want; I need, your trust for my return to be of any value. Only then will I be able to come home Omar; back where I belong."

Omar just stared at it but somewhat bewildered.

"What do you mean by wanting to come home? I don't understand."

"I've been an orphan too long. Out here, in this wretched 'limbo' all this time. I've wanted desperately to protect you, counsel you, and wanted only the best for you, but the more you felt you didn't really need me, the more you drove me away."

"How could I drive you away? I—I wanted to trust in you, but—"

Omar hung his head, unable to convincingly plead his case.

"All is not lost Omar. You still have a chance to make things right again. (the last word of its phrase was repeated several times but fading)

Omar then said, "I don't feel so well." He placed his palm to his forehead, as the voice of the image kept fading, then there was silence.______

He had fallen asleep, but when he woke up he realized he had made it to his bed at least, still fully dressed. It was 2:15am. The effects of the alcohol still depleting his senses somewhat. He turned toward the mirror, got out of bed slowly, and stood to face it from a distance. He stood there for a few moments but there were no signs of any phenomenon from some parallel dimension that might decide to badger him this time.

He then said, "Huh, must have just been a dream."

Clarence had made it to the office the next day a little earlier. The episode with Omar the night before bothered him a lot. He remembered what Melanie had said about the success of the festival hinging on the size of the sponsorships, which meant he really did need to make sure his team was as 'glitch free' as possible. To have his efforts torpedoed by the team leader, who was wary of the assignment in the first place, wouldn't bode well for his own reputation either. He kept his office door closed which was a sign to the staff he would prefer not to be disturbed unless heaven and earth were about to be moved. He logged onto his desktop, watching the cursor flash for almost 3 minutes, waiting on his next command. He then turned to face the big studio chair against the wall that had a framed copy of one of his favorite scriptures inscribed.

'For God has not given us the spirit of fear; but of power,
and of love, and of a sound mind'
2 Timothy: Chp-1, vs-7

He stood in front of it. Staring at it, as if expecting to glean more than it had already revealed. At first feeling sorrowful over Omar's troubles, then suddenly remembering the one thing he had not yet done for him since the first sign of trouble. He had not prayed for him. He dropped his head suddenly, closed his eyes, clasped his hands together, and made an appeal to the Father on Omar's behalf, that his mercy would allow his pain to be replaced with 'perfect peace'. He didn't feel in any way responsible for Omar's predicament, after having pressed him so about accepting the assignment, but he did feel obligated to help him weather this storm in any way he could until he rose above whatever calamity it doled out to him. He opened his door, greeted staff that had already shown up for work, then finished opening up his desktop to start his search into Omar's past. His own personnel file revealed very sketchy information about Omar's time with Dillon. The work history was too far back and included names for job titles that were already obsolete. He decided He'd need to dig deeper, so he called the Human Resources Manager at Dillon for help. After speaking with an assistant twice from earlier attempts, he finally got through.

"Mrs. Sheffield, my name is Clarence Colter. I'm a supervisor in the product development division at Earth Burst Industries. Thank you for agreeing to speak with me."

"Oh yes, my assistant said you had called about information on a former employee. You considering him for employment?"

"Oh, no. He's been with us now for over six years already. I know this is probably unusual to ask, but can you determine from your current file on him if there were any citations of any kind issued while he was there?"

"You're right. It is unusual to be asked at this late date, and privacy laws would forbid us from disclosing any details. We can only say that he worked here, how long, and under what circumstances his employment ended. I'm sorry I can't be of more help. Anyway, his actual employment file has been archived already, and it would take an act of congress almost to justify retrieving it."

"I understand."

'Hold on a minute. When did you say he was here?"

"Around 2003, I believe, is when he left your company."

"There was a guy that two of my staff used to talk about. They were here around that time. They would joke about how the police department would probably be called out today for punching out a supervisor like this one guy did over some rift that had been brewing between this employee and a line production supervisor back then."

"Did they mention the employee's name?"

"I don't recall. Those two guys are no longer here either. They did say the guy must have known he'd be black-listed after that though."

"Why is that?"

"Well in my universe, you don't make too many friends after something like that, and you may just lose a few. He was lucky that supervisor didn't file assault charges."

Clarence said abruptly, almost in Omar's defense, "If he instigated it!"

"Yes, of course. Well, is there anything else I can help you with?"

"Yes. You did say you could at least tell me if he resigned or if he was terminated."

"What's his full name?" "Omar Duncan."

"Give me a minute." Mrs. Sheffield accessed the employee archive for that period and found the 'General Information' database for employees listed alphabetically. It showed Omar resigned after only eighteen months. "Well, looks like he resigned after only 18 months of employment shortly after the incident occurred with that supervisor, coincidentally."

"I see."

"Anything else?"

"No, you've been a great help. Thanks again", then hung up.

Clarence accessed their personnel file again to review Omar's previous employment history. It showed a 14 month gap in employment from the time he left Dillon to his next job. He looked at his actual application more closely this time and noticed he had accepted only part-time employment as a day worker through an employment agency while attending one of the state colleges for his final year to earn his Bachelors in Communication. That twenty one month gap with no verifiable employment, the short time with Dillon, and what occurred after that before being hired by Earth Burst were missing pieces to the puzzle that he now felt compelled to find.

"Hello Munch." (short for munchkin)

"Hi Aunt Evelyn."

"Aunt Ev, why do you keep calling me that? I'll be 21 in a couple of months. Don't you think you should ditch that name by now?"

Munchkin was no doubt more of a term of endearment for Evelyn than for her nephew, but she decided to yield to his sensitivity about it.

Evelyn replied, "I'll think about it", then laughed a little. "Did you get a chance to look at that brochure on the recovery system yet? We're fine tuning the script and it should be ready for you this week to start putting some things together."

There was no response from him. "Richie, are you still there?"

"I'm here. To be honest Aunt Ev, I haven't opened it up yet. Don't get me wrong. I do want to do this for you but I'm also trying to get ready for midterms and it's a juggling act, you know?"

He could hear her sighing from her disappointment.

"Richie, it's ok if you think it's too much for you."

"No, no. It's ok Aunt Ev. I know how important this is for you. I promise, by the time you get me the script, I'll be able to build that system myself I'll know it so well."

"I don't doubt that one bit."

"I really appreciate this nephew. You know I'm gonna take care of you on your birthday, ok?"

"Ah, don't worry about that Aunt Ev. You've done so much for me, it's the least I could do."

"And to think with all this slobbering between us, I've still got to find a new nickname for you." They both laughed a little.

"So, when do I get to meet the other member of your team?"

"Well, Mr. Duncan may be a part of our next meeting even if it's just a conference call. He's the lead on this and I wouldn't want to step on anybody's toes. Not again anyway. He doesn't know about our contact today but it wouldn't have made any difference. Anyway, it's just a follow-up on your progress until the script is completed."

"Sounds like you're trying to convince yourself it's really not a problem with him not knowing about today. You sure you're ok with teaming up with him on it?"

"He's a good guy. Maybe a little touchy at times, but he's ok. I've sort of, adopted him."

They both laughed again. "No, seriously though, we're actually friends. I admire him because he's well spoken, easy going, and thoughtful when he wants to be.

"Sounds like the start of a great romance."

"Oh no, it's nothing like that. Besides, he only turned 41 a few months ago."

"Well now days that's not exactly robbing the cradle Aunt Ev.", then he laughed a little, and so did she.

"I can't believe I'm talking about him this way with you. Must be something in the water."

Her laughter was winding down as her fantasies flirted with the idea for just a moment or two. "You know, he reminds me a lot of your Uncle Alfred, in better days of course; confident when he was in his element. Sort of eloquent in the way he spoke at times. A smooth talker if you know what I mean, but without all the baggage."

"Well, you did say he was a little sensitive. Like they say, where there's smoke there's fire Aunt Ev. I wouldn't let my guard down with him, you know?"

"Yeah, I know kid. That's one of the reasons Auntie loves you so. You're a good listener." "Love you too Aunt Ev."

"How's your mom and dad?"

"They're still dating you know. Got some big plans for just the two of them tonight."

"They must be best friends too to have done this weekly date night thing for as long as I can remember and not miss a beat."

"Well, don't you know by now young man?"

"I guess. They always come back home afterward with big smiles on their faces." They both laughed again.

Evelyn said, "You're terrible. Look, just be thankful you have two parents who love each other enough, that coming home to be together again is still probably the best part of their day."

"I hear you."

"Well, I gotta go, but tell Roxy she owes me a call alright?"

"Ok Aunt Ev. I'll talk at you later, Bye."

Evelyn treated Richie like the son she never had. He made her feel relevant and wanted, even as far back as when the prospect of having children, and her biological clock were still in agreement. She would have been a really late bloomer had it happened, but Alfred still wasn't on board with the idea after 12 years of marriage. It almost drove her into a depression, but letting go of him, for other reasons, was as good a remedy as any to avoid it at the time and to free herself from his rabblerousing tendencies. Her attitude about men, surprisingly, wasn't jaded from it either because of all the good memories he left her with. Alfred was like an uncut diamond, whose real brilliance was obscured by its roughhewed edges, but still special enough to wish for moments when she could still just gaze at it for days at a time. Richie had actually become her sounding board, and moral center. She could let her hair down with him and still earn his respect. It was more than she could say about some other men. She felt Omar could learn a lesson or two from Richie. She didn't like feeling tentative about approaching him, but it crept into her psyche anyway like an unwanted house guest. She decided to relieve herself of the tension and called him anyway about the contact with Richie.

"Hi Omar, it's Evelyn."

"Oh, Hi Ev. What's up?"

"Just wanted to give you an update."

"Update?"

"I spoke with my nephew, Richie, a little while ago to let him know the script is almost done and hopefully we'll have it in his hands this week. He says by the time he's done going over the brochure he'll be able to build that system himself. He can be overly optimistic at times."

He laughed and said, "I understand."

"I'm glad you took the initiative to call him though."

"He's still not talking about fees?"

"He told me not to worry about it. Said he's doing it as a courtesy because he knows how important it is to me."

"Sounds like he's really fond of you."

"It's like I told you before, he's like a son to me. Richie knows me. I even told him to let me know if he felt it was too much for him; to give him an out, you know, but he insisted. He knows we wouldn't try and exploit him. Anyway, he's smart enough to see that coming a mile away. I trust him to be honest about it."

"Nice P.R. work Ev. I guess we really don't have to worry about a budget for his work after all. A real luck of the draw, huh?"

She said re-assuredly, "More like a ram in the bush."

"What was that?"

"Never mind." She then said, "You want to try and button up the script in a couple of days?"

"I guess we should. Any headway with finding actors?"

"I gave a few people a heads up. Got only green lights on two of them though."

"Maybe we should recruit actors with an announcement on the big board downstairs." Evelyn responded quickly. "I'm trying to rely on my hand picked crew to commit first. Maybe in another day, if everybody hasn't gotten back to me by late tomorrow. Is that o.k.? I did give them a deadline."

"Sure, that's your piece of it anyway."

"Oh, before I forget, you might want to see if Theo would be interested in being a part of it in some way. I've noticed he treats you like a big brother; probably wouldn't have to worry about him saying no. He seems to really look up to you."

"I'll mention it to him—By the way, Clarence said we can take whatever time in the afternoons we need to work on it, so let's plan on selecting the cast by tomorrow, o.k.?"

"Alright, sounds like a plan. I'll see you in the morning then. Goodnight."

Clarence caught Omar and Evelyn leaving the conference room about 30 minutes before the end of their shift, and decided to ask for another update on the script. It was his fourth, in as many days. He wanted to avoid making a pest of himself, but felt he could spare them a few editing headaches if he could proof the contents first. Before he could open his mouth, Omar beat him to it…

"The script will be done by tomorrow, guaranteed."

"What makes you think I was gonna ask you about the script?"

"Just a wild guess. Figured you'd want to see it first; you know, just to make sure we don't misrepresent the company."

Clarence looked at Evelyn with a smile. He was amused over how direct Omar had become.

"He is right, isn't he Cee Cee?"

"Ok, guilty as charged. Will I be able to look at it tomorrow?"

"We don't' see why not. It may be near the end of the day but, we should have it to you."

"Ok. That'll work."

He started to walk away then Omar said, "Oh, and Cee Cee, we haven't forgotten you're a part of this team too, so—, the input is appreciated."

Clarence was pleased. He could see Omar finally taking hold of the project too and making it their own. It was a little unexpected coming from the grand procrastinator himself, but a pleasant surprise nonetheless.

Saturday mornings seemed like just another work day for Omar. He jokingly referred to it as 'stuff day', having his waking hours cluttered with chores he'd rather ignore. Although it seemed most of his misfortunes had been self-inflicted, his drinking sadly didn't exactly diminish the glare of shortcomings created by years of having traded purposeful thinking for more wistful pursuits. Neglecting the thing that was most unique about himself had left an almost hollowed out shell of identity, with a seamless cord of sad faces lurking within it. He had been wading through troubled waters left behind from bouts with self-confidence as far back as his childhood. He seemed unable, or unwilling, to rid himself completely of the roadblocks to thinking sensibly, but becoming reckless and impulsive instead. Both traits unfortunately, had been tenants of his character too long; like a house built on faltering piers of self-pity. When he took a moment to think more about it, as he laid there in bed a while before starting his day, he knew the misery had been too much dead weight far too long. If he was ever going to wrap his brain around this project the way Clarence expected him to, he would need to stop letting the lapses in judgment have their way with him. He finally realized there must be something about him that others valued. He knew he had to try and change even though his efforts could be compared to that of a paraplegic struggling to learn how to walk again. Trying to overcompensate in certain situations too, was only going to frustrate his efforts even more. Over-reacting to more than a few circumstances in his past caused him to be a little wary; particularly what happened to Breeland, and what happened at Dillon. They were the closest things to out-of-body experiences he could name, and two he would rather finally count as dead and buried. He finally got out of bed to start his day and checked his itinerary. He needed to call his AA counselor first, to apologize for not showing up at the last few meetings. It was a call he dreaded, but it wasn't as bad as he thought it would be.

"Hi—I needed to let you know, that I fell off the wagon a time or two. That's why I've missed the meetings. I had a few drinks at this place not far from my job just last night, but I did reach out to someone to drive me home. I realized I screwed up big time, and took action, before I had a chance to self-destruct. I'm sorry."

"Well, I appreciate the call and missing a few meetings isn't so bad as long as you're still aware of the importance of why we're here for you in the first place. That won't be held against you Omar. All I ask is that you really examine the reason you broke your sobriety because you've been doing so well."

"Well, what I do realize is that the drinking has always been a symptom of a bigger problem."

The AA Counselor said, "No doubt."

"But I'm getting to work on that too and maybe at some point, all of this will just, go away." There was a brief pause, then the counselor said, "That's ultimately our wish too Omar." "Anyway, I just wanted to touch base to let you know I'm still on board."

"That's good to hear—See you at the next meeting?"

"You can count on it."

He and Evelyn had planned to meet Richie at the Art Institute's film lab at 11 o'clock. It would be his first time meeting him. They had hammered out the script, with Clarence's blessing, and would get a glimpse of the production work that would be involved in completing the video. Richie had done what he promised Evelyn, and had already completed preliminary work on a working 3D computer model from information provided in the brochure. Omar was excited about it and felt Evelyn's advance work was the surest indication of her underutilized talents. He finished his typical Saturday breakfast of fried eggs and a raisin bagel, then called his mom. The call to her was also typical at least once every other Saturday morning...

"Hi mom."

"Omar, Hi. Are you alright?"

"I'm fine. Just wanted to touch base. You guys o.k.?"

"We're fine. Still don't have your license back yet? I hope those AA meetings are helping. They could have at least let you keep your driver's license."

"Mom, like I've been telling you. It's a mandatory 90 day suspension, before I'm allowed to appeal for a hardship. I can't get around that. I'll be ok, as long as I keep my nose clean." He sighed heavily. "Thankfully I don't have that far to go before it's over. I've just got to take my medicine like everybody else, so they tell me."

"Well, whatever you do, keep real friends around you. You know that bottle, can never be your friend. It will always let you down. Trust me on that."

There was a period of long silence as both of them grappled with their emotions.

She then said, "Your Uncle Seth is taking us to Austin's meet today."

Omar replied sarcastically, "Oh, his new protégé."

"He's still waiting on you to call him Omar. Why won't you return his call son?"

"I will, alright? I'll call him. It's just that I've got stuff on my plate right now that needs my attention."

"Well, you always manage to call me."

"That's different."

"Why is it so different? He's also family. He's reaching out. Can't you do the same? He wants to make things right between the two of you. I can't help but wonder why you're hanging on to this feeling for so long. It hurts me, because I know neither of you can reconcile the pain it's caused until you have a one-on-one and hash it out. Your father agrees with me."

"I get it mom. Look, I'm, I'm just gonna need some time that's all."

"He loves you, you know; talks about you all the time." She sighed heavily before a long pause.

"I feel the same mom, it's just that I want to like him too, and that means trusting him again."

"Alright, whatever you say. When are you coming to visit again? It's been a while."

"Maybe when this festival is over, I can catch the train up for a few days before the Christmas holiday"

"I'm hoping you will. It'll be good to see you."

She moved the phone away from her mouth a little and said in a raised tone of voice, "What? Ok, I'll tell him."

She put the phone back to her mouth, "Your Father says Hi."

"Tell him hello for me and, tell him, Go Jaguars!" He started to laugh.

"You really know how to rattle his cage don't you?"

"He loves it. He knows we'll have plenty of time to talk football later, and he can bust my chops about'em then. I'd better go mom. Got a meeting with my team about what we're planning for the festival. I don't wanna miss my ride, so I've got to get my morning started."

"Ok, but let's talk again soon and catch up."

"Ok. Love you guys. Take care."

Chapter 4

G ETTING UP A COUPLE of hours early to get ready for his meeting with Richie and Evelyn was something Omar was still adjusting to. He decided he'd stack the morning with his to-do list, not knowing how long he would be at the Art Institute. He could have felt more alert than he did, but deciding on going to bed earlier that Friday night so he wouldn't rob himself of sleep just didn't occur to him. He was a night owl who didn't see the need to change his routine, even a little. While reorganizing his utility room, he came across one of his banners from high school. He unfolded it, with the image of the school's mascot glaring like bright neon. He sat on the stool inside the room and was suddenly struck with a bit of nostalgia; recalling his junior year there. It was also his breakout year in track. And the 100 meter race, where his posted time was the best in two consecutive races. There had also been talk about Olympic trials for the first time from scouts on the regional committee. It was the proudest moment in his life, realizing he had beaten the odds against him becoming one of the school's best. It brought a smile to his face, but that smile was turned upside down suddenly when he remembered how an incident at one of his meets changed everything. His mentor, Uncle Seth, also seemed to seal his fate after that. His hero, Uncle Seth, was nothing of the kind. It was the most debilitating shot to his confidence after it happened. Seth had owned the record in the same race at the same school for at least three years before it was broken. He had squandered his own chance of getting to the next competitive level because of his overblown ego, by his own admission. The late night partying and rendezvous with young ladies who were nipping at his heels would turn out to be the dead weight he just couldn't shake. It eventually affected his conditioning to the point of him being expelled from the team. (But why did he cast that vote?) Omar had mulled that question over and over, but there would be no placating his bitter-ness—(Was it jealousy?) Thinking about it was beginning to depress him and started to send him to that place where his mem-ories become trapped, involuntarily, inside a bittersweet mirage of his past. Everything he thought about Seth's betrayal only incensed him more. He started to stroke his beard again; closing the door, temporarily, on his indifference toward Seth, only to open another one not too far behind it.

"COACH BIVENS!"

"George, how is it?"

"Fine. Just making my rounds." Omar stopped his stretching routines after the coach called him over.

"Is this the young man you told me about at our function last week?"

"In the flesh. Omar, this is Mr. George Peoples. He's the track coach at Citadel Jr. College. He's part of a pre-recruitment pro-gram for colleges in the area."

"Good to meet you sir."

"Same here young man. Coach Bivens has really good things to say about you, especially how far you've come since you started training."

"Yes sir. He's taught me a lot."

Coach Peoples gave coach Bivens a curious look. "How about a sample then?"

Omar looked at Bivens and said, "Coach?"

"Sure. Let's try the forty. Just to check your form." They moved to the track. Omar started loosening up when coach said, "I've got the wrong stop watch."

Coach Peoples then said, "Don't worry about it. I always keep mine with me. He handed coach Bivens his stop watch and Omar trotted to his mark.

"Ready?"

Coach Bivens raised his hand, then dropped it. Omar's form was a thing of beauty. He was rangy and seemed to put every necessary part of his body into the heat that could improve his performance. When he crossed the line Coach Peoples didn't bother to check his time. He saw the expression on Coach Bivens' face which was good enough for him. He could see that Omar had been well coached and still had two more years of high school left to fine tune his skills even more.

"Well, I'm convinced. He's got talent, and he's not even done yet."

Coach Bivens responded, "Would you believe before I decided to train him, he recorded one of the slowest times in my gym class? Of course he was only twelve at the time."

"Well, if that's the case, he's done an about-face in just a few years."

Omar was approaching them when Coach Peoples said, "Omar, that was impressive. Looks like you've got a career as a runner ahead of you."

Omar smiled broadly then said, "Thank you sir."

"I'm gonna put you on my list for the lottery of pics who might be eligible for athletic scholarships in a few years, but you've got to keep your grades up too. Is that ok with you?" "Oh yes sir. That works for me."

"Well, I'd better keep it moving. It's gonna be a long day. Good meeting you Omar."

"Likewise sir."

"Coach Bivens, I'll call you later."

"Ok George. Thanks for stopping by."

Omar said, "Man; a chance at a scholarship. That's gonna make my parents happy."

"And you'd deserve it. You've put in the work, and it shows. I'm proud of you."

"Thanks Coach."

"Oh, let me get my stop watch and more gator aid for that bunch over there before I forget. Just do some stretches until I come back, ok?"

"Alright."

Omar is energized by what just happened like never before. He's on top of a mountain now that seems unconquerable. For all the adulation he had received, it blinded him temporarily to the fundamentals of preparation he should never have ignored, but he did. He cut his stretching short, took no fluids, and sprinted to the track where the 200 meter runners were. He suddenly joined the race and maintained a good pace until after about 80 meters he pulled up suddenly, grabbed his left hamstring, and rolled over onto the in-field and on his back; his eyes wincing steadily from the throbbing pain. Coach Bivens and two other coaches had rushed to his aid. Omar was Grimacing and moaning, still clutching his thigh.

Coach Bivens sat him up then said, "Here, drink this. Drink it! You're probably cramping." Omar felt he couldn't let go of his thigh, or else his muscles might react like a rubber band. Coach repeated, "Just drink a little more of this then lie still. It'll pass in a minute."

Omar felt guilty for not having followed coach's instructions. He felt like the guy that had lost the Division title for his team…

"I'm sorry coach. I should have listened to you." He was still grimacing, but the pain was disappearing gradually. "I'm sorry."

The other two coaches had walked back to their squads, but the chastisement delivered by Coach Bivens had been earned.

"You hadn't finished stretching and hadn't taken any fluids before you decided to pull that stunt I'll bet. What were you thinking?"

"I just felt I could run with them. I can't explain it. I—I just felt I could."

"Look, I know you feel good about what Coach Peoples said about you but no matter how much something like that might stroke your ego, you can't afford to be impulsive and forget about preparation. It's the thing that got you where you are now. You understand?"

"Yeah, you're right."

"How do you feel? —Still in pain?"

"I think I can get up now."

"Why don't you drink a little more gator aide? I'll be back shortly. Gonna talk to these guys for a minute."

"Ok." He started walking off the effects of the cramps, just as a chorus of horns blowing from the cars of parents who had come to pick up their kids from soccer practice got his attention. He then stopped to watch the runners. The horns still blowing intermittently, as if they were taking turns.

THE HORNS BLARING JUST outside his window from what was likely frustrated drivers inside his parking lot brought him back to reality. He peeked through the mini blinds expecting to find an argument brewing, but discovered the commotion was over a slow moving parade of ducks taking their time crossing the lot. At least the compassion of those drivers toward those ducks was more important than meeting some artificial deadline. When he closed the blinds, his doorbell rang. It was some guy selling Sports Illustrated magazine subscriptions, trying to win a trip to the Olympics next summer.

Omar thinks about it for a minute, then asked him, "Do you play any sports?"

"I'm a swimmer. I'm tops in free-style at my school."

"Well, I guess that counts—I'll pass on the subscription, but here's a donation."

He reached for his wallet on the cocktail table and gave him a ten dollar bill.

"Thanks a lot mister. Have a good day."

"Same to you."

After finishing his cleaning 45 minutes later, his phone rang. It was Evelyn.

"Hi, you gonna be ready at ten?"

"Yeah, I'll be ready. You ok with finding my place?"

"I know where your complex is. I won't have a problem. See you then."

When Evelyn gets to his building, he's already downstairs to meet her.

She parks, then unlocks the passenger side door and said, "Hi, at least you saved me a trip upstairs."

"Hey, truth is, I wanted to spare you the shock of seeing how us bachelors live." Then started laughing.

"Well, knowing you, I'm sure you keep it better than some women I know. I'm gonna call Richie and let him know we're on our way."She got his voicemail and left a message. 'Richie, Aunt Evelyn. Just wanted to let you know we're on our way to the Art Institute. It's a few minutes after ten o'clock, so we should be there before eleven. Will speak to you soon.'

"You'll like Richie. He's a good kid. I could think of a lot more things he could be doing with his Saturday mornings, but he's focused enough at his age to know this experience will probably be good for his resume even though it's not a pay job."

"Or, he's just that taken by his Auntie."

"Well, that too. He told me he and some fellow schoolmates have talked about having their own production company one day."

"Sounds like he's ambitious."

"Yeah, he is. Must be in the genes."

Omar notices young men playing a pick-up game of basketball as they're passing the park some miles from his apartment. It's the same court that's used by some of his co-workers. He thinks he recognizes some of them and wants Evelyn to slow down.

"Slow down for a minute Evelyn."

"What's going on?"

"Pull over by the basketball courts for a minute, ok?"

"We don't have that much time before we have to meet Richie you know."

"It'll be ok. I just want to see who's here is all."

She stops in front of the courts. Omar gets out and stands by the door. He sees Theo and Blake, then walks toward the fence and peers through it like someone who's been denied admittance. Theo sees it's him and says, "Omar, hey. You want in?" Blake sees him and throws up his hand.

"Not today. Evelyn and I have a meeting with someone about plans for the festival. Who's winning?"

A player from the opposing team yells, "Hey man, are we playing or what?"

Theo tells Omar, "Watch us smoke these chumps."

Theo returns to the game, but Omar also stays put. His curiosity over Blake got the best of him and he needed to see if he was the real deal. The mid-morning October sun had begun to beat down on Evelyn after a few minutes. She was irritated from having to sit in the blistering heat, but even more frustrated over Omar's aimless pre-occupations. It's almost as if he had forgotten about the meeting they were certainly going to be late for already. She moved out of the sun to a more shaded spot and honked her horn to get his attention but he just waved her off. He was suddenly fixated on the game, and the one participant who peaked his curiosity. He watched Theo and the third man on their squad pass the ball several times until it was finally in Blake's hands, then the clinic was open. He drove, spun, and then drove again before taking flight for a two handed backward dunk winning the game for them. Theo high fived him, then trotted over to the fence to chat with Omar…

"You sure you don't want in?"

"I'll pass. Another time maybe."

"What do you think of Blake? The boy's got mad skills, huh?"

"Looks like he can handle himself ok."

"Look, I'd better get going. Evelyn's getting anxious."

"Ok, catch you later." When he got back to the car, he sensed Evelyn was annoyed, but then said, "That wasn't so bad was it?" She gave him a stern look then pulled off into traffic.

"Did you really have to make that stop? Now we're already 15 minutes late and I told Richie we'd probably be a few minutes early. You didn't show any consideration for his time when you did that."

Omar looked straight ahead and said nothing. He knew he had triggered Evelyn's hyperactive maternal instincts, especially when it involved how her nephew was treated. But also a much needed dressing down over his own penchant for chaos in situations where it could have been avoided.

She said, "He was good enough to agree to it for no fee. We should at least respect whatever times he agrees to meet with us about it."

She had called Richie again before they left the courts to let him know they had an unscheduled stop, and would be about 20 minutes late.

"When I spoke with him a second time, he said he was already there doing course work and to just call when we got there. He said he'd meet us at the elevators on the 2nd floor and walk us to the lab."

"Look, I'm sorry. You're right. It was impulsive, and it won't happen again."

"Is something going on you'd like to talk about? Because I'm getting the sense that maybe this assignment may not be getting your full attention, when it really deserves it. You know Clarence trusted you with it. Said you were 'his guy' for this. That's confidence that you can't buy."

She paused and said, "There's the school", then turned into the lot to park. Omar was still quiet. Evelyn parked and turned the engine off.

"You know, you don't have to open up to me if you don't want to. Just try not to tip the scales from 'favorite' to 'frivolous' when it comes to Clarence's opinion of you with too many unexpected detours in whatever you're dealing with, because you may never get that back."

She smiled at him to let him know their friendship wasn't in jeopardy yet, but hoped her honesty had spoken for itself. He smiled a little at her then said, "Let's go meet your nephew."

Omar took the folder that contained copies of the script for each of them from the back seat, along with a stack of blank re-writeable CD's.

"I meant to ask you, what are the CD's for?"

"Just in case he might want them for editing. We can't expect him to supply everything."

"Now that's the way a team leader thinks."

Omar said, "And how's that?"

"A few steps ahead. You'll get points for that with Richie."

"Who is this nephew of yours anyway, another Stephen Spielberg?"

She laughed then said, "Don't underestimate him. He's got skills", then walled her eyes at him. He smiled, shaking his head while opening the door for her.

She then said, "I'm just saying, it'll show him you want to help him as much as possible to make it a success. It may not be such a big deal monetarily, but huge when it comes to caring about how he goes about his work and what goes into it."

When the elevator door opened at the 2nd floor, Richie was there waiting. His post-adolescence was trying to make the case for his budding manhood with the stingy facial hair and stilted baritone voice, but the Mohawk haircut and semi-Ebonics dialect were dead giveaways…

"Hey Aunt Ev. You made it in one piece I see."

"Richie, Hi." She hugged him, then pushed back and said, "What's with that 'Do'?"

Looking around his head. Curiously surveying it like it was some unidentifiable object.

"Just experimenting. Anyway, it does grow back you know."

They both laughed. Omar was standing by quietly, waiting for his introduction.

"Richie, this is Omar Duncan, the lead on the assignment."

Omar and Richie shook hands. "Good to meet you Richie."

"Likewise." Richie served as impromptu tour guide while they were on their way to the film lab. Letting them peek inside a few of the classrooms and labs, (most were combined) explaining their purpose and impact in the industry. Evelyn was impressed by his knowledge and obvious commitment to his craft.

"You seem to really be on top of this stuff Richie. I'm impressed."

He smiled at her and said, "Ok, we're here", and opened the door to the lab. Omar remained the passive spectator while looking around the lab as if he was expecting to find eavesdroppers scattered about.

He then asked, "Are we the only ones here?"

Richie replied, "Yep, for now anyway."

Omar then said, "Well, I guess we'd better get to work then." He handed Richie a copy of the script. "We already got the ok from our boss on the script, which should make it easier."

Evelyn smiled, nodding in agreement. Richie took the script and read through a few pages.

He then said, "This is good, but may I recommend a few changes that might make it even better?"

Omar didn't hide his indifference over Richie's remark very well. His body language spoke volumes and Evelyn picked up on it right away and asked, "What kind of changes Richie?"

She looked at Omar who seemed a little shell-shocked. "Well, first of all, I'm only recommending them because based on what your brochure says about what the system can do, I thought some of the dialogue could be more consumer friendly since they're ultimately the ones who benefit from it. They could probably relate better if we change some of the verbiage."

He picked up a yellow marker and held the script in one hand, then he asked, "Ok to mark this up a little?"

Omar said slowly with a somber look, "Be my guest."

They both watched quietly while Richie sat at one of the freestanding tables with a yellow marker in one hand and a pen in the other. Evelyn seemed astounded at how proficient her nephew seemed to be. He was patient and deliberate with the way he approached his work. Reading a page or two first, then wielding that pen and marker with the speed of a seasoned copy editor. It took him less than 10 minutes to change and delete phrases in the first three pages of it. He handed the script to Evelyn when he had finished. She read through it carefully. The smile on her face growing bigger as she went over it, line by line…

She said, "I like it. This is good Richie."

Omar said, "Let's see", and took it out of her hand.

Omar read through it carefully; expressionless, as if looking for a reason to criticize the changes. He folded the flapped pages back to the first page, paused, and then sighed thinking more about how this kid had committed the cardinal sin by butchering their creation in a matter of minutes. He handed the script back to him, then just said, as if he was agitated—"Ok, that's ok."

Richie took it from him but couldn't get a reading on how Omar really felt.

He then said, "I did have one question about the exchange near the end with the woman and the guy from the utilities company. Is she at home when they speak, or?—"

Omar interrupted "Why don't you improvise on that. I'm sure it'll turn out ok. Can we see that 3-D model of the system you said you had produced?"

Evelyn was a little taken aback by Omar's patronizing of Richie by cutting him off and it showed, but she said nothing.

Richie said, "I'm putting the finishing touches on it but I'll show you what I have."

Omar then said, "I brought rewriteable CD's, just in case you might need them for editing, or whatever."

Richie said, "Thanks, but I won't need those", as he moved to one of the editing booths and reached for a CD marked 'Festival – Aunt Evelyn'.

He then said, "Everything's done digitally for the most part. When this is done, I'll let you see the finished product first before I put it on a disk or flash drive."

He looked at them both then said, "Your boss can come too if you like; want to make sure we get it right the first time."

He loaded the program and ran the footage which was about three minutes long.

When it was Done Evelyn said, "You were able to be that detailed just from reading the brochure?"

"Pretty much, yeah."

She then said, "You're good." She hugged him then said again, "You're really good. I'm so proud of you."

Omar then said, "I'll be doing live narration while your mock-up is running so maybe you can slow the pace just a little?"

"Sure—No problem."

Omar then said, "Thanks for your help on this."

He didn't wait for a response from Richie, but just said, "Evelyn, let's let him finish his work. I've seen enough."

Evelyn said, "Alright, but you go on ahead. I'll meet you downstairs."

She stood close to Richie, who still had his back to Omar. Omar then nodded and walked out.

When he heard the door latch, Richie turned to her and said, "You sure know how to pick'em Aunt Ev."

He felt as though he had just gotten a "D" on an assignment as he tried to ward off the effects of Omar's indifference.

Evelyn said, "I'm sorry about his attitude. He likes what you're doing, he really does, it's just that he's got some stuff going on that he won't even share with me and it makes him come off as seeming a little abrasive."

Evelyn knew that trying to defend Omar probably was about as credible as shoveling snow in an avalanche; but it at least served as a band aid for Richie's wounded pride.

She then said, "Just so you know, Omar suggested we compensate you in some way when we first talked about it. He's really an ok guy when you get to know him."

Richie replied, "You seem really sure about that."

"I am, and the other thing I'm sure of is that I'm gonna see your name in lights one day young man."

He smiled at her. "I know Roxy is really proud of you."

She pinched his Mohawk and then said, "Well, I'd better catch up with Omar but, thanks again and looking forward to seeing your final version of that script." She hugged him again.

"Take care Aunt Ev."

"Bye Richie." Evelyn wasn't shy when she confronted Omar about his treatment of Richie when she met him outside.

"You think you could have been a little more civil to him back there?" The irritation in her voice left no doubt in Omar's mind that he crossed barriers that really could threaten their friendship. She didn't look at him while they walked back to the car, and he said nothing, feeling he had ruffled her feathers but made no apologies for his behavior. When they got in the car he finally spoke when she drove off.

"Ok, what did I say that was so terrible?"

"Look, if you don't know then things are worse than I thought."

"What does that mean?"

"You patronized the hell out of him for one thing."

"How so?"

"You seemed about as interested in watching what he had done as you would be in watching mold spores growing inside a Petri dish."

"Ahh, come on Ev. I admit I didn't send up fireworks like you did."

"I get it. You're really upset about the changes he made to the script aren't you? I noticed how you cut him off when he told you he had a question about some dialogue at the end of it."

"What? Come on; you think—" He cut his sentence short after noticing her expression. She only walled her eyes at him, but it shut him down for the moment. It was the opening she hoped he would take to apologize and level with her, but she'd have to wait a little longer because he didn't take it.

"Look mister, I don't know what the real problem is with you lately, and maybe I shouldn't care so much, but what I do care about is my nephew's heart. And frankly, he deserved better from you today. You treated him like some desperate understudy who should have been grateful for the chance. You forgot just that quickly that he's doing this for no fee, even after you saw the quality of his work."

Omar's insides seemed to be churning uncontrollably. Her disdain was baring down on him like a bunch of stacked boulders. Finding himself inside Evelyn's wrath was a distressful place, and one he preferred not to see again.

She then said, "To be honest, it's probably best we not even deal with Richie again on this assignment until you let him know, well, that you just weren't yourself today."

Omar said, "You mean apologize?"

"I guess that's what I'm saying, because if you don't clean this up, he might not be so committed to finishing it. Ok?"

Omar looked straight ahead for a few moments, then said, "Alright. You win."

Saturday night was the real start of Omar's weekend. He stacked his morning time with chores so he could really try and clear his mind and decompress from what went on that week. He had no special lady in his life, and seemed to have little patience for the casual relationships that left him with little or nothing he would commit to. On the other hand, it never occurred to him that the wall of cynicism that surrounded him was something none of them were able to, and in some cases motivated to, try and penetrate. Not having his own transportation compounded the situation even more so he was left, as usual, with the mundane task of trying to entertain himself. Evelyn's browbeating left traces of regret that he didn't want to feel ever again, so before doing anything else, he called her hoping to appease her and remove the jeopardy he had placed on their friendship.

"Hey Evelyn—It's Omar."

"Hi, what's up?"

"Just called to really say I'm sorry about this morning and, I also wanted to call Richie to keep my promise to you."

"Well, as long as you're honest about it."

"I am, but I need his phone number." He paused briefly then said, "What you said is true. He's a valuable asset and it would be a shame to lose that."

"It's good to hear you say that." She paused, then said, "Hold on a second", and left the phone to return with Richie's phone number. "You intend to call him tonight?"

"As soon as we hang up."

"Well, I guess you'd better hop to it then."

"Yes mam. I'll see you on Monday."

He suddenly realized he was brand new at this 'self-recrimination' thing, but admitting to the consequences of his own flaws in this case, was a good first step to erasing the stigmas that had plagued his decision making for so many years. He dialed Richie's phone number and let it ring a few times. Not really sure what to say or how to say it. The phone kept ringing as he had more time to think about how Richie might not even be receptive, then on an impulse, he hung up. He sighed, then raised his head toward the ceiling; dreading what could be a miscalculation on his part. Feeling as awkward as a baby struggling to take its first steps. He sat at his dining room table for a moment, then it occurred to him how a simple act of faith is sometimes the beginning of resolving some things that may seem insurmountable. What Evelyn said about her nephew, and even his first contact with him, proved that he should be less concerned about the likelihood of any resistance, and simply trust in the goodwill that it's intended to leave behind. He dialed the number again, and Richie picked up…

"Hello, Richie, this is Omar Duncan. I hope I didn't disturb you."

"No, not really." Richie was quiet.

"I just wanted to—" Omar sighed then continued. "I'm really lousy at this but, I just wanted to apologize for the way I acted this morning. You didn't deserve to be treated that way."

It became easier to speak as he continued weaving his way through his apology.

"The work you're doing for us is exceptional, and it is very much appreciated."

Richie said, "My pleasure."

Omar relaxed then, knowing he had just unloaded unnecessary baggage.

"You know, my Aunt Evelyn really believes in you, and she'll go to bat for anyone in a heartbeat if she respects them."

"Yes I know. I consider Evelyn to be a good friend."

"Well, if it were me I wouldn't risk losing that respect by sending her mixed signals; know what I mean?"

"I follow you."

Richie paused for a moment, as if giving Omar time to really think about what he had just said. "I'm taking your advice and free-lancing on the rest of the script changes. I can probably wrap it up by tomorrow afternoon."

"That's good. Let me give you my email address at work and maybe you can forward the changes to me. I'll look for them in my in-box on Monday morning when I come in."

"That'll work. Talk at you later then."

Overcoming his ambivalence about calling Richie was a victory for Omar. The idea of being repentant about anything was something that may have repelled him before now, even if his first honest look at himself had to be at the expense of someone like Richie, without the fabled transgressions of others blinding his vision. It was satisfying and regrettable at the same time. He decided to try and watch one of the late NCAA games but only ended up channel surfing. The image of Richie's back facing him when he left the Art Institute kept floating around in his head. He thought it seemed fitting because it was the only part of himself that he had given most people to look at in recent days. There was nothing to gain from that view of one's self; No smiling face to shame whatever vexatious spirit might rear its ugly head, or eyes that could light the path to a place of goodwill. No sound of footsteps drawing near that might just meet you half-way in trampling the pain of a pestilent trial, and no outstretched hands to help muffle the sound of grief when it decides to show itself. It was by all accounts, a breakthrough. Nothing on T.V. peaked his interest to the point of wanting to park at a particular station long enough to get the gist of the show he was watching. His interest had subconsciously been diverted to the success of the sponsorship for the festival. No matter how much he wanted to indulge in weekend downtime, he was about to borrow a page from Richie's work ethic and commit to working on his narration for the video. After all, he had paid the kid a compliment on his work. He at least needed to be as committed to the quality of his own part in the production. While he rehearsed his narration without Richie's completed 3-D rendition of the recovery system, he received a text message from Evelyn that said, 'Thanks for calling Richie. He was relieved that you did. Said he's sending final script changes to your email. Looking forward to seeing them on Monday. Have a great weekend.' He smiled, knowing he had dodged a bullet with Evelyn, but he wasn't home free yet. He realized he couldn't be so careless with Evelyn and still maintain his credibility with her. It really mattered to him now how she felt, and what work might still be ahead of him in convincing her he was not just an 'empty suit'.

"Good morning Chip."
 "Hello Evelyn. Ready to do battle?"

"About as ready as I'll ever be for a Monday." They stepped inside the elevator on the first floor and she asked, "Going all the way up?"

"Yeah, too late to take the scenic route I guess."

"Thanks for helping us on the video for the festival."

"No problem. Glad to do it. Gives me a chance to audition for my trip to Hollywood finally." They both laughed. The elevator stopped after two floors and three more passengers got on, Including Nadine. She greeted everyone in her typical high-energy tone of voice…

"Hey everybody!"

Everybody said almost in unison, "Good morning Nadine!"

Just as loud, and began snickering.

"Well, at least you're all in good moods."

Evelyn then said to her, "Did you know Chip's one of our actors for the video we're doing Nadine?"

Nadine blurted out, "Alright Chip. If you're gonna be my leading man you're gonna have to behave, ok?" She started to laugh, and so did everybody else.

Evelyn then said, "Nadine, cut it out." The elevator opened on Chip's floor.

When he got off he said, "You all have a good day. You too Nadine."

Nadine responded, "Alright, see ya handsome."

When the elevator doors closed it was Nadine's que to kill the silence.

"How was your weekend Ms. Beacham?"

"Oh, no excitement; just a little work for the festival."

"You taking the job home now? Let me check your temperature; make sure you're not running a fever that might be making you a little kooky." She started to laugh as she placed her palm over Evelyn's forehead. Evelyn swiped it away and said, "Will you stop? I'm fine."

Everybody else started to smile as the elevator door opens two floors below theirs, leaving only Evelyn and Nadine on board.

Nadine said, "So, Clarence got you wearing a ball and chain now days?"

"No, it's nothing like that. Omar and I met with my nephew, Richie, on Saturday about producing the video for the sponsors. We showed him a draft of the script and talked about some changes to it. He's supposed to email them to Omar. Hopefully we'll have a version we can all live with by this morning."

Nadine noticed Evelyn's bland expression as they stepped off on their floor...

"Did you guys have a disagreement over it? I'm just getting a vibe, you know."

"It's nothing." She sighed—"It's just that Omar—well, he can be a real 'butthead' at times."

She looked straight ahead as they crossed the breezeway to their department.

Nadine said, "Uh, uh; sounds like trouble in paradise. Anything you wanna talk about?"

"No—No, it's nothing; and this too shall pass, as they say." Evelyn was near her cubicle and said, "I'll see you later on."

Nadine didn't have a good feeling about the friction that may have existed between Evelyn and Omar. She shrugged her shoulders and said, "Ok, but don't let whatever it is screw up your day. See ya."

Evelyn was her friend; Omar not so much. She decided she wouldn't pry but was satisfied with knowing if it really was that important, Evelyn would open up about it in due time. Evelyn passed Omar's desk before getting to her own and noticed he hadn't gotten there yet. She was hoping he may have checked his in-box already to see if Richie had emailed changes to the script. She wanted that issue to be settled so she could concentrate on picking the remaining actors, to get copies to them. She hoped he was o.k. since he hadn't called in sick or anything. Clarence noticed her and approached.

"Hey, speak to your cohort yet this morning?"

Hi Cee Cee. You're referring to Mr. Duncan I take it?"

"The same."

"I haven't heard from him yet, and before you ask we're supposed to have a revised script to look at this morning. Hopefully there won't be any need for you to review this version."

"Oh—revised in what way? I thought it was settled."

"Well, we met with the producer of the video on Saturday, who happens to be my nephew. He recommended them, and to be honest his version seemed better; mostly cosmetic; changes to some of the verbiage for the most part."

Evelyn was still busy setting up her work space and computer while they talked.

Clarence replied, "I see—well as long as he doesn't distort the message, if you get my meaning."

"Loud and clear."

"Maybe Omar will show up soon and we can talk about it."

She glanced up at him, and the clock on the wall, letting him know she was ready to start her day, while nodding in agreement. Clarence drummed his fingers on the top edge of the partition between them in a nervous cadence.

He then said, "Well, I'll let you get to it then."

"WAIT! —HOLD UP!—Wait!—Ah, come on!" ....Omar shouted at the bus again but it was too far away this time. He dropped his bags and stood in the middle of the street; waving his arms frantically, but the Driver didn't stop. He could hear the old bus picking up speed as the driver gunned the engine, watching the exhaust fumes rise above it like smoke from the stack of a refinery. He picked up his bags and sat inside the bus shelter for a few minutes, wanting to kick himself for oversleeping. He had shut off his snooze alarm at least four times before finally getting out of bed. The sun seemed to parch the back side of the bus shelter. It felt like an oven inside; too uncomfortable to sit and wait 35 minutes on the next bus, so he started walking back to his apartment building only about 5 minutes away. He was frustrated, but it did occur to him to at least call Clarence to let him know he'd be late.

"Hey, it's me, Omar; haven't left home yet."

"What happened? You o.k?"

"Yeah, I'm ok; just overslept, sorry."

"Don't worry about it. Any idea how long you might be?"

"The next bus should be here in about 30 minutes, so a little over an hour probably."

"Ok. I'll see you then. Oh, by the way, Evelyn told me about changes to the script you were expecting this morning from her nephew."

"Yeah, he's producing it for us."

"Well, just a heads up. I thought about it and I don't really need to see them unless the content changes. I'll trust your judgment on that, ok?"

"Alright Cee Cee." "See you when you get here."

As he approached his apartment building he noticed the lot had emptied out. He leaned against the rail to the stairwell thinking about how the convenience of having his own transportation was looking more like a luxury with each passing day. He had only been late for work one other time for a different reason, and Clarence also gave him a pass even then. He knew that Clarence had been really flexible with him and didn't want to risk violating his trust. He was grateful for the relationship they had. Had it been anyone else, there might have been a counseling session somewhere in his future. He opened his door and turned the kettle on. He at least had time for one cup of coffee. He stepped inside his bedroom to pick up his umbrella, as a precaution. He remembered getting soaked that morning when he was without it. He was learning. He took the umbrella from the closet next to the full length mirror then stood in front of it again; primping like some 20 year old. He could forget about the real reason for his tardiness since Clarence had all but erased the possibility of any negative consequences from it after they spoke. He leaned forward a few inches toward the mirror; stroking his beard again and turning his face from side to side, thinking it might be time for a new look already. After a minute or two he stood erect again and decided he would leave things as they were for now. When he turned to leave, what sounded like fizzing seltzer suddenly bombarded him. It seemed to envelop the room. He didn't notice workmen outside with machines before he came inside that could have explained it, and it appeared to be coming from inside the apartment. It became so much louder just for a moment that he instinctively covered his ears, then it died down just as quickly. When he moved his hands from his ears he heard that pleasing baritone voice again coming from the direction of the mirror. The same voice he heard the night Clarence picked him up from Dooley's. He couldn't blame it on a dream this time. He was alert and as clear headed as could be, and when he turned toward the mirror again, there it was; that same vapor, in the shape of a man. Omar was rigid suddenly. His speech just above a whisper.

"This can't be—This isn't real."

He turned to his rear; feet still planted, but it wasn't behind him. He turned again to face the mirror and there it was again. He reached out slowly, as if to try and touch it, but his palms were flattened by the glass. He shifted to one side and it moved with him, and then back again as he did. Omar became fretful and slammed his palms against the mirror this time. With his voice cracking he spoke excitedly, and desperately.

"WHAT ARE YOU? WHAT—, what is this? What is it you want?"

There was silence for a moment; then in a voice that seemed to reverberate dramatically with every syllable, it spoke…

"Don't be frightened Omar. I'm not here to harm you." It paused then said, "I'm incapable of that. When I appeared to you for the first time that night, it wasn't a dream. This form; not the best choice I know. Even though you can't touch me, it at least allows me to speak to you. I was desperate, to finally speak to you."

It paused again. Its movements almost rhythmic now as it continued to speak to him..

"This mirror is the medium that lets me assume a visible form of some kind, at least until; until I can once again inhabit the body that bore me; that body would be yours Omar. I'm a part of you, and until we truly become as one again, this form, sadly, will serve as a refuge."

Omar began to break out in a cold sweat. His palms still pressed tightly against the mirror; his eyes bulging as his breathing became labored, but he could not speak.

"You've changed your attitude about some things since our last encounter, and that gives me hope." Its rhythmic motion seemed to accelerate, as if it was expressing cause for celebration.

"When you called Richie to apologize about your attitude on Saturday after the two of you met, it was a big step in the right direction. Even when you decided on something as simple as bringing your umbrella today showed that you can take que's from other people after all. Not taking certain things for granted, especially about your own welfare, is always wise."

Its movements slowed somewhat as it paused once more before speaking again.

"Your tests will be many, and I will be watching; trusting you'll get through them. We're kindred spirits, you and I. It's what completes us."

Omar's hands were still pasted to the mirror like an ornament. Suddenly being rendered mute was so unthinkable, he thought he would have preferred the lash of a whip instead. In the meantime, he could only manage low guttural moans.

"I know you can't speak, and it may be frustrating but just know this, the day will come when the sun will set for the last time in this life, and you will have little proof that you made a difference that mattered in a positive way to someone, unless you walk more in harmony with those closest to you."

It paused again, then said, "There are traces of me yet inside of you; seeds that long for a harvest, but you must seize opportunities when they come your way if ever I'm going to take my rightful place again. I will be waiting patiently for the day you finally mature. Remember, 'starve the beast that is strife, then you can feast on the peace that is life.' I won't have to feel like an orphan any longer when it happens and we'll be as one; as it should be. It's a lonely place out here after you've been cast aside like an old shoe, wouldn't you agree?"

It paused a while longer; its movements more static now…

"Don't keep me waiting too much longer." (Its voice began to fade slowly)

As its voice and image eventually disappeared, the screeching of the kettle was so loud, it seemed to be coming from inside his bedroom. Omar pushed away from the mirror quickly but not realizing why he apparently had been standing there for at least 10 minutes. His memory of it was wiped clean, at least he thought it had been. He couldn't recall one thing that happened, from the time he first faced that mirror. He was disturbed a little by the memory lapse, but managed to pull himself together. He stepped into the kitchen and moved the kettle from the burner, thinking it best to fix the coffee to go. He had less than fifteen minutes to get to the bus stop, but would have minutes to spare this time.

Chapter 5

EVELYN'S ACTORS FOR THE video were assembled inside the conference room for the first reading of the script as she had requested. She also received firm commitments from two other actors that had been holdouts due to suspected conflicts in their schedules, but turned out to be false alarms. Richie had gotten the nod from Omar on the changes he made to the script some days prior, and submitted the changes that Monday morning as promised. Time had become a much needed ally as the plan seemed to be coming together with very little of it having been lost. The experience wouldn't most likely be anybody's ticket to fame and fortune, but they were all eager to be a part of it. They all felt there really was no down side to it. They had already accepted it as a labor of love. Evelyn took a mental roll-call then opened the meeting.

"Hey everybody. First of all I just want to say thanks again for helping us with this, and because you were excited to do it makes me appreciate it even more. A few of you already know Omar Duncan, who is our project lead for this, but those of you who haven't met him, he and I are in the same unit in Product Development, along with Nadine; and well, there couldn't be a better person for the job. So, any drama you got going on, see him."

Everybody laughed, then she asked,"Omar, you want to say anything?"

"Just that I do want to thank all of you for coming on board with this. Your time and talent is really appreciated. We expect this video to impact the company's profile with the public in a big way. The producer, who happens to be Evelyn's nephew Richie, is shooting it for us and from what I've seen it's in capable hands. It's more like an infomercial and it shouldn't be that long, so no need to rack your brains over it. Just have fun with it while getting our message across, ok? Well, this is Evelyn's brainchild so I'll hand it back to her, but thanks again guys."

Nadine blurted out, "Ok, time to rock and roll!", then started clapping.

Everybody else followed her lead. It promised to at least be a lively bunch with Nadine leading the pack. Evelyn chose the few male actors by having them each read all the parts for the men. She selected their parts for them afterward and did the same for the women. She had the luxury of not needing to spar with their egos over who was more suited for each part. After all, they were amateurs but spirited, which wasn't a bad tradeoff given the task in front of them. As it turned out, Evelyn's instincts were exceptional and they each seemed perfectly suited for the roles she had chosen for them. Omar seemed more like Evelyn's assistant but didn't complain. He was pleased, watching her work, but he was also perplexed as to why his friend had not been promoted yet. She was a natural at it and simply relied on her instincts in a big way. She would do well in marketing. He felt so much of her talent had been untapped, yet she seemed less concerned about her own celebrity even after taking on this responsibility. He would get an all-expenses paid ticket toward his earth sciences degree but Evelyn, as far as he knew, was promised nothing for her efforts. The reading ended after about 50 minutes and everybody had their assignments. Evelyn got their attention before adjourning, to let them know what to expect at the next meeting.

"We'll probably be on location, or we'll set up an area similar to where the actual filming will take place so you can get familiar with hitting your spots and how to interact with one another during the filming. I'll have a conversation with Richie hopefully by tonight to find out what's convenient for him, and keep you all posted. Thanks again everybody."

Omar watched how Evelyn had command of the room. She was a natural.

She turned to him and said, "Thanks for the pep talk. It was the perfect thing to say to them."

"No big deal. You know it's pretty obvious, this is your show."

He flashed a broad smile and pinched her curls, as they were leaving the conference room.

Evelyn began to blush a little. "Thanks. It means a lot coming from you."

Nadine approached them from behind. "Alright, break it up you two. You know this is a scandal free zone, so keep it clean."

"Nadine, what are you talking about?"

"Oh, don't mind me sister", then she started to laugh. "Seriously though, this video is a great idea. I can guarantee you, the movers & shakers are gonna take notice. Well, I'd better get back to my cell."

Clarence noticed Evelyn and Omar as he headed to the elevators. "How did the reading go?" "Oh, went off without a hitch. I couldn't ask for a better producer than Evelyn." Omar nudged her in her side as he spoke.

Clarence said, "That's great." He looked at them both, and said, "I know you're well aware that we have only 10 days before the festival opens, so make sure you're on pace."

Omar wasn't really surprised by the reminder. Clarence needed to feel secure by covering his bases.

He told them, "I've already drafted letters to the sponsors whose files you've seen already; just to let them know they should expect to be contacted by our teams, and remind them of the itinerary."

Omar's body language suddenly shifted to defensive mode. He asked, "Did you actually send letters, to all of them?"

Evelyn suddenly looked puzzled; wondering silently, 'why would he not send letters to all of them?'

Clarence replied, "I haven't actually sent them yet; one issue around the itinerary concerning the system demonstrations needs to be dealt with, and a couple of housekeeping items, but we're close to getting them out."

Omar looked away briefly, then back at Clarence again with an unsettled expression. Clarence knew Omar's history with Dillon was most likely the villain that keeps coming back to life. The antipathy for Omar was so thick you'd need a machete to cut through it. The silence was numbing for a moment. Evelyn knew something had crept in again that made him a little uncomfortable. It was becoming a regular occurrence, but she decided to end the exposure at least for herself.

She said, "Well, you two can chat. I've got work to do", then walked back to her desk.

Clarence cornered him again, wanting to know why the 'Dillon issue' was such a thorn…

"You still don't want to talk to me about what happened at Dillon do you?"

Omar said, "What? Where's that coming from?"

"When I mentioned the letters to the sponsors you seemed to get a little uptight. Look, I hope you can understand why I'm at least inquisitive about it because I'm not sure you're totally comfortable with having to deal with them as a sponsor."

"I'll get over it Cee Cee.—Don't worry about it."

"I hope so, because I can't afford to have you wait until the eleventh hour to decide that you can't.. I've got to get downstairs to personnel. I'll see you a little later."

Omar nodded to him as he walked away. He knew then that ditching his insecurities over the issue with Dillon had to take place sooner than later. It was obvious Clarence was running out of patience over needing to resolve this thing he couldn't get a handle on. Omar didn't want to sabotage the project for Clarence or Evelyn. He really cared about the outcome, for their sake. They were his friends, but he seemed torn still between loyalty to what he was entrusted with, or yielding to only traces of a conscious that only made room for hefty doses of cynicism most of the time. He decided to make a pit stop at the men's room to try and clear his head, and ran into Theo.

"Hey Omar, how is it?"

"Theo, hey." He splashed cool water on his face then raised his head slowly; resting his hands on the counter and staring aimlessly into the mirror. Theo took notice before walking out and said, "You o.k. man?"

Omar snapped out of it and yanked a paper towel from the dispenser. ..

"Oh, yeah. I'm ok", He wiped his face hurriedly.

Theo relaxed, then said, "We're planning another pick-up game again at the courts this Saturday, or do you have plans again?"

Still facing the mirror Omar asked, "Who is, WE?"

"Me, maybe Calvin, Blake, and probably a few walk-ons. Everybody else knows you got game, except Blake."

Omar responded abruptly, "I'm not the least bit concerned about Blake, ok?"

Theo said, "What was that?" He responded with a surprised look hoping he had not heard him clearly, but he knew there was absolutely nothing wrong with his hearing…

Omar said, "I mean, I'm not sure about it yet. We're coming down to the wire with this festival business. I might be busy again with that on Saturday."

Theo was insightful enough to know that Omar didn't exactly have a 'warm & fuzzy' about Blake. He picked up on it the day Chris introduced him to their team, and that spoke louder than anything Omar could ever have said about it at the time.

"Ok, Hollywood—Oh, and thanks for telling me about the video. You know you could have asked if I was interested in being a part of it, since we do work in the same unit, and well, you knowing my background with that kind of thing." Theo had propped the door open to leave but decided to step back inside for Omar's reply. Omar stared at him impatiently, needing to avoid a response like he would a leper…

Theo then said out of frustration, "Look, do I have to spell it out? I felt slighted when I found out, ok? You guys had picked the actors for the video and you never even asked if I wanted to help."

Omar answered him in an excitable tone… "Picking the actors was Evelyn's job. Anyway, I thought maybe you were busy with your classes and stuff; didn't think you'd be interested."

He rolled his eyes at Theo as if to say, 'that's my story and I'm sticking to it.'

"Did you really?" Theo felt his body language said just the opposite. It seemed like any old excuse that certainly wouldn't hold up to a little more scrutiny.

"You can be honest with me Omar. I'm not that gullible."

He shook his head, disappointed that Omar didn't even consider him for a role. His mentor had let him down. He had begun to feel Omar was simply ready for him to be weaned from his proverbial shadow, especially since Blake had come into the picture, but he never thought he may have been more of a pest than a protégé. He thought they really were friends, but then again, friends are usually more considerate of one another. He let the door close behind him and faced it for a moment, thinking he had more to say to him, but then he just turned and walked away. Evelyn noticed him when he passed her two cubicles away.

"Theo!" He looked in her direction. "You got a minute?"

He seemed to hobble toward her desk like a wounded animal.

"Hey; Omar said he'd talk to you about helping with the video. Maybe you wouldn't mind being an alternate for one of our actors. Maybe even help with the production off camera, if you're not filling in for somebody with a speaking part that is."

Theo gave her a surprised look and said, "Well I'll be damned", shaking his head and looking away…

"Is something wrong Theo?"

Theo said, "You know I was gonna be ok with him just overlooking me at first. I guess everybody's entitled to at least one of those, but to feel that he just didn't want me in it, well that's another animal altogether."

It was no secret that Theo wore his emotions on his sleeve and he couldn't conceal his disappointment.

Evelyn said, "Theo what's wrong? Who didn't want you, in what?"

"I just talked to your cohort, Mr. Duncan, in the restroom and asked him about you guys having picked the actors. He couldn't even admit that you had discussed me playing a role. He just waived me off with some lame excuse that just popped into his head. Who does that?"

"Ahh, Theo I'm sorry. I asked him if he would talk to you about playing a role when this process started and he said he would. I should have just approached you directly before now, and I'm sorry about that. I did have actors in mind already, but I always felt we could use your help with it in some way."

"You know, I thought he and I were friends. I do reach out to him but I guess he feels he doesn't need to reciprocate. That's not the way real friends behave, is it?"

He kept shaking his head with a loathsome expression—"I guess I was wrong about him."

He hung his head briefly then raised it and said, "No reflection on you Evelyn, but I guess you could say he's really soured the milk, so I think I'll pass. See you around."

Evelyn was dumbfounded as to why Omar keeps leaving so much fallout from relationships anyone else might consider valuable. It left a gaping hole in his personality that continued to bleed from circumstances with people that had deteriorated over the years. Having control of himself was as likely as learning another language. His apologies might as well have been scripted like a part in a play, for all the good they had done. Evelyn was more conflicted now than ever about her feelings toward him. He said nothing to her about not having mentioned the video to

Theo when they were on break. She simply felt it was settled and he would've recruited his help by now. She tried to shake the feeling but knew it was a personality flaw with him that could have really ugly consequences. He didn't just burn bridges, he obliterated them. She propped one elbow in front of her keyboard; resting her chin in her palm with a somber expression. She was still committed to working with him on the project but felt she would need to gear up for more casualties in the wake of his erratic behavior. After a moment she looked in the direction of Nadine's desk. She was really giddy over something and realized Nadine was talking with someone at her cubicle. She was curious why Nadine was standing at her own station and didn't appear to be on a call, but did realize after a moment who the source of her excitement was. Blake raised up partially from underneath her desk. He was setting up her new desktop. His waist-line was almost above Nadine's chest, but despite the mismatch, it didn't stop her incessant flirting with him. Evelyn watched them while pretending to be on the phone with a client. She looked at them with some angst, but a little admiration too over how Nadine seems to just embrace who she is. The unadulterated version always on display, at least in public, but also feeling a little anxious over the liabilities that may be lurking inside of what she knew to be completely innocent behavior by her. If it was her way of gaining validation, then more power to her. She couldn't really worry about what commotion may have been stirring inside Nadine's heart when she was alone. If there was any, she never let it show. She did know one thing for sure. Nadine had a firm grip on who she was and was unapologetic about it; even the parts of her personality that seemed unsavory at times. Nadine turned to see Evelyn watching them and threw up her hand. She then turned in the direction of the breezeway and so did Evelyn, as if responding to some non-verbal cue. Omar emerged from the shadowy opening. His facial expression only drew blanks this time as Evelyn watched him for a few moments. His eyes gave nothing back except anxiety from the frantic ongoing search for whatever he seemed to have lost. A type of villainous desperation that wouldn't let go of him. It was unsettling for her. He had almost become unpredictable. She looked in Nadine's direction again and she had scribbled something on a sheet of paper. She held it up so Evelyn could see and it read, 'You're his next victim', then she smiled. Evelyn was on alert suddenly. Could Nadine be aware of some morbidly extreme character flaw concerning Omar she hadn't bothered to share with her? Sometimes it was hard to know when Nadine was just joking around. It was a troublesome part of her character that Evelyn never got used to. She walked over to her cubicle casually. Blake was crouched underneath the desk again. "Hi Blake". He turned his head around…

"Oh, Hi, how is it? Evelyn, right?"

"Right, and I'm good thanks. Are you gonna be doing more of these this afternoon?", while patting the side of Nadine's new monitor.

"Oh, probably time for a couple more."

Nadine made funny faces standing behind him, making Evelyn grin a little. At that point Evelyn felt Nadine's note had little, if any, to do with Omar.

She then said, "Well, you'll give me a heads up before you're ready for me won't you?"

"Oh, sure. I have to follow this schematic anyway. He stopped what he was doing, sat up and picked the schematic off the floor.

"Let's see, which isle are you?" She found her desk on the diagram and pointed. "If that's you, I'll see you in a couple of days."

"Thanks. That'll work."

Nadine put her finger in her mouth with her head down, like a repentant 4 year old who had just been busted for misbehaving. Evelyn yanked her hand from her mouth and Nadine laughed out loud.

Evelyn laughed too, then said, "What am I gonna do with you?"

Blake ignored them both and kept working. The two of them chatted about other things for a minute or two as Blake was finishing up. The subject of the video came up again.

"I need to talk to you about something Nadine."

Nadine asked, "Ok, when?"

Evelyn said, "I'll call you."

Nadien then said, "Well, I guess it's not the 4-alarm variety, huh?"

"Not quite. I just need to bend your ear about it; you know, get your opinion."

Nadine sidelined the humor, realizing whatever it was, it really troubled Evelyn and she didn't like seeing her friend that way.

"Ok, you know how to find me."

When Evelyn got within a few feet of her own cubicle, Omar was approaching. Nadine trained her eyes on him until he called out to Evelyn, whose back was turned away from him. Evelyn stopped suddenly but didn't turn around. It was as if she had crossed the path of a viper suddenly; frozen, and not sure how to react. Omar called to her again as he approached her. Nadine watched with curiosity as Evelyn's uneasiness was really evident from her body language. She had a sneaking suspicion already about what, or who, the object of Evelyn's dismay was going to be once they had that talk.

"Hey Ev." Evelyn turned to face him, but Omar could sense something wasn't quite right. She seemed really subdued. She stared at him with an almost prickly disdain. Her eyes searched for understanding that only eluded her. She could Say nothing at that moment…

He asked, "Everything ok?"

She sighed heavily. Her posture slumping like an imploded building.

"I'll be ok. It's just; it'll be alright." She stared at him again, and he stared back with slightly knitted eyebrows, thinking he must have done something to force her retreat suddenly behind the wall she had placed between them. He decided to keep it official when he spoke again.

"I just wanted to remind you about letting me know as soon as you talk to Richie about where he might prefer to shoot the video. I'll work on picking some practice sites too; to work with the actors, you know, like you talked about at the reading with them."

Evelyn seemed to have checked out briefly while he was talking. He tried again, to see if she would come clean and asked, "What's bothering you Ev?"

"I'm sorry. You were saying about the location?"

It was obvious she preferred to dodge the issue, but he didn't press.

"I was saying, we can both think about places we can run through the script with the actors until the actual location for the shoot is decided. You agree?"

"Yeah, sure. That'll work."

It would have been easy enough for her to confront him about having overlooked Theo for the video, but at that moment it seemed about as useful as trying to reason with a toddler to stop crying over a missing pacifier. So much seemed to have fallen on his tone deaf ears that she wasn't up to wasting the time or the energy over it. Omar could see that her interest had bottomed out, so he decided to make himself scarce.

He told her, "I'll see you later then."

The bus ride home seemed like a carbon copy of his day at work. None of the usual crew was on board for the ride home for some reason or another. Micki had been missing in action for some days, and Vick had a touch of the flu suddenly. He would have been inclined to even talk to Rupert, who he seemed to avoid, just to feel like he was still inside familiar territory but even he wasn't riding today. His world wasn't exactly collapsing around him, but the absence of those familiar faces was a little unusual. Evelyn's coldness toward him was a shot that caught him by surprise. He was so clueless about needing to check his behavior, it didn't occur to him that who he might have considered to be a friend could easily make the swing to adversary if he didn't treat his relationships with more care. The forty five minute ride home seemed like an eternity, but he got there with no drama.

Omar asked the driver, "Hey, when is Vick coming back?"

"Not sure. I hear this bug he's got is pretty nasty."

The sporadic hiss from the air brakes signaled a full stop, then the doors opened. Omar stepped to the platform to get off then fist-bumped the driver…

"Thanks for the safe ride home."

"No problem. Hey, I wouldn't wish Vick back too soon, but I'll let him know you asked about him."

Omar gave him a puzzled look. "But you don't even know my name."

The driver thumped the name tag on his satchel and said, "You're Omar, aren't you?"

Omar looked down to realize he had overlooked the obvious, noticing his name plate in full View—(PROPERTY OF OMAR DUNCAN)

He smiled, then replied, "Yeah, that's me. See ya next time."

The driver nodded, then quickly reached for the handle to close the door behind him as he was driving off. This driver was older and seemed more settled than Vick, but he didn't exactly have a 'keep out' sign draped around his neck either; an acquired taste for Omar, which meant their personalities could have easily been cut from the same cloth. It occurred to him for a moment, as he watched the bus pull away, that he seemed more courteous to perfect strangers at times than people that were supposed to be closer to him. It was an oddity for him at least, but didn't exactly shake his reasoning to the core; not yet anyhow. The walk back to his apartment with the approaching sunset less than an hour away seemed a fitting climax to an otherwise unremarkable day. He leaned against the banister at the top of the stairwell to his floor to watch the sun as it slipped slowly below the horizon. It was rare for him to pause, and just soak in it for a while. He actually found himself romanticizing about all those rendezvous with young women in his life that were all too brief, and superficial. Getting them to watch the sunset with him was less about being reflective, and more about the strategic role it played in trying to win their juvenile affections. But it was different now. It actually was now more about appreciating the perpetual lease on life for all living things that it gives; at least the kind we know about, and how truly remarkable that is. Whether his sudden attention to it was inspired by the gnawing detachment he felt then, or not, seemed less important than the fact that he finally stopped to meditate on it. The mystery about why, and how it happens with such regularity suddenly ranked high among the lists of things worthy of his attention. He wasn't a 'Big Bang Theory' kind of guy either but in his estimation, if his life depended on needing to claim anything that could be called a spiritual identity, he'd probably be closer to an agnostic. He was at least pragmatic enough to feel deep down, that very little of what occurs in this universe is random, and his reflections at that moment seemed to at least crack open the door to a more thoughtful understanding of truth, and consequences. It remained his center of attention until the dying sunlight gave way to the onset of darkness. Oddly enough, he saw no signs of life around him during his respite there on the stairwell. Nothing, or no one stirred. It was as if his world had decided to leave him alone for that space of time. It allowed him to think more seriously about the impact he wanted to make in this life; no matter that the road to getting there was littered with pitfalls from years of having ignored the edicts of truth; namely about how the rest of humankind might subscribe to that idiom called 'human nature' when it seemed he'd rather ignore it. His ability to recognize it was missing in action, but he did attempt a course correction; like entertaining thoughts on who to trust, not knowing he needed to be trustworthy himself; or whether to forgive, overlooking the fact that forgiveness for his own trespasses was something he longed for. Also, comprehending very little about the motive of goodwill from others; the fact that it is not driven by cynicism and never 'keeps score', but is freely given with no strings attached. Or, did he think it all to be just nonsense. Would he settle for tunnel vision again, which usually left him groping from too many blind spots? If he had, it would probably shove him deeper into that dark corner where he always wrestled with the notion of how he might best dispense with people he thought to be his enemies. The bitterness had become like kindling; already smoldering from too many charred memories. Not far from becoming the raging fire once again, if he wasn't careful. It was exhausting at times, leaving him to rehearse so many twisted fantasies over the tragic characters inside of them; relationships that had become more obscure by this time, but still managed to give him considerable grief. He wondered if he was letting it get a little out of control; but, he was alert enough not to let it become all-consuming, and snapped out of it quickly.

Once inside his apartment, he still felt the tinge of isolation from that day heaped on him like mounds of clay. His home offered safety and a level of comfort he had carved out for himself, but little else. He dropped his bags where he stood and seemed to gaze through every square inch of that space with eyes that were dimly lit from mental fatigue. It didn't keep him from fantasizing though about the obvious signs of life that had been missing from it for too long. Maybe wishing, just a little, for the patter of little feet racing from one room to another; echoing the non-stop 'joyful noise' they'd make, while denying the day's routine of its long awaited tranquility. But even that was ok, until the little ones give in to fighting sleep, and are finally on 'empty' at the end of the day; Or coming home to someone who helps you sum up the hours you've spent apart in a really thoughtful way, while devoted hands labor to prepare a favorite meal; relieving you of that chore, and leaving no doubt about the sweet sensation that emanates from deep within her heart. Or, maybe even the idle chatter from curious neighbors now and again might be tolerable to fill the voids inside his otherwise hollow routine. He realized the serenity had been over-rated. At one time, not so long ago, he relished the idea of being unattached in every way. It provided safe haven for his patented insecurities, because even he considered himself to be socially awkward with only a handful of associates; none of whom were close enough to be called 'best friend'. He was better at making friends as a pre-teen when his biggest concerns were making decent grades and how best to avoid being labeled a geek. His real inhibitions hadn't shown up yet to stir his emotions into a frenzy, and he had gotten better with his social skills. Those thoughts were neutralized just for a while, because it grieved him not being able to grasp the reason for his fall. It seemed to just come out of nowhere, gradually chipping away at his 'armor'. It was in fact a seduction by the promise of 'light at the end of the tunnel', only to suddenly be confounded by the eeriness of dark shadows all around, then having to endure the impish stare of the Grim Reaper in the end. It was unmistakably his conundrum, with no clue as to how he might reverse the cause of it. Trusting in people and their motives had become much less conspicuous, and more cynical. A sure sign of the disconnect, and that more hapless episodes were likely around the corner. What somehow escaped his reasoning was that the spirit, referring to itself as an 'Orphan', held the key to part of his destiny, and it was advantageous to become convinced of how much its influence was needed, if his path was truly going to be illuminated.

Life should have gotten easier then as he grew older, but it didn't. Having to become more responsible, along with the luxury of being able to scale back, if not eliminate, other people's rules from his life was not the honeymoon he was led to believe it would be. It had become the maze he was forced to navigate alone. His sanctum of 'trust' was dealt its first blow when Breeland, his best friend, left town. He felt betrayed after Breeland showed him how to stand up to that bully, Deon, only to eventually move away leaving him to fend for himself. When he found out his dad had been abusive to him, it led Omar to believe it was reason enough for part of Deon's rage. Breeland had admitted to him once when they were in secondary school, that he saw this older guy, that was most likely Deon's dad, curse at him before striking him with a back hand to his face near a store front in town. He didn't know what it was all about, but he saw him grab Deon by the shoulders just as quickly and apologized for hitting him. Breeland said Deon was tough and could take a punch, but seemed to really be hurting more over what this guy had said to him. He said Deon even started to cry after this man just left him there, and knew that he had seen the whole thing. He had never seen a guy Deon's size in tears before. Breeland said Deon then approached him and asked that he not mention what he saw to anyone. Since it was a request and not a command with a fist staring him in the face as an incentive, he figured he'd oblige. Even though the problem of Deon's harassment had been solved, he still missed the companionship of his best friend. Then, he remembered how Breeland seemed to almost flirt with death the day he died. Everything changed after that. It was even harder to accept the fact that his friend had been killed right in front of his eyes. A year after he moved away, he came back the following summer only to lose his life. They had talked by phone a few times since the move. They hadn't actually seen each other all that time in between, but seemed to just pick up where they left off. The horrible images from that day were still vivid, as he was gripped by another one of his flashbacks.

THEY WERE TRYING OUT their new bikes in an unfamiliar area of town and came upon a road expansion crew. Breeland was curious about the massive earth moving machines and wanted to get closer. He hopped off of his bike to push it slowly in the direction of the Loader. Omar did the same.

Breeland boasted, "I'm gonna drive one of those one day, you'll see."

Omar replied, "Yeah, right. Let's get out of here."

Breeland could not tear himself away though. He seemed fascinated by this machine with its huge knobby tires and thunderous engine; like he may have compared it to some large prehistoric predator. The workmen were unaware of how close Breeland was to the restricted area and issued no warnings.

Omar shouted, "Bree, Bree! Where are you going?"

Omar stayed well back, as his plea went unheeded. One of the Workmen finally turned in Breeland's direction..

He yelled, "Hey kid, you're too close to that tape. You need to move back!"

His warning fell on deaf ears as Breeland's head stayed propped toward the cab of that loader. It was as if he imagined himself in the driver's seat. High above everything, and everyone else around him, with the power of the massive machine at his fingertips. It must have given him quite a rush to feel like king of the hill being perched inside that tight steel and glass compartment. Even those warnings of eminent danger did not get his attention. In one horrifying moment, a large excavator digging nearby lost one of its hydraulic hoses. The hydraulic fluid leak sprung like a fire hose at full throttle. (The Operator of the machine admitted to authorities that he was startled from it and lost control of the cab.) It pivoted wildly in Breeland's direction while the bucket was raised.

One of the workmen shouted, "Kid, Look Out!"

He was trying to run in his direction weighed down from the heavy duty work boots he wore, and ankle deep in the mire. Needless to say, it was a lost cause to try and get to Breeland in time before he turned in the direction of the revving engine of the excavator, only to be struck on the side of his head by its bucket. The pinging sound the huge bucket made from the impact, and blood splats on its surface left no doubt about its force, or Breeland's fate. Omar had stayed well back, but what he feared may have been too feeble of an attempt to save his best friend's life already had begun to haunt him..Breeland was pronounced dead at the scene. Omar's eyes were glassy from the onset of tears when he let go briefly of the horror from that day. It was as though it had just happened the day before. His eyes continued to well with tears, thinking about the friend he had lost almost thirty years ago; wishing he could have the grown up version of him back. He and Breeland hit it off right away when they met, and they did everything together. He was like the brother he never had but always wanted. He stared into space searching for answers, as he had done hundreds of times before, but no amount of reasoning could lend itself to the point of understanding why it had to happen; especially someone so close to him. The interrogation by Breeland's family, and even his own, that followed made him really anxious. But then he remembered Breeland's mom who approached him at the wake, and the flashbacks gripped him once again.

She knew the weight of Breeland's death was heavy and tried to ease the misery that was deeply etched across his face. He remembered the care she took with him. There were no glancing blows aimed at his character with questions about the accident, or why he didn't do more to try and prevent it. He had just about had his fill of the proverbial fangs from too many other people that had taken swipes at him about it, but she got to the heart of the matter. He knew the pain of losing Breeland so suddenly would certainly prolong her suffering, but she seemed strong, and felt she would somehow endure its numbing effect. Even so, she understood that it also left a huge hole in his life as well.

"Omar, are you going to be alright?"

She draped her arm across his shoulder and held him close. They both stared out of the large plate glass window inside her breakfast room. His eyes were fixed, but with a pestilent emptiness, and glazed over with tears. They watched her four year old niece play on the swing set she had bought for Breeland when he was about her age. She didn't have the heart to get rid of it after the move.

"I know you'll miss him too Omar. You were his best friend you know, even though he moved away."

"Yes mam, and he was mine."

She turned to him, then gently placed her hands on his shoulders and said, "I need you to try and do something for me."

"Yes mam?"

"Try not to feel there was more you could have done to prevent what's happened. I know you probably saw the danger, and tried to warn him; that I'm pretty sure of."

She brushed his hair carefully with the back of her hand. "My Breeland was a real pistol at times. He liked having his way more often than not. It wasn't easy for me, or his father, to try and get him to just follow the rules." She smiled, as a tear also raced down her cheek—"But you, more than any one of his friends, kept him from becoming some ill-mannered little plebe most parents would have sleepless nights over. Well, maybe I'm exaggerating just a little, but he could be a real piece of work sometimes."

They both smiled. She looked away for a moment; fighting back the flood of emotion lurking beneath her cool demeanor. Omar felt she was simply trying to be strong for his sake. She then proceeded to straighten his necktie in a nervous reflex, but her grimace couldn't be mistaken for a smile this time as she sobbed openly for a few moments. She pulled him close and he returned the embrace. Her pain subsided gradually; more evident by the once constant trickle of tears, drying slowly against her cheeks. With a slight quiver in her voice she tried to gather herself, followed by a deep sigh before speaking again…

"No mother expects to lose a child ahead of herself. That's just not the way it's supposed to happen, but it's really not our call." She paused for a moment; wiping the last of her tears.

She then said, "It's appointed unto man once to die, then the judgment. That's what the bible says, and we know neither the day nor the hour when death will come. It was just Breeland's time, and God decided to just call him home; over our objections maybe, but we hope to see him again in eternity, and so should you. You know, he did leave something of himself behind Omar, and because of that, you must choose how you will honor his memory. Do you understand?"

"Yes mam, I think I do."

She said, "He admired you. You helped him stay inside of himself, and he loved you for it. I just wanted you to know that."

She heard approaching voices then turned toward the archway leading to the breakfast room to see Omar's mom and dad. Mrs. Duncan embraced Breeland's mother.

"Agnes, it was a very beautiful service."

His dad reached to hold Omar close while the grownups talked. Omar noticed there were lots of people at the house, but he was surprised to see his Uncle Seth among the mourners. He thought he hated funerals. At least that's what he'd always say. He looked inside another area of the house and also saw Deon, the bully that taunted him for so long. It was really odd seeing him there. As far as he knew, there wasn't exactly a love fest between Deon and Breeland. He actually looked tame for a change. His rambunctious nature was obviously held in check, but probably hadn't slipped too far beneath the surface, even for an occasion as solemn as this one. Omar thought seeing him without an angry scowl was refreshing; but even more curious was seeing his Uncle Seth and Deon later leaving together. His curiosity really peaked then, and so did his ears when someone apparently rang Agnes' doorbell repeatedly while lots of people were still there. Whoever it was must have felt it would be hard hearing it over the voices inside.

THE RINGING OF THE doorbell to his own apartment brought him out of his flashback. He looked through the peep hole and saw it was the apartment manager. He opened the door and greeted him with a stoic expression.

"Hey; I'm not late on my rent am I?"

"Of course not. I brought you these parcels that the mailman couldn't fit inside your box." "Well, that's a relief. Thanks."

"No problem. See ya."

He took a quick glance at the one box to make sure the addressee was correct for new checks he had ordered from his bank. The other package was somewhat of a mystery. It didn't appear to be bulk mail as part of some promotional campaign, and it came from the 'U.S. Olympic Committee's Regional Office'. At first he thought it must be a mistake, since he had no dealings with anyone connected to the Olympics. He shrugged his shoulders and said to himself, 'some new solicitation no doubt', then he placed both packages on the counter. After pouring himself a glass of fruit juice before heading for his bedroom, a mysterious feeling came over him. He was compelled to glance in the direction of that full length mirror once he crossed the opening to the room. The reason for his fixation fell somewhere between relief, and reproach; more toward the latter of the two. Solving the mystery as to why he was suddenly drawn to that mirror escaped him. After all, the dream he thought he had about that spirit referring to itself as an 'orphan' was just that; at least it's what he preferred to believe. The reshaping of space and time by this 'figment' of his imagination was no small feat, but even more daunting for that spirit would be the task of reshaping Omar's temperament.

Chapter 6

THE EFFORT CLARENCE had exhausted already trying to unravel the mystery surrounding Omar's opinions about himself, and others in his life, were beginning to take their toll. His previous contact with the Human Resource Chief at Dillon left him with sketchy information at best, and any witnesses that could shed new light on the situation were nowhere to be found. Omar's time there was looking more like a 'ghost history', but nothing could be further from the truth. He had dismissed the thought of having reservations about trying to get to the bottom of it until Omar gave him reasons to, after questioning whether he had sent letters to the sponsors; as though he had misgivings about Dillon even receiving one. (So, what was the big mystery about Dillon?) He tried to convince himself that Omar was well aware of his snooping tendencies and may not even hold it against him if he found out about what he was trying to do. A sort of 'shadow surrogate' to clear his path of any lingering hostilities from years gone by, before he and Evelyn set up their initial meeting with their contact at Dillon. Omar could probably be that shrewd; knowing it's something that would need to be settled before he and Evelyn take the plunge. Who better than himself to see to it. After all, it's not like Omar harassed him about wanting to take on the assignment, and he needed to do what he could to insure its success. So, he did what any good team player would do and ditched the notion of having to rely on a clandestine approach. It was also to avoid maybe feeling a little diabolical about it, but decided he'd just have to live with the consequences of his actions.

He decided he'd need to not be so conventional with his methods, but would also need to devote more time to his efforts at unravelling the mystery. So, he decided to take a few personal days from work to dig even deeper. There wasn't much on his plate at work that was pressing, besides preparations for the festival. He had already sent letters to all of the sponsors, including Dillon's C.F.O., so he shifted his itinerary with his manager's blessing. He was due some time off anyway and felt now was as good a time as any to do it. He addressed his team the day before to give them a heads up, and instructions to refer to Regis, the other Supervisor in his department, for issues he'd ordinarily deal with.

"I'm taking some much needed time off before things get knee deep with this festival. It'll only be a few days but better I do it now than later."

They all faked a collective sigh, then all smiles.

"That glad to see me gone, huh?"

Nadine blurted out, "Not exactly. It just means we're already missing you, boss."

Everybody was quiet this time, thinking maybe something was going on in his personal life that was too jarring to try and deal with while at work. Clarence could sense the uneasiness from his team after his announcement. He was well respected and hardly took time off unless it was forecast well in advance. His work ethic spoke for itself, and he could sense the troubling undercurrents from his team, which meant their anxieties were raised about sudden departures of certain employees, especially in recent memory. It was unsettling, but also reaffirming. He knew then that they would have his back, come hell to high water, and unlike some of the others that couldn't make the cut, he'd be back. He sat on the edge of Nadine's desk and continued speaking to them.

"It's not an emergency or anything like that, just so you know."

They all let go of a collective sigh again, only louder this time, and again ending in smiles all around. Nadine then said, "Thank God for that!"

"Any problems beyond your scope to handle, just refer to Regis, ok? Just behave while I'm gone, and don't let Nadine give any of you a hard time"

Nadine said, "Had to throw that in, huh?", Nadine replied. She then said, "Just make it back without any drama."

He was headed back to his office when Omar called to him. "Cee Cee, got a minute?"

"Sure, let's talk in my office." Evelyn watched the two of them; trying to get a bead on Omar's body language. She had hoped she wasn't the subject of their meeting. Clarence closed the door behind him..

"Sit, please. So, what's on your mind?"

"Just wanted to let you know we're trying to decide on a location for the video shoot. I had a temporary location in mind, just so the actors can get used to interacting with each other. It'll give them a head start on working together until Evelyn and I can agree on a definite site. Unless you can help us with that."

"Well, I hadn't really given it any thought, but the company's employee park adjacent to the main building may not be such a bad choice. You at least wouldn't have far to go."

"Ok; something to think about. I'll run it by Evelyn. Also I've picked the core courses for my first semester this coming term, and totaled the costs, but I can share the details of that with you when you get back."

"Ok, sounds good."

Clarence noticed he seemed reluctant to get right up and excuse himself, as if another issue was clawing its way to the surface but reluctant to show itself…

"Was there something else you needed to cover?"

"Well, not really just, enjoy your time off."

Omar opened the door slowly, feeling he had just foreclosed on his opportunity to find out if the sponsorship letters were sent yet.

"Look, it's not like I'm taking a leave of absence you know."

"Yeah, you're right."

Omar's movements still seemed to be in 'stall mode'. He was desperate for another opening but not quite sure how to seize it. Clarence let him off the hook..

"Oh, by the way, I did get letters to all of the sponsors and gave them a time when they could expect contact from our team."

The news seemed to jolt Omar from the expression on his face; like he had just been hit with a stout punch to the chest from someone's fist.

"I didn't give your names in the letters though. I figured you and Evelyn can introduce yourselves when you make your initial contacts, ok?"

Omar seemed relieved at the news, which still raised questions about his commitment to courting Dillon as a sponsor. It also meant Clarence was more committed now than ever to finding out why Omar's contact with Dillon was turning out to be more like an incarceration of his will.

"Ok, that's a bet."

Omar turned quickly to leave, sensing Clarence knew his 'Dillon' issue was the real reason he wanted to see him. Omar walked back to his desk feeling more eyes were watching him than usual, but it was more evidence of a manifestly insecure self-image as no one hardly noticed. Theo wasn't chasing after him, and Evelyn had not spoken to him yet since the work day started. The morning break time was even approaching but no word from Evelyn yet whether she wanted to meet in the atrium as usual. With Evelyn and Theo not nipping at his heels, he came to realize how lonely life can be there, and with Clarence being gone for a few days he had almost begun to feel like a man without a country.

No one else there was any particular friend; certainly not anyone he'd want to hang out with. Not that he hadn't received overtures from other people in the building, but he never bothered to reciprocate. It re-affirmed the old adage, 'no deposit; no return' as a stark reality he would need to reckon with. Just when he felt he might take the initiative to invite Evelyn on break, to at least let her know what he and Clarence had discussed, he saw her walking with Nadine toward the breezeway, presumably heading for the atrium. His efforts at damage control had been thwarted, at least temporarily. Missing out on time that had become almost automatic with Evelyn was now in real jeopardy. He could only hope it was not too late for a reprieve. Nadine and Evelyn sat in a secluded spot inside the break area. Evelyn seemed to want to be out of sight of Omar just in case he walked inside while they were there.

"So what's so important that we needed to be 'cloak & dagger' about it?"

"Cloak & dagger?"

"Well, with all the other seats you passed up, I guess the only things missing are trench coats and dark glasses. You know, that 'black bag' look."

"Nadine, come on."

"Ok, maybe we could lose the trench coats then."

"Can you be serious now? I just don't want anyone else to hear."

"So what's troubling you?"

"I'm worried about what's going on with Omar, or what's not going on with him."

Nadine didn't let on that she suspected Omar was the subject of her concern when she said she needed to talk to her. She just responded with, "What exactly do you mean?"

"He's showing me a side of him I didn't know was there before. Like the way he treated my nephew, and even his attitude toward Theo lately." She shook her head and cast her eyes toward the table top in obvious despair over it. "It almost seems like he's become petty and really insecure. Like somebody who always feels threatened, you know? He's not the guy I had come to know."

"That's a surprise. I thought you two were good?"

"It's not like he's put a wrecking ball to our friendship, but he doesn't seem to have a clue about how his behavior affects people around him. I got first wind of it when he and I were on break shortly after we got the assignment for the festival sponsorships. He actually got annoyed when I first mentioned the idea I had about how we could make the presentations even better, and he didn't even want to hear the idea initially; said we shouldn't get ahead of ourselves. I felt cornered from it. I thought I should re-assure him that I wasn't trying to rain on his parade since he was the lead on the project, before he could bring himself to apologize for over reacting. He then decided it was ok that I tell him about my idea. What kind of attitude is that to have with me when we're supposed to be in it together? It's like whatever I wanted to contribute wasn't worth talking about."

Nadine was silent but her meter was running and ramping up the negativity leveled at Omar for putting her friend through the paces. She had good reason to shelve the humor for a change and just be the sounding board Evelyn needed her to be. Nadine knew Evelyn's heart all too well. It was brimming with good things to sow in as many lives as she had the privilege to touch, and didn't need that quality about herself stunted by Omar's reckless meandering. It was bad enough that she hadn't been pro-moted for as long as she had been with the company, but to make her feel she was probably pigeon-holed for certain types of jobs because she hadn't yet, well, it wasn't a good sign.

Nadine said, "You talk to him about it yet?"

"No—He wanted to talk the other day, after I found out what went down with him and Theo, but I pretended it was nothing. I guess I should have gotten it off my chest then, huh?"

"It may have been best, since you guys are still supposed to be doing this video together." "What happened between him and Theo?"

"I found out from Theo that Omar pretended we hadn't dis-cussed him playing a role in the production of the video when we had. Well, he actually told me he would mention it to him, to maybe recruit his help, but he didn't when Theo asked him about wanting to be in it. I just thought that was a blatant disregard for what he and I had talked about, and inconsiderate to Theo, who is supposed to be his friend. What do you think is going on?"

"Sounds like a guy who's running on automatic who really needs to think before he acts. Maybe he hasn't heard, but relationships between people don't just happen in a vacuum. Sounds like he's missing the part about cause and effect."

"It happened with Richie too that Saturday we met with him at his school. He just had to stop at the basketball courts after I picked him up to see who was there. We had already agreed to meet with Richie at a certain time, but he decided he'd be impulsive. Needless to say we got there much later than we had agreed, but it never occurred to him to apologize to Richie for being late. He then treats him like some low level grunt after Richie read the script and recommended changes to it. I know he was irritated over the changes and he may have been taken aback by it a little, but it didn't justify his reaction to it. Actually, the changes made it better after all. He forgot just that quickly though that my nephew is doing this for no fee and he needed to be more appreciative of what he was doing for us."

Nadine had already heard enough, and was ready to pronounce judgment based on her body language. Her opinion of him had already been reduced to a cautionary tale, but these new revelations about his character were enough to justify her full-throttled animosity.

She then said in a menacing tone, "Why don't we tranquilize him, put him in a box, and then ship him to the North Pole?"

"Get serious will you?"

"But wait a minute. Since he's so cold blooded, he'd probably be right at home there, don't you think?"

They then looked at each other with curious expressions, as if it was something they might actually consider, then both laughed out loud over how ridiculous it must have sounded.

Evelyn said, "Really, that's no solution. Anyway, I'm not ready to just write him off. After I had words with him about how he treated Richie, he did apologize to me, and he called Richie to apologize to him too. Well, you heard what he said about him at the reading we had with you guys. I'm still not that convinced he won't do it again though. I guess that voice that speaks to most of us, especially when it comes to taming our emotions, may just be missing in his case."

"God forbid. Oh, look at the time. We'd better get back."

"NATALIE, SWEETHEART, YOU AWAKE?"

Clarence sat on the side of the bed and sipped on a glass of ice water while waiting on her to come around. It seemed to defy conventional wisdom but for him, it was better than coffee to help him kick start his mornings. Natalie rolled slowly onto her back, but not before letting go of a ferocious yawn that seemed to keep her in suspended animation for a while after Clarence had nudged her a few times. She had been interrupted from really sound sleep, but the time was close enough before her alarm was due to go off. She reached for her 'companion pillow', pushing it carefully against her back. Her eyes were still closed as one hand shielded them from the glaring lamp light, while the other instinctively rested on her precious mound. She opened her eyes slowly. Still emerging from her deep sleep.

"Morning sweetheart. What time is it?"

Clarence kissed her on the lips, then kissed her stomach. She quivered slightly from the cool of his lips against her lukewarm skin.

"It's almost 6:30 sleepy head."

She looked away then sighed, knowing there was no need to try and get back to sleep.

She said, "You're dressed already?"

"Almost there. Still missing shoes and socks."

She sniffed the air that was saturated with aromas from the breakfast he had also prepared for her. It was something he usually did on the weekends anyway, so he didn't have to worry too much about messing it up

"And smells like somebody's been rattling pots too. So what's gotten into you mister?"

"I figured I'd try and beat some of the traffic and get an earlier start for my trip to Dillon. I cooked your favorite and left it in a covered plate inside the microwave. Since Nathan's a little finicky, I figured you'd want to fix his yourself; just a hunch."

She placed her palm against his cheek; the blush in her own bloomed like freshly cut rose petals. She was grateful for his initiative, knowing he would be expected to do more of that soon enough, but without needing to be asked. He held her hand closer with his own, carefully brushing her locks away from her eyes with the other.

She smiled and said, "It was a good hunch."

He walked to the closet to get his shoes and socks and slipped them on. Natalie was sitting up by this time.

She then said, "It's kind of odd seeing you dressed down in the middle of the week, but you're still as handsome as ever."

"Thank you my queen."

He kissed her twice again. "Well, I'd better get going before the traffic gets too heavy. See you later this evening. Be careful, and take care of our little ones while I'm gone."

"Don't I always?. I hope you find what you're looking for."

She sat on the side of the bed, shoved her feet into her slippers and whispered, "I Love you."

The sixty two mile drive to Dillon Industries was as he had hoped. There were no tie-ups, except for the last few miles before reaching the outskirts of the city, and no bouts with any self-proclaimed road hogs itching for a confrontation either. He hadn't been to Gleason, Florida except for one other time after accepting the supervisory position at Earth Burst. He recalled having attended a 2-day seminar there for new first line supervisors sponsored by the company. It was unremarkable to say the least. What he got from the workshops then could have easily been obtained through an internet platform, but it seemed more about the importance of fraternizing with likeminded personalities than anything else. It became more accepted as part of the scripted itinerary for that weekend. Besides, he wasn't about to say no to a pricey company sponsored hotel suite and a generous expense account to cover the cost of incidentals. He was so modest about it, he referred to it jokingly as 'excessive privilege' while speaking with Natalie about it when he returned home. The place had gotten something of a facelift since then. Some aesthetic upgrades had replaced the bland, pedestrian profile of the downtown area he remembered. Pavers with unique concentric patterns and colors had replaced the aging and battered concrete and asphalt streets and walkways within a half square mile radius from the main hub of activity. Elaborate landscape designs were also a nice touch, topping off its new 21st century look. A new amphitheater had been built not far from city hall, as well as two new banks. The usual compliment of fast food restaurants had also arrived, but the main architectural feature, that also pinned a piece of Gleason's history, was unchanged. It was the First Baptist Church of Gleason, with its impressive steeple whose spire looked to be just shy of piercing the clouds. He took a moment to stop and read the inscription on the marquee during his first visit. It reminded him of when he toured old town in Savannah. He was struck by its architectural style and its size then. The original sanctuary building had remained the same since it was built after the town was founded, and it was almost like looking at a snapshot. The large SUV and dated four door sedan were parked in the same spots on the south side of the sanctuary, even though he wasn't quite sure if the color of the SUV was the same as before. The kids' playground at the rear of the church appeared to have new pieces and the previous vacant lot next to it now contained a basketball court. Two 10 cubic yard storage containers were also at the far end of the property, but he also noticed someone he hadn't seen before; an apparent caretaker, with garden tools in hand, that instinctively looked up and in his direction at the moment Clarence laid eyes on him. It was a little mysterious with him being so far away but yet, it happened. The man wore rustic colored coveralls and a hat that was a little tattered around the brim. He was tall, and fairly grizzled as far as he could tell. The most noticeable thing was that he walked with a considerable gimp, and seemed to favor his left arm; not the kind of job someone in his condition would consider a wise career move, but he must have made it work. Clarence looked away for a few moments to return the greeting of someone leaving the donut shop. When he turned back toward the church again the caretaker, was in the same spot, staring again. The eeriness of it seemed too much of an omen for the upcoming 'trick or treat' atmosphere to suit Clarence's taste, but at least there were no jack-o-lanterns being sold on the church's lot in advance of Halloween. That would have sent a mixed message if ever he had seen one. The building had been declared a landmark by the historical society, and the city had devoted a portion of its budget for monuments restoration. It occurred to Clarence that for the people of Gleason, some things truly were still sacred. Just before arriving within a block or two of the street the hotel was on that sponsored that weekend seminar, he decided to stop at the new Dunkin Donuts shop for coffee. The unseasonably cooler weather, even for that time of year, made him wish he had brought a light jacket at least. The clear skies meant it would probably be around for a little while. The coffee would at least warm him up a little. When he parked he noticed a paper dispenser with several area newspapers inside. That's something he hadn't seen in a while. He also happened to glance in the direction of a large billboard off in the distance. It was a Dillon Industries advertisement. It contained a large red arrow at the bottom and the phrase '¼ mile west' in the direction of the arrow before reaching the main plant. The newspaper bin in front of the donut shop even contained a matted bronze label with the inscription, 'Courtesy of Dillon Industries'. He also noticed an abstract sculpture on the grounds of a Veterans park next to the Donut shop that clearly showed the Dillon Logo. Now things were getting a little creepy. He pulled one of the papers from the bin, tucked it under his arm, and stepped inside. He was just inside the doorway but couldn't go any further for the line of people waiting for a breakfast sandwich and coffee. No one seemed interested in dining in, so he felt he could at least have a chance to have his blueberry muffin and coffee inside. It was evident to him that it was most likely a blue collar town, based on the way the people were dressed that paraded in and out of the place. The lot was filled with pick-ups rather than sedans, and several of the men wore caps and long sleeved button down shirts with the Dillon logo stitched on the front. It was pretty clear to him that this stop was a daily ritual. The majority of them seemed to know each other well, including the store's staff. They all seemed to be on a first name basis, and what may have been viewed as idle chatter to some, was a 'rite of passage' to them. Having so much in common obviously made it easy to become comfortable with one another. From the overzealous hype over the winning touchdown drive by a favorite son at the local high school game, to the fiasco that took place at the recital of one mother's ten year old; it was earth shattering stuff, but it was their 'stuff', and it probably ranked almost as high as regular church attendance on Sunday mornings. The expression of common courtesies was as important as giving first aid to someone that needed dressing for a wound. They must have known, it has a claim to stake all its own when it comes to medicine for the soul. He was sure that their social order left no room for suspicious 'side eyes' hatching non-stop tales that could eviscerate someone's character without real evidence of foul play. They seemed to have a regard for one another that probably treated gossip like some pesky airborne virus that needed to be avoided at all cost. He got the impression that integrity to them was important; really important. He could sense it. It was clear to him that they appreciated the simplicity of their lifestyles, rather than the anti-septic and impersonal variety that is oftentimes typical of bigger cities. It was also clear that Dillon Industries had put its stamp on this town, and some of what he came for at least, may have been right under his nose. The line moved fairly quickly after only a few minutes of waiting. It seemed the most popular items on the menu were predictably prepared well in advance of the demand. When Clarence was about to be waited on, a uniformed deputy walked in, and his deep baritone voice matched his 6 foot-plus frame.

"Morning everybody!" He had the strut of a marine T.I., moving to what was probably his favorite place to sit. He removed his hat, placed it on the table top and took a seat next to the fixed glass panel. A few of the others made sure they said hello to him as well before walking out. The manager emerged from the food prep area when she saw him.

"Morning Ronnie. Good to have you back. How are your folks?"

"Hey Maggie; their ok. Got my grandad squared away finally."

The manager asked, "You want the usual?"

"Sure, that'll be just fine Maggie."

"Alright, I'll bring it out to you. You eating in right?"

"Of course."

After getting his order Clarence took a seat a few tables behind the deputy. He felt at one point he may have wandered inside a real live Mayberry, (that fictitious town from that sitcom back in the sixties era of television), but he wasn't completely surprised by the attention paid to the officer. The uncontroversial ones deserved to be held in higher esteem. Clarence opened his paper while his coffee cooled a little. The front page of 'The Gazette' featured an article about the Gleason Chamber of Commerce members and new initiatives planned for the city. All seven members of the board were represented in the photo, which included the reigning Chamber president, which was also Dillon Industries' Public Relations Director, Priscilla Eagan. Clarence had already stumbled upon a piece of Omar's past without even realizing it. The Dillon P.R. Director in the photo was none other than Omar's childhood crush. The paper contained mostly ads for other companies in the area. Very few human interest stories were featured in the 15 page periodical which, for the most part, was a classified ads publication. As he thumbed through the pages he noticed an article in memory of the pastor of the First Baptist Church not far from the restaurant. It spoke about the shock of his untimely death at age 62 years, and his outreach to the community and beyond. As he continued reading he was a bit startled when the manager dropped pieces of silverware on the floor after bringing the deputy his order. He took sips from his coffee as the manager apologized to the deputy for the mishap.

"Oh! —Clumsy me. I'm sorry Ronnie."

She set his tray on the table carefully, then stooped hurriedly, trying to pick up the utensils off the floor with a napkin to get him another set…

The Deputy said, "Don't worry about that Maggie. I'm a country boy. We know how to improvise, even without real silverware" He laughed about it, then she relaxed, remembering she had another set in the pocket of her apron.

"Here you go. I gotta sit for a minute. The morning's already got me in a tizzy; you mind?" "You know you don't need to ask."

Clarence checked the time. It was a few minutes before 8:00 am. The administrative offices at Dillon would not be opened yet, so he sat a little longer to finish his coffee. It was entirely co-incidental, but overhearing the conversation between the deputy and Maggie couldn't be helped, unless he would have decided to plug his ears with cotton, or move to another table; neither was really an option…

"You said you got your grandad squared away. Is he still in High Springs?"

"Yeah. Found a group home there that he likes a lot. He started flirting with a few female residents not soon after we walked through the doors."

They both laughed a little about it. "That sounds just like him. If it's ok, I'd like to send him a bowl of my home made peach cobbler next time you make the trip. It was always one of his favorites."

"He'll like that a lot." The deputy became somber suddenly; ignoring the rest of his breakfast which might as well had been a prop at that point. He looked out for a moment through the fixed window pane; silent and reflective. What little light that was shown through his eyes grew dim from fast moving shadows of what seemed to him, the absence of grace for his brother and grandfather's circumstances…

He said, "The P.A.'s at that home said they can only make him as 'comfortable' as possible, but the dementia will eventually claim his memory, even for basic functions. You know it was him that taught me how to ride my first bike; took me to ballgames too cause dad wasn't around much."

"I'm so sorry Ronnie, but he's in a good place and he has family around him that love him." She patted his hands in a maternal gesture; trying desperately to trace the missing light in his eyes with her own..

"For what I know of your grandad, that's one thing he knows for sure, and I'm almost certain that's something that sets his mind at ease."

"I know the time will come when we should anticipate his passing. I just hope it doesn't happen like it did with Pastor Rueben. It was so sudden for him. Everybody was just really caught by surprise."

She said, "I know. There's another nice article about him in the Gazette today. Just goes to show we need to be ready when our time comes." She decided to change the subject before stepping too deep into his despair.

"Ever see your dad? You know he's still somewhat of a hero to us old heads who knew him back in the day, being a track and field star and all. I believe we've got some of those old articles somewhere from when he was at the top of his game too."

"Yeah, a game that fizzled out; but to answer your question, no, I don't see him much these days. Not since Dee's, incident."

"You mean what happened at Dillon?"

"None other." He shook his head then covered his face with both hands, as if trying to halt the arrival of his distress over the subject.

"When I think about where Dee could be right now if it wasn't for Pastor Rueben; it was a miracle that he took him under his wing when he did. I was bitter about what happened to him after that guy attacked him. I wanted him arrested, but dad wasn't having it. He said he made Dillon's Management team swear to secrecy too, as well as any witnesses of the incident that he knew about. He said what I felt like doing was only gonna burden me with also having to grieve the suffering I would have caused that guy, not just Dee. He had no appetite for vigilante justice you know. He kept hammering it into me; 'you're a better man than that', but I didn't want to hear it at the time; Said it was Dee's choice, and I couldn't make it for him,. It was as if he felt he owed it to this guy not to have Dee press charges. He told me some day I would understand it all."

Maggie became curious about it and questioned him further.

"Did you ever get any closer to finding out who this guy was that attacked Him?"

"All I know is, he got out of dodge shortly after the incident; supposedly moved to Mumford so they tell me."

Clarence's ears perked by this time. He was sipping on coffee that had cooled to room temperature by the time he picked it up again.

"You gonna look in on him this morning?. He's at the church today you know."

"I had intended to before making my rounds."

One of the employees yelled from the kitchen, "Maggie, you've got a call."

"Be right there. I'd better go. The natives are getting restless. You take care Ronnie. See you next time."

"Take care Maggie, and thanks." He discarded what was left of his breakfast, placed it in the trash can and got up to leave. As he was passing Clarence their eyes met, he nodded, then his country manners compelled him to greet this stranger —"Morning".

Clarence said, "Morning officer", but noticed his badge number (442) and made a mental note for later reference. His instincts told him he had hit a treasure trove of information already and hadn't even made it to Dillon yet. He ordered another small coffee to-go and stepped outside to follow the deputy's movements as he left the lot. As he sat inside his car he noticed the deputy turning into the church's lot. He watched him get out and stand by the door for a moment when he saw that same grizzled caretaker approach the deputy. He dropped his hand tools on the ground, then they embraced. The caretaker then patted the deputy on the back repeatedly as they hugged each other. He was obviously glad to see him. Clarence watched them converse for a few minutes. The caretaker stood back from him for a moment, with both hands gripping the deputy's shoulders; their faces fixed on one another as if they were basking in the joy of fond memories. The caretaker then said something that caused the two of them to laugh out loud. It was clear to Clarence they had a bond, and based on their body language, the caretaker was most likely the person the deputy and Maggie were talking about. Clarence sat inside his car for some minutes before leaving the lot. He felt he had been handed a gift just on the suspicion that the caretaker of that church shared a wrenching past with Omar; a past Omar still chose to keep hidden from view. Clarence also knew, that no amount of secrecy would ever eliminate the veil of uncertainty that covered his friend day after day, and having to confront his past head-on was the only way to really put it behind him. When he thought about it more, it became more important suddenly, as a matter of principal, to see Omar free of his predicament with Dillon, than trying to insure the success of the sponsorship. To him it was reasonable to trust that a permanent resolution of the Dillon problem would likely guarantee a successful campaign to win the sponsorships.

He was also well aware of the risks, that undressing old emotional scars only to expose a more festering wound, could spell disaster. He decided, it would be a gamble he was more than willing to take. When he started his car the 'private eye' in him kicked in and his mind shifted into overdrive. First he would need to contact the Sheriff's office there to try and verify the full name of the deputy at the donut shop. He could then search the public records for other legal names associated with him. He would also have to invent a reason for the call that was plausible without sounding suspicious. It may have been easier just to ask the manager at the Dunkin Donut shop for his full name, but he needed to remain as anonymous as possible while he was there. Besides, being a stranger there may have raised too many questions about the reason for his inquiries. He took a few sips from his coffee while mulling over what he would ask of the Sheriff's Department once he called. When he settled on a story, he was not entirely comfortable with his reason for calling since it wasn't exactly true, but if it was going to open up access to a deeper understanding of why Omar went 'dark' about his history with Dillon, then so be it. He called the Sheriff's Department and a pleasant sounding, older woman answered.

"Lake County Sheriff's Office, may I help you?"

"Good morning. I just wanted to know if you could give me the name of one of your deputies. His badge number is '442'. I saw him at the coffee shop this morning and I overheard him speaking with the manager, Maggie, about a group home in High Springs that he had visited on behalf of another relative."

"Yeah, you're talking about Ronnie Bristol, and it was probably about a place for his grandad."

"I didn't think to ask him for the name of the place, because I might need to find a place just like that for a relative of mine, but he had left before I could approach him. He seemed pretty satisfied with it."

"You must not be from around these parts because everybody knows Ronnie."

"You're right I'm not from around here, and I kind of got the impression he was pretty well known when he came into the shop."

"You maybe, want him to try and call you back?"

"Well, it's not official business so, he might not be good with that."

"I see what you mean. He's listed though; lives just outside of Gleason off McKnab Street."

"Ok, that's helpful. Maybe I can speak with him before I leave the area. Thanks a lot for your help." Finding the deputy's phone number was easy enough and Clarence wasted no time in placing the call. After getting his voicemail he decided to try later to see if he'd catch him at home. In the meantime the trip to Dillon was next up. He wanted to at least get a feel for the place that drove Omar's confidence into hiding. The scene of the crime always harbored clues long after the deed was done, and in Omar's Case he felt there were things yet to be revealed that might paint him as the villain, or maybe the victim. The amount of traffic on the county road that led to the Dillon plant reminded him of an evacuation out of the city. It seemed at least half the population must have worked there. It occurred to him that this place accounted for a big piece of the local economy, and it seemed unthinkable that anyone would risk losing a job there because of a temporary lapse in judgment. If Omar was the culprit in the incident with the caretaker, or anyone else for that matter, there must have been other factors that contributed to his meltdown. Clarence finally was free of the thickening congestion after traffic cleared the main gate. The sprawling twin marquees, 'Welcome to DILLON INDUSTRIES & PHARMACEUTICALS, INC.' flanked the gate house on both sides. The usual compliment of informational signs followed once inside the gate which made it easier to locate the administrative offices. After finding a parking space he sat for a moment trying to decide where to go first. The Visitors Center seemed the safest bet, since his visit wasn't exactly official. When he walked inside the reception area there was a larger replica of the photo he saw in the paper inside a glass covered bulletin board. There was also a plaque underneath it; a commendation to the chamber president, Priscilla Eagan, for her service to the community. Clarence looked very much like a first time visitor and was approached by the receptionist.

"Good morning. First time with us?"

"Yes—yes it is. I'm from Mumford; just passing through but was persuaded by someone I know to stop by and take a look at your facility while I'm in the area."

"Well, it's not the science fair but most people that come through here know a lot more about what we do once they leave. Our interactive displays are some of the best in the state for this type of facility. Not to brag, but people seem to have only good things to say about us. She reached out to shake his hand, "I'm Eileen."

"Clarence; pleased to meet you."

Clarence got the impression she was kind of chatty, but then again, for the people of Gleason it was the nature of the beast. He was the only one in the place then, so she took time with him to point out the photo displays that showed the history of the plant from inception as well as colorful maps showing key sectors. When she directed him toward the interactive displays, a small group of about six people came in.

She excused herself and said, "That's my small group for this morning, so I'll leave you to it. Any questions I'll be in the area alright?"

As she was approaching the small group, a woman dressed in a smoke colored business suit squeezed past one of the visitors who was just inside the doorway. She wore dark designer glasses with her hair up in a flattering style that complemented her 'cover girl' features, and walked with the confidence of a runway model. As she was approaching Clarence, another voice from behind him called to her…

"Oh, there you are. I was just about to ask Eileen if you had called."

The woman pulled her shades off and was the same woman

in the photo; the chamber of Commerce president, who also happened to be the Dillon Public Relations Director. Clarence was almost caught staring at her, to make sure it was the same woman but there was no doubting it. Her eyes caught his and she did greet him. She was also pleasant, but sounded rehearsed…

"Good morning, how are you?"

Clarence said, "Morning, I'm fine thanks."

Clarence wanted to give her credit just for being courteous by nature, but felt the greeting was more about arresting his tendency to keep staring at her and erasing any suspicion as to whether she was some rigid task master. It was ok with him either way. After she disappeared with the other woman into another room, he spent time at some of the displays, not sure how he and this woman's paths might cross again. She seemed as good a candidate as any to try and dissect Omar's history and what really happened there. When he stepped to one of the displays that included a recorded narrative about testing procedures for syringes, the voice in the recording sounded a lot like Omar. When he looked at a photo of the staff for the Biologists Lab in the year 2001, there it was; a shot of Omar in a white lab coat, standing alongside four other people, also in lab coats. The video portion did not include footage of him, but the inscription beneath the photo did list him as a Junior Lab Technician. He finally had something concrete. When he resumed the video, he heard voices coming from the room where the P.R. Director was. No one was approaching him but the door must have been left ajar for a moment just before they walked out, and he overheard them conversing…

The young woman asked, "You mean you almost gave in?"

"Not even. He could have gotten further, but he wasn't a closer; started talking a lot of nonsense that had nothing to do with what interest me, but yet he takes me to what was supposed to be a secluded spot better suited for his 'pillow talk' if you know what I mean. In the end, he was just really shy about expressing himself openly to me."

They both started to laugh a little.

"These closet Don Jon's are gonna wear me out. He sort of reminds me of the guy in high school I told you about; the one that used to work here, Omar Duncan."

"Oh, yeah. The one in the pic out front."

"We were kids then, so it was easier to excuse that kind of behavior from a guy. Actually, in his case it was kind of cute, but you don't expect it from a grown man, you know?" Priscilla paused, then said, "I wonder what's he's doing these days? I actually saw him again during spring break my sophomore year. I think he thought for a moment we were still in grade school the way he came on to me. He was a good guy and all, at least the one I remembered, but I had moved on."

Clarence couldn't believe what he was hearing. I'm sure he felt the receptionist must have been at least curious why he spent so much time at that one display. He casually glanced in her direction, but she was so engrossed with the small group that came in behind him, she must not have noticed. Ms. Eagan and the other woman were coming back into the reception area when he decided to move to another display at that moment. He couldn't believe his good fortune in just a short space of time. Ms. Eagan got the receptionist's attention briefly while heading toward the door but looked to be holding several briefs this time.

"I'm headed to the other side now Eileen. See you later on."

"Yes mam—Knock'em dead today."

"I'm gonna try."

When the door closed behind her, Eileen excused herself from the group and headed back to her desk. Clarence decided it was a good time to pick her brain a little about Ms. Eagan. She was making entries in a log when he approached her.

"Seems she's somebody with influence." He motioned to Ms. Eagan as she was getting in her car…

"Oh, yeah. She's the one with the chops alright. She's the Public Relations Director, and President of the chamber of commerce. The company's C.E.O. has her ear first over anyone else in his senior staff. She's a mover and a shaker alright."

"Is that so?" Clarence was watching her pull away with a fixed stare. Somehow he knew Ms. Eagan and Omar were destined to meet again, and soon. It was clear she was one ingredient inside Omar's bittersweet concoction of a personality that kept him off balance at times. He knew he had to somehow make Omar aware in advance that she was on the executive staff at Dillon and possibly someone he would need to confront for the sponsorship, unless he already knew about her being there. There was one sure way to find out, and guarding that paper with his life was part of it. He said goodbye to Eileen as he was leaving and decided to try and contact the deputy again. He did reach him this time…

"Hello, is this Deputy Bristol?"

"Yes it is, who is this?"

"My name is Clarence Colter. I'm visiting from Mumford and I wondered if I might speak to you about something. It's pretty important."

"Ok, I'm listening."

"I was in the Dunkin Donut shop this morning when you were talking with the manager about your Grandad, and also about the caretaker at the church not far from there."

Clarence winced a little, not sure how the officer would accept his remarks. He responded in a slightly agitated tone.

"You weren't eavesdropping on us, were you?"

"Oh, no; nothing like that. I just happened to be sitting not far from you and could overhear what the two of you were talking about pretty easily. The truth is, I'm here as a favor to a friend. Someone who has a history here that I believe still haunts him a little. He doesn't know I'm here but it's something that won't let go of him until he faces the truth about what happened, and the people that were affected by it."

"Alright. You've said a lot, but who is this friend of yours, and what does he have to do with me?"

"The man you visited at the church, the caretaker; he's a relative isn't he?"

"Yeah, he's my older brother." He paused briefly, then asked, "Are you a private eye?"

"No, nothing like that. Just somebody seeking answers, like you seem to have wanted concerning the attack on your brother."

Clarence had moved into unchartered territory with the Deputy when he mentioned the attack. He didn't know how he might react, but he chose to commit to it as willingly as someone might, facing a hail of gun fire without any body armor. He held his breath, waiting on the deputy's response. There was a long pause. Clarence could hear clearly the rapid breathing by the deputy. Something was triggered in Deputy Bristol then, but he couldn't be sure if it spelled anger, or just anticipation of a chapter in his life, and that of his brother's, possibly coming to a close finally.

"Do you know anything about who may have done this to my brother? Who attacked him and almost left him a cripple?"

Clarence could tell in his tone that the bitterness had resurfaced once again…

He then said, "I can't be sure to be honest, but I believe that friend I told you about at the start of the conversation, and the man that injured your brother, may be one in the same person."

Chapter 7

OMAR'S DAY AT THE office without the watchful eye of Clarence was as he had feared since Evelyn was treating him with a long handled spoon. He did find an email from Richie, letting him know he had made space on his schedule to rehearse the actors by the beginning of the week, and he had also copied Evelyn on the email. It seemed the closest thing to human contact for him since he stepped into the office. The script wasn't that long and Richie assumed the actors would have had more than enough time to commit it to memory. He hadn't gotten feedback from Omar or Evelyn about the changes he had made, so he assumed the script had a green light. Omar was at least curious. Surely Evelyn had gotten the email but she hadn't mentioned it to him yet. He knew he needed to at least find out if she did, and to talk about deciding on a place to rehearse the cast. He also knew that ultimately, he was the man in charge, and Clarence entrusted him to make sure this sponsorship campaign would go off without a hitch. He couldn't rely on Evelyn to make a move this time. Avoiding being chastised by her was reason enough not to face her; but he felt it best to take the plunge and approach her. Besides, something he did must have really 'gotten her goat' to just shut down the way she did, so he called her just before the afternoon break to test the 'emotional' waters.

"Hey Evelyn—it's me, Omar."

"Hello Mr. Duncan." Her voice was laced with so much skepticism, she even sounded like someone else to him.

"I wanted to know if you got Richie's email about wanting to rehearse by next week."

"Yeah, I got it."

"Well, why didn't you call me about it?"

"You're the lead, and since he addressed it to you, I figured it was your call. No need to chase you about something you already know about, right? I felt you'd touch base when it was convenient, so here we are; two colleagues, having a meeting of the minds."

He took her sarcasm with a grain of salt, or two…

"Well, since he's your nephew, I figured__"

"You figured what? Look, it's like what you said to me once before about getting ahead of you, and believe me I didn't want to be accused of that again. You're the lead on this, so just take the initiative when you need to. That's what's expected of you; by me, and everybody who has a hand in this."

It was an awkward moment for him. His friend had never been so official with him before. Evelyn, on the other hand, felt she was swimming against the tide of their relationship all of a sudden; trying to find vindication of some kind to try and flush out his nemesis. What was more troubling was the fact that he seemed completely unaware of what may have caused it.

"You're right-You're right, it is my responsibility. I know we didn't give Richie a 'yay' or 'nay' on the script changes but I'm o.k. with them; how about you?"

"I'm good with what he's done."

"Why don't we get copies of the changes to everybody and schedule a walk-thru of it for Monday or Tuesday of next week. That way they'll all have a chance to meet Richie."

"We didn't talk about a place yet you know."

"Clarence suggested the employee park before he took off. It's practically next door and may even be good enough for the actual shoot. We can take a look, and the three of us can make a decision at the rehearsal; how's that?"

"Ok, that'll work."

"Can you check with everybody today or tomorrow to see if they can make it on one of those days? That way I can confirm with Richie."

"Sure. I can do that."

There was a long pause; neither one of them was ready to end the conversation without an attempt at repairing the breach between them. Evelyn felt he did assert himself moments earlier but also feeling, for Omar, it must have been like someone who had never seen snow before, suddenly being pounded by too much of it in the middle of a blizzard. It was clear to her he was still skittish about assuming the role of a leader. It made more sense now why he hadn't posted for any supervisory jobs since he had been there. She got the feeling it was truly virgin territory for him. She did learn something about him during all those times on break together. She thought it was just a phase, but something had spooked him to the point of feeling it would probably be a lost cause anyway. At that point she pitied what little was left of his confidence, after so much of it had presumably been chiseled away by misfortunes that had become, to a degree, self-inflicted. He was talented but lacked discipline; the luxury sedan that performed more like a jalopy. She couldn't risk a serious gaffe with the presentation to the sponsors and decided to not be so delicate with him.

She asked, "Look, can I be honest?"

"I'm all ears."

"I've been uncomfortable with you lately."

"What do you mean?"

"I want to trust you but you weren't honest with me when I asked you to speak with Theo about a role for the video. You said you would, then when I spoke with him he said you didn't mention it because you thought he wasn't interested. I don't want to play games, especially with the lives of people who are supposed to be our friends. That includes me. They deserve better than that. And there can't be any place for your impulsiveness either, especially while we're trying to work this project. I need you to be focused on what we're trying to do here. Clarence also needs you focused, so get a hold of yourself and understand you have a job to do and there are people that want to help you do it. Just start putting some purpose ahead of your pitfalls and your pride, and understand that it's something he's counting on you to do. That has to happen if we're going to succeed at this."

Omar's armor had been tarnished just a little more after Evelyn opened up about her concerns, but he needed perspective and she had no qualms about being the one to give it to him.

"Ok, I'm sorry." He said. "Is that what you want to hear?"

"It's not about what I want to hear but how you must really feel about it that matters here. Haven't you been listening to what I've been saying? You've done some rotten things, to people that are supposed to matter to you but you've developed this Teflon approach to life that you feel everybody else should have too. People aren't built that way Omar. You can't expect things just to bounce off people the way they might with you."

"Just don't preach at me alright, I'm—"

She interrupted and raised her voice. "Will the real Omar Duncan please stand up!" Everybody in her row looked up suddenly; the melodrama startling them somewhat. She continued....

"You have to ditch your fear Omar. You've built this fortress around yourself, thinking it will hold your demons at bay, but you're still forced to live behind that wall as long as you don't step from behind it to see what's on the other side. Your Demons won't stop pestering you; it's just in their nature. You just have to learn to show them whose boss. You won't score points playing defense all the time you know."

"Are we done?"

"Yeah, we're done. I'll let you know when I've talked to the actors about next week—talk at you later."

"Hey Regis, it's Clarence."

"Hey man, enjoying your time off?"

"Well, let's just say it's more productive than I thought it would be. No fireworks so far?" "Well, not yet anyway. Of course the day isn't quite over yet so, you never know. Your team seems to be doing o.k. on their own though. Too bad I can't say the same about mine."

"I needed to speak with one of them; Omar Duncan, if he's around. I tried to get him on his extension but got no answer."

"Hold on a minute. Let me take a walk to see if he's in the area."

Just as he placed Clarence on hold he saw Omar walking back to his unit…

"Omar!" He turned to see Regis holding up the receiver. "You've got a call!"

When Omar reached his desk, "It's Clarence."

"Hey Cee Cee."

"Hey man. How are things going with the video?"

"Oh, they're going. Waiting to hear back from Richie about a date for our first rehearsal next week."

"Yeah, bout time we tried to nail it down; clocks ticking you know. I discovered something that might really be useful for you and Evelyn during the production of it, but I can share it with you when we talk again."

"Oh, ok.. I hope it doesn't involve a rewrite of the script. I felt we were done with whatever editing we were going to do."

"No, nothing like that; at least not that kind of editing anyway. I'd better give Regis his phone back, but I was just checking in. Don't keep me in the dark about anything you feel you need my ear on, ok?"

"Alright, take care."

Omar walked back to his desk, less than a minute's walk away, but enough time for him to think about Clarence's statement about the discovery that might help him and Evelyn. He mentioned editing of something, but not in the usual sense. He knew Clarence had a penchant for wanting to be cryptic, but it was a curious reference to make. If not editing of the script, then what could he have been referring to exactly? He dismissed it quickly when his attention turned to Blake and Theo, who were at Theo's desk. His computer was next on the list to be replaced and adjustments were being made to the desk module to accommodate it. Theo saw him looking, but turned away quickly. Nadine and Evelyn were walking back to the unit from having been on the afternoon break together and approached the two of them. Evelyn also looked Omar in the eyes, then turned away. Omar watched the chemistry among the four of them, mixing like some popular weekend cocktail. He had become 'the odd man out'. He sat down slowly, feeling very much like the invisible man in a room full of people. It was a feeling that would have distressed anyone else but curiously enough for him, it was about as potent as a rubber ball hitting the side of a brick building. The fact that it didn't seem to bother him much was a little troubling even to him. That brief flirtation was undoubtedly a remnant of his conscious, crying out to show itself; struggling to get its legs; eager to stand on its own; but the impulse still remained too fuzzy to even name. He became aware at that moment, that loneliness can almost be compared to 'Kryptonite' for some people; himself included, when describing the thing that makes them feel less relevant, but he had become almost neutral; knowing deep down it wasn't exactly emotionally healthy. He was losing himself to a past that literally held him captive; trailing off into his daydreams at the spur of a moment; boosting his indifference even more. Today was no exception. He stared into space, while stroking his beard again. His phone extension rang repeatedly but he tuned it out. He had stepped inside one of his time portals again, where real time almost stood still.

"OMAR, ARE YOU READY YET?"

He yelled from the bedroom, "Just about mom—Gotta get my gym bag. Is dad still gonna meet us at the track?"

He rushed downstairs to see his mother waiting, holding a set of freshly pressed street clothes for him…

"Mom, you didn't have to bring those. I can carry a change of clothes in this bag."

"Well don't you want to look neat after you've gotten sweaty from all that running? There's probably gonna be a lot of cute girls there you know."

She smiled, fully expecting him to agree with her.

"Believe me; a lot of 'em would rather see me all sweaty—Must be a 'chick' thing."

She shoved him on his shoulder and they both laughed about it.

"I can shower at the stadium, but let me think about those clothes, ok?"

"Oh, alright; but I'll bring them just in case you change your mind."

Omar put his gym bag in the back seat and also noticed the portable oxygen tank in the trunk area. His Mom had covered it up partially, knowing it sometimes interfered with his mental preparation for his competitions. He turned in his seat with his arms folded, but a little agitated.

"I won't need that tank either mom. I wish you hadn't brought it."

"It's just a precaution son, that's all. I know—I know, you don't want to think about an episode on the track but suppose the medical team there doesn't have what you might need? Do you even know if there will be a team on standby?"

"Mom, come on. You're being paranoid. I haven't needed that thing for over a year now."

"But this is different. It's too important. It's the meet that will decide if you get that scholarship help you've been wanting, and frankly you'll probably need. Besides, why take a chance on your health when you don't have to? That's what's most important to me, and should be to you too." Her cell phone rang as she was turning onto the street the stadium was on—It was Omar's dad…

She said, "Hi—are you at the stadium?"

"I got here about 10 minutes ago. I'm talking with Seth. Are you close?"

"Less than 5 minutes away. Why don't you meet us at the main tunnel?"

"Ok, see you in a few minutes."

The training Omar received from Coach Bivens for almost four years, along with having overcome a rare respiratory malady from birth, had erased the distinction he had of least likely to even complete the forty yard dash. He had become the most celebrated runner in the 100 meter sprint. His uncle Seth attended almost all of his meets, and was also his 'de facto coach' due to Coach Bivens' recommendation. Seth and Coach Bivens ran track together when they were in school. Seth was the Pre-Olympic hopeful during that tme but his appetite for mischief seemed to matter more than his career as a runner. The bright light of his celebrity dimmed rather quickly when his coaches became aware of his behavior. His backsliding eventually led to his suspension from the team after being given several chances to get his act together. He was bitter about it for a long time, but after befriending Bivens, and getting to really know him, he couldn't help but respect his attitude about life in general as much as anyone he had known. He showed him how an athlete is like a finely tuned machine that will eventually fail without proper maintenance, especially if the choice is made to willfully shorten its life by adding things to it that don't belong. Bivens never disputed Seth being the better athlete, but he had the edge when it came to much needed discipline. Bivens knew Seth still wanted to be around the sport after 'hanging up his spurs' for so many years, so he let him serve as one of Omar's coaches during practices and at the meets for his first two years on the team. Seth lost his opportunity as an Olympic hopeful, but gained much needed perspective about responsibility; to himself and to others that depended on him. Coach Bivens even submitted his name to be selected to the Pre-Olympic selection committee for the southeastern region of Florida, which he eagerly accepted once he received the formal invitation. Omar never knew his Uncle Seth had a history with

Coach Bivens. It was one of many surprise revelations about the people in his life that would impact him some years later in the most dramatic of circumstances.

OMAR'S MOTHER PARKED NEAR the opening to the main gate as a throng of spectators seemed huddled around it, slowly making their way inside. As he was collecting his gym bag from the back seat, someone touched him on his shoulder. It was none other than the infamous Miss Priscilla Eagan. She had become quite the young debutante since they were in grade school, but he was no less smitten by her coquettish behavior…

"Hello Mr. Duncan."

"Oh!, Priscilla. What are you doing here?"

"Came to watch you run silly." She greeted Omar's mom with a somewhat plastic facial expression, "Hi Mrs. Duncan."

His mom's reply was flat—"Hello young lady."

Based on Priscilla's reputation, his mom could think of other reasons for her being there; the kind that were also muscular with close cropped hair, and maybe a 'bad boy' signature tattoo on one arm, but it didn't interfere with Omar's attempt at an overture…

"You here by yourself?"

"I brought my niece and nephew. Sort of babysitting, you know how it is."

Her nephew ran over to her from the car and asked, "Aunt Priscilla can I have my bun now?"

"They've been bugging me about these things since we left the store." She took a cinnamon bun from her bag, opened it, and broke off a piece for him. She ate a piece of it herself, then offered Omar some of it…

"Here, why don't you finish it—Maybe it'll give you a boost."

"Maybe I shouldn't. I'm not really supposed to have anything but fluids."

"Here silly; this little bit won't kill you."

The way he looked at her, you'd think she was puckering up for a kiss. She put it up to his mouth and he took two hefty bites of it anyway. She said, "See, that wasn't so bad was it?"

His mom had seen enough and said, "Omar, we'd better get going if you're gonna have time to warm up."

"I'd better get inside, but maybe I'll see you a little later?"

"Maybe; we'll see."

His mom was a little upset at him for bowing to Priscilla's will. From one female to another, she knew that performance by Priscilla was more of a power play than genuine affection for her son. She almost scolded him as they made their way up the tunnel…

"If you ask me, I think she's got at least a few fellas tugging on that skirt tail, if you get my meaning."

"She's not that bad mom; a little dramatic maybe."

"You ever been on a date with her?"

"No, not really."

"Ever talk to her on the phone at least a few times a week?"

"No, so what's the big deal?"

She tugged on his arm to slow their pace a bit.

"You're my son, and I care about your feelings, and I just don't want any skirt with a flashy smile messing over you, understand?"

He almost stopped, thinking about what she had said, with an ominous look on his face. She kept walking to meet his dad. Omar eventually made his way down to greet him too, then trotted to the track where his team was assembled.

"Hey coach; Uncle Seth."

Seth high-fived him then helped him loosen up before warm ups. Coach reminded him of the miraculous journey he had made to get to that point, and how the race should really be his to lose…

"A lot of blood, sweat, and tears to get here Omar, but this is it. This is what you've worked so hard for. You remember when I used to preach at you about preparation being everything, well it is; this is proof of it. The fact that you're among the elite, means you belong here. Do you believe it?"

"Yes sir."

"Is it yours for the taking?"

"Yes sir!"

"Alright, get prepped. Your qualifying heat is up second."

As he progressed through his warm ups, his skin suddenly became a little blotchy from redness, and he began to cough in sporadic burst only a few seconds apart. The crimson tinge in his eyes that followed put Seth on alert right away. He stopped his warm up abruptly and confronted him…

"Omar, look at me." He put both hands at his cheeks. "Are you feeling alright?"

"Yeah, just a little something in the air probably."

The coughing was further apart, but didn't disappear. Seth got Coach Bivens' attention right away. ..

"Something's not quite right with Omar. You should take a look."

Omar continued his warm up but seemed to move in slow motion. Some parts of it he didn't even bother with.

Coach asked him, "Are you ready for this?"

"I'm ok; I'm ready."

But he was far from being ready. His palms were beginning to sweat and the hair on his arms and legs stood erect; moving like blades of grass against a mild gust of wind.

Coach Bivens said, "Your qualifying heat is next up. I guess you would know better than either of us how you feel."

His mom watched from the bleachers with a look of foreboding. There was too much activity around her son suddenly. A lot more than usual. She remained quiet, hoping her worst fear would not be realized. His dad seemed unfazed by it all. Minutes after the first race, Coach Bivens gave him the green light.

"Better get to the track; you're up."

Omar's trot seemed listless. He was the last runner to his blocks. It was a qualifying race, but then again it was Omar

Duncan, 'the meteor man', on the track which meant all eyes were on him. When the gun sounded, he had one of his fastest starts ever. He simply willed himself through the heat as his body continued giving him conflicting signals. His lead was never threatened until the last 25 meters when it was apparent his speed had fallen off a bit. He was first place in the qualifying heat, but still had given up a full two and a half seconds before crossing the finish line. He waddled to the infield and stopped to sit down on the turf. The race shouldn't have taken that much out of him. Coach approached him with a few squirts of Gatorade. He took the fluid then just fell on his back. Coach Bivens checked his movements to try and gauge the level of his physical distress.

"That took a lot out of you; more than it should have I'm thinking. Looks like you gave out of gas."

"Don't worry coach. It's like you said." Panting heavily between phrases "It was mine to lose." His breathing though was too labored for Coach Bivens to be convinced of his claims about feeling fine.

Seth walked up and asked the coach, "You want the medic to take a look at him?"

Omar interrupted as the rest of the squad looked visibly concerned.

"Coach, I'll be ok; just need to catch my breath that's all. I'm fine, really. There's too much riding on this."

"Your race is only about half an hour away. I'll take a closer look at you then, but if I have any reason to be concerned about you—"

Omar interrupted, "I get it; It'll be your call."

Seth looked on with concern but said nothing. Omar's victory today would be a vicarious win for him as well, but the possibility of double jeopardy rearing its ugly head at this point in time was unimaginable. Omar had overcome tremendous odds just to make the team, let alone becoming a featured athlete. It was unthinkable, but not improbable as competitions go. He would be holding his breath, hoping fate would have dealt him a favorable hand when it was all over. Omar felt his mental preparation at this point in the meet would give him the edge; all things being equal with his physical conditioning, but things were not equal. He knew his body was out of sync but he couldn't put his finger on the problem. He isolated himself from the rest of the team, which he did often to clear his head before getting ready for his next race, but the anxiety rushed in like a flood. He paced back and forth for several minutes attempting to recharge despite it clinging like an alcoholic high. He sipped on his Gatorade again with wind sprints mixed in. The coaches left him alone, thinking the qualifier was just an anomaly. His next race was only about 10 minutes away now. The other runners on his team were pumping each other up for their upcoming events, but Omar stayed away. He almost treated the fraternizing like the kiss of death before a race but the isolation proved to be the real culprit. He performed a few more short sprints, then got ready to move to the track. His time had come. As he approached his lane, he seemed to lose his equilibrium suddenly. He stopped short of it, then kneeled for a moment; the skin on parts of his arms had become blotchier with the look of flamed out ashes this time.

One of the other athletes asked, "You up for this chief?"

Omar stood slowly, trying to disguise what he suspected might be a medical problem.

He replied, "Yeah, I'm good."

After the gun sounded, he was already in trouble. His start out of the blocks was lethargic and did not get much better. He picked up some seconds after the first 50 meters but his form made him look like he was tracking through mud. His mom went on alert and rushed to the car to get the oxygen tank just in case. Her son's health was most important now, even at the expense of relinquishing the thing he had fought so hard for. During the last 20 meters or so, it was clear the race was lost. He would be lucky to place in the top four. Coach Bivens didn't hide his disappointment sensing the inevitable. He looked at Seth with a slumped posture.

"Damned; I knew something wasn't quite right with him—I felt it."

Omar did finish 5th place, but had barely crossed the finish line when he pivoted to the infield and collapsed. Coach, Seth, and a few athletes from his team rushed to his side. His nose was running mucus and seemed to be struggling to breath. His eyes were also a little hazy.

Coach tried to keep him alert. "Omar can you hear me? Someone get the medic over here."

One of the other athletes rolled up his windbreaker to put under his head and noticed his arms and face..

"What's happening to his skin?"

His mom and dad rushed up with the oxygen tank at the same time the medics got there. There was a hush over the crowd as Omar's crisis had taken center stage. His breathing was rapid and he seemed delirious.

His mom shouted, "He needs oxygen; please let me get this to him, please!"

She was trying to position the tank when one of the medics stopped her cold.

"Hold one second mam; that may not be his problem." He checked his lips which were still pinkish. He then pulled a small bag with a half mask attached from his kit and put it over Omar's nose and mouth.

He then said, "He's hyperventilating. He should start to breath normally in a little while, but looks like he's got something else going on here too."

When they sat him up his eyes were blood-shot and his sinuses gushed uncontrollably.

"Get the truck here, now! He needs to be taken to the hospital."

Omar's mom was in tears as they placed him on the stretcher. His dad, Coach Bivens, Seth, and other members of the team looked on in disbelief. Their world had suddenly come tumbling down in one fell swoop; no one knowing what, or who, the real culprit was that may have caused it all. Omar's eyes were barely opened but recognized the voices around him. His mom and dad held his hands, trying to reassure him that everything would be ok. He could barely grip them; an indication of how the episode had sapped his energy. Seth also was trying to process the hit that the team had taken that day; but more importantly the colossal disappointment it must have been for Omar, and for himself. He prayed silently for a moment, then watched them position the stretcher for the ride to the hospital. The sorrow he felt for his nephew at that moment gave him chills. It subdued him; the way sheets of ice might mercilessly stress the tiny branches of a young willow in winter; weary of its frigid bondage; weeping for the urgency of spring. He had hoped it would not mean the end of a stellar career for Omar. His saga didn't deserve this type of ending. Just before Omar's stretcher was placed inside the ambulance, he caught a glimpse of Priscilla, standing in the bleachers as she watched the entourage that followed him. His celebrity seemed certain by all the attention from the crowd. The clapping and cheering as he exited the stadium caught him completely by surprise, but the image of Priscilla standing there, with an expression that seemed to curtail any sympathy she may have felt for him, had a surprise of her own. The arrival of another suitor had gotten her attention suddenly. He saw the two of them embrace, followed by a passionate kiss. Omar was crushed. As miserable as he felt, it had been multiplied many times over at that moment. His mother's suspicions about Priscilla were justified after all. He would have given anything to confront her about him; who was he, and how long had they been a couple, but more importantly, why would she give him hope when she knew there really wasn't any to be had? It was, in Omar's estimation, a senseless act of betrayal. His mom had decided to ride in the back of the ambulance with him to the hospital while his father would meet them there with the car. Seth and Coach Bivens were also making the trip. As he lay there in a semi-conscious state but with stable vital signs, he peered through the transparent IV bag supplying a saline drip to his body, and fixated on a reflection of the red and white strobe effect bubble atop the ambulance. His eyes welled with tears as one raced down his cheek. The lights and siren did help to ease anxieties about his own mortality once he realized he was in capable hands. His mom gently squeezed his hand making sure her maternal bond had not been broken, as his eyes remained fixed on the reflection of the flashing lights.

THE INTERMITTENT RED AND white flashers and sirens from two police cruisers that had parked in the swell just below his office window brought him back from his flashback. He was a little surprised that no one in his unit had been curious as to why he seemed motionless for so long, but when Regis approached him and asked if he was ok, he found out why.

"You seem a little listless Omar, you ok?"

"Oh, hey Regis. I'll be alright; had something on my mind is all."

His body language told a different story though…

Then he asked, "Did you need anything from me?"

"No, but unless you've been in a bubble for the past ten minutes, most of your team has already left the floor and headed home."

Omar, looked at his watch and said, "Oh, man. I need to catch my ride too. Thanks for the heads up; See ya."

He collected his satchel and the other bag and rushed to get to the elevators. When he exited his building he could see his bus from a distance getting ready to turn toward the bus stop. He double-timed it for the one and a half blocks to make it just in time.

The driver said, "Just under the wire Mr. Duncan."

Omar replied, "Hey man, how is it?"

He was about to take a seat when he noticed Micki a few rows back.

"Mick, where have you been?" He took a seat next to her.

"Hey Omar, you miss me?"

He tried to play it off by pretending her absence wasn't that big of a deal…

"No, just curious."

He realized just how big of a role Micki's bus rides with him played when he saw her again. Just hearing the playful vibe of her voice was like a much needed massage for him. He smiled at her, feeling the ride home would not feel like an eternity now that he and Micki could pick up where they left off with their jousting.

"I took a couple of days to scout space for a second shop; think I may have found something too."

"You're moving fast."

"It's what planting seeds will do for you. Look at this."

She took her cell phone out and showed him a face book post of a response to her comment about 'living the dream' and how her own journey had taken her from her mom's basement, to renting her own chair, to having her own shop in just three years..

"It was typical enough, you know. I talked about the virtues of hard work and where I really expected to be in another four years. Just trying to encourage somebody, you know what I mean?"

She scrolled through her post and landed on the reply by someone who wanted to know more about her plan to expand and wanted more details about it.

"At first I thought it was just a gag, but when we started exchanging posts, I found out she was legit. She pointed me to an article in 'The Entrepreneur', published some months ago, that featured her company as financier for other smaller companies wanting to grow their business. She liked my business model and, well the rest as they say, is history."

"Good job Mick." He patted her shoulder, but not without also submerging himself inside a putrid tinge of failure. She became light hearted again, which was what he liked most about her.

"You'd better get some of this Duncan."

She high-fived him and sat back in her seat again. "Rupert's already on board. He's putting his plan together for them too. That's why you haven't seen him lately. He and I might be sharing plaza space again soon. She looked straight ahead with a satisfied expression…

"Like I said, plan the work, then work the plan; never fails."

The bus pulled into Micki's stop not long afterward. She then said, "See you in the A.M.?"

He replied, "Probably—Take care."

As the bus pulled off he watched her slender but buxom frame, with dancer's legs, for some minutes moving with a pace that was only exceeded by her ambition. Omar knew it wouldn't be long before her business expansion would demand the need for her own private transportation again, but she was holding out as long as she could for what she really wanted in a 'lady's chariot' as she always called it. He would certainly miss her personality during those bus rides to and from work when the time comes. When he took a moment to really think about it, he had started to miss her already.

Omar was disappointed that he hadn't heard anything from Evelyn about the actors being available to rehearse the video next week. Her opening up to him about her concern agitated him. He was thinned skinned when his character was being questioned, but he needed to consider the source. Evelyn had pumped him up to other people whenever she had a chance. It was never anything that was solicited, but being aware of his inclination to second guess himself made it a much needed gratuity. She felt he needed as much encouragement as possible about his abilities if ever he was to be free of the thing that hounded him so. The friend in her had always felt that not knowing the real source of his troubles made her efforts seem benign, but whatever accolades were doled out to him in the meantime should help to reshape his outlook about himself and those around him. When he paused to consider their relationship, the 'Foe' in her was someone he never thought he would come face to face with, but he had undoubtedly fanned flames of discontent so unsettling that for Evelyn, and maybe even Theo, being in his presence seemed almost toxic. He felt suddenly like a two-sided coin. With certain people he was congenial most of the time. Maybe it was because of the limited exposure in those cases like his attitude with Vick, and Micki, and even the replacement driver for instance. But for some, there were more impactful consequences, and he chose to squander them recklessly. He was at a crossroads. He at least had the presence of mind at that moment to understand he had lost a part of himself, especially after feeling marooned by two people he really did care about; but it was by his own hand that those relationships had mutated from a hefty dose of mistrust. He wasn't schizophrenic, but he needed to find his way out of the wilderness that had turned his thinking upside down. He decided tonight was as good a time as any. His AA meeting was tonight. It would be his first one since admitting to the group leader about breaking his sobriety. He was never that vocal in the five meetings he had attended since he joined the group, but tonight would be different. He would take a chance and 'air his laundry' with the group, if only to recruit an advocate willing to step inside of his misery along with him. At least he wouldn't feel so alone in it. When he reached his bus stop and started the short walk home his cell phone rang; it was his Uncle Seth again. He became annoyed at first, thinking he might answer it but with a harsh rebuke of whatever Seth may have to say to him. He then decided he'd let it go into voicemail again. He stopped to check his mailbox and thought about the envelope from the Olympic Committee that was still on his counter at home that he never bothered to open. His curiosity got the best of him and he thought he might as well take a look at it when he got back to his apartment. It was the envelope he had hoped he'd see when he was competing, letting him know he had been accepted on the Olympic team for track & field. It was sort of like the feeling he'd get when buying a lottery ticket for the power ball; knowing you had a snowball's chance in hell at best of winning, but a chance nonetheless, so you buy it anyway. When he got inside his apartment he dropped his satchel in the big chair and headed for his bedroom to get comfortable. He traded his dress shirt and tie for one of his oversized college T-shirts, and his loafers for a pair of house slippers that had seen better days, but they were comfortable. While sitting on his bed he was struck by a strange sensation; as if being beckoned by an unknown force. He suddenly stood up and turned toward that full length mirror, and it was as though the light of his expression went dark. He walked slowly toward it; the hissing sound that he had heard before had returned and was getting stronger with each step. Its hypnotic effect seizing his mind and emotions for the moment. As he stood in front of it the hissing sound died down suddenly, then that vapor reappeared. Omar's reaction to it was much less dramatic this time. It was as if his memory had somehow allowed him access to previous encounters with it; reassuring him how it wasn't there to haunt him, but to help him. He responded with a slight smile this time and placed his palm gently against the mirror, as if greeting an old acquaintance.

⁂

"WELL OMAR, WE MEET AGAIN"—its throaty baritone voice seemed amplified throughout the room; speaking slowly but with a sympathetic tone—"I had become worried not having seen you for a while."

Omar responded as though he had certain expectations about its influence over him.

"But, I thought, you had summoned me here?"

"Summoned? Oh no, I don't have that kind of power. Even if I did, it would somehow make our time together seem, less meaningful."

It paused briefly then said, "Maybe it was your own subconscious desire to reconnect with me that drove you here. Do you think that's possible?"

"I'm—I'm not sure; maybe that's what it was."

The image suddenly became sharper and appeared to display faint outlines of facial features this time. Its movements also accelerated like before; evidence of something having excited it, but in a joyful way.

It replied, "If only you knew how good that makes me feel to hear you say that. You're aware there is a problem and you need help solving it; that's promising."

Omar said, "There is something—I've alienated my friends, and others, close to me." He paused briefly, shaking his head to signal his regret. He continued—"I should feel really bad after it happens; things I might have said or done, you know; but when I'm reminded about it, I don't seem to want to accept responsibility for what may have caused it; It's as though I can't bring myself to do the decent thing, so I'm told, and I'm left groping for reasons how that could happen."

The image replied, "There may be something that's blocking the pathway to you getting where you want to be emotionally; perhaps, recurring memories that are too painful to just bury. They can become really big road blocks you know."

The image, and what it represented, was already aware of Omar's unexpected trips inside his past but needed him to acknowledge them as possible reasons for his behavior himself. It was necessary in order for him to willingly receive whatever remedies were in store for him.

Omar replied, "I do have these periods where I daydream about my past; things that may have happened as far back as my childhood; unfortunate things that I couldn't really control. They seem to want to monopolize my memories; not leaving much room for the ones that can bring a smile to my face. I feel helpless to stop them."

The image paused again before speaking. Its tone more strident this time.

"As much as you realized some of those circumstances you couldn't control, did you ever think about the ones that you could; decisions that only you were responsible for?"

"I do, I suppose, but something usually forces me to make the kinds of choices I may not have made if things were different."

"You mean like being petrified of Deon when you all were kids, and taking his abuse when you thought you needed Breeland's help to gain the courage to stand up to him?"

"Well, yeah, something like that. How do you know about that anyway?"

"I told you. I've always known what you were thinking, even now, outside in this prism; but it seems you blamed your friend for moving away, and somehow it left you ill-equipped to handle whatever challenges came afterward."

"That's the way it felt, at the time. He was my best friend."

"And you were his, but what occurred in his life couldn't be centered on what happened in yours, no matter how close you were. Wouldn't you agree? "

"I guess so, but I was a kid; things were different then."

"You're right; you were a kid, but it doesn't diminish in any way the truth about what happened. Breeland had no say in whether he could stay or leave with his parents. He was their child and their responsibility. It wasn't his fault that he moved. They were a family like yours, and no matter the drama swirling inside of it, or the harshness of its reality, most families choose to stay together because they love each other, and their stronger because of that. I believe it was as traumatic for him as it was for you, but you should learn to adjust to new situations in your life. There should be only one place reserved for your pain, and that is, to be trampled under your feet. It's necessary if you're going to grow. So, don't think of him leaving as a betrayal. The two of you were too close for his memory to have been marred that way. Wouldn't you agree?"

Its movements were fluid and rhythmic now; the subtle facial features had become even sharper now with faint definitions for arms emerging as it spoke.

Omar said, "I suppose, but what about—what about when he died? I still can't seem to accept the way that it happened, and

right in front of me. It's been hard. All this time, and it's still hard."
"You have to remember what his mother said to you about it. You tried to warn him, but he preferred to follow his own mind. You can't accept Breeland's decision that day as your own; you're not being fair to yourself. You did what you could by warning him, because you cared about his safety; that's what's important for you to remember. You should expect the same of yourself. Own your decisions, because others shouldn't be made to share in suffering the consequences for them; Remember—(the spirit's voice faded gradually as it repeated the word 'remember', then there was silence)—The bond had been broken abruptly, but subtle imprints of the experience were left behind this time.

OMAR'S ARMS DROPPED TO his side. He was unaware but had fallen to his knees during that episode. It happened to be the perfect position for someone like him who, until then, had avoided a genuine birth of humility. It seemed to have also sapped some of his energy as he stood slowly; feeling like he had just emerged from a sauna. His brow and arms were beaded with sweat, but he had only been in front of that mirror for about ten minutes. The reality was, he felt revived and on a mission to becoming more emotionally grounded. Whatever that entity deposited, or resurrected in him during their recent encounter had apparently taken root. He was actually eager to get to his AA meeting; confident that he wouldn't self-destruct, but also hoping this new outlook wasn't just a fluke.

Chapter 8

THE PENDULUM HAD INDEED begun to swing for Omar. Getting comfortable with his new civility would at best become an acquired taste; needing to be weaned to some degree from his penchant for isolation. He was at least taking the initiative to deal with it, but doing that meant admitting some things about himself that were previously taboo. He had come to realize that living inside his despair for so long had robbed him of any chance of success. It was a reality that sadly resembled nothing more than a pipe dream that never broke free of his imagination. History had not been kind, in his estimation, but he needed to shed its negative influence and extract whatever lessons from it that might help in his quest for some normalcy. Realizing that time in the 'valley', even as an accidental discovery, is not about feeling like it is punishment, but about reaping the reward from being truly committed to maneuvering his way out of it. He had unwittingly embarked on a path to finding that out. His decision to open up at the 'AA' meeting was a first step in really subjecting himself to closer scrutiny. He wasn't going to let himself get distracted while getting ready for it either. He muted his cell phone and suddenly the symbolism shaping his desire to change became heightened when he stepped into the shower and opened the control valve. He imagined the pulsing bursts of water slowly purging his body of its host of sorrows, partially enabled by the sins from his past.. His shackles were loosed and sent tumbling at his feet in a mangled mess, but still under the watchful eye of a 'renewed purpose'. The bursts of water from that nozzle had become a moniker for his will, and it was satisfying. At least that's where his optimism had led him for the moment. He finished his shower then dressed quickly, feeling he'd be among anxious commuters still on their way home from work. He had a ten mile stretch to cover to get to his meeting so time was precious if he was going to try and get there before it started. He decided to bring a few mixed nuts and a peach for a snack because it was too early for dinner, but before leaving his bedroom he was compelled to face that mirror again. Its effect seemed almost hypnotic. His encounters with that 'spirit' had re-emerged in flashes. It had become difficult all of a sudden to distinguish reality from fantasy. He turned from the mirror and sat on his bed but a little dismayed. It felt like a literal tug on his psyche trying to get his attention. He couldn't understand where it was coming from. It was a little spooky, but he snapped out of it; determined to stay clear of that mirror, as if to break what he felt might be some mysterious connection to it. He put on his shoes, then to the kitchen to collect his snacks before leaving to catch the next bus. The trip wasn't as incident free as he had hoped. He was met with at least two severe traffic jams not far from his apartment before coming upon a working accident that appeared to be only minutes old. Traffic was being diverted to only one lane on the four lane county road for this particular bus route. It was a little longer in distance, and he believed it wouldn't take as long with fewer stops, but his instincts had failed him again. He pushed aside his frustration over the delays to at least sympathize with the driver of one of the vehicles that had over-turned on its side, as EMS workers hastily attended to his injuries. He had hoped no one was seriously hurt in the mishap.

The traffic crept at a snail's pace while he counted down the minutes that would put him over the threshold for getting to his meeting on time. At the rate things were going, it seemed a lost cause already. He removed the ziploc bag containing his snacks and decided to munch on some of it as he watched the eclectic collection of passengers making the trip with him, react to the delays. A number of them stood up to watch the spectacle outside unfold as if their attentiveness had bestowed some quirky entertainment value to what must have seemed a 'side show' to some of them. Others went on alert and into nonstop texting mode for fear of being subjected too long to an untimely gap in their sensory universe. Then a few of them just couldn't bridle their tongues; expressing their outrage, laced with an excess of 'salty language', over a situation no one in their immediate sphere of influence had any control over. He thought for a moment how he may have reacted not unlike some of them some months ago, but held his peace, even surprising himself. He was patient, and realized there was nothing he, or anyone on the bus, could do to provide the relief they all wanted, including the driver. It dawned on him that some things are simply outside of our control to resolve, and patience seemed at least expedient then. They were moving out of the congestion finally from what he could see about twenty yards ahead. As he continued to munch on his snacks, the words quoted to him by 'the orphan' during one of their encounters suddenly glared like bright neon— *'Remember, to starve the beast that is strife, then you can feast on the peace that is life.'*—Those words had been seared into his memory without him even being aware of it. He tried to recall where he may have heard them, or even seen them somewhere but nothing came to mind. He did suspect one thing; those words would become someone's mantra; maybe even his own. The bus had cleared the accident after about fifteen minutes, and arrived at the bus stop only 10 minutes later after making up some of the lost time. Omar's stop was first, and he did something that was uncharacteristic, for him. He fist-bumped the driver, then paused, waved at the others with a parting phrase.. "I hope the second leg of your trip is better than the first. You guys take care."

It must have been contagious since the body language shifted for most of them suddenly. They smiled and waved back at him letting Omar see firsthand how deciding to extend a simple courtesy to strangers even is not such a bitter pill to swallow, and almost always pays dividends. It was a short but brisk walk to the community center less than a block from the bus stop. As he approached the entrance it was almost like entering the doors for the first time. He became a little uneasy; remembering how it was during his first meeting and how he chose to only become a spectator then. Choosing to not unload the baggage that drove him there, courtesy of his drinking; reluctant to open up to this group of outsiders who could choose to violate their oath of confidentiality and reduce to a cautionary tale, what may have been left of his reputation. He was terrified of being judged too harshly over his troubles. There was a new outlook now, but it still did not diminish the anxiety he suddenly felt. His pace was reminiscent of someone about to face the gallows for his crimes, as he slowly made his way up the single flight of stairs to the meeting hall. When he opened the door to the room the group was already in session. The group leader, Mr. Chalmers, greeted him as the rest of the group turned toward the door. His presence was met with muted enthusiasm to say the least, once they realized who it was. It made him really uncomfortable, but Chalmers broke the ice for him.

"Omar, welcome back. Glad you could make it."

He replied, "Thanks," then nodded to a few members of the group and half-heartedly waved to them. One of the guys named Nelson Kindle, (AKA 'Noggin') eased his anxiety a little...

"Good to see you back man. Thought you had put us down."

"Got sidetracked some, but I'm back now."

Their attitudes about his return seemed to thaw gradually. There wasn't a great deal of guess work going on about why he really dropped out of the loop. The prevailing thinking was that if he did happen to fall off the wagon, it was the reason they were there in the first place; to give support to one another and try to get a fix on the real issues that plagued them all.

Omar tried to dismiss his jitters quickly and said, "So, what'd I miss?"

He smiled, but just slightly as he surveyed the room, only to be met with blank stares that he mistook for contempt but it was nothing of the kind. He shifted quickly thinking his return may have been too soon after all, but Chalmers reassured him that his being there couldn't have been timelier.

"Don't worry Omar. You're just in time."

One of the other men named Fred, who was the new guy in the group since Omar's absence, was in the middle of admitting something that was disturbing, Chalmers asked him to repeat it for Omar's sake. He also embellished more during this account.

"Well, like I said, I loved my son and I couldn't understand what went wrong. He was a good kid with a bright future; told me he had wanted to be one of those high paid 'Tech guys', you know, those Silicon Valley types, but, he rubbed shoulders with the wrong crowd; Sounds familiar?"

He looked down at the floor, rubbing his hands together and bobbing his head; his reasoning hitting a brick wall. He continued…

"I tried to get him help; so did his counselors at school but for some reason, I went from best friend to mortal enemy, only because I tried to show I cared. Maybe if his mom was still alive she would have had better luck with him, you know?"

No one spoke up yet but just listened and let him unload. It was an unspoken rule.

He said, "Her death took a heavy toll on him; on all of us. I tried to convince myself that her passing was the reason he suddenly changed; a good enough reason for any kid I guess when they've lost their mother."

He began to brush his hair back repeatedly and raised his head a few times to look into their eyes finally, as if seeking consensus over the pain that still racked his consciousness. He continued…

"She was my queen, and there was nothing she wouldn't do for our son."

The memory of her stirred mightily, and his voice began to quiver. His eyes had become glassy, then he paused for a while before continuing the story.

"Truth is, we both dealt with her loss in different ways. The devastation that followed was no less for either of us. Just so happens he chose heroine, and I chose the bottle. Some 'role model', huh? That's when I hit rock bottom myself. I could no longer help; couldn't help my son. How could I? I could not even help myself. I gave up. I—I backed away from it; from him. That's when I got the call one night from the police that he had overdosed. One of his addict friends called it in from some vacant house in the outskirts of Tampa. They had become squatters there of all things. I went into a tailspin after that. How do you keep it all together after losing the two most important people in your life? It was then I decided—He took a deep sigh before delivering the bombshell.

"I was drunk, but it was clear what I had to do. I decided to take the revolver, put it to my temple and squeeze the trigger but it didn't fire. I checked the magazine clip and it was fully loaded. I tried again, and it did the same thing. Somehow I felt it was 'just punishment' for my crime of not being able to protect either of them. I don't know why the gun didn't fire. I found out from the gunsmith there was nothing wrong with the weapon. That's when I felt I was being given another chance. I'm not a religious person, but there was a reason for that happening. That's when I was told about your group, by someone who cared about how my life ended up; someone who saw my problem for what it was, when I couldn't see it myself.. It's been three weeks since I took a drink, but the pain of losing them will probably stay with me for years to come so, I'm going to need help dealing with that; that's why I'm here. I need to be here."

Noggin patted him on the back and said, "We're here for you man. One hurdle at a time." Chalmers asked the group if they wanted to say anything to Fred about what he had shared. Omar decided to test the waters and spoke up about his own situation.

"I can relate to Fred's grief and how it can turn things upside down. I lost a really good friend; a childhood friend actually, in a pretty gruesome accident that I witnessed. It hit me really hard because I tried to keep him out of harm's way before it happened, but he decided to trust his own instincts about it rather than mine. I don't know why I was that surprised. Most of us are that way aren't we?"

He looked down at the floor and began stroking his beard. Chalmers had a satisfied look on his face knowing Omar needed this moment to lay it all out. He knew this was Omar's first step in charting his own path to becoming whole.

"It's that way sometimes with people you care about I guess; not that you've done anything wrong in trying to deal with their obstinacy, but the end result certainly makes you feel that you did. It's been over 28 years since I lost my best friend, and because of what's happened since then, it seems hard to trust anyone else that's tried to come close."

He stopped talking, clasped his hands and just stared into space. There was silence for a moment, then 'Noggin' connected right away. He looks to be in his late twenties but had already seen his share of bumps and bruises throughout his life, and decided to speak.

"Hey man, I can relate. I took my first drink at fifteen. It all started after I lost my best friend in a knife attack by some doped up gang bangers. We were just kids, you know; wanting to grow up in a hurry."

One of the other men said out of frustration, "How many times do we gotta hear this story Noggin?"

Noggin snapped back, "Well, Omar hasn't heard it yet"

Chalmers said, "Let him talk Bean."

Nelson Bean, the antagonist, sat back with his arms folded, forced to listen out of respect for the group's creed.

Noggin continued—"After his funeral I went home and took

a shot of my old man's stash he thought no one knew about. At first I did it out of frustration over missing my buddy, but then the booze became my hiding place when I got depressed, over anything. Once a week turned into twice, then three times. Pretty soon I was paying the wine-o's to get replacements for me with money from my paper route."

Most of them were amused by his 'paper route' remark, but Bean still seamed agitated over having to hear another version of Noggin's story one more time too many, for his taste… Noggin continued—"Course I had to stop when my old man found out about it, but it was like trying to 'unlearn' how to ride a bike after you've been doing it for so long. I've burned a few bridges since then; letting the alcohol speak for me at times when it should have been silent, but, that's why I'm here; to get some perspective, as they say."

Omar chimed in—"You know, even though I was reassured by my friend's mother that the cause of his death was out of my hands, it was still hard for me to accept because it didn't erase the pain of his loss. I haven't had a friend like him since."

Omar thought maybe he should stop talking; as if he had said enough; feeling they may have trivialized his story since it happened so long ago but no one was expecting him to stop, until he was ready. He had finally opened up to other people, and started to feel relaxed with them.

He continued—"There was a sickening hollow feeling inside of me after my friend's death. I know it might sound strange but I seemed to just empty out after that. Breeland sort of rode shotgun for me when it came to relationships, cause I was never that good at making friends. When he died, it was sort of like being stranded on a deserted island, you know?"

He leaned forward on the edge of his chair; brushing his hair back several times while his composure hung on by a thread. I don't want to take up too much time, but this one thing I did scared even me. I've sort of been out of sync ever since."

He hung his head again and looked at Chalmers, not sure

whether he should reveal it. Mr. Chalmers got a whiff of his body language and decided to reassure him.

"It's ok Omar; nothing you say here leaves this room. Everybody o.k. with that?"

It was almost a unanimous response with them agreeing, except for one. His silence could have easily been overlooked unless there was a show of hands that would have flushed him out, as well as his diabolical intent. He had decided not to volunteer too much information about his own situation with this group but instead, allowed the veil of secrecy to access whatever cloaks and daggers were at his disposal and exploit secrets about them when the opportunity presented itself. This Judas decided he would lay in wait; eager to leverage his sinister plot with privileged information disclosed by one particular member of the group. He ignored his oath of confidentiality, setting into motion a destructive sequence of events.

Omar said, "When I worked for Dillon Industries a while back, I was involved in an incident with a Supervisor there. It was a situation that had festered for some months, and just came to a head. It got really heated between us, and it became violent. It felt like I had no control over myself; like I forgot where I was even."

He began to move his hands nervously in a continuous twirling motion. He was reluctant to go on, but Chalmers reassured him …

"It's ok, you can continue with what happened Omar."

Everyone else sat quietly and attentive, especially that 'Judas', Nelson Bean. Omar clasped his hands together then placed them under his chin. The sting of what happened that day seemed all too real again. Bean was intrigued now. He crossed his legs and rested his chin on his knuckles; squinting curiously as if to try and incite more quickly the mode of thinking he was truly after. The initial shock from the familiarity of Omar's story was momentary, as Bean's plan of betrayal had already begun to take root…

Omar said, "I hit him and threw things. He got banged up some from where he was hit in the head, and other places. I didn't know how bad it was until later on, when he started showing signs; started having problems, you know."

Omar stared at Chalmers with a look of desperation. His voice also began to crack as the memory of it came rushing back.

"I didn't mean to, it just got out of hand. I wouldn't wish that on anyone, even if there was bad blood between us. It's—It was like something, or someone else, just took control. I'm sorry, really sorry it happened."

Chalmers could see he was becoming unglued and said, "Why don't we take a break; be back in ten minutes."

Omar remained in his seat, barely shouldering his regret. Noggin patted him on his back as a show of solidarity.

Chalmers then asked, "You going to be alright Omar?"

"Yeah—yeah I'll be ok."

Mr. Bean on the other hand took the opportunity to place a certain person on alert, based on Omar's revelation. He made sure he put enough space between himself and everyone else before making the call.

"Hey, it's me, Bean."

"Hey Bean, what's up?"

"I'm at my AA meeting, and you're not gonna believe who's a part of the group."

The remaining time at his AA meeting produced a few funny stories from three of the other men during their turns at the 'mic'. They were much needed anecdotes for the gloom that hovered over most of them after the first part of the session ended. Noggin was without a doubt the most free-spirited of the bunch. He seemed eager to want to make friends with Omar. He could sense he was a kindred spirit who had tread some of the same emotional ground that he had, even though they were more than a decade apart in age.

Omar asked him, "So, where'd the name Noggin come from?"

"My mom gave me that name. She said when I was a kid I was always falling or bumping my head on something, but I'd whine a little afterward, then keep on trucking. She would always say I had the hardest 'noggin' she had ever seen." They both laughed a little. "It finally just stuck, except the bumps and bruises in my life got a lot more serious, if you get my meaning."

Before Chalmers adjourned the meeting, he handed out a new roster to each of them…

"This is the updated roster as of tonight's meeting. A phone number has been included for each of you if you feel you need to reach out to one another outside of this place. That's something that was discussed when you decided to become a part of the group so it's not anything that should be a problem for anyone I hope. Remember, I'm also just a phone call away if you need to talk to me, about anything, ok? See you next time, and don't forget to pick up your literature on the way out."

Omar and Noggin were walking out together as Bean trailed them; tagging behind them suspiciously; surveilling Omar like some high-profile mark being set up for a wicked 'sting'. They eventually trailed off in opposite directions but Bean was just getting started. He had more than enough information for his friend to exact his vengeance on the 'villain' he so often spoke to him about and, until now, had remained anonymous. Omar had walked with Noggin to the parking lot on his way to the bus stop in the meantime.

Noggin asked, "So you've been catching the bus all this time; to and from work too?"

"That's right. I've gotten used to it now though. When I do finally get my license back, it's going to feel kind of funny getting behind the wheel again."

"I'd give you a lift, but I've got another stop before I make it home; you know how it is."

"Thanks, and it's ok. The bus shelter's not that far. I just can't afford to miss this last bus. Well, good seeing you again Noggin."

"Likewise Mr. Duncan. See you next time."

Omar's wait for the bus was short but it felt like an eternity. He felt certain he had been followed from the parking lot of the center to the shelter. He looked back several times to see someone ducking; trying to avoid detection, but the sound the soles of their shoes made against the hush of the night in that area of the city sounded almost like taps against the concrete. When the bus pulled up, he could see the silhouette of someone against the pale moon light moving from behind a retaining wall. The figure of a man just stood there for a moment, then seemed to hobble away as Omar was getting on the bus. He felt it was a missed opportunity for that would-be assailant, for now anyway. He didn't feel altogether safe having to wait on a bus in that part of the city at night. He had already decided it was best to try and hitch a ride home with someone next time. Either that or get strapped, God forbid. He put his anxiety about it behind him and concentrated on the good vibes the outcome of the meeting left him with during the bus ride home. He thought it to be a 'free fall' into the pit of more fractured personalities like his own, when he first considered joining the group. He could only see more misery being heaped upon him to the 'Nth degree' in those sessions, with a court of only sad faces testifying to most likely exaggerated claims about each of their troubles. It was a page from the pessimist's playbook back then, but after this meeting, he had a new appreciation for its purpose, and Mr. Chalmers' efforts at making sure it worked for them. The reaction to his absenteeism was expected. He knew it made his commitment to them seem shallow, which painted him as being less reliable to call upon in a time of real crisis. It was supposed to be a type of brotherhood, where the only dependency each of them was expected to boast, was about being able to lean on one another when it really mattered. He decided from now on, he would give it the attention it deserved, but it wasn't lost on him that he was just beginning to get his 'legs' with it. He could only hope there was nothing waiting on the horizon that could derail his progress. He decided to call Evelyn once he boarded the bus.

"Hi Evelyn, it's Omar."

"Oh, Hi—Are you at home? Sounds like a problem with the reception."

"I'm on the bus and on my way home from the community center; must be the satellite. I didn't want to bother you, but I wanted to know if you spoke with everybody about what day next week would be good for rehearsal?"

"Yeah, I did." Her reply was bland and business like. It put him on guard right away.

"Did they agree on a day we can all meet?"

"They all said Monday would be o.k., after the shift is over."

He was curious why she had not called him earlier to let him know, but he didn't press knowing he was walking on shaky ground already.

"Ok, Monday it is." There was silence. It was obvious the chemistry had fizzled out. She felt it was poetic justice for the way he had behaved, but staying cross with him was about as practical for her as bungee jumping. It would need to come to a head eventually, but not just yet.

"Can we talk about this in the morning Omar? It's getting late and I've got things to do yet." "Ok, sure. I'll call Richie and let him know it's a lock for Monday then."

"Alright, see you in the morning."

The words that the orphan conveyed to him were imbedded in his consciousness more often now; like the appeal of stylish tattoos—'*Own your decisions, because others shouldn't be made to share in suffering the consequences for them*'—'They had become permanent, but poignant reminders for him to try and embrace sentiments he could no longer afford to ignore. He was forced to reckon with them as he walked from the bus stop to home. Once inside his apartment, he opened a can of soup for dinner, and let it simmer on low heat for some minutes while he headed for his bedroom. He thought he'd call Richie at that moment before he let himself get distracted. He slipped out of his loafers as the phone was ringing, and slid into his house slippers just as Richie picked up.

"Hello Richie, it's Omar Duncan. How is it?"

"Hey, I'm good. What's up?"

"Just wanted to let you know everybody is o.k. with Monday after work for rehearsal on the video. Is that good for you?"

"It's fine, but where at?"

"There's an employee park on the grounds of our office building. It may even be good enough for the actual shoot. My boss suggested it. I'm somewhat familiar with it, but you can judge for yourself and, well, maybe we can decide together if it's suitable or not. I've discussed it with Evelyn and she agrees."

"Alright—Is five o'clock o.k.? That way nobody has to leave and come back."

"I'll give them a heads up."

"I know where your building is so, unless something comes up I'll see you then."

"It's a bet. One of us will wait for you inside the lobby. See you then."

Omar had mixed feelings suddenly. Even though he was encouraged by what occurred at the AA meeting, but in contrast, he had to consider his careless alienation of Evelyn and Theo. It's effects were obvious; suddenly deflating his spirit. His melancholy searched for light, where there were only shadows. It was crippling, and stalled his outlook about his recovery. He needed to be ready to try and cover any possible damage control with them on Monday. He knew his challenge would be trying to prove they could really trust him again. It would, mean him needing to be as transparent with them as he was with his AA group if he was ever going to feel untethered from a history that kept him off balance and on the defensive. There wouldn't be anything he could sidestep his way out of with any degree of success. That approach usually served as a band aid anyway which left him unfulfilled, so he decided he would just 'brave the elements' and absorb whatever punishment may be in store for him. He checked on his soup and decided it needed a few more minutes to cook down to his liking. Covering the pot with a perforated lid kept the steam to a minimum. The apartment manager hadn't gotten around to fixing the fan on the range hood yet so he improvised by also opening a few windows to ventilate the space. His first impulse while he waited on dinner usually was to grab the remote and catch up on news or sports, but after changing his shirt, he was inclined suddenly to glance at that mirror in his bedroom. The glance became glaring, then it mysteriously seemed to call to him. He was several feet from it but moved toward it slowly, as if being placed in some type of hypnotic stupor. The high pitched fizzing sound returned and engulfed the room as he stood inches from it, slowly placing his palms against the glass and granting access once again to the spirit within that vapor.

The fizzing stopped abruptly, then it appeared; much sharper now with more discernable features. It was closer in proximity to Omar's reflection this time, and seemed to mimic exactly the subtle swaying of Omar's body before it spoke.

"Hello Omar; seems you've decided to reach out to me again."

"Hello, spirit." He was now able to speak to it, like he would an old acquaintance, but not unlike conversing with someone in one of his dreams. He would forget sharp details about it once the episode was over, and after becoming aware of himself and his surroundings again. Slight impressions that were meant for its eyes and mouth changed their shapes as it spoke; as if to convey its struggle to claim its identity.

"You reached a milestone tonight and it pleases me. You're beginning to put into practice some things I've shown you by opening up at the AA meeting. You've started to actually slay the demons that have brought you the most grief. You're beginning to see the light Omar."

Its speech reverberated to the point of almost becoming garbled from the stirring of its emotions. Witnessing Omar's progress was reason enough for jubilation.

"I laid it all out tonight. I did—I didn't hold back, and it felt like a great weight had been lifted from my shoulders. There were men there with problems, like my own, that listened to me, and didn't judge me; it was, liberating."

"It's interesting how something as basic as being open and honest, and unselfish with people, especially the ones that will listen who have the same motives as you, are the best pathways to creating relationships that last. Imagine how well that works with the ones you already consider to be friends? They've wanted to show you that in many ways. It's about time you showed them that side of you, don't you think?"

Its movements became erratic suddenly; evidence of having detected something disquieting about Omar's behavior.

Omar then said, "Feels like I'm all thumbs all of a sudden. How do I show them they can trust my motives? I've only let them down lately. How can I repair what I never really tried to build? And what about the ones that really did let me down; like Priscilla, and my Uncle Seth? How do I square it with what they did to me? Who do I really trust? How do I know their motives are genuine?"

Omar's 'rosy' outlook had suddenly become infested with its share of doubt as his blitz of questions was more evidence of his uneasiness about his anemic pace toward repairing his relationships. His hands slid down the face of the mirror as he almost collapsed to his knees again.

"Don't be alarmed Omar. There are some things you have not yet considered, but the solution is already within your grasp."

THE DYING ECHO OF the word 'grasp' eventually faded to silence, and the connection was broken once again. Omar seemed dazed. He pushed away from the mirror with his hands still raised; frustrated as to why he was on his knees and in front of it again, but not being able to recall why. He snapped out of it once the smell of the scorched soup and the howling of his smoke alarm put his senses on alert. He almost sprinted from his bedroom into the kitchen. Someone was also pounding on his door as he was taking the pot from the stove, pouring cold water into it right away. He turned the cap off, then the smoke alarm.

He shouted to the person at his door, "Just a second, I'm coming!"

He opened the door and it was his neighbor in the adjacent apartment…

Omar said, "Oh, hey man."

The guy lived that close but he didn't even know his name.

"I saw what looked like smoke or steam, or something, coming from your window and heard your alarm sounding for some minutes. Just thought I'd check and see if everything was alright"?

"Yeah—everything's ok. I was in the back and just took my eye off my soup too long is all, but good of you to check. Thanks."

The guy just nodded and turned to walk away.

Omar asked, "Say, ah, what's your name?"

"I'm Rob." Omar reached to shake his hand..

"I'm Omar. Good to meet you. You know I don't really see you much, maybe except on the weekends, and from a distance."

Rob said, "I work twelve hour days most of the time."

"I guess that explains it then. Like two ships passing in the night."

"Yeah, I guess."

He appeared to be in his thirties; a little older than Noggin, but seemed personable. The fact that he was considerate enough to check on his safety was a solid indication he could be a good friend, so he took the opportunity to become conversational.

"I work days and usually inside hibernating until morning, but I still try and make time for a little recreation."

Omar could see his countenance change a little as though he might have anticipated a few questions he would rather not answer.

"Me and some of the guys I work with shoot hoops at Regency Park on the weekends sometimes. You know it's not that far from here."

"Yeah, I know where it's at."

"You play?"

"I play a little bit, but I'm no Michael Jordan."

"None of us are either; well, maybe one of us is a little closer to him than the rest."

They both laughed a little.

Omar said, "Maybe you can join us one weekend, soon; when you're not busy."

"Ok, sounds good."

Omar then said, "Hang on a second." He stepped back inside the apartment with the door slightly ajar to get his phone.

"You got a cell number Rob?"

Rob gave him one of his cards that showed a cell number and email address. Omar held it up to read it: 'Robert Rugby' Community Relations Officer, Sumter County Department of Corrections'.

He then said, "Oh, you're a "G-man"

"Not quite. I'm a lot less threatening, and I don't have to carry a firearm."

"I'll text you my number, if that's ok, and I'll give you a few days heads up about the pickup game at the park, ok?"

"Ok man. I'd better get back. See you later then."

Just before he closed his door he noticed someone in the parking lot below just across from his apartment, who seemed eerily similar to the person he thought may have been following him on the way to the bus stop. He seemed about his height and he just stood in front of his car, against the hood, motionless. Omar could sense his eyes were on him like a predator on its prey. It made him uneasy now, believing this person's victim of choice could not be random, especially after hearing the faint sound of 'taps' like he did before, as the man walked around to the driver's side, got in, and drove off slowly. He closed the door, locked it, and leaned his back against it thinking maybe he was just letting his imagination run away with him. He then took a deep breath, feeling he may have been overthinking it after all. He pivoted then, grateful he was able to avoid fighting an actual fire that could have quickly gotten out of hand; thankful also for at least one thoughtful neighbor he can account for. He was finding out that letting his guard down almost becomes a reflex during time spent with good natured people. There was never a reason to suddenly become postured for 'warfare', when no shots were being fired. He still considered it to be a slow advance through a minefield though, being so new at it; but he was advancing nonetheless. What he wasn't aware of was how the orphan's influence had become woven into his subconscious, and would ultimately allow him to confront the meaning of forgiveness as well.

Clarence's meeting with Officer Bristol at a local Bistro in Gleason was at least cordial. The officer had decided to accept his invitation to drinks after his shift, to talk in more detail about his suspicions concerning what he overheard at the restaurant. It was meant to provoke a bit of calm inside the storm that could erupt from Officer Bristol, who may have still harbored feelings of retaliation against the person responsible for his brother's injuries. It was also meant to remove once and for all an obstacle that stood in the way of Omar getting rid of anxieties that seemed to have boxed him in for too long. Clarence wisely didn't feel the need to patronize him with sympathetic remarks about his grandfather. He did get the impression the officer treated it more like a business meeting and preferred to dispense with formalities, but he seemed agreeable. Clarence was careful not to call Omar by name, but tried to paint a picture of his personality that would cause the officer to feel less vengeful about punishing his brother's attacker. He couldn't point to any particular admission by Omar that could finger him as the assailant. Based on his reluctance to even want to talk about what happened at Dillon though, and the account of the incident from two former employees repeated to him by the H.R. Manager, it all seemed to fit. Officer Bristol was quiet; he hadn't taken one sip of his drink since Clarence started talking. He seemed to grow impatient, and interrupted him surprisingly in mid-sentence.

"You don't want to tell me his name do you?"

Clarence was put on alert; measuring his response very carefully.

He then said, "Maybe I shouldn't; not right now anyway."

Officer Bristol now seemed torn between what his emotions were telling him to do and his oath to also uphold the law, as well as bring to justice those who choose to violate it. Clarence let his comments rest in a more peaceful atmosphere and became silent; sensing that what he said to him may ultimately arrest any ideas of retaliation; but after the officer excused himself for some minutes to take a call and then returned, he sensed his retribution had been aroused once again. Officer Bristol didn't bother to sit again but seemed agitated when he said he had a slight emergency and needed to leave.

"Thanks for the talk, and the drink Colter. It was, eye opening."

Clarence watched him walk hurriedly to his SUV, almost slamming the door and speeding out of the lot. He sat back down not knowing if what he said may have actually triggered a delayed reaction. Based on the Officer's behavior, it was hard to detect if what he said to him had any positive impact at all. He breathed a sigh of relief; certain that not giving him Omar's name was the right call. The waitress approached the table shortly afterward.

She asked, "What happened to Ronnie?"

"Oh; said he had an emergency and had to run."

"You want another?"

"No, thanks." She placed the check on the table and said, "I'll just take this up when you're ready."

He nodded to her but sat a little longer; feeling somewhat shell-shocked over what had just happened. He had to count the meeting as a 'bust' for now, feeling he'd still need Omar to admit the truth about what happened to even feel comfortable with pursuing the sponsorship at this point. He got the waitress's attention to pick up the check, then called Melanie to let her know he was on his way home…

"Hi beautiful."

"Hello Mister. Got lost on you way home?"

"No, nothing like that. I probably should have called you earlier to let you know I was going to meet with a Deputy here after work, at a local Bistro to chase a lead about Omar's situation."

"This deputy wouldn't happen to be female who's built like an amazon would she?"

He laughed a little and said, "Not even close. He looks to be at least 6 feet, four and built like a Mack truck; not exactly my type."

"Well, that's a relief." They both laughed.

"So, are you on your way back?"

"Just called to let you know I should be home in about an hour. How are the little ones?" "They're good. Nathan's missing you already. The baby must be too cause she has really been active. You see the trouble you cause when you're away? Besides, I miss you too."

"Miss you too, but the trip up here was more productive than I thought it would ever be after just one visit. I hadn't even made it to Dillon and felt like I hit the mother lode shortly after I got here."

"Really, how so?"

"Let's just say, it was a little bit of luck, and a lot of grace that placed me there today."

"I guess you must have asked the right questions of somebody, huh?"

"To be honest, it's what was just handed to me that's really remarkable. The timing in which things happened; it couldn't have been accidental. Anyway, I'll probably need to plan a second trip, but I'll need to see if Omar will come with me this time."

"You think it'll be necessary?"

"Well I have to admit; something occurred with that officer that was kind of strange. Maybe it's nothing, but I did plant some seeds; just have to see if they sprout or not. Look, let me tell you more about it when I see you, ok?" He then imagined giving her a long kiss through the receiver with the puckering sounds he made, then said, "Love you," then ended the call.

Chapter 9

O MAR BARELY SURVIVED A contentious bout with restlessness overnight, and managed what could only be described as twilight sleep before tackling a full day at work; at least that was the plan. His alarm clock sounded at 6 a.m. but his body clock told a different story. Most times he could explain not having slept over something he ate, or just having eaten too late the night before that seemed to interfere with it, but that wasn't the case this time. His anxiety over what he might say to Evelyn and Theo turned out to be the real culprit. He had never treated the quality of their relationships with so much scrutiny. It had become second nature to be coy with Evelyn about so many things she had said to him that were meant to be complimentary. It occurred to him how his preference for remaining neutral about them lately, and not responding to her at all most times, must have left her feeling like she may have violated him in some way. He realized he had taken too many things for granted with her. He would need to tread carefully if he was going to try and salvage whatever confidence she may have still had in him. There really was no price he could put on their relationship, which meant there was no debate worth having about whatever he must do to make things right again; her input on the sponsorship notwithstanding. Theo, on the other hand, seemed to insulate his abrasiveness toward him most of the time because he was his mentor, who most likely had earned a waiver for his transgressions. He recalled how he admitted to him that he reminded him of his older brother, and his father. He held him in really high esteem, and seemed to say to him often when they chatted, and in response to some of his opinions, "that's what my dad would say", or "you sound just like my brother." He finally realized, that was credibility he could never buy. Having thought about it, Omar conceded it was probably validation for Theo that his point of view carried so much weight, and it spoke to his loyalty to him as a valued friend. His reluctance to tackle both problems confounded him only for a few moments. He had begun to embrace a more compassionate outlook that let him see more clearly now, attempting to salvage what may have been left of his character. He followed his morning routine as usual, with particular care given to his diet still; making sure he continued to eat healthy, even though the attention he had given to improving his social skills seemed to be on life-support. He felt he needed to consume as many energy boosters as his body could safely absorb during the course of the day. He even packed a few energy drinks as insurance just in case he bottomed out before his shift ended. Since it was Friday he would at least have the weekend to regroup, if he tanked too badly with trying to repair the damage with Evelyn and Theo.

Getting to the bus stop 15 minutes early was also brand new for him. It was a short enough walk from his apartment but he felt he'd try it on for size as part of his new 'M.O.' He also took a pair of headphones, that piped tunes from his favorite playlist while he walked. The smooth jazz melodies proved to be the perfect companion to channel his mood as he approached the shelter and sat down. He was the lone rider, as far as he could tell. It was almost like watching a silent movie as the minutes counted down. He pulled the headphones off for a moment, just to keep his senses in check from the familiar sounds of the morning bustle; thankful he didn't have to be in the middle of it just yet. He started to put them back over his ears when he suddenly heard it again. It sounded like taps; eerily similar to the sound he had heard the night before after the AA meeting, and across from his apartment. It spooked him a little, so he turned slowly in the direction of the noise. He notice it was only a kid with his book bag strapped to his back, at the back of the shelter. He was knocking a pair of bamboo sticks together rocking to his own playlist, unaware of what was going on around him. Omar had to grin knowing he let his paranoia get to him a little, but the bus was pulling in front of the shelter around the same time, and he noticed Vick was behind the wheel this time. The doors swung open with that all too familiar rattle, and Vick wearing a broad smile. Omar's attitude toward Vick was puzzling; his contact with him was limited, and the superficial brand really didn't test the extent of his affection despite some irritating exchanges in the past.

"Hey Vick. Guess that bug let go of you, huh?"

Vick replied, "I must be seeing things. You mean you're actually waiting on me today?"

"Well, it 'ain't' my clone you're looking at."

They both laughed a little and high-fived each other.

"Good to see you back in the saddle man."

"Good to be back. So, I guess you finally decided to roll your butt out of bed on time, huh?"

"A man's gotta know what side his bread is buttered on at some point I guess."

Vick cut his eyes at him as he whipped around the intersection opposite the bus shelter and onto the street for his next stop.

He then said, "You haven't been smoking anything other than cigarettes have you?"

"You know I don't smoke; and No! It's nothing like that. Just trying to change the way I do things that's all."

"Hearing you say that seems a little odd, since you didn't seem to care much about that kind of thing before."

Omar looked away this time, trying to absorb the sting of what he felt was a well-deserved critique. He then said, "Well, people can change, you know."

Vick replied under his breath, "Huh; about time."

Omar put his headphones back on until the next stop when he realized, it was also Rupert's stop. He saw him at the shelter just before Vick pulled in. He pulled the headphones off, realizing it was his chance to show Rupert a 'kinder, gentler' version of himself to at least open the door to a more amicable relationship between them; maybe even the start of a friendship. Whatever the case, he'd have to be a little careful about it since he hadn't so much as given him the time of day before. He couldn't really hold it against Rupert if he happened to be a little suspicions over his sudden 180 degree shift in his attitude. When the air brakes sounded signaling a full stop, doubt had crept in like a thief in the night; but then the words imparted to him by that spirit suddenly came to mind; when he reminded him during their last encounter, how he should only expect to mend old relationships, and maybe even create new ones with people who are like-minded, and whose character speaks louder than anything that may raise suspicions about them. It challenged him on how much easier it should be with people who are already in his life who may fit that description, and who had not completely withdrawn from him because of his unwillingness to reciprocate. He didn't quite understand why that idea suddenly seemed bur-rowed inside his consciousness, but there it was and it could not have been timelier.

Rupert saw him and threw his head back, then said,"Mr. Duncan."

"Hey Rupert."

Rupert walked by him and took a seat a few rows back. Omar didn't want to spend time second guessing himself about what he felt he needed to do next. He hadn't exactly been a model of goodwill since first meeting Rupert, but knew that the wall of cynicism must come down now. Rupert had done his part by reaching out. It was his move now. He got up and walked back to sit across from him. By the time Rupert looked up, Omar was standing across from him. He was unresponsive but understandably curious since Omar's reaction to him, even wanting to chat during the morning bus rides, could only be described as allergic. Omar had hoped the tension he sensed from him did not suddenly take the shape of a closed fist to his jaw, but decided to try an open a dialogue.

"Hey man." He sat slowly, not sure if Rupert was going to tell him he'd rather be alone.

"What's up Mr. Duncan? What's on your mind?"

His tone was bland, and he resisted eye contact with Omar.

Omar said cautiously, "Well, first of all I just wanted to apologize for being such a jerk lately. Lots of things on my mind; things that I really let distract me, more than they should have, and I've taken my eye off of things that should have been more important."

"Can I be honest about something with you now?"

"Yeah, ok."

"I don't need to make friends at any cost. It just so happens to be the most beneficial way for me, and probably most people, to satisfy our urges to be sociable. It's just built in, and truth is it shouldn't cost anything and should never come with a list of pre-requisites; like making sure you catch somebody in a good enough mood to expect a little civility. So when you turned me off all those times, I felt it must have cost you quite a bit judging from the way you would react. So, that being said, I wouldn't want you to do anything that you feel might break you, or cause you too much emotional distress, so I accept your apology, but why don't we just call it even and leave it at that."

Rupert put his headphones on, smiled but with a smirk at Omar, then turned away from him and toward the window. Omar walked back to the front of the bus again; disappointed but not surprised by Rupert's less than enthusiastic reception. He realized it would more than likely be a slow thaw with Rupert, but he would also learn to be patient. He was preoccupied with licking his wounds for the remainder of the bus ride hoping he would see Micki at the last stop before getting off, but she was not riding today either. He could only imagine how well she must be doing with her planned expansion, unless she was out for other reasons. He wanted to approach Rupert to ask about her, but thought he'd better leave him alone, at least for now anyway. Vick was pulling up to Rupert's and Micki's bus stop when Rupert got up and was walking past him to get off, and didn't even look his way.

Omar said, "Have a good one my man."

Rupert turned back toward him with a curious glance, as though he was wondering why Omar even bothered. Omar realized he had grossly under estimated him, and would first have to earn his respect. The walk to his building was less spirited than most times. No snapshots of anything, or anyone for that matter, came to mind during the hike to his building that could have relieved his semi-depressed state. Rupert's pelting of his confidence after his apology made him more aware of how deep he really had driven those pangs of animosity, especially to people that seemed to care about him. His instincts told him that Evelyn and Theo would be even bigger hurdles to overcome. He did his best to mask his uneasiness about facing them. The stilted tone in his 'good morning' greeting to people he rarely laid eyes on when he walked inside the lobby to his building seemed, artificial. Seeing Evelyn and Nadine at the elevators didn't help either.

"Good morning Evelyn, Nadine."

They both seemed mechanical in their responses…

"Hi Omar"… They then turned abruptly to face the elevator doors. Nothing was said by either of them during the ride to their floor. The anxiety was stifling for him. He loosened his tie just before the doors opened, then stopped Evelyn in what seemed a pre-emptive bid for redemption…

"Evelyn, you got a minute?"

Nadine paused for a moment, but realized it would probably be a 'hashing out' session between the two of them and walked ahead. Evelyn then said, "I'll see you later this morning Nadine."

Evelyn lifted her eyes reluctantly, staring into his with a look of resignation…

"What's on your mind Mr. Duncan?"

"Ev, look, I know it's been hard to try and read my behavior lately and I've created doubt in your mind about who I really am, and what I want."

He looked away a few times, clearing his throat; thrusting himself into an awkward space he felt he might have trouble making a graceful exit from.

"I guess what I'm trying to say is—"

Before he could finish Clarence was approaching.

"Hey you two. Glad I caught you before you logged on. Why don't you step into my office for a minute? I just need to run something by you concerning the sponsorship."

Omar replied, "Alright Cee Cee—We're right behind you."

Evelyn just let them lead the way but said nothing. Clarence had placed his copy of the local newspaper he picked up from the donut shop in Gleason on the chair Omar usually sits in, but it wasn't exactly accidentally placed there, and positioned to where the headline and photo could be easily seen.. Omar was about to take his usual seat when he noticed the paper. He picked it up and put it closer to his face to make sure he wasn't seeing things. Clarence detected his surprise at seeing Priscilla's photo and the caption; but Omar probably was equally surprised as to how Clarence came across a Gleason periodical when he didn't sub-scribe to it, and the town being so far away. Evelyn sat patiently, waiting for the meeting to be over and done with.

Clarence then said, "Let me make this pit stop before we get started. I'll be right back."

Evelyn noticed Omar seemed pre-occupied with the newspa-per article, thinking he might take the opportunity to finish telling her what he started to before Clarence interrupted. He kept his head inside the article for some minutes; almost forget-ting she was even in the room…

She called to him—"Omar, Omar!"

He replied with his head still fixated on the newspaper, "Yes Ev?"

"Don't you have something you want to finish saying to me?"

"What?—Oh, yeah I do." …But he looked up just for a second, then turned his attention back to the paper again; shaking his head but with an empty stare. She glared at him with knitted eyebrows and pinched lips, thinking his disorder had reached a new high, when he lowered the paper but still held on to it. He then refocused, feeling he should at least state his case starting with an apology. Uttering the words again would at least establish his intent; proving it though, would be another matter.

"I wanted to say I know my behavior hasn't been worthy of your friendship Evelyn. You've never let me see anything but honesty and integrity in you, and maybe I got a little sloppy and took it for granted when I shouldn't have. But your instincts were right, as usual. I do have some stuff going on, but I'm finally trying to work it out. I'm getting help actually, to try and work it out." He looked away and paused for a moment. She was left wandering if he had gone so far as to seek help from a therapist. She wasn't ready to let her guard down just yet either, but his admission neutralized her irritability a little.

"I guess what I really want to say is—"

Clarence came back in mid-sentence, interrupting him again…

"Ok guys. Just wanted to know first of all if you had decided on the company's employee park for the rehearsals?"

Omar spoke up. "Actually we did, and our first run-through of the script is scheduled for Monday after the shift ends."

"Good. That'll give me time to give security a heads-up to let them know you'll be on the grounds for a few hours afterwards. They patrol the site 24/7, so it's best they know the people they see are gonna be our own. Anything you guys need from me?"

Clarence got wind of the negative energy between the two of them, but felt it may have just been a case of needing to get through some 'rough air', and of no real consequence.

Omar said almost under his breath, "No, nothing yet Cee Cee."

Evelyn simply shook her head in agreement, but her expression was one of dubious consent. "We've got eight days left guys, so I'll be expecting you to make your initial contacts with the sponsors by Monday, ok?"

They both stood up. Omar still held the paper in his hand. Clarence excused Evelyn, and said he needed to speak with Omar for a minute longer. Omar sat back down; tossing the paper on Clarence's desk. The suspense was eating away at him, so he had to ask…

"So how did you come by a copy of the Gleason Gazette.?"

"Oh, that; picked up a copy when I was there the other day. I thought it best, as coordinator for our group, to visit the sites we'd be pitching for sponsorships; to get a feel for the culture there, you know? Not just confine our relationship with them to data on a spreadsheet."

He could see Omar struggling with how to reconcile his upcoming contact with the Dillon Rep., feeling that a meeting with Priscilla was probably inevitable. Omar began to wring his hands, then stroke his beard; a clear enough indication to Clarence he was probably dreading what could be the thing that might cause their pitch to implode, unless the issue of 'Priscilla' was resolved before hand. Clarence decided it was as good a time as any for his invitation, without giving Omar any clues about him being aware of his history with Priscilla.

"Look, I've decided to plan a second trip to Dillon, and I'd like you to come with me."

"Well, what's the up-side to that? I'd like to concentrate on making sure this video is going as well as it should be. I think I should stay close, to make sure there aren't any unexpected glitches that might be a problem for Evelyn to handle alone."

"I hadn't intended to take away time you'd need on the video. It would actually be a field trip during business hours; maybe only for half a day, then back here."

"Look Cee Cee that may not be so good for me. I mean, I'm just not getting a good vibe about it."

Clarence felt like he was subjecting him to torture based on his resistance to the idea. Omar's confidence seemed to be in a tailspin. His movements reminded him of a caged animal, looking for an escape. Clarence was tempted to admit to knowing about his relationship with Priscilla, and the conversation with Deputy Bristol, but thought better of it and provided the escape that Omar was after…

"Alright Omar. We'll just table that for now."

Omar replied, "Are we good then?"

"Yeah, we're good, for now."

"I'll see you later then."

He left his office knowing Clarence's bloodhound tendencies were at a fever pitch, and his pursuit of the Dillon trip had only been placed in limbo for now. He headed for the men's room to try and regroup; locking himself inside one of the stalls to allow the anxiety to pass, but then his phone rang. It might as well have been a bugle horn from the way he reacted to it. It was his Uncle Seth again. He watched the screen as it rang repeatedly. The number pulsing, as though it could have been a stout shove from Seth acting out his frustration over not being able to reach him. Omar was then reminded of the orphan's words about needing to re-acquaint himself with people already in his life, but Seth had hung up by the time he thought he might answer it. It occurred to him at that moment that he did not bolt out of the starting gate of his new outlook, he wobbled. It wasn't the way he imagined he'd start his Friday, but there it was. He opened the door to the stall knowing his absence would be noticed by this time, and began walking slowly toward his desk. His eyes then fixated on recurring images of Evelyn, Nadine, Theo, and Blake. When he reached his desk, he had to fight the urge, but their images seemed to play over and over in his mind, like a looped video reel; souls to be reckoned with on some level for sure, but how exactly still escaped him. He tried to harness his thoughts to start his day, but they were suddenly re-directed to images of Priscilla on the front page of the Gazette. He was caught completely by surprise seeing her photo. His brief and forgettable rendezvous with her only resulted in many unfulfilled fantasies that covered his mind like decades-old wall cloth, but very real consequences to his career as a sprinter. Forgetting to log on first, he assumed the position once again. The scratching of his beard and slumping posture preceded, what proved to be, another sacrificial leap into his past.

The ringing of his hotel room extension might as well have been a klaxon alarm going off inches from his ear. He certainly could have used the extra hour of sleep, after the hotel clerk called him for his wake up an hour too early. The 'Bayview Hotel' on Fort Lauderdale Beach was a budget hotel but at least the rooms were clean and it had a comfortable bed. It was 'no frills', with doses of gratuitous door knocking, lots of laughing, and fits of running along the corridors throughout the night for College Kids like him, who didn't bother to shut down even after spending all day on the beach, then binge drinking after night fall. There was no continental breakfast, and the T.V. set didn't work half the time but, it was home for the week he would spend there. Evidence of his drinking the night before wasn't without its tattle tale signs either; but for a 21 year old on spring break, it was treated like a badge of honor just to survive it without having up-chucked just about everything he had eaten earlier that day. It was bad enough that he had to endure the racket throughout the night, but when it showed up at his own door just after 7:00am he was beside himself with frustration.

He shouted from his bed, "Who is it!"

"Hey Omar, rise and shine!"

He stomped to the door in just his shorts, and almost ripping it from its hinges when he opened it…

"Hey man, time to get at it. Let's go son!"

"Smook, don't you ever sleep?—and time to get at what?"

"You suffering from amnesia all of a sudden? We're supposed to get an early start at the pier down at Dania Beach, you know; your vacation piece for the radio segment? You know you never should have volunteered to do it; and you know you can't afford to come back empty handed and disappoint your fans either."

"Ahh man; I thought that was tomorrow?"

Smook, his on-air side-kick (aka, Dwayne Stokes) pushed on the door slightly, letting himself inside..

Omar said sarcastically, "You wanna come in?" …Closing the door behind him and shaking his head as he collected what he was going to wear before heading for the bathroom. Smook made himself right at home and flopped on the bed of tangled sheets, expecting to stay put until Omar was ready to go. Omar yelled from the bathroom with the door propped slightly..

"Are we supposed to get rain again today? That'll ruin our set up for the remote for sure. You checking the weather?"

Smook said, "As we speak." Smook was channel surfing, trying to get a weather forecast for the day, but the T.V. set wasn't cooperating. It only had limited programming and fuzzy reception for the channels that were available.

He said, "We might as well forget about this set. Maybe we'll pick up something inside the lobby, and if that doesn't work, we'll just ask around."

When Omar stepped back into the big area to finish dressing, Smook couldn't resist.

"I still can't believe you didn't pounce on some of that action last night Omar. That's the real mystery son."

"No mystery; just didn't suit me that's all."

"Yeah, that's what you say, but you can't really prefer getting cozy with a six pack of Heineken in a corner somewhere for hours, to the point of blending in with the furniture. We're here to have fun man; so, let's go have some fun."

They never got a heads-up on the weather from the desk clerk, or two other people they asked before leaving the hotel. Omar was driving a rented car, courtesy of his dad, and decided to just make the trip down to Dania Beach anyway. If today didn't work out for the radio piece, then they could always try again tomorrow. They each got a bottle of O.J. and chips from the vending machine just outside the lobby, then headed out the door.

Smook said, "Why don't we just head on down there. At least we'll be early enough to pick our spot for setting up."

Omar seemed in no hurry to get to Dania. His near misses, which earned him 2 misdemeanor violations in recent months, was reason enough for him wanting to creep inside of traffic. The eastern sun was already high enough to almost roast anyone's skin that had been exposed to it for too long, and the A/C unit in the rental left something to be desired.

"You know it's already hot, so why are you creeping Omar?"

"Just being cautious, and taking in the view."

"Yeah, right."

A cream colored Malibu convertible with at least 4 girls inside pulled beside them and honked, then two of them waved. Smook leaned forward with a predictable animated response; waving frantically and wearing a pasted smile. He leaned back in his seat again, feeling the day was already getting off to a promising star.

He said, "The natives are already getting restless my man."

Omar suddenly sped up to pull alongside the car again.

Thinking out aloud he said, "Well, I'll be damned."

He seemed desperate to find out if his mind was playing tricks on him, when he became fixated on that convertible suddenly while trying to keep his eyes on the road too.

Smook then said, "Say, what's going on? What's the deal on those girls?"

"I can't be sure, but I think I might know one of them. Someone I've known for some time." They stopped at a traffic light, side by side; and there she was; Miss Priscilla Eagan, in all of her bombastic glory.

She shouted,"Omar! I thought that was you. You down here on break too?"

"Yeah, you could say that. I'm really surprised to see you here."

She replied, "No more than me seeing you."

They glanced at each other with no words between them; just lots of awkward body language...

Omar said, "We're on our way to Dania Beach to take in the pier."

Priscilla responded, "So are we. We'll probably see you there then."

"Ok, sounds good—Bye."

She flashed her infamous coquettish smile at him, leaned back in her seat, then the driver of the convertible suddenly sped up and out of sight after a minute or two.

Snoop said, "Well, looks like somebody's worthy of your attention Mr. Duncan."

"Really surprised to see her here. Would you believe we go back as far as grade school?"

"Yeah, I can believe it, knowing you. You guys, have a particular history together?"

"Not exactly." Omar shook his head a little, sighed, then said, "More like a handful of false starts that might have been; you know what I mean?"

"Yeah; loud and clear."

When they reached the bridge before crossing the intracoastal, traffic was already backing up for several hundred feet because of the bridge being raised for boaters. It was drive-time for commuters on their way to work, but also for eager beachgoers who preferred not wasting one minute of daylight by lounging in their beds too long. He and Smook realized it wasn't quite the 'master stroke' they imagined by getting out as early as they did with the intent to beat traffic. They soon got over it when the bridge lowered after a few minutes, and traffic resumed with no more delays.

Omar said, "There's the pier. We can see the cruise ships make their way to and from the port authority from there too. Not a whole lot's changed since I was last here."

Omar was about to unpack some of their equipment when Smook got his attention…

"Hey, check your 'two o'clock'. Looks like your girlfriend's ride."

Omar turned to his right and noticed the cream colored convertible parked several rows over from them, but no one was in it.

Omar replied, "They must be on the beach already."

"Let's go find out." They both carried pieces of the recording equipment, and a beach umbrella so they could catalog random shots of beachgoers. They had walked the top edge of the shoreline for about 30 yards in the direction of the pier, when Omar noticed four girls in swimsuits on a large beach towel. He felt it might be Priscilla and her friends; at least he was hoping it was. He almost raced ahead of Smook, hoping to reach the girls before they'd decide to hit the water, but as he got a little closer he noticed Priscilla wasn't among them. He wasn't up to walking the entire beachhead to try and find her; and he did want to catch up with her in the worst way.

Omar then said, "It's not them."

"Yeah, I can tell by the look on your face. Looks like she was the one that kind of got away, huh?"

Omar didn't answer him but just gave him a blank stare.

He then said, "Let's walk down further."

Then a woman's voice behind them shouted, "Omar!" They both turned around. It was Priscilla, and she was walking toward them, alone. Smook could see the light return in Omar's eyes once he saw her. He could also see that his infatuation with her was the 'coal fired ember' that was taking forever to extinguish, but he already felt he needed to at least be cautious with her.

When she caught up to them he said, "I thought you would have been at the pier by now."

She replied, "Headed that way." They seemed undecided about whether they should hug each other, but finally did…

She then said, "Well, you're as handsome as ever."

"And you look, stunning. Oh, this is my friend, and co-host, Dwayne."

They shook hands.. "Nice to meet you Dwayne, but, Co-host?"

Omar then explained. "For the campus radio show we do together. It's one of the reasons we're here; to do a piece on the culture this time of year. If the student body likes it, maybe it'll be an annual thing; hoping so anyway."

She said, "Sounds ambitious. You getting ready for 'Inside Edition', or something?"

"Just a thing that I do; following my nose if you know what I mean."

"I know exactly what you mean." He then asked, "Where are your friends?"

"Oh, they're at the showers, getting wet. They wanted to get right in the water; me, not so much. I'm a bonafide land lover."

They both laughed a little as they continued walking toward the pier.

Omar then said, "You know what? You can kick this off for us."

She slowed her pace a little, curious as to what he had in mind. "Why not let me interview you, right here, right now. You'll have the distinction of being our very first for what we'll call, the inaugural season of the segment.. How about it?"

Her expression seemed to pierce his heart with expectation all over again. She was impressed with his ambition; a side of him she thought she might never see. She got much closer to him; her face perched only inches from his with shifting bedroom Eyes. Smook watched her work him like a master puppeteer. They had just met, but he already had an uneasy feeling about her.

She then asked, "You have a name for this segment yet?"

"No—Hadn't given it any thought, until now. See how you bring out the radical in me?"

She grabbed his hand and said, "Maybe we can both decide on a name, later, if you'd like."

"Oh, I'd like, very much."

Smook decided he'd interrupt the bliss.

Then he asked, "So, are we gonna do this?"

She replied, "Sure, why not?" They set up their equipment where they stood while Priscilla laid out her beach towel and uncovered her bikini clad body to take in the sun. When Omar asked during the interview what was the most memorable thing she had done so far, she seemed to give Omar signals that only aroused his expectations all over again.

She then said, "Well, I saw this guy that I've known since grade school here. I was really surprised to see him, but delighted at the same time."

She held the microphone as if she was caressing it tenderly; like some precious possession that would cause her serious grief once they parted, but in that instant, her gaze had cornered his heart once again.

"Me and this guy, well, we sort of have a history together that was involuntarily interrupted; but I'm hoping there's more of our story to be told yet before this week is over."

She lowered the microphone and smiled at him. Omar was speechless and just stared back..Smook looked at them both but was puzzled. He didn't think Omar would be stopped dead in his tracks suddenly by this woman who had been part of a sorted past at best. It explained his reluctance toward the other girls he had met since they were there. He stopped the footage while they talked. Obviously hip-deep into plans for a rendezvous later that night with her. When they got back to the hotel, Omar was really animated and couldn't stop talking about Priscilla.

"You gonna make that run with me tonight on the strip Snoop?"

"You know three's a crowd. I'll be a part of the landscape though, somewhere."

"We had a pretty good day with the footage we got for the segment. I think it's gonna turn out ok."

"Yeah, especially with the way your girlfriend brought you back from the dead at the beginning of it."

"Why do I get the feeling you don't really care for her?"

"I wouldn't go that far; just not a 'warm and fuzzy' about her, know what I mean?"

"She's not the same person I remembered. I feel certain about that."

"Whatever you say man."

Omar showed up at the 'Seafarers' Restaurant & Lounge' almost 20 minutes earlier than the time Priscilla said she would see him there. He was curious though why she seemed a little vague about treating it like a real date. He left Smook at another place on the north end of the strip. They had agreed to check in with each other periodically to try and determine when they might both be ready to head back to the hotel. Omar saw one of Priscilla's friends at the bar finally after waiting almost 45 minutes and approached her.

"Hi, Sheryl."

"Hi—Omar, right?"

"Right. Is Priscilla here yet? She said she'd meet me almost 45 minutes ago."

Sheryl gave him a quizzical look…

"Oh, you still interviewing her for your segment? Getting something about the night life too I guess, huh?"

"No, not really." Omar suddenly had a strange sensation in the pit of his stomach that felt a lot like 'dejavu'. He was bracing himself, but for what he had no idea.

Sheryl replied, "Well, there she is over there, with her beau."

She pointed to a far corner of the room and there she was. She was with the guy that looked a lot like the one he saw her necking with at the track meet that day; the day he had to be carried away in an ambulance; the day his world fell apart. He couldn't believe it had happened again. It seemed too unlikely that it would, based on her behavior earlier that day, but he had to know. He walked slowly toward her table. The chemistry between her and that young man was unmistakable.

"Hello, Priscilla."

"Omar, Hi; been here long?"

"Not quite an hour." There was awkward silence for a moment, then she introduced him..

"Omar this is Derrick." They shook hands loosely, but he became noticeably wary of his place in her hierarchy of suitors suddenly.

"He was my second surprise today; you being the first of course."

She reached across the table and held Derrick's hand…

"We've been at it since high school; didn't expect him to show up down here of all places."

Derrick then said, "I couldn't let you get away with having all the fun baby."

After he said it, Omar thought, 'how original'.

Derrick then said, "Why don't you have a drink with us Omar?"

Derrick beckoned to the waitress after he offered him the drink.

Omar said, "Would you believe I'm almost at my limit already? Designated driver, you know how that is; so I'd better pass but thanks anyway."

Priscilla asked, "Did you finally think of a title for your segment? I know it was something we talked about working on together after I saw you this morning."

He wanted to appear as sturdy as an oak, but he felt his pride had been punctured; so much so, that after what just happened, the slightest turbulence might just shred him to pieces, but he did manage a reply…

"No, I hadn't even thought about it yet, but after today I know whatever I decide will fit like a glove. See you around."

He turned and walked away. His face had turned to stone, but he felt his heart had just been mauled by her. He dialed Smook's cell phone just before leaving the place.

"Hey, where are you?"

Smook answered, "I'm at Ricardo's. I believe it's not quite a block from where you are."

"I know where it is. Look, I'll see you there in a few minutes, unless you're into something."

"Wouldn't matter if I was anyway. I'll see you in a bit. I'm in the back."

When he found Smook, he was in the company of two girls.

"Hey man. Didn't expect to see you so soon." Smook introduced the two girls and they excused themselves soon after for a run to the ladies' room but were coming back.

Smook asked, "Did she even show up?"

"Yeah, she showed, but it wasn't what I was expecting."

"What do you mean?"

"Her 'Number 1' showed up unexpectedly, so she was locked up with him. He even rubbed my face in it by inviting me to have a drink with them."

"Well, did you?"

"No –no way."

"Good, because he probably knows how she is, and did it just to make a statement about how confident he is knowing he's the one who has her heart, no matter how much of a flirt she is."

Omar hung his head, knowing what Smook said was most likely the truth. She had toyed with him yet again, piling even more of his over-blown fantasies on top of an already smoldering ash heap.

"You want a drink Omar? " Smook got the waitress's attention quickly.

He asked, "Can you bring my friend here a couple of Heineken?"

Omar interrupted and said, "No, something stronger." He just stared at the stage, with only instruments on their stands, but no musicians yet.

Smook asked, "Ok, what's your pleasure? "Omar, Omar, Omar!"

Omar didn't respond but seemed shell shocked. The delayed reaction to Priscilla's masquerade had been numbing.

CLARENCE WAS WALKING UP, and calling out to him—"Omar, Omar!" —Shaking him was the only thing that brought him out of his day dream.

"Are you alright? You haven't signed on yet."

"Oh, yeah; just a little housekeeping I had to take care of first. I'm good."

But he was anything but good. The daydreams persisted and his anxieties had ramped up again. He knew he couldn't go into Monday's rehearsal without having finished his talk with Evelyn beforehand, so he picked up the phone before having time to think twice about it, and called her extension.

"Earth Burst Industries, Evelyn speaking."

"Hi Ev, it's Omar."

"Why are you calling on the outside extension line?"

"I didn't want you to not pick up if you saw it was me calling."

"I'm not that petty Omar; really."

"Look, ah—can we go on break together this morning? I just need to finish saying what I started to earlier; need to clear up some things."There was silence for a while, then she responded…

"Alright Omar. I'll go on break with you."

Omar managed to get through the first part of his morning with relative calm. He was relieved that Evelyn agreed to meet him on the morning break. He may have been a little melodramatic by feeling their relationship may have only been on life-support, but if that was the case, he'd make it his duty to try and resuscitate it. He hadn't seen Theo yet, and was curious about his absence. He saw Clarence standing at an associate's cubicle a couple of rows from him and got his attention.

"Hey, Cee Cee?"

"Yeah Omar."

"Is Theo out today?"

"He's taking some personal time this morning; has a medical appointment, but he should be in before noon."

He was in no hurry to confront Theo, and felt the more uninterrupted time with Evelyn for now, the better off he'd be. They agreed to meet at ten o'clock, but the sting of isolation was even more pronounced when Evelyn apparently didn't care to walk with him to the break area this time. Even that little feature that was evidence of their bond for so many months, was missed in a big way. He got there before she did, but when he saw her coming, he bought her favorite drink from the vending machine, and one for himself, then took a seat where he could be easily seen. She noticed him and waved, then headed for the drink machine.

He stopped her and said, "I've got you." He wanted her to notice the bottle of soda he had bought for her…

She turned and said, "Thanks, but you didn't have to do that."

He said, "It's not a problem."

She opened the drink, took a sip, and then asked, "So, is this your confessional then?"

"To be honest, I just didn't want to accept what was happening to me Ev—I've been shooting blanks so long when it comes to really connecting with people, I've become almost immune to its effects, but not anymore."

He looked around the room; anywhere but in her eyes, as he nervously tried to construct his apology. He was really sincere this time, but also hoping it wouldn't fall flat with her since he had been there several times before recently, but with negative results. Evelyn did get the sense there would be full disclosure this time; a road less travelled before, in favor of the promise of safe harbor for problems he chose to defer, until now.

He continued, "I've carried some baggage in my life that I just couldn't unload. I'm ashamed to admit most of it, but I've committed to an Alcoholics Anonymous group I've been a part of for some months but just now opened up to them about my own past. I never told you about it because, I just didn't want it to affect your opinion of me."

"Look, I'm still your friend, and friends help one another. It doesn't mean we won't ever have a falling out, and I'm still a little mad at you."

She wagged her finger at him, to put him on notice.

"Just trust the relationship enough to know it will survive it. So take some advice from somebody who's lived a little longer than you. Every disappointment I've faced, and believe me there have been many, have made me stronger. I've taken something good from every one of those experiences and tucked it away like it was currency. I couldn't just lie down and let them take me out. So I just decided I would become bigger than my problems. It's also not good to treat your friends like some chore you happen to get stuck with when you feel more like sulking while going through your 'stuff. Real friends will stick around for the ride right along with you, no matter how bumpy it gets."

"I hope you can forgive me Ev, because the truth is, some of my history may seem a little 'dark' with people I have yet to reconcile with. Just giving you a heads-up, in case that part of it is not altogether cooperating once I try to make things right."

She became noticeably alarmed when he said it… "Omar, are you in some kind of danger?"

"I wouldn't say that; just hoping for a peaceful outcome that's all. Not to worry."

He smiled at her, unconvincingly, then said, "It's that time. Can I escort you back?"

"Yeah, sure; let's walk."

The alarmist in Evelyn was always triggered by her protective nature. She now had something new to worry about concerning Omar—his safety.

Chapter 10

"HEY SIS, IT'S YOUR brother, Seth."

"Oh, Hi Seth, how are things with you?"

He spoke in a low monotone voice; a clear indication he had labored over some issue, he thought, ultimately, might be a lost cause...

"I suppose I'll survive."

"Umm—You sound stressed. You sure you're ok?"

"Truth is, I still haven't heard from Omar yet. I know he must be getting my messages. I've left enough of 'em."

"Malcom's not home yet, but did you try and get him to talk to Omar for you?"

"I called Malcolm on his cell, but got his voicemail the times that I did call; thought if we triple-teamed him, it might make a difference, but I guess he's sticking to his guns."

His tone was sorrowful; like a lion's roar having been reduced to a whimper, because its instinct to hunt had mysteriously vanished. This posture was unnatural for him. The doting but high energy Uncle Seth that Omar had come to know as one of his coaches and friend, seemed to be subdued by the persistent badgering from what had become his unpardonable sin. Elizabeth became well aware that the anguish over Omar's break with him had taken its toll.

She said, "I'm sorry Seth. Whenever I talk with him I do my best to try and persuade him. He needs to talk, if he's ever going to understand what really happened. I'd hate to call him at work and make him think it's some type of emergency at home, but maybe it's worth a shot. I can at least set up a 3-way to put the two of you together finally."

"I've been wanting to sort of extend an olive branch by letting him know I took the liberty and submitted his name for consideration as a judge on the Pre-Olympic Committee."

"Oh Seth, that's great!"

"The committee sent him the initial letter for candidates who may have been recommended by a sitting member, like myself, to see if they are even interested. I don't believe he's responded to the letter because the chairman of the committee hadn't heard from him as of two days ago. That's one of the reasons I've been trying to reach him. He may not talk about it but I know he still loves his sport, and any chance to be around it, especially in an official capacity that also pays him a stipend, well, you'd think he'd jump at the chance."

"You'd think; but he's been bitter for so long that being involved again in some way still may not be enough to bring him around. It's just where his attitude's at right now."

She pivoted for a moment, to reflect on Omar's experiences growing up, as if to justify his indifference to some degree.

"He was always so trusting of other people, even when he was a kid. He would say to me sometimes, he felt like some 'lab rat' because of so many visits to the doctor, and how careful we needed to be with him."

Elizabeth paused, deciding to commit to a plunge into Omar's past. Seth was familiar with that side of her, and just listened.

"I remember once, when he was about four years old, he asked me if I knew what it was like to die. Huh, I gasped; wondering where that came from. I just sat him on my knee then held him close; doing my best to suppress this urge to just cry out over a stigma he had carried like a mule all of his young life. He looked at me with those little innocent puppy dog eyes, and I explained as carefully as I could that, dying was like going to sleep for a really long time only to wake up in God's Bosom where he'll never have to sleep again, or know pain ever again. He gave me this serious look then asked me, "Am I going to die soon momma"?

I told him no, of course he wasn't; told him he was going to do great things long before that ever happens. It seemed to cheer him up, but to be honest I wasn't so sure myself about how much longer he might be with us. He was insightful to be so young, but he must have felt he was different than other kids when he couldn't run as fast and jump as high as they could before giving out of breath in a matter of minutes. I guess he felt he had to compensate by going out of his way to try and make friends which, unfortunately, didn't always work out for him. Some of that attitude must have stayed with him, even after overcoming his birth defect like the doctors said would probably happen. It was nothing short of a miracle what happened to him after he grew out of it. He so far exceeded what we could have ever imagined you know, but he just couldn't embrace how he had been gifted in spite of it. For some reason, he felt he was still limited by something he had already overcome, and felt he still needed to almost apologize for it. Kind of like the caged elephant who finally has its chains removed, not understanding that it can walk out of that cage to freedom any time it wants, but chooses to stay as if it's still in bondage. It's the reasoning that causes him such disappointment in someone he cares about, even if it's a question of choices he may have made that cast dark shadows over the relationship. He always makes it seem monumental."

Seth responded, "Omar was like a son to me; you know that. I would have done anything for him; tried to have his back when it mattered. I'd give anything to take back what I did, but I can't."

"Don't beat yourself up all over again Seth. Anyone in your situation at the time, may have done the same thing. You had to think about the team."

"Yeah, the team; who I cared deeply about, but didn't think it would mean being at odds with my own blood. To betray his trust in me, was just too high a price to pay."

"You might think that it was, looking back, but if he was any other athlete on the team who had suffered the same thing that day, would you have the same regrets? You also had a responsibility to the team. You had to know you needed to be as objective as possible about your decisions when it came to evaluating their fitness. Casting the deciding vote to advance another team mate to that Pre-Olympic squad rather than him was the responsible thing to do. Had you let him retain his spot and the team suffered because of it, then it would have been a lot worse."

He replied, "There's no guarantee that would have happened."

"Maybe, but was it really worth taking the risk? Then you really would have been made to be the 'heavy,' and besides, you tried to persuade him to maintain his training to get ready for the next Olympics but he declined, so that wasn't on you."

"Then why is he being so obstinate about talking to me at least? I'm not his enemy. I knew he was in trouble that day when it seemed all the world was watching, but he kept insisting he was alright. Coach Bivens and I wanted to pull the plug, to opt for a medical deferment maybe, but he wasn't having it, so we let him humiliate himself in front of all those people."

"Seth stop! You only did what any coach would have done. You followed your gut. Besides, after Omar found out it was all caused by an allergic reaction to cinnamon of all things, he admitted to me and his father how he came across it."

"How?" "Some little girl he was sweet on was there that day and persuaded him to take a bite or two from a cinnamon roll she had bought for her nephew."

"You mean, he ate some of that just before his meet?"

"Yeah Seth, he did. You see that little detail he left out when he decided to crucify you. He had broken that rule about his training on his own because he lost focus for a moment. But that's all it takes isn't it, for the house to come crashing down around you? Remember that was his choice not yours; and who I think he's really disappointed in, is himself. You just happened to be a convenient target for his rage. Sort of reminds me of a certain brother growing up in our own household as kids, who took everything so seriously; sound familiar?"

"Well, we had a military father who was in my face often enough about it, who almost ordered me to change my ways."

They then laughed about their father's antiquated rules.

He then said, "Well, target or no, I can't leave things like this if I can help it. He's always been like a son to me, you know."

"You keep saying that as if it's some wishful thinking going on when it comes to your own son. Am I wrong?"

"Not entirely. Even when Agnes told me she was pregnant with him, I had already decided I couldn't really be a father to him. She was barely engaged after she found out she was pregnant, but her fiancé knew we had a history before they did. He's a better man than me, to stick with her even after the baby was born. They never postponed their plans to marry either. She even told me he was willing to adapt the baby as his own if they needed to, knowing how she felt about it. I guess that's what the phrase, 'love is blind' means, huh?" "Yeah, it is blind, but it doesn't mean you can't see where or when a situation might actually suit whatever purpose love may have in store for it."

"Maybe you're right. We both decided we'd give him up for adoption to a relative, on her dad's side; me being so mobile then, and her wanting to avoid the stigma of having to raise a son that's not her husband's in the same household. She would show up on his birthday and Christmas time with gifts, and sometimes just to take him on an outing; almost trading places with the woman that was raising him. When their first son was born, all that changed. She barely came around then, and so did I. The kid suddenly had a big hole in his life."

Elizabeth said, "Agnes cared more for him than she let on Seth. I think the mistake you guys may have made was not telling him sooner who his real parents were. She said when he got older he became a bully; taking out his anger on other kids, especially after Breeland was born. It was tougher then to show him affection when his behavior only irritated her more, but she didn't love him any less."

"Deon is my son—my son, who I really didn't try to get to know until things went south with Omar. Is that screwed up or what? It's punishment for my own sins. That has to be it."

"Don't do this to yourself Seth. I'm a firm believer that things happen for a reason. None of what goes on in our lives is all by chance Seth; not any of it. It all comes full-circle at some point, and that's where the blessings can be found."

"Would you call the attack on Deon at his work a blessing? "

"I'm sorry Seth. I didn't mean to"—He interrupted.

"It's ok Elizabeth. I know Omar was in a bad place that day, and Deon may have been too, but what's done is done."

"Did you decide to keep quiet about it because of the history between the two of you?"

Seth was silent for a moment; groping for words while still wrestling with his despair ..

Then he said, "I don't know; maybe that had something to do with it. Whatever the case, I didn't want Deon to get the police involved. It would have only made matters worse, you know. Omar doesn't know about Agnes and me does he? He and Breeland were good friends weren't they?"

"Best friends. Omar took it really hard when he died."

"If he's ever going to find out, I'd like to be the one to break it to him, ok?"

Omar's Friday at work went as well as could be expected. He felt he had crossed a major hurdle with Evelyn after creating some daylight between them following the morning break. He hadn't seen Theo yet and wondered if he was going to show up at all. When he had a moment to think about it, he really wasn't in a big hurry to see him. Theo may not have been as agreeable as Evelyn, and he didn't want to run the risk of ruining his weekend by having him topple his attempts at reconciliation. He decided it was probably something better left for Monday, or the day after. He was more upbeat about the rehearsal for the video on Monday now and had already started counting down the minutes left in his day. The entire department hummed at high energy. They all seemed to be synchronized by the pre-weekend ritual of non-stop, high pitched chatter. The 'twenty somethings' were hip-deep into spinning fables filled with plenty of exaggerated claims about their carnal pursuits. The intrigue was often kept alive by their self-proclaimed, but careless, spending habits and the sort of behavior that bordered on little or no restraint. In the end, it all seemed made-to-order for the comic relief served up to their audience. And then there were the aging 'peacocks' and 'lions', in all of their salt and peppered glory; secretly humming their 'swan song' lullabies but not quite ready to fall asleep; whose desires for just a few days of solitude were well disguised inside all the noise. But then, there were those in the middle, like Clarence. He seemed unaffected by the revelry; almost touting some immunity to it as though it was expected for someone in his position. He happened to be close by, performing quality control checks with one of the IT Techs on upgraded software they had also installed with the new desk top terminals. After completing the last checks, he approached Omar at his desk before heading back to his own.

"Hey, mister."

Omar replied, "Cee Cee, how is it? "

"Just wanted to let you know I put Security on notice about your rehearsal on Monday at the park. I didn't say how long you'd be, but I assumed you'd be leaving before dark since there's only pole lighting out there."

"Yeah; no longer than an hour or so should do it."

Clarence folded his arms and rested his hips against the corner of Omar's desk. Omar knew him well enough to know when he was getting ready to probe, and simply waited for it… "Sure you won't change your mind about making that trip with me to Gleason? It won't be as bad as you might think. You can delay your first contact with the Dillon rep at least until Wednesday, if you make that run with me by Tuesday."

"It's probably best to let sleeping dogs lie Cee Cee."

Before Clarence could reply Omar's extension rang, and he answered it hurriedly…

"Earth Burst Industries, Omar speaking." He waited for a moment but no one answered…

"Hello, this is Omar speaking—Hello!

He could hear background noises and someone's steady breathing, but still, no reply..

"This is Omar, who's calling?"

The person's breathing became louder, then they hung up. Omar shook his head and said, "Sounds like the cat's got somebody's tongue."

Clarence raised up, then said, "I've got to get to my office, but think a little more about Gleason, ok? I don't think you'll regret it."

Omar was truly a lone wolf within the pack. His attempts at being sociable had become so brittle, that his pride might have just snapped like a twig from the slightest misstep. With the exception of maybe Evelyn and Clarence now, he needed relationship 'training wheels' for his new outlook, but until he could be fitted for them with help from people he already trusted, and family, his ineptness would have to do. Standing in front of the plate glass window behind his desk seemed to be the perfect refuge until the bell tolled, but just as he decided to get up and take in the view, his phone rang once again…

"Earth Burst Industries, Omar speaking."

He held his breath this time while he listened intently to the sound on the other end of the receiver. Still no one answered, but a sound that seemed amplified a thousand times was eerily similar to the sound of taps. The same taps he heard near the AA meeting hall, and at the parking lot inside his apartment complex. It suddenly became more rapid, as if someone's footsteps were closing in on him, then it stopped. A dial tone had interrupted what seemed to be a virtual chase. He was a little on edge about it, and almost slammed the phone down. He suddenly felt light-headed and called Clarence right away.

"Cee Cee, would you mind if I leave now. There's only about 15 minutes left before the shift ends, and I don't feel so good."

"Well, I hope you're not catching what Theo has. He wanted the rest of the day for himself too. The TGIF syndrome I guess."

"It's nothing like that. Anyway, I still have to catch the bus to get home; just thought I'd sip on some tea from the shop downstairs while I wait on the bus. Maybe it'll make me feel better."

Clarence said, "You don't have to sell me on it. It's ok to leave. Just take care of yourself, and let's hope we'll see each other on Monday."

Omar then said, "Thanks, and have a good weekend."

He wasted no time logging off and collecting his belongings. For once he seemed to blend in with the rest of his unit when he stood up just before leaving. Associates in front and behind him, whom he rarely socialized with, were relieved to see him finally break protocol thinking he may have decided to escape his shell. It turned out to be a 'false positive' as he locked his desk and slung his satchel over his shoulder.

One of them asked, "You leaving early Omar?"

"Yeah, not feeling so good right now."

Omar turned in Evelyn's direction to see her looking at him, then she waved, with a half-smile that she struggled with. It was an expression that seemed to coddle his need for her approval. It wasn't evidence of a full pardon, but was still enough to set his mind more at ease. He smiled and waved back, then said goodbye to associates in his row before leaving. He sipped on the tea he had picked up from the kiosk in the lobby while he waited. He at least understood it was better to be consistent with his claims to Clarence about how he was feeling, even though the truth may have been stretched way out of proportion. He had just missed a bus headed in the direction of his neighborhood, but when the next bus did arrive he said hello to Vick, took his seat, and exhaled a big sigh of relief. The work week was finally done. His phone rang as he was getting ready to decompress; it was his mom…

"Hi mom, everything ok?"

"Yeah, we're fine. I've got somebody on the line who wants to talk to you."

She had set up a three-way connection with Seth, who didn't bother to wait for a cue..

"Hello Omar; it's Seth. How are you?"

Omar's tone and expression made it seem as if he had suddenly been hit with a rancid odor after hearing Seth's voice..

"I'm good, but what is it you want?"

"I just want to talk; to maybe try and explain again what really happened concerning my committee vote back then, for one. I don't want you to be at odds with me forever over this. You're like a son to me Omar, and you've got to know I wouldn't have done anything to deliberately destroy your shot at the Olympics."

"We've been over this Uncle Seth. The simple fact is you betrayed me. I don't know why, but you did."

Seth then said, "That's not true. My back was against the wall. I had no choice. We had to think about fielding the best team at the time. I was obligated to vote the way I did son. There were obvious concerns about your conditioning after that episode at the track, and I didn't find out until recently that—"

Omar interrupted him. "Forget it. Just forget it. What's done is done. What was it really? Was it because you lost your own shot at it and you took it out on me, huh?"

Seth could sense Omar was becoming unraveled, even though his venting could easily have been body blows to his gut. At least they were talking, finally.

"Omar, you know that's not true. I knew how hard you had worked; what you had to overcome to get there, and I couldn't have been more proud. I wanted to protect that, but something happened then, that none of us could explain. To be honest, I've been waiting all these years for you to shed some light on that situation, since it sort of came out of the blue, you know? There's one other thing I wanted to discuss with you, that's strictly business. It concerns that same committee; a position I thought you might be interested in. Correspondence was sent to you about it some time back; thought you would have responded by now."

Omar was quiet. Something nudged his thinking in a different direction to at least consider what Seth had said to him. It was the thoughtful thing to do, and he couldn't put his finger on the reason why his attitude might be shifting, but he resisted anyway and clung to his oath of bitterness just the same without hearing him out about the judge's position on the Olympic committee.

Seth called out to him—"You still there Omar?"

"I'm here, but there's nothing else to say about this Seth. Sounds like you're just throwing a dog a bone anyway with that business about a position on the committee."

His mother was saddened, again, but also irritated as to why Omar somehow couldn't accept the role he played in his own failures, despite the history that followed him. She interrupted sharply.. "Omar, you really should apologize to your uncle. I'm ashamed of you!"

He huffed and puffed for a little while; avoiding any apology to his uncle…..

Then he said, "Look, I'm on the bus, and I'll be getting off soon, so let me talk to you maybe tomorrow, ok mom?"

He disconnected; not waiting for a reply. Frustrated with himself, he shoved the phone in his satchel faced with the realization that he'd need to, at some point, reckon with his own guilt. His new outlook seemed to have a really short shelf-life. He tried pushing the idea aside as if it had violated him, but it kept coming back like an ocean tide, helplessly lapping beneath the glow of a full moon. He was noticeably agitated just before the bus stopped to pick up Rupert, and three other passengers. Seeing Rupert wasn't exactly a bright spot in his day, but he didn't feel pressed to try and converse with him either. His efforts at 'fence mending' with him would come at a price after finding out he couldn't be so easily manipulated into submission. He wasn't quite sure how deep into the well he'd need to plunge to make peace with him. He knew he didn't want to aggravate an already festering climate of mistrust, but really had no clue about what villains might be lurking inside Rupert's personality. He may have had his own revelation that demanded a change in his outlook too after their morning bus ride, but if there were any he needed to appease, Rupert's new attitude could easily spell trouble for him.

Rupert made eye contact with slightly knitted eyebrows; rocking his head back to acknowledge him. Omar returned the gesture and casually waved his hand in front of his chest. No words were spoken between them. It was the kind of behavior typical of common foes, fiercely protective of their territories; namely their egos. Attempting to masquerade their desire for respectability with tiny doses of common courtesies, while at the same time planning the next offensive against one another. Omar was content to table his attempts to be sociable with anybody on the bus, let alone Rupert. Micki wasn't riding again today and he could have really used a potent injection of her humor then, but it was the type of withdrawal he would have to endure for only another twenty minutes. Just before putting his headphones on to listen to more smooth jazz, he was caught off guard suddenly by that sound again. The sound that began to haunt him at every turn. It was the rhythmic sound of taps again. He casually hung the headphones around his neck and stared out of the window. Not wanting to seem too conspicuous, as if it mattered, he turned slowly in the direction of the noise to find it was coming from Rupert. Omar stared, motionless and Rupert stared back, expressionless. He already had his headphones on, knocking two chop sticks together near his face. It was as if he imagined he was drumming the sticks against Omar's face, beating it to a pulp, as the drumming of the sticks became more aggressive. He kept staring at Omar for a while longer. It was a menacing stare as the clatter began to swell to a crescendo. He must have known it made Omar uncomfortable, yet his still but shadowy eyes pierced his, until it suddenly stopped. Rupert's expression also shifted. It seemed to be more passive now, as he tucked the chop sticks in-side a pocket to his satchel. Omar's imagination went into a free fall during the walk to his apartment from the bus stop. He felt the exchange with Seth was a test, but he had failed miserably. It was clear he had not turned the corner on his animosity yet when he chose not to hold his tongue when they were speaking. It didn't occur to him that Seth was the person he could most easily make peace with, since he had been lobbying for it for so many years. It was everyone else that he needed to be more concerned about; especially since a stalker had presumably been added to the equation. Rupert was the last person he'd think would actu-ally want to harm him, but he couldn't rule him out altogether. He began to appreciate how costly it had been to show an amica-ble side of himself to only a select number of people. The coolness shown to him by others, after their overexposure to cer-tain of his prejudices, was manifesting itself in ways he was ill-equipped to handle. It never occurred to him that, whatever standards of perfection he expected of other people, in order for him to call them friend, was truly subjective; and the distance he might choose to put between himself and someone else because of some perceived flaw that unfairly depicts the heart of their character, could also be the standard by which he is judged. Needless to say, it was time for him to appreciate the fact that all of human kind is 'a work in progress' seeking perfection in most things, especially in our relationships; but really being o.k. with just getting something as close as possible to it.

When he unlocked the door to his apartment, he tossed his bags on the couch and flopped in the big chair next to it. He kicked his shoes off, grabbed a juice from the 'frig' and sipped on it while he listened to a local news segment. He was amused by the piece that reported on the upcoming festival in Mumford. The guy doing the report was probably well worth what he was being paid with the way he embellished the story. It was the type of publicity the area needed anyway, but he would also be instru-mental in its impact. That made him feel even more committed to making sure the video was a success. He still felt a trip to Dillon with Clarence though would only amount to a stroll down memory lane that would most likely be littered with pot holes. In his mind, there wasn't a bribe big enough that would let him commit to it. He remembered he hadn't checked his mailbox on the way up, so he slipped his shoes on again and walked downstairs. The box was half full but mostly with solicitations for one thing or another. He looked through the envelopes to discard what he didn't need before he made it back upstairs. When he returned, he tossed the mail he decided to keep on the kitchen counter and headed for his bedroom. The brightness of the sun with its orange tinge was fading as it began to slip below the horizon, but still bright enough to cast a reflection in the full length mirror in his suite, like a halogen in the dead of night. He pulled the shade to the window to extinguish the glare, but even in a room now filled with only shadows of its contents, that mirror still revealed the presence of light within the reflection, but nowhere inside the room. Omar stood still for a moment. His eyes were stretched wide, searching for the mysterious source but there was none that he could point to. He stepped back near the door to flip the light switch on but it was as though power to his entire apartment had been cut off. He started to breath rapidly as the room became almost pitch black immediately, but that light still emanated from the reflection inside the mirror. It didn't occur to him to check his electrical panel box for faulty breakers. It was as though the light was calling to him. He was now more driven by his own curiosity as he stepped slowly toward it, somehow knowing there was something startling waiting for him. Pieces of his previous encounters in front of that mirror suddenly bombarded his memory. They were vivid at first, like dramatic color bursts against an ebony sky, but then quickly became grossly distorted; reduced to a distressfully opaque image with little, if anything, that was identifiable. As he became aware of the high-pitched fizzing sound, it grew louder. The bright light slowly dimmed, then the fizzing stopped; and there, in all of its benign splendor, was that spirit, the Orphan; much sharper now in its likeness to human form. Omar seemed to almost expect its arrival; placing his hands against the mirror as the image began mimicking his exact movements. It seemed more integrated with Omar's reflection now. Omar reacted to it as if he was gazing at some new exotic species. He marveled at it, and in that moment, was also under its spell. It's deep but paternal tone had command of his attention once again.

"You've been naughty recently Omar; finding it harder to keep your vow than you thought it would be I see."

Omar replied curiously, "What do you mean; what vow?"

"The promise, scribbled across your heart; a vow that was inscribed by a committed hand once; a pledge to becoming more approachable and sociable with the people in your life. It seems now, it might as well have been written with a withered hand."

It paused for just a moment, in obvious distress over the set back of its host, but continued speaking…

"You let anxiety back in again because you were faced with something you didn't expect." "What do you mean?" What didn't I expect?"

"Well, your reaction to Clarence's invitation to Dillon, and your suspicions about Rupert since you didn't get the response you were counting on when you finally reached out to him. Not to mention being alienated by Evelyn and Theo. But probably the most troubling is the bitterness toward your Uncle Seth; just to name a few."

"Well, with Rupert and Evelyn, and maybe even Theo, I'll have to be more patient I guess, but with what happened at Dillon, and with my Uncle Seth, there's too much history there to just let go. I can't just let it go."

"But that's exactly what you must do. Bury that pain, while you dig to uncover the real root of the problem. Decide you're going to become that instrument that wants to reconcile with whoever used you, lied to you, or shamed you into a corner. That includes things you've done to others that have left their own scars. This fear or pain you feel has duped you into feeling you have to haul it around, like some beast of burden."

"I've got that under control, as long as I don't have to—"

The Orphan finished the sentence for him—"As long as you don't have to relive the experience by putting yourself in situations that might trigger it. Isn't that what you're saying?"

"Well, what's wrong with that?"

"Because you'll always be looking over your shoulder; hoping to avoid those triggers you really have no control over. Why not seek the peace-of-mind a permanent solution can give you, rather than facing the prospect of dealing with a problem that will only leave your conscious cluttered with indecision. That approach only lets you kick the can down the road for a while anyway, until it decides to show up again later."

Omar listened with nervous energy. The Orphan matched every gesture he made with his body no matter how subtle, except for when it spoke. It was clearly knocking at the door of its home again...

Omar said, "That's a lot easier said than done. It's not like some magic trick where a puff of smoke, or a trap door determines whether I've been persuasive enough with people I meet."

"I'm not saying it is, but like most things of any real value, it's a process that has to mature with time. You can't plant tomato seeds and expect bananas to grow in their place. It's a ridiculous notion isn't it? If you sow seeds of contempt, that's what will come back to you. It's also just as naive to believe that whatever you've sown will also sprout in just a day or so. Besides, you can be your own worst enemy at times, when you decide to overlook your own faults."

"I haven't done that, have I?"

"Do you recall the parable repeated to you by your mother when you were eleven; about the consequences of casting seed on stony ground rather than fertile soil. Those seeds can't really produce whatever fruit they're meant to bare, until that ground is tilled, and scaled of its crusty exterior, like the fish you might catch before you'd be expected to have it for dinner. They must be cradled within that soil; unmolested by driven wind, or trampling feet, or some fowl's beak, until their roots are stout enough to call that place home and the place where they will flourish. Curiously enough, that crust bears a striking resemblance to someone I know. You'd think his heart hovers just above freezing sometimes based on the way he always responds to one person in particular, but it's badly in need of thawing, wouldn't you agree?"

It paused as if expecting Omar to respond, but he was too busy pondering those nuggets of wisdom from the 'Orphan', who had rightfully assumed the role of his companion. After a moment he pulled back from the mirror; on his knees again but stood to his feet suddenly. The light within the reflection was gone.

THE CONNECTION TO THE Orphan had been broken abruptly. Omar could hear knocking at his door, also realizing the lamp light in his suite was on now. As he left the room to see who was knocking, he could trace only a few remnants of what had just happened, but he was starting to remember. He looked through the peep hole but couldn't quite make out the image of the person standing there.

He asked, "Who is it?"

"It's your neighbor, Rob." He opened the door to see Rob, still in his uniform; a jacket and tie.

Omar said, "Hey man, how is it?" They shook hands.

"It's good—Had to come back home for something. I'm on my dinner break right now; just thought I'd stop by and hit you up first about a game of round ball at the courts tomorrow. I've got the morning off and wanted to get in some practice. You know, if you're not busy."

"Ok. That's a bet. I'll make sure I get my chores out of the way early."

Rob asked, "How about 10 o'clock?"

"Sounds like a plan."

"Ok, I'll swing by on the way down. We can take my car."

"We'd have to anyway because I can't drive yet; been catching the bus to work, and whatever else is too far for me to hike."

"Oh; what happened?"

"License suspension; too many DUI's. It's almost over though; another 2 weeks or so and hopefully I can get my car off my parents' property and start driving again."

"Alright then; in the morning. Take care."

Omar's punctuality had proven to be habit forming. He actually rolled out of bed an hour earlier than usual to start his Saturday morning routine. He felt good that he and Rob Had made a connection. It had the promise of a good friendship which, in his case, had become as unlikely as snowfall in the panhandle. He at least humbled himself enough to count his blessings for the much needed break in the redundancy, but still took time to call his mom as usual to check on her and his dad. She answered the phone as though she had been awaken from a deep sleep. It was only a few minutes after 9:00am.

"Hi mom."

"Omar, hi; you're really early today. You ok?"

She was trying to fight back her yawning between phrases.

"Yeah, I'm ok—Sounds like I woke you up."

"No, I'm up and walking around but yeah, still trying to wake up. We had Seth over last night for dinner, then he wanted to go bowling of all things, and that ran a little late. Your dad is still in bed. Why are you calling so early?"

"I'm going to the courts with my neighbor to shoot hoops. He invited me so we can get in a little practice before we take on the guys from work, so I'm getting my chores done early." "Oh, alright. You're still trying to run with those young bucks, huh?"

"It's just good exercise for me, mom. I can't speak for him though.

Look mom, I'm sorry about yesterday. You were right. It was a little aggressive."

"Does that mean you'll talk with Seth again, to really try and iron things out?"

"I wish I could say yes to that, but I guess I'm still trying to make my way there. I can at least promise you though, I won't light into him again without good reason, and hopefully if, and when it happens, it'll be for something totally unrelated, ok?"

"Well, I had hoped for more but I guess I can't make you feel anything you're not ready for yet. You know I guess I shouldn't tell you this, but for what it's worth, he admitted to me yesterday that his affection for you was greater than that of his own son, before that vote changed everything. He said he didn't really try to reconnect with him until it happened. He gave me the impression you filled a space his own son never could. To be honest, he hasn't been the same since."

Omar was quiet for a moment. Hearing about Seth's admission to his mom started to at least soften those stiff edges of his contempt; enough to maybe lend a sympathetic ear the next time he and Seth spoke…

"Well, like I said, I'll try and be more open-minded about it. By the way, who was it that came out on top with the bowling last night?"

"Your dad, who else? He's a bigger competitor than Seth. They're two of a kind you know." Omar suddenly experienced flashes of his uncle's days as one of his track coaches; remembering how Seth would constantly bend his ears about his knowledge of the sport; even away from the track, and at family gatherings. His nuanced conditioning approach set him apart as a mentor. He seemed doting at times, but felt it was just one benefit of being his blood. The significance of it hadn't really occurred to him, until now.

"Omar, you still with me?"

He replied, "Yeah, I'm here mom; just had a flashback for a moment. Look, I'd better get myself together. Rob will probably be here soon, but tell dad hello for me and tell him I'm hoping I can make arrangements to get my car off your property soon, ok?"

"Alright, I'll tell him—You take care son."

Rob seemed less intimidating after Omar opened the door to see him in gym clothes. He also seemed a little shorter, but he was obviously pumped and ready to get at it..

"Hey man, you ready to do battle?"

Omar was a little amused seeing Rob in his matching 'NBA' monogramed outfit, but he didn't bother to bring his own ball, even though he was the one who extended the invitation to play. Omar felt this was something he probably didn't do very often; besides, it was his opportunity to just socialize which proved to be more ambitious for him anyway. He left the door slightly ajar, remembering to pick up his ball...

"Oh, let me get my ball."

When they got downstairs to the parking area, Rob unlocked the doors with his key-fob, and Omar noticed the headlights flash on a late model nickel colored BMW SUV at least 20 feet away. Omar said, "Looks like law enforcement pays pretty well."

He opened the passenger side rear door first and placed the ball on the floor, but noticed the new car smell still lingering inside....

"Smells like you haven't had this for too long."

Rob replied, "About three months", as he pulled out of the lot into traffic.

Omar asked, "Ok to put my wallet in your glove box?"

He opened the glove compartment as he was asking the question and noticed Rob's revolver.

He then said, "Oops! I guess I can just hold it."

"It's ok. It's not loaded. Just move it aside. I keep the ammo in a separate place; and don't worry, its department issue."

Omar said, "I thought you said you didn't have to carry a weapon?"

"Well, I'm just not forbidden to carry. It's my choice. Besides, it's also for personal safety."

"I take it you're not comfortable with firearms."

Omar replied, "Haven't thought about it much to be honest; never felt I'd need to use one for any reason."

"Well, it's probably not a bad idea to at least get yourself a handgun, even if you'll keep it inside your apartment. Lots of bad people out there who wouldn't think twice about coming in on you, even in the middle of the day."

Omar responded, "I guess I'm trying to avoid being paranoid about it. Too many weapons floating around as it is."

"Suit yourself."

As Rob approached the courts within 50 yards or so, Omar could see two other guys were already involved in a shoot-a-round. As they got closer he could see one of them was Blake. They parked and walked slowly toward the court. Neither one of them had the stomach yet for a two-on-two; especially not having a clue about each other's skill level yet. Blake recognized Omar right away and invited him in.

"Hey, Looks like you came to play today."

Omar said, "Not really; just here for a little workout."

He turned to Rob and introduced them.

"This is my neighbor Rob. We live in the same complex. Rob this is Mr. Blake Bristol. He's the company pro."

Blake smiled and said, "He's exaggerating", then gave Rob a stout handshake and said, "Good to meet you Rob."

Rob replied, "Likewise."

Omar then said, "I'm surprised Theo's not here with you."

Blake said, "Yeah, I spoke with him earlier about trying to make it, but he's still under the weather. You sure you don't want a run at it?"

The other guy that was there decided he would just sit out for a while, then Blake took the opportunity to get Omar isolated in a one-on-one competition; something he preferred to do anyway, having been told about Omar's reputation. He had been chomping at the bit to find out for himself.

"Look, why don't we just play to eleven; just to get warmed up?"

Omar thought for a moment, handed Rob his ball, then turned his back to the goal…

"Ok, let's do it."

Blake felt as if he had been handed a loaded weapon and Omar was his target judging from how he jostled Omar's 40+ year old frame around like they were in a demolition derby. Omar did have enough skill to mount a three point lead over Blake because of his ball handling ability and a killer mid-range jumper. For an older guy he still had impressive skills. It seemed to frustrate Blake somewhat as he tried to get inside Omar's head with the trash talking, but Omar was disciplined enough to ignore it and remained focused. After scoring his next point, He felt he'd return the favor and managed a little trash talking of his own.

"What's the matter young blood? Running out of gas?"

Blake seemed desperate now as Omar had gotten inside his head. It was clear he must have under estimated him, and it was costing him some embarrassment, which he probably was not accustomed to.

Blake said, "Careful old man. Don't hurt yourself."

He scored three consecutive points closing the margin to a one point lead for Omar, but then suddenly, his style of play looked less like basketball and more like a brawl; and it seemed personal. It was clear he wasn't accustomed to losing, especially to who he felt was an inferior opponent. Rob and the other guy stopped their shoot-around; turning their attention to the game. He had knocked Omar down twice and clipped his ankle while driving to the basket. He made sure he scored first before even checking to see if Omar was ok. He then turned around slowly with the ball in the air; Glaring at Omar with a scowl as if he could have slammed the ball on the side of his face. The expression quickly vacated his countenance, remembering where he was, then tucked the ball under his arm.

He asked Omar, "You ok, old man?"

He reached his hand out to help him up, but was obviously

more concerned about winning than any injuries Omar may have sustained.

Omar said, "I think I may have twisted my ankle a little; think I'll sit for a while."

"Ok. I'm gonna get a bottle of water from the car. Sorry I don't have enough to go around."

"It's ok. There's a water fountain right over there."

Omar knew it was best he do a little acting with Blake to exit the competition early. He didn't like the vibe he was getting from him. He had even more cause for alarm when Blake returned with his bottled water. It was wrapped in a towel along with a pair of loafers. He sat next to him with the towel between them. Omar suddenly was uncomfortable with him. He felt his behavior on the court was unsettling for just a pick-up game. Blake said nothing; apparently savoring his victory as if he had bested an opponent in some major tournament. Omar decided to crack the wall of silence thinking he needed to try and clear the way for it, but also to vie for much needed reassurance concerning Blake's temperament.

He then said, "Looks like you haven't lost much, if anything, when it comes to your skills brother."

Blake just rocked his head back and gave him a quizzical look, as if the thought of him losing any of his skills was a ridiculous notion. He decided to unfold one end of the towel to expose the water and the partial sole of one shoe. When he took the water out, the sole of the shoe was fully exposed and revealed a heel that showed an obvious discoloration from what looked like the shape of steel taps. Omar noticed it and bolted upright almost immediately. His uneasiness about Blake, from the day they met, may have become a little hyperactive suddenly, but He felt with that revelation, his time on the court with him may have truly been a dance with the devil. He yelled to Rob letting him know he felt he should probably leave to nurse his ankle.

"Sorry to spoil the party, but I'd better get back to get some ice on this ankle."

Rob said, "Got a little too rough out there, huh?"

"Yeah, for my taste anyway."

Blake turned to him with a bland expression and said, "Hope your ankle gets better soon."

Omar looked back at him and just rocked his head back, faking a hobble. Then he told Rob, in an agitated tone, "Let's get the hell out of here."

Chapter 11

OMAR FELT A LOT safer once he was back in his own apartment. He had survived what could have turned into a brawl with Blake at the basketball courts. He felt his suspicions about him were probably justified. Even though he faked his injury, Blake had succeeded in at least wounding his pride a little. Omar had never been bounced around that way before, especially over a pick-up game. He could easily accept Blake feeling a little intimidated by his competiveness and eventually laughing it off, but was surprised by his hostility toward him. The look on Blake's face when he stood over him at the courts, after he had knocked him down for the last time, didn't exactly raise his comfort level either. His eyes suddenly seemed black with rage, and he wore an angry scowl that became the window for his aggression; but just as quickly, the expression disappeared; like goblins being chased away by the appearance of angels. Omar was perplexed. They had only met that one time when Chris introduced him to the team. Their meeting wasn't exactly memorable, but it wasn't hostile either. There was no reason Blake should treat him like an adversary; at least none he was aware of, which made him even more curious now about that imprint he noticed on the sole of his shoe at the courts. If the person he saw outside his apartment in the parking lot some days earlier was stalking him, then he felt even better about having a new friend, who happened to own a gun, living across the hall from him. He felt he'd better switch gears before letting his preoccupation with Blake ruin his day, so he decided to take a chance and call Theo just to see how he was feeling. He really didn't have an ulterior motive, but did actually feel concern for his friend who he hadn't talked to in some days. The subject of the video wasn't as important as him simply wanting to know if he was alright. He realized finally, that Theo deserved better than being treated like some chore he needed to just get out of the way, and real friends didn't exactly come a dime a dozen. Theo picked up after only two ring tones. He coughed a little before answering, and sounded like the 'bug' had a firm grip on him.

"Hey Theo—it's Omar. I heard about you being under the weather, and called just to see how you were feeling."

Omar could hear him sighing between his coughing and sneezing.

"Omar, why are you even bothering to call me? "

"Ok look, I'm not gonna pretend I don't know what you're talking about. I guess I do deserve that comeback after dismissing you the way I have lately."

Theo said, "You've talked with Evelyn about me haven't you?"

"Yeah, I did, and I really feel bad about not being straight with you on some things."

Theo said sarcastically, "I guess you needed a little extra motivation to see the light, huh?"

"Yeah, maybe I did; but it wasn't the only thing that made me realize you deserved better than what I was giving, and I'm sorry. I like to think of you as a friend Theo; A better friend than I deserve right now, but I wanted to say I'm sorry; sorry I haven't given you the respect you deserve. I just hope we can still be friends. I've been walking around with a lot of baggage for years, and it's interfered with my judgment to say the least, when it comes to people mostly, but that's changing."

"What kind of baggage are you talking about?"

Omar replied, "Stuff that goes back for decades man. I won't go into details. Just know that I'm finally getting help to deal with it; real help, and just try to be patient with me if you can. I wasn't gonna bring it up today, but there's a place for you in the video production we're doing, if you're still interested."

"What place would that be? Now that I'm down with this bug, nobody's going to want to come near me."

Omar said, "I know about your experience in those theatre groups, and you can still contribute with your creative input. You know our first walk-through on location is Monday. Evelyn's nephew is shooting it for us, but I can make sure you have a chance to look at what he's filmed and maybe give us feedback on the actors' performances, or whatever. You can be our 'creative consultant'. How about that?"

"I'm not hung up on titles Omar, but I do appreciate you asking and I'll help in any way I can, ok?"

"Thanks Theo. By the way, I saw Blake at the courts today; said he talked to you earlier." "Yeah, he called; said he was hoping he'd see you there so he could clean your clock. He made it sound like he's already got an axe to grind with you. Did you guys have words already?"

"No we didn't, which is why this is so strange."

Theo asked, "Why what is so strange?"

Omar said, "I didn't want to say anything but he got a little rough with me today in a one-on-one; he had this 'hit man' mentality that came out of nowhere. I didn't want to hang around for the finale, thinking I might not leave in one piece, so my neighbor and I just left. You're getting to know him pretty well aren't you? I mean, you guys talk right?"

"Yeah, we talk, about girls mostly; nothing earth shattering. Why?"

"How does he seem to you? I mean, does it seem like he's playing with a full deck?"

Theo replied, "You mean like, if he's nuts or something?" Theo laughed a little.

"I can't say that. I do know he's a little touchy about some things; like not wanting to talk about his family much. He sort of shuts down when it comes to that. It's almost like he's ashamed to talk about them. When we first started talking he opened up a little."

Theo coughed and wheezed between phrases, but was committed to the conversation now. It seemed like old times again, and it appeared the breach between them was close to being repaired.

Theo said, "He said his mom was a big time executive with some pharmaceutical company, but his dad had gotten hurt real bad at his old job, and works somewhere now doing odd jobs. He said even though they live in the same town, they don't really see each other or talk much. He wouldn't say anything else about it. It seemed to really depress him, so I backed off."

Theo had provided clues to unravelling the mystery about Blake, but Omar missed it. He was just glad he and Theo seemed to be back on speaking terms. He had begun to feel the coughing was wreaking havoc on Theo's throat and decided to end the conversation.

"Well, I'm gonna let you go; sounds like your throat's taking a beating man."

Theo said, "I'll live. Soup and hot tea always makes me feel better when these things come calling; just has to run its course I guess."

"Well, if I don't see you Monday I'll at least let Evelyn know you've agreed to help, and can expect input from you on the video."

Theo said, "Ok chief; sounds like a plan. Oh, and Omar?"

"Yeah Theo?"

"Thanks for calling."

When Omar put his phone on the counter, he reached to pick up clean linen from the big chair that had not been folded yet before he left with Rob. It was an awkward stance that caused him to put too much weight on his left foot and he felt a slight pain from it. He was a little surprised by it, thinking he had escaped any real injury from being jostled by Blake at the courts; then again, maybe he was just suffering from a hyper-active imagination. It felt real enough; a mild sprain maybe, but didn't appear to be swollen. So before doing anything else, he managed to grab his ice pack from the freezer, sat on the sofa, wrapped the ankle with the ice pack inside, and rested his leg on top of the foot stool. College Game Day broadcasts were up and running, but he only wanted to watch once the games actually started. UCF would be playing Grambling at 1:00pm in South Florida but he had almost an hour to wait before kickoff. He decided he'd try and do without the noise until then and take in the silence while he laid there for at least 20 minutes or so. His imagination would only lead him to one place; reliving the drama at the basketball courts. Blake had become a real mystery and it dawned on him that he could have been in real danger not really knowing much about the guy. He scooted a little to get more comfortable, as his head plunged into the cushiony backrest of the couch. He stared at the ceiling; aimlessly stroking his beard again and casually wiping new beads of perspiration from his bare arms and forehead with the hand towel he used at the courts. The perspiration was almost mysterious to him since it occurred inside an apartment that had been cooled to a frigid 69 degrees; but it was a cold sweat and an obvious sign of his uneasiness about his safety. He felt he needed to stay put and let the coolness of the ice around his ankle do its thing. He also knew that he had no real evidence that could point the finger at any one particular person that had it in for him. He decided not to give life to a 'boogeyman' that may not even exist by letting his imagination put a name and face to him, at least for the moment. He focused instead on his narration for the festival and how he might need to adlib much of his presentation to sound unscripted. He then remembered how that talent was something that he struggled with as a fairly new member of the team of lab techs at Dillon Industries, and how he was selected to be a spokesman for a marketing film the company was ready to produce. His communication training had become common knowledge among the staff and he seemed a shoe-in for the company's public relations and media department, but his trials at it were unremarkable to say the least. It turned out to be too much, and too soon for him. The attention seemed to intimidate him. He realized that being behind a microphone, like during his college radio segment, and invisible to his audience, was far less demanding than being on camera with notes and a teleprompter. His attempt at it was more like watching a 'Bloopers Reel' and he had to try and live with the embarrassment of being dropped from consideration. He felt he at least may have avoided jokes about it by the people he worked more closely with. His success at it was something most co-workers thought would be a forgone conclusion, but instead they were disappointed at the thought of not seeing his face on camera. They got over it though, and returned to business as usual afterward; appreciating the good work he did do as a lab tech. Omar however couldn't quite let go of what he felt was a colossal failure. His eyes were suddenly fixed and unblinking. The shadow of foreboding had overtaken him as the vaulted chalky colored ceiling above him became the portal for another trip into his past. He tugged on his beard nervously; wishing his imagination might respond to his plea, and halt the arrival of this particular episode. For this trip inside what seemed like Death Valley, he yearned for mercy, hoping to be spared the anguish of having to relive details of that fateful day. His eyes closed partially with a sullen appearance; the bleakness of descending shadows had suddenly replaced the bright light of his consciousness.

"OMAR, THESE SAMPLES FROM the animal lab needed to be run like yesterday. 'Reliability' has been asking for them since Wednesday morning. Weren't these given to you a couple of days ago to handle?"

"Yes sir, they were and I'm sorry. I'll get on it right away."

David, the Senior Lab Tech, had mentored Omar since he started there, and felt he needed to mention his less than stellar work ethic lately.

"Hold up a minute. Look, it's not like you to be late with workups from your samples. You're usually early, but it's been three days in a row now. Is there something you wanna talk about?"

Omar replied, "No—Just a few things on my mind Dave; nothing you'd be interested in."

"News Flash young man—If it's affecting your performance, well yeah, it does interest me. Better to avoid a counseling letter in your file while there's still a chance to fix the problem, don't you think?"

He gave Omar a serious look, then smiled slightly. "It's ok.— You can talk to me."

Omar put down the tray he was handling on a small metal roll-away table, then shoved his hands in the pockets of his lab coat in frustration.

He then said, "I blew it. I just blew it, and—and I don't know how I could have let it happen."

David replied, "Look man, everybody knows how disappointed you are in not being selected for the film, but it's not the end of the world. Just don't hang your professional hat on that experience. There will be other opportunities for you."

Omar was still hung up on it and said, "I took too much for granted I think."

Dave tried to repel the doubt that had started to consume him by stroking his ego a little...

"The rest of us kind of always thought of you as somebody more suited for a bigger stage anyway. You know, the Inside Edition type."

Then he nudged him in his side with a broad smile. Omar was not amused.

He then said, "I should have brushed up, but I was too cocky;

too sure of myself." He turned away from Dave then leaned against the wall with his arms folded.

"I really screwed up big time, and I let you guys down too."

"Omar, you gotta get over this man. It's affecting your work. Look, we don't think any less of you because of what happened, but you've gotta move on, ok?"

Dave checked his body language. He picked up vibes that led him to believe there was more to Omar's obsessing over his performance at the audition for the company's film.

"Is that the whole story Omar? Is that all there is to this, problem?"

Omar said slowly, and unconvincingly, with an unsettled look, "Yeah, that's all there is."

"Well, just put it behind you then, and get focused, ok? I really would hate to have this discussion again. Get to work on those samples for me."

Dave patted him on the shoulder and left him alone. He had finished the samples two hours later, but still stressed over the unsettled chapter of this saga he chose not to disclose. A midline supervisor on another floor had started to double-down with his badgering of Omar, and his mission of maligning his character even more. It was especially hard to deal with because of who this person was; a character from his childhood, whose attitude toward him had not mellowed, but had morphed into something even more sinister. It was non-other than Deon, the bully, who had beat him down on a regular basis as a kid, and whose memory of that time had not grown so trivial that he no longer got a rush from it. He seemed to gloat over the fact that he had authority over Omar as a supervisor this time and was more persuaded to commit the abuse because of it. Omar walked hurriedly from the 'Reliability Department' after delivering the samples and headed toward the elevator, but it was also on the same floor as Deon's unit. Deon noticed him from a few feet away and pounced on the opportunity.

"Hey matchsticks, what's the hurry?"

Omar turned slowly in his direction. "Look, I told you, don't call me that, ok?"

Deon still seemed to tower over Omar as an adult. They both seemed to have growth spurts that mirrored their childhood years, but Omar had fleshed out with more muscle this time; evidence of his conditioning as an athlete.

Deon said, "Hey don't get so defensive."

Deon rocked his head back, as Omar ignored him and started to approach the hallway leading to the elevators.

Deon shouted, "Heard about you tanking on the audition for the company's film. I knew you weren't a good fit when I heard about it."

He chuckled with a menacing smirk on his face. Omar stopped, then turned and started to walk toward him slowly.

He then asked, "What did you say?"

"I said, this is the real world Mr. Duncan. Not for college egg heads like you to try and dabble in. You should go back to your Frat house and play."

Deon started to laugh out loud. It got the attention of everybody within several feet of them, but he didn't let up. It was as if he was facing him down again during another one of those epic beat-downs after school many years ago, but the physical battering had been replaced with words this time that were more blistering.

Omar said, "Do you even know how long I've been out of college dipstick? Just shut up about it you understand?"

Deon said, "Or what? It's the same reason you've never been promoted. Just can't stand to really be challenged, about anything, and always moping when things don't go your way."

Omar stared at him, with his fists clinched slightly. Deon noticed and tamped down his assault. He seemed to become serious suddenly, and scolded Omar about his attitude.

"Stop thinking there are no rules that you should be bothered with trying to follow, when the rest of us do every day of the week. That's life, man."

He stepped closer and stared Omar in the eyes followed by a verbal thrashing—"Nobody's gonna give you anything. You gotta pay your dues and earn it; you get my drift?"

Omar responded with, "What do you know, crybaby?"

Deon balked at that remark. The confrontation had become a sideshow for onlookers, not thinking it would erupt into violence.

"Crybaby? What are you talking about?"

"I know about you, back in the day; whining like some toddler from being smacked around by some guy downtown."

"Where'd you get that from? Was it that flatfoot Breeland?"

Omar then said, "Don't talk that way about him ok? He was my best friend. You don't mention him, you understand?"

"Oooh—Looks like I struck a nerve. Yeah, I see why you two were so close; you were two of a kind. He was a knucklehead too."

Deon then started to laugh again and didn't seem to stop, but he had stopped. Omar was dazed by the comments about Breeland and kept hearing the laughter, in his mind. Deon decided to thrust the daggers even deeper with a claim that sent Omar over the edge.

"I even ended up with your girl; the one you could only fantasize about; almost pleaded with me to get her pregnant; said she didn't want to be caught with a biological clock that just stopped ticking all of a sudden."

Omar interrupted sharply, "She had a kid for you?"

"Yeah Sherlock, but I got double for my trouble if you know what I mean. Priscilla never would have given you the time of day. She was too slick; way out of your league man. You were just too dumb to realize it."

Omar had stepped outside of himself, and what happened next came out of nowhere. As Deon turned thinking he had ended it, Omar's fist caught his right shoulder....

He shouted, "I told you to shut up you snake!"

His fists were finding their target as he flailed relentlessly striking Deon several times in his abdomen and a stout punch to his forehead that sounded like something had cracked when it landed. Deon tried to run but was dazed as Omar tossed a scented candle at him from a nearby desk that was still inside its metal stand, striking him on his nose, creating a stream of blood that seeped inside his facial hair. Omar was a man possessed. He said nothing, but with a crazed look in his eyes, seemed to be acting out the revenge he always wanted to inflict on Deon from all the times he willingly took punishment from him as a kid. Deon had fallen and was on the floor writhing in pain, and seemed unable to defend himself as Omar's arms moved in rapid fire motion until three young men rushed up and pulled him off, but not before a swift kick struck Deon's lower back causing him to jerk uncontrollably for a few moments. They pinned him against the wall next to Deon and a few feet away from him, thinking his feet might take a shot at Deon's head. He wrestled with them for a few minutes before finally settling down as a Security Team rushed up to apprehend him. When he realized what he had done, watching several people crowd around Deon who seemed to be lying still and unresponsive, he pressed his palms against his ears as if trying to silence the voices inside his head lamenting over his meltdown. He began to sob openly then whispered in broken phrases as he stared at Deon, then at the men who had restrained him...

"Oh no, what have I done? "

The security officers loosened their restraint on him noticing he was no longer a danger to anyone. One of the security officers, who knew Omar, grabbed him by the forearm.

He then said, "We'll have to call your supervisor to let them know what happened, but you'll need to come with us to the security office for now, ok Omar?"

Omar nodded his consent. His lips slightly contorted and trembling; trying to wrap his brain around the assault he had just carried out. He continued to look back at Deon's still body as a medical team had also been called to assess his injuries.

He kept repeating, "I don't know what just happened. I—I just don't know. He's gonna be alright isn't he?"

He sighed heavily, looking down for the most part, then said, "That wasn't me."

Turning to one of them, then the other several times, he repeated..."It just wasn't. You have to believe me."

The two men just looked at each other with pitiful expressions, feeling some type of intervention might be needed for Omar. Dave, his team leader, had been called in place of his immediate supervisor and arrived at the security office when they did. The officers sat him down at a large rectangle table inside what appeared to be a small meeting room draped only in shades of grey from floor to ceiling. It also happened to be reflective of Omar's mood. Omar sat quietly and unresponsive. Dave questioned him while the two officers left the room for a moment.

"Omar, what happened?"

Omar stared aimlessly and said nothing. "You could be facing assault charges. Are you aware of that?" He still sat quietly; shaking his head in disbelief. "Talk to me Omar. Just tell me what happened."

Dave had his arm across the back of Omar's chair as if to try and console him, but dropped it when the two security officers returned.

"We've talked to witnesses who came forward and said as far as they could tell, the two had words but nothing that should have provoked the attack. Protocol calls for immediate 3 day suspension for fighting until things get sorted out as to what provoked it, and the Director agrees. We were on the phone with him before we came back in. We'll also need to escort him out to make sure he exits the building. That's also protocol. Just so you know, we're keeping this in-house for now."

Dave said, "I understand. What's the condition of the guy he injured?"

"He's in the infirmary. He got banged up pretty bad, but should be ok, in time. His next of kin is on the way here to get him checked out by his own doctor from what I've been told."

"Does he intend to press charges?"

"Too early to tell. I guess you'll know before too long though."

After taking Omar's statement, they had him sign a couple of affidavits, then collected his lab coat and badge.

One of them asked Omar, "Can you drive yourself?"

Omar replied just above a whisper, "Yeah, I can drive myself."

"We'll have to escort you out of the building, but you'll need to leave the premises, ok?"

He said again, "Yeah, I got it."

Dave then said, "I'll go up and get your belongings and bring them down to you."

"Ok, thanks man."

As they were walking him out, Dave said, "We'll sort this out Omar, ok? We will."

Omar nodded then barely kept pace with the officers, still with a dazed look on his face. It seemed the entire population at Dillon was aware of the incident by this time and the action seemed to come to a dead stop as he and the security officers approached the main lobby. As the three of them crossed the archway that led to the infirmary, Omar's Uncle Seth was entering the building from behind them and heading that way in a hurry. They had just missed noticing each other by only a few seconds. As the three of them approached the entrance, someone at the canteen had dropped a bucket of ice, spilling the cubes into the edge of the area.

THE SOUND OF THE ice hitting the ceramic tiles brought him back from his time warp as the bag containing the ice against his ankle had become undone and spilled almost all of the cubes on the hardwood floor. He sat up quickly and dropped to his knees to retrieve the cubes that had spilled several feet on all sides of him.

Thinking out loud he said, 'Ah!, clumsy oaf', as he scrambled in frustration to collect them all. He sat quietly on the couch again after putting the cubes away, and decided at that point he would try and fill the rest of his day with enough mundane things to keep him from becoming idle. It seemed to be the gateway for his flashbacks, and he was at his wits end at trying to stop them altogether. He realized he still had plenty of work to do with his narration for the video, and decided he would dedicate the rest of the weekend to it.

Omar was committed to avoiding more trips into his 'time portal', and realized having a more amicable attitude couldn't hurt; starting with the bus driver, Vick…

"Hey Vick. How is it?" He high-fived him and said good morning to everybody…

"Hello Mr. Duncan. You're smiling. Looks like your weekend must have been o.k."

"Yeah, it was. Got a lot done for a change. How was yours?"

Vick said, "Nothing to write home about, and I must be allergic to Mondays. They always seem to hang on and take forever to end; like a bad cold you just can't wait to get rid of, you know?"

"I know that's right."

Someone yelled, "Omar!"

He looked down the aisle and saw Micki beckoning to him. He was glad to finally see her again, still making his way back to her row as the bus was pulling away…

"Hey stranger. So where have you been? Thought you had put us down."

He sat next to her quickly as the bus rocked and swayed almost knocking him against her as it made a sudden maneuver to avoid a pedestrian.

Micki jokingly said, "Missed me that much, huh?"

He replied, "Sometimes I feel it wouldn't hurt to have seatbelts in these things, you know?"

"And how are you sir?"

Omar replied, "I'm good. So, what's up? I thought maybe you had your own wheels or something."

She said, "I wish. I've been at a workshop for that Company I told you about who wants to help small businesses out. I finished it Saturday. Gonna get mentored by one of their pros too to walk me through my progress. It's more than I could have ever expected."

Omar said, "Sounds like you struck gold."

She said, "Seems that way; which reminds me, I wanted to talk to you about producing a radio spot for me. It's one of the things the workshop stressed about marketing. It should go a long way to help me get exposure to a larger clientele. How about it?"

Omar seemed to ignore her question as Vick was pulling up to Rupert's bus stop but he wasn't among the passengers waiting at the shelter.

Omar noticed it and said, with a little suspicion, "I guess Rupert's put us down now."

Micki said, "I don't think so. He's probably starting his workshop this week. I know he was expected to commit when I last spoke with him. It'll be a good thing for him too."

"Oh, I see."

Omar somehow didn't share her optimism. He tried to be upbeat and positive about what she had just said, but couldn't shake the annoying feeling that Rupert might possibly be his stalker. Micki sat back in her seat, a little taken aback by the fact that Omar had ignored her question about doing a spot for her shop. She had hoped he'd really be excited for her and would jump at the chance. She noticed he seemed to have checked out, apparently pre-occupied; thinking about something else. She knew his habit of stroking his beard was a dead give-away. As the bus was approaching her stop, she decided to ask him again about doing the spot.

She asked him again about the radio spot, but with a little agitation this time..

"Did you even hear what I said back there about doing the spot for my shop?"

It was obvious he had tuned her out when he asked, "I'm sorry Mick, what did you say?"

"Never mind. Have a good day. Maybe I'll see you tomorrow."

The early morning blitz to get to his office was at its peak when he made it to the south entrance. It was the preferred route by Earth Burst employees who always shaved it close to the 8:00am bell; mostly by necessity if they took public transportation like he did. It did allow them to avoid the traffic from employees of two other companies who were on the main floor and at the opposite side of the building. Omar always liked to be on his floor at least a little early when he had his own wheels to avoid the bottlenecks. If things went as he had hoped, he would only have to endure the bus rides for another two weeks before getting his license back, as long as he kept his nose clean. The morning bustle was a mixture of conversation that hummed along in surround sound, interrupted by sporadic outbursts of high pitched laughter, and the random cadence of high heels hitting the Mediterranean tiled floor of the lobby. Omar had just gotten through the doors and headed for the elevators when he detected the distinct sound of 'taps' suddenly. How he was able to distinguish the subtlety of that sound above the others, that had already bombarded his hearing, surprised even him. He did not bother to look around to see where it may have been coming from but simply reacted and walked a little faster to get to the elevators. He stood in front of it for only a few moments, but relaxed, realizing he was in the company of familiar faces. When he turned around as the sound tapered off, he noticed it was coming from the shoes of a uniformed deputy headed in the direction of the canteen. He was curious as to why he was even on the premises since there were only private companies that had space in the building. Just as the elevator chime announced its arrival, Omar noticed the deputy handling his cell phone. He appeared to be placing a call to someone as he stood in front of the counter at the canteen. His surveillance ended when the elevator doors opened and he stepped inside for the trip to his floor. The deputy had ordered coffee and a Danish and sat inside the canteen while he waited for something, or someone. He checked his watch a few times, impatiently, and was putting the final piece of the Danish in his mouth when the man he waited for walked up. They greeted each other with a firm handshake, but the Deputy seemed agitated from the start. The young man hung his head in shame from what was to be his chastisement over certain behavior from him that was apparently taking place much too often.

"Your mom called me again; said you harassed some guys at a pool hall over some petty nonsense. You've got to stop this. This town is not even my jurisdiction, but she wants to make sure you're not looking out from the inside of some jail cell if it keeps up, and so am I. Look, I know you don't really have the relationship with your dad that you'd like because of his—well, because of his situation, but you can't expect me to rescue you every time this sort of thing happens either."

"I know Uncle, and I'm sorry. It's just that I wish things were different between them, in spite of dad's situation."

The Deputy said, "And I feel you on that. I do, but you can redirect your frustration and anger onto other things without always wanting to pound somebody's head when you get the urge."

He clasped his hands together and confided in his uncle.

"You know every time this happens, I'm really only thinking about how to avenge what happened to him. Trying to decide on a 'just punishment' seems to be the only thing that matters to me, especially after what I found out recently."

The Deputy replied, "Well, that in itself is enough to let you know it's something you should just forget about. There's no upside to what you feel you should do about it, except to try and get to the place your dad is at emotionally. I know it's not easy, but you should try, like the rest of us that care about him are also doing; for his sake."

"I am trying, but you're right; it's not so easy."

The Deputy asked, "You're still on your meds aren't you?"

The young man said, "Yeah, I'm still taking them."

"You make sure that doesn't change, you understand? You're on them for a good reason. And forget about this vengeance thing that's festering inside of you. I don't know if you think you can finger a particular person for what happened to your dad, but you forget about that you understand? That can only spell heartache for you and everybody else."

"Yes sir—My shift is starting, so I've got to get upstairs; talk to you later?"

The Deputy's tone had mellowed when he said, "If you'd like. I'm never so busy that I can't talk to you."

He stood up and put his hat on, then shifted his gun belt a little…

"I'll call your mom later today to let her know we talked. See ya kid, and say hello to your brother for me."

They shook hands again then went their separate ways….

"EVELYN, IS IT MY imagination, or did you change your hair again?"

"No Chip. I'm not that vain about it; just didn't have time to, you know, fuss with it after it got a little damp. Truth is, I need to get back to the salon so they can fix it for me."

"Well, for what it's worth, I was still complimenting you."

"Why thank you sir."

Nadine joined them at the next elevator stop and asked her the same thing…

"Hey—Did you change your hair again?"

"No I didn't. Just didn't know what to do with it I guess."

Chip and Nadine smiled at her, then at each other just to see if it would make her uncomfortable…

Evelyn then said with a serious expression, "Looks like crap doesn't it?"

They both put their hands to their chins, as if looking more critically at her hair..

Then Nadine said, "Now that you mentioned it—"

Then she and Chip laughed out loud as the elevator reached Chip's floor.

Before getting off he said, "Alright superstars; have a great day."

Blake happened to be on the floor chatting with Regis, the other supervisor, about installs that were set up for that day in his unit. Some of Clarence's team were also scheduled for installations of new desktops before the end of the day. Nadine winked at Blake as they passed them…

She then said, "I think I want to adopt him Evelyn."

Evelyn said, "Why do I keep having this vision of you being escorted out of here for sexual assault on a minor?"

Nadine said, "Nothing wrong with window shopping."

Evelyn then said, "If I don't catch you at afternoon break, I'll see you at the company park later. Don't' be late."

Omar was already at his desk and setting up when Evelyn walked up….

"Hey Mr. Duncan."

"Oh, hey Ev; ready for that dry run today?"

She replied, "I guess. Good thing we changed the time; wouldn't have had much day light otherwise."

Omar said, "I happened to speak with Theo over the weekend. I think we've got an understanding now, and he's agreed to help with the video any way he can. I told him he could be our creative consultant. He said he wasn't hung up on titles, but I really wasn't being sarcastic when I said it. I think maybe he thought I was, just a little."

"Well, I'm glad you two got through your own rough patch. He's a good guy."

Omar said, "Yeah, he is."

Evelyn was getting ready to walk away when she paused and asked, "Wanna break at ten to see if the script needs any fine tuning?"

"Ok, sounds like a plan."

Clarence walked up in the middle of their chat. "Morning guys."

"Hey Cee Cee."

Clarence said, "Omar I need to see you before you log on, ok?"

Omar replied, "On my way."

Evelyn had gotten used to the abrupt meetings between them, especially when she and Omar happened to be talking about something. It was annoying at first, but then again, she couldn't overlook his prerogative as their boss either, even if it was about the sponsorship. She shrugged it off then walked to her cubicle. Omar sat in his usual chair inside Clarence's office not sure if he was already in trouble over something.

Clarence asked, "Have a good weekend?"

Omar said, "It was ok; got some things done."

Clarence said, "I wanted to give you one more chance to reconsider the trip to Dillon tomorrow. I think it might help you resolve some conflicts you're having about what went down there."

"I don't think so Cee Cee. I'm trying to bury that part of my past."

Clarence responded, "Can I be honest? I don't think you're doing a very good job of that."

Omar asked, "How do you mean?"

"Those times when you seem to just check out, like you're in another world or something. Other people have noticed it too. Am I wrong?"

Omar said, "Look, I've got a few things going on right now that I'd like to get behind me; like getting my license back, beating my drinking problem, and finishing my schooling. I could be thinking about any one of those things at any given time that might distract me."

Clarence said, "But those things are kind of detached from this sponsorship campaign. No, I'm referring to something that may be directly connected to your experience there. I haven't forgotten how uneasy you became when I first mentioned Dillon as a sponsor, so I don't think you've quite put things behind you, as you said."

"You're beating a dead horse Cee Cee."

Clarence sighed before unloading the bombshell.

"Just so you know, your old fling, Priscilla Eagan, is the Public Relations Director for Dillon; found that out when I was there the other week. You may have to go through her for this campaign."

"Priscilla? She works there? How did you find out about —?"

Clarence interrupted—"I actually said hello to her at the visitor's center, but more than that, I overheard her and an associate talking while I was there."

"About me?"

Clarence said, "Indirectly, yeah. She said that—"

Omar interrupted him this time—"You don't have to tell me. I don't want to know."

Clarence said, "Look, it may be your chance to set things straight with her. Somehow I get the feeling you guys have a history that's still not settled yet."

He responded sharply, "Don't concern yourself Cee Cee! Really, it's ok."

"Whatever you say. I'll reach out to her office to let them know our team will be in touch." Omar stood to his feet suddenly—"Is that it?"

Clarence said, "Yeah, that's all."

Omar walked out with a rigid posture, and with fists clinched so tight his palms were almost a rosy red. He was definitely rattled over the news about Priscilla. He sat at his desk, brushing his hair back several times; staring at a blank computer screen. He knew he couldn't let himself get lost in the revival of his animosity toward her, so he took a moment to call his friend Noggin from his AA group about hitching a ride home with him after Thursday's meeting. It would take his mind off of her, and maybe foil the plans of whoever might have ideas about trying to ambush him that night….. "Hey Noggin, it's Omar from the AA group."

"Oh, hey man. How is it?"

Omar said, "I'm good. Listen, I wanted to know if I could maybe hitch a ride with you back home after Thursday's meeting."

"Ok. Well, let me get back with you on that, because I might not be headed in that direction right after the meeting."

Omar said, "Alright then. Can you let me know maybe by Wednesday? That way I can make other arrangements for a ride if I need to."

Noggin said, "That's a bet. You'll hear from me one way or the other ok?"

Omar said, "Thanks man. I appreciate it."

Omar felt a little uneasy throughout the day. Even during the morning break with Evelyn he revived his old habits of detaching from whatever may have required his undivided attention at that time. Evelyn wasn't amused and felt that trying to get him to talk about the script was a bust.

She said, "You know it occurred to me that your body is present and accounted for, but your mind is nowhere to be found."

She gave him a serious stare, and he responded.

"Sorry, but I got a bit of news today that was a little unsettling. I should have told you maybe we could actually work through any tweaking of the script at the rehearsal today, if that's Ok."

"It's fine with me, but I gotta tell ya; I'm a little dizzy from your mood swings Omar."

He said, "We'll be ok at rehearsal; I promise."

"Well, the jury is still out on you keeping promises you know."

He looked away; flexing his jaw muscles in frustration over the truth in what she said.

Omar said, "I'll call Richie when we get back, just to make sure we're still on for 4:30 today. I called him about the time change, and told him he should still come inside the lobby and call me when he gets here."

Evelyn checked the wall clock. "It's that time. We'd better get back."

Officer Ronnie Bristol's posture was rigid and official this time when he visited his brother at the small efficiency apartment he rented. It was a decent place, with part of his rent being paid with a portion of his disability subsidy. What little he was expected to pay on his own was done through the First Baptist Church's benevolent fund in exchange for his grounds keeping duties. The job was simply a way to justify the generous contribution to his care without referring to it as a gift. They were pleased to see each other as usual, but the enthusiasm was guarded this time because of the nature of the visit…

Officer Bristol said, "I went by the church, but Mrs. Rueben said you had already been in the chapel for your afternoon prayers; thought maybe you were a little under the weather." Deon wrapped himself in a blanket and plugged in a space heater before he sat in his favorite chair.

"The landlord hasn't fixed the furnace yet, and it may get nippy tonight."

"It's what I heard too. You need anything big brother?"

"You know I travel light. Anyway, the church takes pretty good care of my basic needs; can't expect anything more than that." He sat awkwardly to relieve the stress on his spine. It looked uncomfortable to his brother, but he swore it wasn't.

"I know when your visits are this frequent they're not altogether social. So what's on your mind? Is it my son again?"

"None other. Priscilla called me again about him rough-housing it with some guys at a pool hall. I talked with him yesterday morning and told him I couldn't keep covering for him. He told me he was still taking his meds, but I'm not so sure. The other thing that disturbs me is, I think he might know who your attacker is. He said something about only thinking about what 'just punishment' might look like for him. It didn't sound good. I told him to let it go. I also said, it's what you would want him to do."

"You told him right. It's the one thing I pray for every day; that his disorder won't send him off the rails." The officer just listened realizing the emotional hit his brother was taking from talking about his troubled son.

"I know where he's headed because I had a violent streak when I was young; even as a kid. It's a dead end street. I never told anyone this, but what happened to me that day was most likely instigated by me."

"What are you saying?"

"I'm saying I taunted that guy; had been for years even as kids, and I never let up with him."

"Wait a minute; you're not telling me you deserved what happened to you, are you?"

"No; not saying that, just that I may have lit the fuse that caused the explosion." He adjusted himself in his big chair; pulling his stocking feet up onto the seat with his good arm and staring into space.

"Our father gave me the skinny on him afterward and it forced me to think differently about things; what happened and why. And when I met Pastor and his wife, well, they introduced me to the one who helped me really see the light. I know this might sound crazy to you, but I've never been more content in my life as I am now; with who I am now, inside. I need you to promise me something; that you won't let him dive into that black hole like I did thinking there was no way out. His bipolar disorder may never be cured but it can be controlled, at least that's what the doctors say about it. He'll probably always need help trying to get to a good place emotionally. I rarely see him and his brother now, and I never see their mother. I might as well be dead to her it seems. That's why I trust you'll do the right thing and not abandon him. Promise me you won't, please. You're the one bright light in this Ronnie."

"I promise big brother." He patted his arm affectionately and repeated, "I promise."

Chapter 12

OMAR BUSIED HIMSELF WITH a little housekeeping at his desk until he was ready to meet the cast for the first rehearsal. He had hoped Richie hadn't forgotten about the time change and decided to trust that he would get a call from him any minute. Evelyn saw him on her way to the elevators and approached him...

"Hey, you coming over to the park soon?"

"Hey Ev; just waiting on Richie's call to let me know he's downstairs. I didn't want to seem like a pest by calling to remind him."

"He wouldn't forget—He'll call. I'm meeting Nadine so I'm gonna head down."

"Alright; see you in a bit."

When Evelyn was out of their department his phone rang. It was Richie.

"Hey; it's Richie. I'm inside the lobby across from the canteen."

"Ok, I'm on my way. Evelyn is already on her way down, so I'll see you in a minute."

After locking his desk and collecting his belongings, he looked up and suddenly had a sense of foreboding. He surveyed the floor from one end to the other, and was surprised at how quickly the staff had vacated it. He was the only soul that could be accounted for. He tried to dismiss the eeriness he felt at that moment; imagining the walls starting to slowly close in on him only to collapse suddenly on top of him, pinning him underneath as his nemesis stands victorious atop the rubble .He started walking to the elevators quickly to relieve his anxiety. When he was inside and the doors closed, he breathed a sigh of relief, feeling he had sidestepped the paranoia that was tightening its grip on him. He hoped it would be an express ride down but it stopped at the sixth floor. He moved to one side instinctively near the control buttons just before the doors opened. A tall hooded young man stepped inside. He recognized Omar and looked at him with knitted eyebrows. Omar's glimpse of his face was too momentary to identify him clearly as he focused on the panel for the elevator buttons.

"Headed for the lobby?"

The young man replied in a deep baritone voice, "Yeah, thanks."

His face was partially hidden by what seemed an ominous draping of the hood over his head. He then pulled a pair of dark sunglasses from his pocket and put them on, as though he was already outside in the glaring sunlight. He clasped his hands in front of him, then stepped almost directly behind Omar as the elevator doors closed. Omar was immediately put on alert. This guy seemed a little creepy. He wondered why he would choose to stand directly behind him when they were the only two people on board. It was as though he wanted to conceal his identity (but why?) His imagination went into overdrive wondering if he may have been an employee whose idea of dressing down after his shift also meant needing to remain anonymous. Omar shifted slightly to his right and turned his head to the left, only to fill his peripheral vision with this man, who seemed to be reaching into the pocket of his hoodie but was otherwise as still as a mannequin. Then after a moment, the creaking of the elevator floor from the subtle movement of this man's 'six foot plus' frame was barely audible, but after feeling his lukewarm breath against his neck he knew he had moved much closer to him; too close, for him to feel comfortable. He wondered if this guy could be his stalker. Perhaps the same person that called his extension that afternoon when Clarence was at his desk but wouldn't answer. And maybe the same person in the parking lot of his apartment some nights before. It seemed far-fetched but not improbable. He started to hum random notes to try and relax as the elevator ride seemed like an eternity, then the chime signaled his rescue, as the doors opened to a bustling lobby. He stepped off hurriedly, thinking the man could have been Blake. He was tall like him, but why would he act like a perfect stranger? Then again, why not, given their encounter at the courts? Even then he seemed to morph into someone with destructive tendencies, so it wasn't a stretch. He noticed Richie right away, as Evelyn and Nadine sat at a table inside the canteen. When he picked up his pace he also heard the faint sound of taps behind him. He stopped and turned to see the man from the elevator disappearing behind a column, as the faint sound of taps followed him. Omar was about to chase him when Richie called out, thinking he may not have noticed Him.

"Mr. Duncan!"—Omar felt his opportunity to follow the man was already lost, so he turned toward the canteen and threw up his hand on his way to meet Richie. Evelyn and Nadine were also coming out.

Omar said, "Hey man, how is it? "

"I'm good. Should I follow you over there?"

"Well, I don't have my car back yet so I guess I should ride over with you. Is that okay?"

"Sure, no problem."

Evelyn walked up then said, "We'll just see you there."

Richie noticed Omar looking back behind them a few times as they left the building and on their way to the guest parking lot. Omar had a look of urgency in his eyes that peaked Richie's curiosity…. "Are you looking for somebody else to show up too?"

"What?"

"You keep looking back as if you're expecting to see someone."

"Oh, no. It's nothing." After they had walked out and gotten past the covered circular drive at the edge of the building, Omar could see a hooded figure at the corner of the entrance to the parking garage about a hundred feet away. After a closer look, it appeared to be the guy from the elevator. He wasn't moving, but just stood there with his arms crossed in front of him again. Omar could sense his eyes were locked onto him. He imagined they were the eyes of death. He was shaken, but tried to conceal it realizing then that he most likely had been targeted by this guy. He needed to take every precaution now. The threat seemed too real to ignore. He didn't want to alarm Evelyn any more than she already had been concerning his safety, so he asked Richie if he was ok with dropping him off at the bus stop to catch the last bus.

"You mind dropping me off at the bus stop after rehearsal? It's only about two blocks from here."

"No, I don't mind." He had given this mystery man too much power over him, thinking he could probably follow him anywhere, just waiting on the ideal opportunity to strike. He hadn't quite shaken his uneasiness about it, but decided to hold his peace while they rehearsed for the video. The rehearsal was going much better than expected. Evelyn's thespians seemed more like seasoned pros than novices. They surprised even her, whose work was made much easier by the little direction they needed. They were hitting their spots almost perfectly after the first walk-through. She knew her instincts had served her well after having hand-picked each of them. No one forgot their lines, which was a real concern, so she pumped their egos a little.

"You guys are nailing it. You sound like you really studied each other's lines too. There weren't any awkward pauses in the dia-logue, except for a couple of bobbles, but great job. Let's run through it again and speak just a little louder this time. Richie plans to have a stronger microphone mounted to the camera next time we meet and for the actual shoot, but it still needs to pick up all of you without being right in your faces, ok?"

She glanced over at the sheltered table where Omar was sitting and noticed he almost had his back turned to them, looking off in the distance at something, or someone. She called to him. "Omar, what did you think!?"

"I'm sorry, what!?"

"What did you think about our dry run?"

"Oh, yeah. It was, good—yeah."

She felt he gave the patented answer for someone who sounded like his favorite sporting event had just been interrupted.

"What did you like, or dislike about it? How about a little feedback for these guys from our leader?" She smiled, feeling they really needed very little tweaking, if any, before filming. She needed to hear him utter the words not just for the actors' benefit, but also as a show of confidence in her ability to lead. They all stood by; quiet and attentive with eyes fixed on Omar; like tryouts for a Broadway casting call; patiently waiting to see who made the cut. She was disappointed in his response. He trotted out what sounded like unintelligible babble which meant he was afraid of being honest about his true feelings, or he really hadn't been paying attention. She chose to believe the latter; it would be easier to remedy. She told the group to break for 5 minutes and decided to speak with him privately.

"You know it's obvious you weren't paying attention to their performance, am I right?"

"Ok, I'm busted, but then again, I do have confidence in your own assessment of it."

"Oh, no. You don't get off that easily. Would you at least watch all of it this time, just so you're sure you're ok with it as 'project lead'? You really should you know."

His stomach was tying up in knots. The more urgent business to him was just needing to stay alive, and avoiding his hooded rival who seemed to be as driven as a blood hound. He didn't want to tip Evelyn off, or anyone else either, about possible threats to his safety, so he felt it was best to oblige her…

"Ok—You've got my undivided attention this time."

The second walk through of the script went off without a hitch. After Chip and Nadine's exchange near the end of it, both Evelyn and Omar were really excited about what they had produced. The cast knew they had pulled it off; high-fiving each other after it was over and getting handclaps from Evelyn, Omar, and Richie. The entire infomercial would last only about twelve minutes. The sun had already fallen below the horizon when Evelyn spoke to the actors.

"Great job everybody. You knocked it out of the park today. I believe this video is gonna do what it was intended to do for the company, and I've been around long enough to know that something like this is always good for the resume."

Evelyn wasn't one to be that vocal about the company's agenda, but it seemed to fit since she was as loyal as they come, and more importantly the video was her brainchild. She continued as Omar just listened intently as Evelyn echoed exactly what he was thinking.

"And we'll make sure Clarence gets all of you featured in the company's newsletter after the festival is over, as a show of thanks. You know it's one of the best ways to 'name drop' if you're bucking for a promotion you know."

They all laughed, and so did she and Omar. He had actually taken his mind off of his immediate problem to focus on the job Clarence trusted him to do. Evelyn's comments somehow made it easier to forget, at least for the moment. The comradery this group showed became a safe haven suddenly. It was the kind of setting he chose to steer clear of until today. This would be a refreshing change for him.

Evelyn continued.. "I want to thank my nephew Richie who is volunteering to film this for us."

They all applauded Richie. Some even whistled their approval. He took a bow, grateful for the acknowledgement. Omar smiled, realizing then, when he considered the company of the people he was with and how committed they were to its success, he was getting a pretty hefty dose of what it means to be humble. Evelyn then reminded the group about the final rehearsal on that Wednesday and the actual shoot would probably take place that Friday…

"Everybody good with those days?" Most of them nodded with approval.. "Omar will make sure it can happen for any of you who may have a conflict, ok? Alright, we'll see you guys back here on Wednesday, same time."

Omar thanked them as they were walking off, but Nadine used the opportunity to do her own name dropping on Evelyn's behalf.

She then said, "Ok Omar, now is a good time to get in Clarence's ear about a raise for my girl." She then draped her arm around Evelyn's shoulder. Evelyn appreciated the plug.

Richie then said, "Sounds like a bet to me."

Omar was about to say something when he turned in the direction of the east shelter and saw the hooded man again standing behind the chain link fence. He might as well have been a silhouette as the approaching darkness erased any distinguishable features. He still had his hands in his pockets and did not move. Omar's anxiety had suddenly returned.

"Hey Richie, can I still get that ride to the bus shelter?"

"Whenever you're ready."

"I'm ready now."

Evelyn then said, "I'll see you at the office tomorrow Omar. Have a good night, and thanks for giving this project its due. I'll see you nephew." Evelyn kissed Richie on the cheek and walked to her car. Richie collected his camera and tripod, then he and Omar started walking to his car. Omar kept looking back toward the fence, then all around them but noticeably unsettled.

Richie asked, "Omar, is everything ok? You seem nervous about something."

He didn't want to admit to Richie what may be happening with him. Besides, he didn't feel comfortable telling someone like

Richie about it. Because of the way he treated him at first, he may have felt he had it coming.

"I'm good. Just had a flashback about something. I'll be alright."

Richie was also intuitive and felt something was wrong. When he stopped in front of the shelter, Omar sat for a minute as though he wasn't sure whether he should get out of the car. His stalker probably had followed them there as well, and no one else was there with night fall approaching. He also didn't want to impose on Richie any more than he had. He took his time getting out of the car as he thanked Richie for his help.

"I really appreciate this, and thanks again for your help on the video. I've got a feeling we're gonna get really good feedback from it."

Richie wasn't as cynical to believe that Omar was fishing for a ride home, but just felt he would be rescuing him from something if he did. He just had that kind of heart, so he asked the question Omar really hoped that he would.

"Say, why don't I just give you a ride home? That bus could be really late, or never show up; then you'd be stuck."

"Ah, you don't have to. Besides it may be too far out of your way."

"Well, if you're near Regency park it's not much of a detour at all."

"Well, it just so happens that's where I practice hoops, and so do some of the guys at work sometimes on the weekends. It's only ten minutes from my place."

"Well, buckle up." Omar knew Richie was a Godsend that day. If only he knew what he had helped him avoid. Even though Richie was a 'young blood' he had a nose for trouble, and somehow he already suspected Omar was struggling with an issue he preferred to keep silent about. Richie didn't go as far as escorting him upstairs to his apartment once they got there, but his conscious was telling him Omar may be in real jeopardy. Once inside his apartment, Omar took a quick look down both ends of the hallway, then closed and locked the door quickly, with both locks. He had made it a habit since his first suspicions about a stalker. He threw his satchel on the couch and went to the area of the counter where his mail had been untouched for at least 5 days. He was about to search for the letter from the Olympic Committee Seth kept after him about when there was a knock at his door. He turned on the outside light and noticed it was Rob. When he opened it, Rob seemed a little uneasy.

"Hey Rob, everything ok?"

"Hey, I was on my break again and just left the apartment manager's office. He told me there was a guy at the mailboxes today; a stranger, who seemed suspicious. He said he was caught peering at the boxes as if he was looking for something, or someone's name in particular. When security noticed him and was about to approach him he took off."

"You know I've heard about these guys who wind up with people's social security checks and stuff by heisting their mail."

"I don't think it was anything like that because when security checked the boxes he had only tampered with one. It seemed to be the only one he was interested in, and it happened to be yours."

Omar said, "Really?" , trying desperately not to let his uneasiness about it show.

"Fred said he would leave a note on your box to see him before making it upstairs. This guy apparently tried to 'jimmy' the lock but botched it so bad the keys won't work now. He said it looked like he even tried to pry it open judging from the damage. Fred's not aware we know each other. He was just giving the residents a heads up to be on the look-out for anybody suspicious looking. You should go see him now."

Rob asked him jokingly, "You don't have any arch enemies on the loose do you?"

He grinned a little, but then he noticed the anxiety scorching its way through Omar's coolness like a wildfire. He was suddenly concerned about his safety now and got serious.

Rob then said, "You let me know if you need anything, ok?"

Omar shook his head with a look of desperation in his eyes.

"Ok, man. Thanks for the heads up."

Omar stepped back inside momentarily to grab his keys, then walked down to the manager's office. Fred was at his desk and on the phone with the head of the investment group that owns the building, letting them know about the incident.

"I'll keep a lid on it; wouldn't want something like this to become public knowledge either and drive tenants away. I'll talk to you soon, bye", then hung up.

He noticed Omar at the desk while walking out front.

"Mr. Duncan; saw my note on your mailbox I take it."

"Hey Fred—No, actually my neighbor, Rob, told me about the incident at the mailboxes and said I should come see you. I haven't been down there yet."

"Come on. Let me show you what security found."

He locked the office and they walked down to the area where the mailboxes were.

"Well, you can see everything looks normal except for yours. They even tried to pry it open and just left a mess."

Omar tried to be casual about it and said, "Good thing I didn't get any mail today, huh?"

He knew the situation had become more serious than he may have originally thought. The stalker's interest in him had turned into an obsession.

He asked Fred, "Did you notify the authorities?"

"Of course. They came out, but couldn't pull any prints. The security officer on duty at the time said he noticed the guy at the boxes during his initial pass but thought nothing of it, but during his second one he saw that he was still there and peering into someone's box; most likely yours."

"Why didn't security approach him then?"

"He was about to, when our guy was spooked after he saw him open his door, then double timed it away from there. He said he did notice he seemed to be wearing a law enforcement I.D. badge on his belt."

"You think a cop may have done this?"

"Anything's possible, but he don't live here. The only resident in this complex that's in law enforcement is your friend Rob."

Fred shook his head while tugging on the jagged metal that was once Omar's box, then looked at Omar and asked, "Any ideas?"

Omar said, "Not a clue."

"Could just be a random attack, but who knows. I'm having the door and lock replaced and will get the new key to you when it's done. I don't have a vacant box I can give you, so I'll collect whatever mail comes for you in the meantime myself, and let you know if you have any that needs picking up, ok?"

"Ok, thanks Fred." Just before they split, and Omar was walking back to his apartment, Fred remembered something else about the intruder.

"Oh, there's one other thing which is kind of odd."

"What's that?"

"Security said the guy must have been wearing taps on his shoes; At least that's what it sounded like as he was getting away. Imagine that—For somebody who's trying not to be so obvious, he got really careless."

Omar winced, then shook his head and thought, 'Or he may have just left his calling card.' He started to stroll back to his apartment, in no big hurry. He had begun to feel almost like prey who couldn't avoid being hemmed in by this predator, no matter where he found himself. He suffered a momentary lapse that could have invited his peril, thinking there was little he could do to stop him. With his head down, driven only by his despair, he couldn't help but wonder why it was even happening to him. His own behavior was so often riddled with completely undeserved opinions about certain people in his life. Opinions frayed with hostility, but left to rot from gross neglect; neglect by an un-forgiving spirit inside the souls of those same people. Souls that could probably enrich his life if he would let them, but instead seemed only suited for his bonfire of tattered egos. If his suspicions were correct, it was most likely the thing that incited the stalker's relentless pursuit of him. It was nothing short of robbery for him then; as if the wind gust that surrounded him had suddenly carried with it any remnants of his fractured spirit, while in the midst of trying to mend itself. When he did make it to his place, he headed for his suite and fell on the bed, as if the trials of that day had shoved him down hard; Only one light was turned on once inside the place; cloaking himself in a blanket of darkness, except for a dimly lit foyer. He kicked his shoes off, then turned over on his back to gaze at the ceiling that had become gloomier by the minute. His mind continued to search for answers inside the darkness that greeted his eyes with a stark emptiness. He seemed sure it was his punishment being carefully crafted by this nemesis, but at a loss as to who exactly, and why in particular. He raised up and sat on the side of the bed with his head in his hands; hoping to reshape his thoughts into something more palatable when suddenly, it called to him. The pitch blackness also enveloped the apartment like before, except for the light within that mirror again. It might as well have thrust itself into space like outstretched arms; clutching Omar's hands, and pulling him closer to it. His eyes were wide; curiously fixed, and his pace slow and deliberate, but it was also eerily quiet. Only inches away from it, the light stopped. He was partially aware this time; suddenly submerged into twilight, but not disturbed by the appearance of it. Somehow he knew he had been here before. The parade of calamities that plagued his life had forced his reasoning into hiding for too long. That darkened corner of his mind had become his sanctuary, where most of his days were spent in hopeless isolation. Except for the wisdom disguised as flashes of light in recent days by 'the orphan', Omar's thoughts would most probably continue to careen listless in search of that light. Somehow he knew deep down, 'the orphan' wanted to be his friend. He flattened his palms and slowly placed them against the mirror, then the image appeared. Incredibly, it was Omar's own reflection, but this time also carrying with it a sad countenance. He gasped then withdrew quickly, not quite wanting to believe what he was seeing. It's entire outline became like liquid, but matched every move he made no matter how subtle, until it decided to speak in that familiar throaty tone of voice. Omar backed away again, but was startled a little since it was the first distinct sign of it being something more than just his reflection. Then just as quickly, he pressed his palms hard against the glass again, signaling his alliance with it; then it spoke.

"OMAR, YOU'RE TREMBLING WITH uncertainty, and it troubles me to see you this way."

"I am, somewhat. I believe someone is stalking me, and who knows what his plans are for me." He sighed heavily. "I feel powerless to stop him. The thing is, I don't have any idea as to who it might be, or why exactly. I don't have a clue as to what's coming."

"I think you know why it might be happening; at least your reasoning opened the door to the likelihood of it just a while ago."

"What do you mean?"

"When you thought about how you closed the door on reconciling with certain people in your past, and how giving those relationships no attention was just as bad as giving them the wrong kind. You're sort of like a gardener in a way Omar; A gardener who needs to try and cultivate a field whose crop happens to be his relationships with other people."

"I don't understand."

"A good gardener knows that tending that field takes care and nourishment with all the things needed for a great harvest. Things like patience, longsuffering, kindness, charity, and humility. What becomes even more urgent, is him recognizing God's call for him as the faithful steward who has also been given dominion over his creation; a steward whose heart was meant to beat with the strength of the Father's own character. For all of the wholesome things that garden is expected to yield in its lifetime, weeds might also gather like bands of thieves to frustrate the harmony within it; agents of the enemy committed to draining its lifeblood and giving nothing back in the process."

It paused for a moment, sensing the swell of Omar's sensitivity about what he was trying to convey. He also felt at that moment, he was much closer to becoming re-acquainted with Omar's soul. Omar's eyes became glassy, but did not blink. His fingers flexed as if he was grasping at something that was still not quite within his reach.

Omar asked, "Is that what I've done; let the weeds gather for too long?"

"It would seem so, and in most cases they're circumstances created from your own insecurities. It's time you got rid of those weeds so you can really dress that field the way it should be. Your hands may get calloused and you may suffer bouts with fatigue, but don't get hooked by the lure of complacency. You should keep your hands to the plow and realize that no one is perfect, but everyone is worthy of saving. It's always good to try and connect with what's honorable in whoever crosses your path, because during those times when you'll need to tread those troubled waters of discovery about someone, it will give the relationship buoyancy when it's most needed. You've made progress, but choosing to alienate yourself from people that truly care about you, while excusing the faults of those who would rather exploit you is not the solution. If it's real justice you seek, it must be even-handed. You shouldn't treat that notion like it's a fifth appendage that still makes you feel more normal somehow, even though you still choose to ignore your own faults. It's time now to really think about the kinds of seeds you wish to sow, and how you will distinguish yourself for those who choose to sow into your own life."

"I guess I've squandered lots of years just playing the defensive, haven't I?"

"Perhaps you have, but just remember, the best relationships are also a result of having made wise choices about your associates. Choosing not to be unevenly yoked with someone whose friendship seems to come at a price may be virtuous, but to also despise the gift of genuine friendship when it is offered just seems, reckless."

Omar let go of a mournful sigh with a bewildered look on his face.

The orphan then said, "Still not convinced?"

"To be honest, I let myself become consumed over what happened to my friend Breeland. It was so long ago, but I've always felt I let him down somehow. We were just kids, but it almost seemed like a part of me died with him that day. Trying to make friends afterward was like trying to learn how to ride a bike all over again. It's been hard to really trust anyone since."

He shook his head in obvious frustration; confounded by his inability to reconcile his feelings. "What can I do to fix this?"

"You did change you know, but you grew in other ways, in spite of missing Breeland's watchful eye. Seems to me it's you that can't be trusted; feeling betrayed when he moved, then blaming yourself for a failure that never happened on your part when he died. It has always kept you guessing about your own destiny. Try and think more about how you overcame your own problems, and realized one of the things you were gifted to do with your running. Coach Bivens saw in you what you couldn't see in yourself, and maybe would have overlooked altogether. That was no accident Omar."

"What makes you say that?"

"Because, sometimes we need the help of others in finding the wisdom in some things. Someone to set us on a path that we may otherwise miss, because of preconceived notions about what we feel we can't possibly achieve. Coach Bivens allowed you to see yourself as someone who could become an accomplished athlete, and you got part of that right."

"What do you mean?"

"Well, you can't claim wisdom without discipline, and that also could have been yours until you were persuaded by Priscilla to do something you never should have done before your meet that day. And what about your Supervisor, Clarence?"

"What about him?"

"He seems to have nothing but confidence in you to lead the promotion for the company's sponsorship. Seems he held out only for you on that one. I wonder what he remembered that you apparently decided to forget?" Omar looked away then hung his head in disgust.. The orphan continued…

"Then there's your uncle Seth, who was there with you from the start."

"I'm not wrong about Seth. I know I'm not."

"And why is that? Because he and your coach wanted to pull you from the competition when you insisted you were ok? That wasn't on them that was all you. And when he had to vote on the best squad to field for the Pre-Olympic team afterward, your fitness was called into question. That was also as a result of a decision you first made by bowing to Priscilla's will. He's only been trying to make amends all these years for a decision that was really agonizing for him, but unable to justify any other choice in the matter. That's life Omar. Sometimes we're faced with unpleasant decisions that affect those we love, but can't be helped because that someone can't seem to get out of their own way. You have to believe that whenever that happens, wisdom will show up at the end of it like a mob screaming for justice, and getting it."

"With all that's happened to me and for me, like you said, why do I feel so incomplete? Why has wisdom passed me by?"

"You can start by forgiving yourself for the things you've done while you're busy forgiving others. It's always good to try and understand someone's motive for doing something before pronouncing judgment on them. You can't change what's already happened, and whatever you've done has consequences you know; good or bad. What you can decide to do from now on is choose weapons of warfare that are pleasing in God's site, against an enemy that wages war on the same battlefield; that is your heart and your mind. Always remember this passage; *'No weapon formed against you shall prosper.'*—When you do, panic is replaced with real power; power derived from that spirit who wants to live inside of you, letting you face any challenge that comes your way with confidence, and a winning outcome that's yours for the taking."

Omar's face became flush, his eyes welled with tears, and his lips quivered as he tried desperately to contain his emotions.

"Why would that spirit want to live in me? I'm a mess inside, and I don't feel worthy of it."

"No one is worthy of it, but it's only by God's grace that anyone has the chance to be made whole again after having been broken, for whatever reason, but there is one condition."

"What's that?" "It's by invitation only."

"What do you mean exactly?"

"You must invite him to come into your heart. He's no different than you in that respect, in that he's not going to stay where he's not wanted."

Omar's eyes became bright, as if his consciousness was suddenly bombarded with the light of reason…

"You know Clarence, my Supervisor, talks often about why he prays, and how he will never stop doing it. He said he knows he must ask God daily for those things he needs to sustain him for whatever trials he might be facing, and have faith that he's the one that can provide it. I never gave it much thought really. I always believed it was a little over the top, you know; even when I was young. I treated it with the same seriousness as when I would make three wishes before blowing out my birthday candles, or something like that; knowing in all likelihood none of it would ever come true."

"Oh but that same assurance he'll give to you too, if you have faith and truly believe that he can."

It was surreal for him to be staring at his own likeness with such a mystic predilection, and engaging it as if it was someone else entirely. The Orphan was eager to hear his response, feeling it was also in its final trek toward home, but knowing it all hinged on Omar's willingness to submit.

The orphan then said, "Since you recalled so perfectly what Clarence said to you about it, I believe his words were more important than you thought they were at the time. The good thing is, you can never be so far outside of God's will that he'll refuse to throw you a lifeline, if you really want it. You see, he's already forgiven you, and he expects you to do the same for others; starting with you forgiving yourself. It's the only way you'll ever truly be free." (The orphan's voice gradually faded before the connection was finally broken).

OMAR'S PHONE BEGAN TO RING. The orphan believed it was close to a breakthrough during their previous encounter, but it would have to wait for it yet again. Omar stood up, somewhat dazed from the experience, but remembering vivid details about it unlike before. His phone kept ringing instead of going into voicemail, so he answered it.

"Omar, it's Theo."

"Oh, hey Theo—how is it?"

"I'm good—Just wanted to let you know I plan to be at the next rehearsal for the video, if it's ok with you guys."

"Oh, yeah Theo, I'm glad you called. We're meeting on Wednesday at the company park around 4:30 again. Since it's the last planned rehearsal before the actual shoot, I'll get a copy of the script to you tomorrow so you can review it. Maybe you'll still have some ideas on how we might tweak it."

"Ok man, and thanks for thinking about me."

"Not a problem. You feeling better?"

"Yeah. I'll probably see you guys tomorrow."

"I guess that bug wasn't about to keep a good man down, huh?"

Theo paused, feeling he was dealing with a new and improved version of Omar.

"Yeah, I guess it wasn't at that."

Omar said, "See you in the morning."

Omar had already decided he would put his trust in the orphan. It never did sugar coat his situation, and did let him know his journey was not without perils; but none he couldn't overcome with God's help. He headed back to the kitchen counter to find the envelope from the Olympic committee again, with the intent of actually calling his Uncle Seth. After he clipped the edge of the envelope and pulled the one page letter, his phone rang again. It was Clarence.

"Hey man—Thought I'd give you one last shot at making that trip with me tomorrow to Dillon. We can leave at the start of the shift and be back before one o'clock. At least that's the plan."

Clarence felt it was a long shot at best, but followed his instincts and went for it anyway. Omar was quiet for a moment, then recalled the orphan's words about forgiveness and how he was being given another opportunity to really heal the wounds from his past. It was his chance to really start looking forward now to a future without being haunted by the unsavory truth about himself. Those ghost were finally being silenced now as he embarked on his trip toward wholeness. He didn't waste time waffling in his response to Clarence…

"You know what, this might surprise you but I've changed my mind. I will go with you. I need to try and put this stuff to bed once and for all."

"If only you knew how good that makes me feel. It's the right thing to do; you'll see."

"I hope you're right boss; I really do." He had forgotten just that quickly about the letter from the Olympic committee, and about calling his uncle Seth after hanging up with Clarence. They apparently still were not high on his list of priorities.

Omar made sure the first thing he'd do after getting to his floor that morning was to Find Theo and hand him his copy of the script. It was all about trust now, and he needed to keep his promise to him before the day was spent. He didn't seem concerned about his stalker so much now as he was about just trying to be obedient to what the orphan had said to him the night before. If God's plan was to make his enemy his 'footstool' then he had nothing to worry about. Just as he boarded the elevator to his floor, he saw what he thought was the same hooded figure walking through the double glass doors to the lobby. He made sure the elevator door remained open for a moment to try and get a good look at the man. Oddly enough, the man walked with a peculiar gate that slowed him down some, but his hood still covered too much of his face before deciding to wait and pull it off of his head once he was well outside of Omar's field of vision. The man took an adjacent hallway to another part of the floor by the time he got passed Omar, then he said to himself, 'Stay focused Duncan; stay focused', then abandoned the idea of following him. Getting the script to Theo was more important now. At least he might have time to look it over while he and Clarence were gone. When he got to his floor, he approached Theo.

"Hey man, I believe this is yours."

"Hey Omar. Is this the script?"

"Yes sir—Me and Clarence are going on a field trip to Dillon Industries for a few hours this morning; thought I'd get it to you now in case you want to look it over while we're gone." "What's at Dillon?"

He said jokingly, "It's classified."

"Yeah, right."

"We're meeting some VIP's about the sponsorship before the actual pitch."

"Ok, above my pay grade anyway so I'll leave it alone, but thanks for the copy man."

Omar noticed Evelyn walking through the breezeway and approached her…

Good morning Ev."

"Hi; going on a field trip this morning, huh?"

"How'd you know already?"

"I saw Clarence on the way up, and you didn't even invite me."

She put on a sad face and pretended to wipe her eyes. Omar

smiled at her, but couldn't really be sure if she was upset over it, until she smiled back.

"You boys have fun. You can tell me all about it when you get back."

Clarence emerged from the breezeway and beckoned to Omar right away…

"Hey Omar—Let me check my mail, then we can ride. No need for you to log on. I'll only be a minute."

Drive time traffic to Gleason was as predictable as ever with bottlenecks occurring almost every four or five miles until they were 20 minutes into the trip. Clarence regretted leaving so late, and made Omar aware of his disappointment in himself.

"It probably would have been better had we left an hour earlier and not bother showing up at the office first. Didn't count on it being this stop and go."

"Well, seems like we're gonna have lots of time to chit chat. So, you want to tell me what you hope we'll find when we get there, because I have no idea what we're looking for."

"It's just a hunch. When I found out your former girlfriend"— Omar interrupted sharply..

"She wasn't my girlfriend, alright! She was just a teaser."

He let the window down completely and put his hand at the top of the opening; drumming his fingers against it in obvious frustration."

"Sorry, I guess I struck a nerve. This thing—it must have really been a thorn for you."

"You could say that, yeah."

"Sorry man, but it's really one of the reasons I wanted you to come. This kind of stuff eats away at you like a cancer until you can find some way to bring closure to it for yourself, and maybe for that other person too. Honestly, even though I do care about how this campaign turns out knowing this trip will probably remove any stumbling blocks for its success, I care a heck of a lot more about what it's gonna mean for you, personally. You're still my friend you know."

"I know, but how do you know we'll even see her? There's got to be other people on staff that can serve as her surrogate, or something like that."

"I already called ahead and she agreed to take a meeting with me—with us."

Omar shook his head and looked straight ahead.

"She doesn't know I'm coming does she?"

"Well, I didn't want to take a chance on spooking her if she knew."

"You know I thought this might not be such a bad idea, but what am I supposed to say to her? "

"Don't worry, it'll come to you."

Omar then said in frustration, "Can we just go dark for a while? I need to think."

The uneasiness was etched across his face while he stared into the side-view mirror. He had ignored the flicker of light inside of it that actually pierced his consciousness in an instant. He mistakenly thought it to be sunlight that had not yet escaped the clouds. Clarence knew he had rattled him but ended the chatter like he asked, and turned the radio down low. They had to travel at least another 40 minutes before reaching the outskirts of Gleason.

Chapter 13

Theo had taken Omar's advice and started looking over the script on his morning break. He decided to wait until he actually saw the cast run through it to give his opinion. Richie's rewrite obviously wasn't an issue, and it didn't seem to matter if he had a speaking part or not. He seemed content just to be a part of it. Blake was on the floor to set up more terminals and noticed him after deciding to take a break of his own.

Blake said, "Hey man, how is it?"

Theo replied, "Hey, I'm better. Glad to be back. How about you? I heard you and Omar sparred a little at the courts on last Saturday. How'd that turn out?"

"Ok, I guess. I think he banged his ankle a little; had to end it early. Is he here today?"

"He was—He's on a field trip with Clarence for a few hours. His ankle seems ok though."

Blake pulled an orange crush from the soda machine and sat with him for a minute. Evelyn and Nadine walked inside the area just as Blake was taking his seat.

"Hey Theo, Blake—how are you two?"

Theo said, "Hey Evelyn, Nadine—and we're good."

Evelyn asked, "Ready to get back in the saddle so soon Theo? Haven't you accrued sick time yet?"

"Yeah, but I felt well enough to come in, so I did. I don't like being out."

Evelyn and Nadine looked at each other curiously, then shrugged their shoulders.

Evelyn said, "Ok; different strokes I guess. I see Omar got a copy of the script to you like he promised. He's trying to do better, except for not telling me about him and Clarence deciding to play hooky with their little field trip to Dillon this morning. Neither one of them thought to invite me. It's not like he's riding solo for this sponsorship, you know."

Theo said, "I'm sorry Evelyn."

Nadine's remark was less congenial.. "True to form isn't it? You men are too much!", then she turned away, in a huff.

"Oh, it's not that serious Nadine." She turned to Theo again..." I busted his chops before he left, so I'm good now. "

She and Nadine both laughed about it, then said, "See you gentlemen later."

Blake seemed a little agitated suddenly and asked, "Dillon huh? The plant in Gleason?"

"Unless there's another one we don't know about, yeah. He said something about needing to meet with some V.I.P.'s about the sponsorship; told me it was classified."

Theo laughed a little, but for Blake it was no laughing matter. He had only finished about half his drink before bolting up suddenly, then tossed the soda in the trash.

He then said, "I've gotta run man; gotta make a call before I get back to it, but I'll see you around."

He was already in the process of making that phone call before he was out of the break area. Theo said to himself, 'I guess if I was either one of them, I'd probably avoid me too after the first day back'. He raised his bottle of OJ as if toasting himself, then said aloud, "Welcome to the lepers club Theo."

He then chugged the last of it and started walking back to the unit. Blake had made it back to his floor but with his phone practically pasted to his ear hoping the person he was trying to reach would pick up. He had made several attempts after about ten minutes straight. He didn't want to leave a message but had run out of time before he was expected back on the floor to continue his installations. He had to leave a message on the final attempt hoping it wasn't too late.

"Mom it's me, Blake—Call me as soon as you can. It's important."

Clarence was as quiet as a mouse during the remainder of their trip to Gleason. He decided to turn the radio off after a while with only the hum of the engine and intermittent noise from other traffic breaking the silence. Omar had seeped into a twilight sleep. That flicker of light from the side view mirror had become another gateway for the orphan's' way back home. It was desperate for its reunion with Omar, but the way it must happen could not be changed for it to really matter, so it simply counted on patience to be its ally. Omar's eyes struggled to stay open, and whatever occupied his thoughts at the moment had sealed him off from the rest of his universe. His breathing was quiet and steady, giving Clarence the impression he was probably in an o.k. place, wherever his dreams had taken him....

IT SEEMED REAL ENOUGH; him sitting on the passenger side in front. It didn't matter who was driving. His trip had turned into a cinematic reel for more of those triggers that opened the door to memories he'd rather do without, but memories holding pieces of the puzzle that sadly, had shaped his outlook until now. A reel that first showed him a field where the tare stood as tall as the wheat, and the wheat in an endless struggle to subdue it. The orphan had called him out about it; how trying to avoid those triggers was pointless. He was now being guided subconsciously through that field by the orphan's outstretched hands; crossing dimensions of time and space in a last ditch effort to help Omar come to terms with what he must do to get him back home. The imagery that followed depicted all too well the unexpected drift through Omar's past. A past that left his spirit scarred with deep caverns, where the hope of his own glory once stood majestic and proud. The task of reviving those hopes had been troublesome. With what seemed like only minutes now, it would have to be time enough for the orphan to finally clear a path to an open door. Omar's eyes darted frantically back and forth signaling the arrival of 'REM sleep'. The orphan kept a watchful eye, but still in another dimension. Unable to harness specific memories, as if the power to do so would guarantee its passage but it trusted what fate had shown it to be; the hour of its reckoning.

A YOUTHFUL OMAR DUNCAN, barely 22 years old, taking 3 years to complete a two year program, seemed bright enough, but had just wasted enough time in school to the point of boredom. It just didn't seem real to him. He was still floundering and not sure of the path he wanted to take. He could at least count on a soft land-ing at his parents' house until he was sure. He didn't relish the idea, but the stigma of being an underachiever continued to badger him for another three years. Hanging around the local track meets where his uncle Seth coached, didn't help either. He yearned for the feel of the asphalt under his feet again. The scorching of his own world record speed along with some others, and the setting of new ones gave him chills. His dream had died on the vine, but only from his own neglect. He never took Seth's advice about training for the next Olympic trials, even after knowing Seth would make himself available to train him, alone if need be. Seth made that clear. It was that important to him. Omar however, thought of himself as damaged goods and let his animosity overrule his good judgment, thinking it no longer mattered. He'd just fill the void with other things, but he knew deep down even Breeland wouldn't approve of the path he had taken. Breeland was fearless and took risks, but Omar was quite the opposite. As much as he felt desperate enough to want to trade places with Breeland at times back in the day it just wasn't possible, but there was nothing stopping him from learning by example. He forgot just that quickly about what makes good friendships work. It didn't occur to him that for all the reasons why he admired his friend, Breeland also saw character traits in him that he wanted to live up to as well. Three years of just scratching the surface of his potential by working dead end part-time jobs didn't exactly cause him to salivate over the possibilities for his future. His motivation for trying to finish college for his communication degree, with only 13 semester hours to go, had all but evaporated, along with the finances he needed to finish. His parents had helped as much as they could already. He even ignored the interview with an Army recruiter arranged by his dad, which was a real head scratcher because of the possibility of Uncle Sam covering the costs of finishing school. His dad didn't help his motivation much afterward by brow beating him over it. Omar's attitude was, it just wasn't his 'bag', and his dad did eventually understand. His uncle Seth was the one person he could always talk to; about anything, but his guilt wouldn't let him open that door just yet so he was content with showing up at the track, secretly, to get his vicarious shot of glory until the next fix.

The reel continued spinning, showing him at the end of his emotional collapse over his lack of options when Dillon Industries hired him at 26 years of age. The company was in the middle of a hiring binge at the time, but even that was courtesy of his uncle Seth, who found out about the job openings through a friend that also worked there, and passed the information on to Omar's mom. (That was one thing he had conveniently forgotten) It seemed things were looking up, but then took on nightmarish proportions after finding out Deon also worked there. The discovery was less dramatic for Deon. He felt he could just pick up where he left off with Omar, so the constant collisions between them endured. Omar had not yet earned a reprieve from the taunting and mocking after all those years, until it all came to a head on that fateful day. It was another opportunity lost after only eighteen months of employment, just shy of his 28th birthday. And again, he invoked the memory of Breeland to try and salvage what remained of his dignity. At the time, it was like he had been gut punched over and over again. He recalled how the drinking started shortly after that, once he had to move back home with his mom and dad for another three years. The reel continued to spin; letting him see how hitting almost rock bottom wasn't far behind with no job, no money, no girl, and very little left of his ambition. Run-ins with the law and a litany of traffic citations initiated the era of his strolls through 'death valley'; at least that's what it felt like, except when he was at the track, watching those young protégé's strut their stuff, then afterward gather obediently under Seth's 'wing'. He at least had to admit, in spite of his break with Seth as his confidante, he was still an exceptional teacher and the track was the one place that still made him feel at home. Away from the athletes he notices two young boys for the first time, about 8 or 9 years old at the edge of the in-field where the athletes are warming up. He thinks they're probably kids of one of the parents or younger sibling of one of the athletes. They capture his attention because one of the boys seems to suffer from super hyperactivity with the constant running and flipping; pretending to be an athlete himself, while the other boy sits quiet and subdued on the single bleacher designated for the athletes. The only sign of life from him is the mild shuffle of his legs as they dangle just slightly above the ground. He barely turned his head the whole time he sat there. Seth beckons to the active one to stay clear of the teams' warm up routines. He then walks over to the quiet one, says something to him, then pats him on the head. For all the times he visited the track after that, he witnessed that same behavior with those two boys. For them to be allowed to get that close to the athletes, must mean they enjoyed their own version of V.I.P. status.

The scene shifts yet again to his melt down with Deon. He knew the fact that he did not at least face jail time for the assault was a miracle. Deon however, was facing injuries he may never fully recover from. With that reckoning, the guilt had become overwhelming. The reel rolled on; showing him the successive close calls behind the wheel after he had been drinking too much. His routine had already pegged him as an alcoholic, but he stayed in denial about it. The mercy God had shown even then escaped him, as if the prospect of his own untimely death was no cause for alarm. His parents had seen enough, and the blow up between them was inevitable. What happened that day was still vivid. His dad had to confront him after getting a whiff of his breath which wreaked of alcohol at 8:30 in the morning…

"Why do you torture yourself like this son? Nothing good can come from this."

He could barely stand wearing only his shorts, his bath robe, and one sock which was about halfway off his foot as he stumbled his way in front of his dad again. They stood inside the doorway of his bedroom, when he raised his voice with a considerable slur in his speech…

"I'll be o.k. dad. I will—so don't you worry ok?"

"No, you won't be ok; not until you get help. You're spiraling out of control son. This can't go on."

"Ok—ok, here we go again." His dad reached out to steady his wobbling when Omar snatched his arm back and snapped..

"I said I'm alright!"

His mom was around the corner from the room with her hands to her face, fighting back the tears. Her son was in a free fall and they seemed at their wits end to try and stop it. His dad dropped both hands to his side in disgust.

"No Omar, you're not alright. I'm getting you help, today."

He collected his car keys and stormed out of the house. Omar had fallen to his knees and began to sob openly, as his mom approached him and helped him to his feet then back to his bed to finish sleeping it off. For a brief moment she pitied him; but knew tough love was what he needed now. She felt at that moment it would probably be a long way back for him, but he needed to at least start the journey.

The reel then showed him at the end of his year in rehab. His dad followed through with his promise to get him help letting him dry out for almost thirteen months at a facility not far from his parents' home. He was a resident-patient there for the duration but didn't complain since there were too many other things there to enrich his mind, rather than him saturating it with alcohol every day. He was grateful at the end of that experience, and insisted on moving into a halfway house to try and re-establish himself, even though his parents offered him his room again. At age 32, he felt it was time he stood on his own feet again. Deciding to work the 34 hour a week job set up by the staff at the halfway house was a virtual crawl back into the traditional work force but he was committed to it. His dad offered to buy him a car to get around in since he had wrecked the previous one. He was grateful for the help and felt maybe he really should count his blessings since he now had a way to get around on his own; maybe even look in on the track & field squads again. He hadn't touched a drink since his stay there and felt good about himself, but the reel pivoted suddenly to a scene where he had visited the track to watch the teams practice. He always sat high on the bleachers, presumably in disguise in his panama brim and dark glasses. He watched Seth, who was really in his element as a coach. Omar felt then, even if he hadn't run track, he probably would have been a coach at something. He scanned the crowd near the field and noticed a man who was beginning to grey and who walked with a hobble. His face wasn't that visible, but he was tall, like Deon. Omar watched him as he slowly moved toward the squad and reached out to embrace his uncle Seth. They chatted just for a moment and he suddenly had a flashback to the time he saw Deon and Seth at Breeland's house the day of his funeral. He never knew the connection between the two of them, and still didn't, but it did peak his interest suddenly even though he couldn't be sure the man he saw hugging Seth was in fact Deon. He then noticed those same two little boys, both a little taller now, at the edge of the in-field coming up behind him.

Curiously enough, the one boy was predictably active, but the other boy walked slowly, with feet that appeared to be turned slightly inward. The kid wore a blank stare that said very little about who might really be lurking inside that mind of his. Omar felt sad for him suddenly; feeling he probably felt he had to remain a recluse thinking he just didn't fit in. Omar thought about his own challenge as a kid in that instant, and the problem he was able to outgrow eventually. He hoped this kid would be as fortunate. The kid took his usual spot on the bleacher until, to Omar's surprise, he suddenly came to life when a couple of Sheriff's Deputies' squad cars pulled up near the end of the bleachers and parked. The kid waved frantically at them, and they seemed to know him too as they waved back and turned on the 'party lights' atop the cruisers, then a brief flash of the sirens which got him really excited. Omar was glad for him, but it was short lived when they stayed for only a few moments then pulled away. The boy then returned to that 'altered state'. His excitement terminated just as quickly, as if someone had turned off the lights in the dead of night.

The reel spun again, showing a new and improved Omar Duncan, whose search for meaningful and goal oriented employment was like trying to find that needle inside of a haystack. He couldn't boast of a resume that distinguished him above the competition, but instead only relied on the hand of grace to make a way for him. He was at least confident enough now to realize that if he was granted an interview he could probably make enough of an impression to land the job. Earth Burst Industries hired him then, which happened to be close to his 34th Birthday. They were a relative newcomer in the county with a plant in Mumford, and the pay for an analyst in the product development area was enough for him to get his own apartment and to cover relocation expenses. Lots of prayers, including his own, had gone up for him during his job search, and he felt God had been faithful in providing what he desperately needed at the time. His tenure there was off to a pretty good start, until subsequent visits to the track to watch the squads reminded him of that dark place in his past. Seeing that same man there several times at the infield, with that hobble; presumably escorting those same two boys, who were more like young men now, revealed obvious chemistry between them and his uncle Seth. The fraternal bond was unmistakable. He was too proud to admit he had been sneaking visits to the track by asking his mom, Seth's own sister, about it. He couldn't seem to put his finger on his indifference either since he had practically alienated his uncle. It shouldn't have bothered him so much, but it did; so he turned once again to an old acquaintance that couldn't really talk back so that he could really hash out his feelings about it; it was none other than his companion in a bottle; Hennessey and seven.

"OMAR!" CLARENCE SHOOK HIM a few times—"Omar wake up. We're here."

Omar's eyes stretched wide as he sat erect. He stared at Clarence as if he had something to be embarrassed about.

Clarence said jokingly, "You know you talk in your sleep?"

"No I don't!"

"Ok, whatever you say." He rolled his eyes and pushed his hair back. He was already uncomfortable the moment he saw the large Dillon billboard from a distance.

While pointing at the billboard he said, "You know I haven't been back here since I left the company."

Clarence said, "This should seem brand new to you then. There's probably a whole different crew at that plant now."

Clarence was trying to ease his anxiety by making him think he might not see anyone he had known when he worked there, but Omar wasn't so optimistic.

He replied, "Yeah, but what about the locals that might still be around?"

Clarence wanted to change the subject when he pulled into the donut shop.

"I need a cup of coffee, and maybe something to much on. You want something?"

Omar responded, "Maybe just a coffee for me, thanks."

Clarence said, "Let's go inside. We've got a little time before we need to be at the plant."

Blake's mom interrupted her usual morning meeting with two of her assistants to return his call. He made it sound too urgent to ignore it, especially since the subjects of the message were headed her way. The name showed up in his caller I.D. and he wasted no time picking up.

"Mom, thanks for calling back."

"Hey—What's going on? You ok?"

"I'm fine. I just wanted to give you a heads up about the people that are on their way to meet with some Dillon Reps this morning about our upcoming festival. I just wanted to know if you happened to know who was coming."

"Yeah, I know who it is. I was told they wanted to do a preview of their pitch before the actual presentation. Everyone here is o.k. with it."

"Well, in that case, be kind then. A lot's riding on the success of it, for all of us here."

"Seems like a lot of drama over nothing, coming from 'Mr. cool and collected'. Anyway, other department heads will have to weigh-in before a final decision is made. I wouldn't be that concerned about it if I were you though. That new system of theirs is already getting a lot of good press. It doesn't seem likely that we'd deny the sponsorship, but don't repeat that to anybody ok?"

"You got it. Have you talked with dad lately?"

"You know that's a road less travelled for me these days. I respond sometimes to phone messages he might leave with a text, or I might decide to just send him one, to let him know I'm still alive at least."

"Mom, why so crass, and impersonal?"

"Well, I don't mean to be. It's just that we don't have much in common anymore."

"By that I guess you mean he doesn't compliment your life-style anymore?"

Blake had always been sympathetic with his father once his circumstances changed and the prospect of gainful employment for him again seemed less likely over time; let alone a thriving career. He knew she no longer looked at him the same way.

"I guess that's what I'm saying son. We're simply moving at different speeds now, that's all. I still care for him though. I really do, it's just that—"

He interrupted—"Don't bother to explain. I'm trying to understand. How about Nate, have you talked with him recently?"

"No I haven't, but I'm going to make it a point to try and see you boys more; I really am. I've been so busy lately. You know how it is. It's a demanding job and things could come apart at the seams if I'm not on top of it. I owe that to the company at least."

"Funny, I had hoped you would have the same attitude about your family." She got quiet for a moment because she had no come back for his remark.

She then said, "If you speak with your brother, tell him to call me; it's been a while since we talked."

"I'll try and reach him today. I won't keep you then. Good hearing your voice mom."

"And yours; you take care, ok? I love you."

"Love you too—Bye."

Blake was a little curious about how mild his mom's response was to the news about who was coming to see her group about the sponsorship. He thought she would be at least a little apprehensive but with the heads-up from him, she would eventually settle into her role play like she always does; working the room like the master that she's always been. He had gotten used to her stalling tactics and dismissed whatever promises she made as soon as they hung up with one another. He did try and keep his promise to her by visiting his brother's department at Earth Burst to give him the message from their mother, but his Supervisor said he had called in sick the last two days.

Fred, the manager at Omar's apartment complex, was approached that morning by someone claiming to be a technician for the company that provides cable service for tenants in that complex. He's courteous and seems clean cut, as the bright orange company logo stitched to his shirt pocket seems to conspicuously glare at Fred, along with a name tag below it and a tool belt around his waist that are intended to arrest any suspicions he might have about his identity. He's actually a former employee of the cable company, who has gotten access to the service schedule for communities in the area and discovered today is the day that households in that area are to receive quality control checks. The shirt he wore was one he never bothered to turn in when he was let go. The company didn't need the I.D. Badge, so he kept it as a memento, but changed the name on it. He improvised with the tool belt. He then recited an improvised script to Fred that explained the purpose for his visit.

"I'll be checking routers for a couple of the apartments here for signal reliability. There was a report from central there might be some issues. I'll need access to apartments #210 and #217 while we're in this sector. If you need to call the tenants to let them know, we can set it up for another time if it's not convenient, but then again they run the risk of the service being interrupted if there is a problem that needs to be addressed. There would probably also be a service charge added in that instance. This one's on the house at least."

Fred gave him a curious look, as though he might not really be trusting what he was saying. The guy took a gamble.

He then responded, "You can call the office and check if you want."

Fred noticed the cable company truck at the pole then said, "That's ok. I see your truck at the pole. I'll let the tenants know after you leave. It should be alright. Let's go."

He stays a few paces behind Fred as they approach apartment #210, which happens to be Omar's apartment. When Fred unlocks the door and opens it, the man casually sprays a substance inside the keyhole to the deadbolt. It's a fast-acting polyurethane resin, only available on the black market. It stiffens after a few minutes allowing it to be extracted with an impression of the tumblers so that a key can be made from it. According to the 'dark web' the method was at least ninety percent reliable if the gelatin like substance wasn't disturbed after being removed. He'd find out soon enough.

He asked Fred, "Do you know where the router is here?"

"I'm sure it's in the big area, because I don't believe there's a T.V. set anywhere else."

He looked at Fred with a half-smile and said, "You must know this tenant pretty well."

"Yeah, I do. Omar Duncan; good tenant. Never a problem with him."

The technician shook his head; thankful for confirmation of the occupant's identify, then walked to the area where the big screen T. V. was. He pretended to check something on the router, then excused himself. He stepped outside pretending he needed to make a call. He pulled the door closed enough to conceal himself without latching it, then extracted the stiffened resin from the lock and placed it inside a plastic sandwich bag. He stepped around the corner to the apartment for a few minutes then returned. He tampered with the box for a little while too to make the routine seem more believable.

He then said, "No problems with this one; signals ok here."

He needed to look inside the other apartment just to keep up the charade, but after Fred had let him in, he noticed the cable truck leaving the complex.

Fred said, "I think your ride is leaving."

Without looking up the man said, "He'll be back."

After checking the router to that apartment he said again that he found no problems there either.

"I guess sometimes it's a wild goose chase with these things, huh?"

He smiled at Fred, then said, "Sorry for the inconvenience, and thanks for your time," then left.

Blake became really concerned about his brother after the news from his Supervisor about him calling in sick. It wasn't like him to miss more than one day from work, and he never seemed to get sick. He thought he was in better health than he was; physically anyway. He took an extended break and decided he'd check with people in his inner circle; starting with his grandad see if anyone of them had heard from his brother…

"Blake, how is it son? Good to hear your voice."

"Hi gramps. Good to hear yours too. You doing o.k."

"I'm keeping my head to the sky. No worries."

"Listen, I wanted to know if you've talked to Nate lately."

"As a matter of fact he called me this morning, just to chat. You sound a little worried; something new going on with him I should know about?"

"To be honest I'm not sure. I talked with his Supervisor this morning; said he had called in sick the last couple of days. It's not like him to just miss work like that."

"Well, he didn't sound like he was under the weather to me when we spoke. He did seem a little agitated though, come to think of it; like he needed to get something off his chest. He got into this deep discussion about how some of us seem to be dealt a really lousy hand in life; something about chasing the rainbow but no chance of ever really catching it. I tried to get his mind off of that by changing the subject, but it was clear he wasn't in the mood for any small talk."

Blake let go of a big sigh then said, "I'm worried about him."

"I'll contact his uncle and see if he's spoken with him. They're pretty close these days."

"Ok. If I don't hear from you by the end of my shift I'm gonna go by his place."

Clarence and Omar hadn't really become caffeine addicts all of a sudden, but having drank six cups of coffee between them said more about their need to kill time than it did about how great the coffee was. Before his cup cooled too much, Omar decided to order a Danish. Melanie called when he left the table to order it.

"Hey mister. Just wanted to know how your trip to Dillon is going."

"Oh, it's going. We're inside the Donut shop killing some time until we're expected to be there. We may be climbing the walls later if we drink any more of this coffee though."

"Is Omar behaving?"

"As a matter of fact he is."

Omar was sitting down again with a piece of the Danish in his mouth already.

"Someone wants to say Hi."

She put the phone to Nathan's ear so he could say hello to his Dad.

"Hi daddy."

"Hey tough guy. You ready to see the Doctor with mommy this morning?"

"Yes sir."

"You gonna be strong for mommy and daddy and not cry this time?"

Omar was a little amused by the line of questioning by Clarence to his three year old; as if shedding tears from being poked with a needle was an act of cowardice from which there was little chance at redemption. He was sure his kid wasn't that reflective about it, but understanding Clarence's relationship with his family made him more aware that it was only meant to boost Nathan's confidence about it being something he need not fear. Not having the good fortune of trying to raise any kids yet, he did soon realize he still had more of his cynicism to shed, but it was a work in progress.

"You gonna bring something for me when you get home daddy?"

"Don't I always?"

Clarence could here Melanie asking him for the phone back.

"Bye Daddy. Here's mommy—Bye."

"See ya tough guy." Melanie was back on the line…

"Well, I guess I'll see you at dinner?"

"Yes mam, God willing."

"Ok; hope it goes well."

"Me too. See you tonight."

Omar was finishing up his Danish and coffee after Clarence hung up with Melanie. It was obvious he wasn't that comfortable sitting in a place that seemed so popular with the locals. His head seemed to be on a swivel the entire time Clarence was on the phone. Even though he wore a beard now, he was still nervous about maybe needing to duck a familiar face that could walk in at any time while they were sitting there, but it provided pretty good cover for him after all; or no one there was really that interested. Clarence looked at his watch and collected the used plastic ware and coffee cups.

He then said, "We'd better get going."

When they stepped outside a stiff breeze had kicked up, which carried a slight chill with it. They both turned up the collars to their light jackets and watched as a plastic lid to a waste barrel at a nearby storefront become airborne. Clarence followed the path of the lid until it landed against the fence surrounding the lot to the First Baptist Church. Clarence raised his eyes above the fence line, only to be met with that caretaker's gaze again. Omar also saw him and gasped. The caretaker dropped the tool he was holding at the same time, realizing who it appeared to be from that distance. They both seemed startled at the sight of one another and just stood frozen for a moment…

Clarence saw what was happening and asked, "You know him don't you?"

Omar didn't turn to him but simply said somberly, "Yeah, I believe I do."

They got in the car and pulled away. Omar still couldn't believe who it was he thought he saw, after so long. Clarence was about to pass the church as Omar continued to look in the direction of the caretaker, but he suddenly turned into the church driveway, headed in his direction.

Omar asked him, "What are you doing?"

"I'm not sure, but just trust me."

The caretaker picked up his tool, dressed in the same coveralls and wearing the same tattered brim. He stood patiently as Clarence got out of the car to approach him.

"Hello sir." The caretaker nodded his head and said, "Morning."

"My name's Clarence, and I couldn't help but stop to introduce myself. I saw you when I was here before. You were speaking with Deputy Bristol in the lot that day."

He nods his head again. "That's Ronnie—he's my younger brother."

He keeps his eyes trained on the other occupant in Clarence's car while they speak; needing his suspicions about his identity to be confirmed in the worst way.

The caretaker asked, "I know you're not from around here, so what brings you by?"

His injuries were more obvious now as Clarence could see the effort it took for him to perform something as simple as getting a good grip on the handle to his rake. Clarence could also see, it was a routine he had simply grown accustomed to. There was something about him that made Clarence believe he was content to still count his blessings in spite of what happened to him.

"We have a meeting at Dillon Industries this morning in a little while about our upcoming Festival. We've got a little time before we're expected there, but the man that's with me—well, I believe you know each other and I know it may not be the best time for this, but I believe he has something he needs to say to you.

" The caretaker looked off into the distance, as though it was something he had secretly hoped for. Omar somehow is compelled not to delay the inevitable, and also got out of the car. He approached the two of them slowly, stopping just short; astonished at who it was.

He then said, "Deon, it is you. But—how—?" He seemed to struggle with what he wanted to say.

"I never thought I would see you again in this lifetime Duncan."

The age lines in his face became sharper from the emotional jolt. Omar looked at his disheveled appearance, and his eyes began to well with tears. He was about to say he's sorry, but Deon raised his palm and shook his head to stop him….

"No, It's me that's sorry; sorry for devoting so much energy into shaming you for so long."

He then took his hat off slowly and extended his hand. Clarence looked on in astonishment, understanding that he's about to witness the closing of a painful chapter between the two of them. Omar and Deon clasped hands, then hugged each other. Omar let the tears rain down as they continued to embrace. The sorrow that had been bottled up for so many years making its plea for redemption. He repeated over and over, "I'm sorry, so sorry. Please forgive me."

Deon grabbed his forearms, looked at him squarely, and said, "I did that a long time ago." Clarence is still an observer at this point, understanding that what's happening between them is deeply personal.

Omar asked, "How did you end up here, and with this job?"

They all sat on the bench that was at the edge of the drive to chat. Deon was patient when he spoke, as though it was something he needed to talk about.

"After our incident, I spent three days in the hospital getting my injuries checked out. There was nothing broken, but I did suffer a severe pinch to some nerves from cracked vertebrae and a wicked concussion. My godmother couldn't manage the rounds of medical attention that I needed afterward, so my dad found a facility that took me in, whose expenses were partially subsidized by the outreach of this church. That's how I met Pastor Rueben and his wife. They were a real 'God send' for me."

Omar and Clarence could only be sympathetic and quiet, feeling Deon needed to unload. Omar seemed convicted in his guilt more than ever now, but Deon would soon put it to rest when he continued with the story of his rescue by Pastor, and Mrs. Rueben.

"Long story short, they were able to help me cut through my own bitterness to see that I mattered more than I realized, in spite of how I felt about my situation. I learned how much my dad really did care during that time, after I had doubted him so much before then. What you see isn't always what you get, if you also see with your spiritual eyes. They introduced me to Christ, and how his love for me is unconditional, regardless of where I've been in my life. That's when I decided from then on, to follow after him, and that includes forgiveness."

He stopped talking, and looked at them both with a passive expression. Omar and Clarence were blown away by the character of the man. To Omar, it was as if the soul of the Deon he knew had been turned inside out, and his anxiety vacated him like a bandit suddenly on the run. Omar recalls the remark Deon made about finding out his father cared more than he thought he did during his trial, and tells him about the times he showed up at the track when Seth was coaching his teams.

"I have to ask; what's your relationship to my uncle Seth?"

"Seth is my father." Omar is blown away by the news; not just about the level of secrecy about it for all those years, but also finding out that Deon is actually family.

Omar replied, "I would sneak and watch him and his squads practice, when I was going through my own changes after what happened. I saw this man that I thought might be you approach him and embrace him during my visits sometimes, but I couldn't be sure it was you."

"It was me you saw. Agnes, Breeland's mom, is also my mother. She and dad had an affair before she married Breeland's father. It was all kept on the hush, hush. I used to always feel I was the one they wanted to throw back."

He chuckled a little, but Omar and Clarence knew it was pain that still needed masking to some degree. Deon also could see it was a lot for Omar to process.

He told Omar, "You should talk to dad more. He's probably got a lot more to say to you about it."

He managed a slight smile, letting them know he'd prefer to end that discussion.

"Alright, I'll do that."

Omar patted him on the shoulder and said, "I'm glad we had a chance to see each other, really."

"So am I."

They all stood, at the same time the SUV pulled up to leave the lot. It was Mrs. Rueben. She simply waved at them on her way out before moving into traffic. She felt certain Deon was about to get back to work in a minute anyhow, so she didn't prolong the break by stopping to talk herself. Omar and Clarence then said their goodbyes and left him to his work. As they got ready to leave, Omar decided to stroke Clarence's ego a little after realizing his decision to stop at the church was the right call. He told Ce Ce to keep following his instincts, as they approached the on-ramp, headed toward Dillon.

Chapter 14

OMAR'S VISIT WITH DEON impacted him in a way he never thought it would, in his wildest imagination. He couldn't stop talking about his transformation on their way to Dillon. Clarence knew Omar was finally able to exhale a lot of bottled-up tension from his history with Deon, and how seeing and listening to him might just be a safe bet for his own path toward redemption. He even felt they could become friends now. Clarence also knew it was nothing less than divine intervention that persuaded him to suddenly turn into the church's lot, because his friend was even closer now to becoming 'whole' again. After reaching the plant they stopped at the Visitors' Center as Priscilla's assistant had requested. They were ten minutes early. The assistant had them wait in the conference room until a few minutes after the hour when Priscilla walked in.

Clarence introduced himself first.

"Ms. Eagan, I'm Clarence Colter. We spoke over the phone. Pleased to meet you."

"Mr. Colter—my pleasure."

Clarence then said, "This is actually the 2nd time we've met, unofficially that is, but weren't introduced. I'm sure you won't remember."

She said, "Oh, try me."

"Ok—I was here the other week, alone, doing advance work for the sponsorship team; I spoke to you in passing while I was in this building checking out your displays. You had just come in, and wore this smoke colored outfit that day."

"She said, "Hmm; you're right—I don't remember. I'm sorry."

She smiled as her eyes shifted to Omar. She stared curiously at him as he stared back. Clarence is quiet and lets the drama play out. She's noticeably shaken, when she finally recognizes Omar underneath the beard. Omar is cool about it and speaks first. Surprisingly, he feels no bitterness, not after seeing evidence of Deon's transformation. Even at that moment, he was secretly wishing for an awakening of his own.

"Hello Priscilla."

She responded, "Omar, you've grown a beard."

The discovery was obviously awkward for her. She managed a pasted smile again just for a moment, then turned to Clarence.

"I actually thought you were the only person we were expecting."

Clarence replied, "Omar is our 'project lead', and I thought it best he also attend."

She's noticeably embarrassed about facing the guy she only toyed with, but didn't seem to be caught completely off guard by seeing him again. Omar opens the meeting sounding very official, as if he had put their history behind him already. The reality was, he was starting to do just that. He and Clarence gave her a preview of their pitch and she was quite impressed. She was even more inspired by Omar's performance.

"It seems pretty ambitious, and you Mr. Duncan didn't miss a beat. Your confidence in this new system is pretty obvious. Why don't we set a date for your presentation to my team for next Wednesday; 10:00am ok?"

Omar responds ahead of Clarence, "Ok, we can arrange that."

Clarence smiled; pleased to see Omar taking the lead. He then excused himself to use the men's room, leaving the two of them alone to talk. Priscilla suddenly converts to 'shy school girl mode' with nothing to say. Omar didn't want to clutter his objective with a lot of senseless small talk, and decided to cut to the chase…

"It's ok to look me in the eye Priscilla", as she looks away. "It's no secret that what happened between us wasn't as important to you as it was for me, and I was hurt over it and bitter for a long time. It really sent me into a tailspin, but that's over now."

She turned to him and said, "I've often thought about how completely selfish I was when it came to you; how I toyed with your feelings, not really appreciating how that must have affected you. I've regretted it for a long time now, and I'm sorry, really sorry it happened."

He looked into her eyes, searching for the sincerity in what she had just said, and seemed satisfied that he had found it.

"Before our meeting, I met someone at the First Baptist Church this morning that I never thought I'd see again before our trip here."

She interrupted him and said, "You mean Deon."

Omar is surprised she knows who he was talking about.

"I even know about the incident between you and him here at the plant some years back."

Omar replied, "He's done an about face in his attitude. He seems so at peace now, even in spite of—what happened to him."

Omar was visibly agitated; recalling how he seemed to step outside of himself that day; his expression slumping like a lump of soft clay, until he suddenly snapped out of it.

He said, "You know, I never would have thought you two would have a fling. When he told me about the two of you, it was one of the things that sent me over the edge that day with him."

"When he said to me how you went ballistic after he told you, I realized then how much I must have deceived you. I'm so sorry Omar."

Omar hung his head slightly, then said, "The kid that you guys had; was it a boy or girl?"

"How about boys, as in twins?"

"You're kidding, really?"

"They're fraternal twins actually; twenty one years old, and trying to scratch out a living. It's not such an easy thing for one of them though."

"How do you mean?"

As she was about to get really personal with him and reveal secrets about her boys she would usually keep closely guarded, Clarence came back in and they tabled it for another time, but she was suddenly hit with a bit of nostalgia.

She tells Omar, "I want to show you something." The three of them moved to the display in the reception area and she showed him the photo of him and his team in their lab coats being featured among the displays. It's the same one Clarence saw during his first trip there. There is silence for a few moments. Omar stares at the photo, knowing it represents a chapter in his life he's finally about to close. Clarence is understandably less reflective than either of them and breaks the silence.

He tells her, "Well thank you for meeting with us. I trust you'll verify the date and time for the presentation with your P.R. team in a follow-up email to me then."

"I will, and as far as I'm concerned it's probably already a done deal letting you have the sponsorship, and you can expect my email within 24 hours, ok?"

Clarence collected their materials and they got ready to leave. On the way out the door Omar stopped to say goodbye to her…

"It was pleasing to see you again Priscilla."

"It was good seeing you too; really it was."

As they leave the building Priscilla has a new appreciation for the adult version of Omar. She is also unaware of how important it was that she swore to secrecy the name of Deon's attacker to anyone, at Seth's request, since she was the mother of his grandsons. She had hoped after today's face to face encounter between Omar and Deon that it's discovery would be of no consequence.

Clarence shut the door to his office around 1:30pm after he

had treated Omar to lunch on the way back to their building. He needed to place a call to Deputy Ronnie Bristol to let him know his suspicions about his friend were correct. He was only able to leave a voice message again requesting a call back as soon as possible. He felt the deputy may have the notion to only run interference against Omar's attempt to rid himself of his dilemma, so he felt he needed to at least let him know about Omar and Deon having met, and seemed to have made their peace with one another hoping he would understand. In the meantime Omar had become quite sociable with his co-workers for a change, and was enjoying the freedom of not feeling so tethered to his past. He mistakenly forgot just that quickly, that there was a stalker on the loose who seemed intent on robbing him of that bliss. He decides to chat with Evelyn and Theo about the upcoming final rehearsal of the video for the next day.

"I hope everybody's sharp tomorrow because we won't get another chance to get it right before the real deal on Friday you know."

Evelyn replied, "They'll be ready. No need to doubt them now after what we've already seen. Come to think of it, they didn't need nearly as much coaching as I thought they would, even from day one."

"I just hope you're right about it. Theo, you still plan to be there right?"

"Yes sir, I do."

They were all in the process of shutting down their terminals and clearing their work stations. Omar then said, "Well, I'd better get to the bus stop. I'll see you guys tomorrow."

On his way to the elevators Omar decides to look in on Clarence before leaving the floor. He knocked on his door, but was already opening it when Clarence said, "Come on in."

"Hey, heading downstairs to the bus stop, but just wanted to say again, I thought it was a really good day, and thanks for inviting me. I'll try not to second guess you so much from now on. It's clear to me that your instincts are pretty reliable."

"Yes they are, especially when you consider the source."

Omar just smiled, realizing he was speaking about his faith.

He nods his head, then says, "See you tomorrow."

As he makes his way to the elevators he runs into Blake. "Omar, hey. How's your foot?"

"It's better; just iced it afterward. Not much swelling."

"Good; glad to hear it. I'll see you around then."

As Omar boarded the elevator he was reminded of the young man that got on the elevator that day he had his bout with paranoia. He felt he could rule out Blake as his stalker because he was too personable, unless he was schizophrenic; but he really couldn't be certain of that either. When he got on the bus he saw Micki, and she confronted him again about doing the radio spot for her…

"Hey mister."

"Mick, how have you been?"

"I guess I should be asking you that question because of the way you checked out on me the other day when I asked you about doing that spot for me. Is it that unimportant to you?"

"Micki, you've got it all wrong. My mind had trailed off into the stratosphere the last time we saw each other and I wasn't paying attention to a lot of things that day. I've been dealing with something that had been keeping me preoccupied to say the least, but I believe it's over now. I'm sorry if I gave you the impression I didn't care. Of course I'll do the spot for you. I just need to see what you have so we can get to work on it, together."

"Thank you, Mr. Duncan. You said you've been dealing with some stuff; anything I can do to help?"

"Well, let's just say, the worst of it is probably over. I think I can deal with what's left as it's doled out to me." Micki wasn't altogether convinced of his optimism. She then said with some reluctance, "Ok, whatever you say."

"What's the deal with Rupert; haven't seen him in a while?"

"He's supposed to be taking part in his mentoring sessions this week for his business, but I can't swear to it."

As the bus approached Micki's stop, she stood up then told Omar, "I'll let you know what I had in mind for a radio spot by Thursday. I need to think about what I really want to say in it so I can try and drive as much traffic to it as possible. That air time can be pricey, so I don't intend to go there that often; know what I mean? Have a good night and maybe I'll see you in the morning."

Omar is curious why Rupert has been 'missing in action' since he hasn't had any contact with Micki, who helped him connect with the mentoring program in the first place. He decides to not dismiss the idea of him being his stalker, despite Micki's claims. When he gets home he decides to stop by the office to see if Fred has any mail for him.

"Hey Fred, any mail for me?"

Fred reaches into a cubby hole reserved for correspondence and hands him two envelopes.. "Just this; looks like junk to me."

Omar looked at it then said, "It is."

"Oh, before I forget, there was a guy from the cable company inside your apartment this morning; said he needed to check 'signal reliability' or something concerning the router, so I took the liberty to let him in; said you'd have to pay a service charge if you needed them to come back, in case you had a problem after the fact; hope you didn't mind."

Omar is noticeably uneasy when he said, "I guess it's ok. Did you check him out?"

"I did—The company's truck was scheduled to be in this area anyway, like he said, and he had his uniform and I.D. badge on. I was even with him the whole time he was inside. He looked at one other apartment too, but left afterward. He said everything seemed ok with the signal."

"Well, that's a relief. Ok, Fred I'll see you later, thanks."

When he reached his apartment, he dropped his satchel and tossed the envelopes Fred had given him, but decided to finally open the envelope from the Olympic Committee. It's an invitation to succeed Seth as a judge because his tenure is ending. The letter explains the pre-requisites for each candidate but also the perks. The first part of the letter contains a paragraph that includes Seth's recommendation for Omar to succeed him. Omar is flattered but also depressed. He reflects on his treatment of Seth through the years and how it was really undeserved. He thought about how Seth had endured his brow-beating for so long, but never lost sight of what Omar meant to him as his protégé but more importantly, as his blood. Seth obviously felt it was more meaningful then to remain committed to regaining his trust, even while he was being pummeled about his motives. He decides to just sit for a moment to soak it all in.

Clarence was enjoying quiet time with his family just before Nathan got ready for his bath. He was still relishing in the favor that Omar was shown that morning during their visit to Dillon, and how his former nemesis actually became a source of inspiration for him. As he and Melanie sat together on the couch while watching Nathan entertain himself, his phone rang; it was Deputy Bristol returning his call. He told Melanie he would take the call in the other room.

"Deputy Bristol; thanks for calling back."

"Hi, what's so important?"

"I just wanted you to know that the friend I mentioned to you when we spoke last; well, he is in fact the guy that attacked your brother."

Clarence could hear him sighing, feeling that his anger was also about to resurface.

"You're not that surprised are you?"

"I couldn't be sure, and that's the truth. I wanted to let you know though that he and I were actually in Gleason this morning, and the two of us met with your brother at the church where he works."

"How did that happen?"

"I remember seeing him with you the last time I was there, and well, I just had a hunch and stopped while he was outside, to chat with him."

Clarence paused for a moment. "He's a remarkable man. It was clear he had really changed. The two of them talked about what happened and actually made their peace with one another. I have to tell you, it was an amazing thing to witness."

"It's an unusual thing for all of us to grapple with, but that's who he is now, and I guess he wants us to honor that. To be honest, this guy's identity really doesn't matter to me anymore if what you say is true. If Deon has decided to let it rest, then so will I."

Clarence felt he should at least let the deputy know about the meeting between Omar and Deon, and how they seemed to 'bury the hatchet', just in case he had thoughts of interfering with Omar's attempts to truly put the episode behind him with possible threats of vengeance. The deputy's sudden disappearance the day they met was still a curiosity, so he had to ask..

"I've always been curious about you leaving suddenly the day we were at that Bistro for drinks. It didn't have anything to do with this did it?"

"No. My nephew's mother called; said she hadn't heard from either of her sons and wanted to know if I could try and reach them. I don't know why she always bugs me about that. They live and work in Mumford and I live in Gleason. It's not even my jurisdiction. They both work for 'Earth Burst' which isn't exactly a mom & pop operation, if you know what I mean. It should be easy enough to track them down there."

"I'm a Supervisor at Earth Burst; been there for going on three years. What departments do your nephews work in?"

"Well, Blake is an IT Tech, and—" Clarence interrupted.

"Yeah, I met Blake the week he started with us. I didn't know he had a brother that also worked there. We're supposed to have a date on the basketball court soon; nice young man."

"Yeah, he is; a little cocky though. As for his brother, well, it's information better kept under wraps without going into details."

Clarence didn't press but just said, "I understand. I think you and Omar should meet."

"If you say so. I guess I need to sort of purge some negative feelings of my own over this"

"I'll be in touch with you about it as soon as I can arrange a meeting."

"Alright, but I won't hold my breath."

JUST BEFORE THE END of the work day on Wednesday, Omar touched base with Richie to make sure he'd be at the company's park at 4:30pm.

"Hey Richie, its Omar. Just wanted to give you a heads up about rehearsal today. We can just meet you there because I can hitch a ride with Evelyn this time."

"Ok, no problem. I have the other microphones too I told you and Aunt Evelyn about last time, so they should pick up the actors' voices a lot better."

"Ok, that'll work. We'll see you at the park."

Evelyn stopped by his desk on their way to the elevators and asked, "Are you ready?"

He locked his drawer, posted two notes to his board, and then said, "Let's go."

THE REHEARSAL WENT OFF without a hitch as Evelyn had promised. The cast gave themselves a handclap, knowing the actual shoot was the last time they would have to do it. Each of them was already getting set to at least spin what would become a source of overblown nostalgia for each of them for as long as they could breathe life into it; especially for people they knew outside of the Earth Burst family. It might have earned them a little more credibility as amateur performers; but in reality mostly for the fun of it, since the content of the film would speak for all of them in the end. Evelyn gave them 'props' as usual for a great job, and was in the middle of giving them a checklist, including what to wear, and the time to meet on Friday. Omar took a moment to call his friend with his AA group, Noggin, to make sure he could hitch a ride home with him from the meeting on Thursday.

"Hey Noggin, it's Omar."

"Hey Omar, how are you my man?"

"I'm good. Just touching base about that ride home on Thursday after the meeting. Is it gonna be ok?"

"Sure man; I've got you."

"Thanks Noggin. I owe you brother."

"See you tomorrow Omar."

When he hung up with Noggin the group was disbursing, when Richie approached him.

"You need that ride home again Omar? It's ok if you do."

"You're a life saver Richie. Yeah, I sure could man, thanks."

Evelyn tugged Omar on his arm, then said, "You see what I meant now about my nephew, right? He's got you covered in more ways than one."

Omar smiled and said, "That's a fact. Looks like we should be ok for Wednesday's presentation if there aren't any gaffs at the shoot on Friday."

"I'm sure we will be."

"I've decided I want to treat the cast to lunch at 'Bottoms Up' after the screening of the film; maybe Monday or Tuesday. They deserve it. Richie and Theo are invited too."

"Oh, they'll really like that."

"Minus a bar tab of course."

"Of course." She smiled then said, "Well, I'd better hit the road. See ya Richie, and thanks for everything! I'll see you in the morning, Omar."

"Have a good night, Ev."

OMAR'S SLEEP WEDNESDAY NIGHT had been one of his best ever,

without having to get up two or three times to relieve himself. It was obvious his efforts to expel the nervous energy that usually showed up in the form of destructive negative thinking, and at times a weak bladder, was loosening its grip. He was beginning to discover that real trust through friendships won't come, unless he proved himself to be friendly and also trustworthy. He felt that people in his circle were more eager in recent days to open up to him more since he had mellowed some. It made him seem more relevant; more connected. So, with that reckoning he felt his day just might get off to a promising start. When he made it to the bus stop, his greeting to Vick was noticeably upbeat.

"Morning Vick, how is it?"

Omar; you being on time now has gotten to be habit forming."

He rolled his eyes at him and said, "Now that's a habit you ought to keep."

Omar replied, "Oh, I intend to."

When Vick pulled up to Micki's stop, Rupert wasn't there again…

"Hey Mick."

"Hi Omar. You know, it seems kind of odd to not see you chasing the bus down anymore. So what's gotten into you?" She took her seat next to him laughing a little.

"Well, it's not like I got hit over the head or anything you know. I just, woke up I guess; about a lot of things. It's part of my new M.O."

"Whatever you say, but it's a good look. I did hear from Rupert finally. I told him about you agreeing to produce the radio spot for me. I suggested he consider the same thing for himself to sort of get ahead of the curve you know, but his response seemed a little cryptic. He said he did feel that the two of you probably had some unfinished business to take care of anyway. Any idea what he might be talking about?"

Omar got quiet for a moment, feeling more than ever now that Rupert might be his stalker.

He looked away then said, "None whatsoever."

Omar double-timed it from the bus stop to his building. He suddenly felt the need to isolate himself inside one of the restrooms on the 3rd floor that were rarely used, until the nervous energy that drove him there subsided eventually. Most of the office space there had been vacated recently, so it was the perfect hideout. He needed to be at his desk in less than ten minutes. As he splashed cool water over his face, he placed his hands on the counter. An empty stare greeted the image in the mirror. Then moments later the lights dimmed; their luminescence almost non-existent. Suddenly, the flicker of a bright, but momentary flash within the mirror signaled that he was once again under the influence of the 'orphan'. Its image almost super-imposed over his reflection now which was even sharper, except for the movement of its lips when it spoke.

"OMAR, THE TIME IS growing short and I can almost see my way home even from here, but there is one test you have yet to face; maybe the most important of all that will determine if we're ever to be reunited."

Omar responded, "How will I know when the time has come?"

"My hope is that courage will rush in like a flood in what will prove to be your most desperate hour, and that it won't abandon you at the time you will need it the most. I'm counting on the humility you must also possess, to become the trusted ally for that courage once you've reached the crossroads that await you. If your faith truly becomes your armor bearer, then you can be confident that together they will fortify you, and allow you to weather those storms that threaten your own survival. Even so, make sure you will choose to answer the call to service where the lives of others you are destined to touch can be blessed, before your time in this realm is over. Nothing less will do for our reunion to be meaningful; so stay vigilant Omar. I will be watching, and waiting" (The orphan's words faded gradually as before until the connection was broken once again).

THE LIGHTS RETURNED TO normal as he pushed back from the mirror in a cold sweat. He felt he had been transported to another dimension, but his recollection of it was foggy at best. He trusted that whatever impressions it may have left him with, were at least useful. He checked the time and had a couple of minutes to spare before he needed to log on to his terminal. When he reached his floor it seemed to already be humming at midday speed. Just before he made it to his desk Evelyn called to him…

"Morning Mr. Duncan."

"Hey Evelyn. How is it?"

"Just wanted to let you know before you sit, I got a text from Richie; said he'll be leaving town late Saturday morning, but will spend time with editing the film on Sunday to make up, that way we won't lose any time and he should still have it finished by Monday. He also wanted me to remind you about recording all of your narration, and to get it to him no later than 10:00am Saturday; or Friday if it's convenient."

"Richie is really on top of this thing. I like that. He's a pro."

Evelyn said, "Yeah, he is isn't he? So remember that, if he might need you for something."

"Copy that."

Just before he broke for lunch Omar noticed Blake setting up Theo's terminal and stopped to chat on his way out.

Theo said, "Omar, the 'house pro' here wants a rematch."

Omar responded as he looked at Blake, "So soon; I'm still on 'injured reserve' you know." "Look, he's kidding; ignore him. I was just saying, you do have pretty good skills, you know, for somebody your age."

Omar said, "Well, I'm not exactly ready for a rest home, young blood."

"No, I didn't mean it like that."

Omar looked at him with a stern expression, then smiled and said, "I know what you meant." Blake said, "You remind me of my uncle. He's a cop, and he's not that much younger than you, but he's got game too."

Theo asked, "Isn't he the one you said gave you and your brother all that stuff when he was in the Marine Corp.?"

"That's him; gung-ho as hell, but really a decent guy."

Blake was still well into setting up Theo's new work station while he talked. Omar decided to stay for a few minutes and socialize for a change. Blake continued to talk about his uncle, the cop…

"I remember once, when he had just gotten out of the Corp., he bought each of us a pair of those black brogans he used to wear as a T. I. at basic training camp. They even came with those taps they wore that was supposed to sound so cool."

He laughed a little while telling the story.

"I think they were meant to intimidate the trainees myself. I gave him props for thinking about us, but I wasn't really feeling' um; know what I mean? I wear the shoes sometimes, but those taps had to go. I took them off of mine, but my brother still wears his a lot; even with the taps. I think being a cop has always been one of his pipe dreams. He thinks the sound they make is so cool; makes' um sound like they're musical or something the way he talks about it; weird huh?"

Omar suddenly became anxious again after listening to Blake's story about his uncle, and his brother. He thought it odd that Blake would mention the shoes, since the sound of taps seemed to be his stalker's 'calling card'. The news about Blake having a brother was even more surprising. When he took his morning break, he had already decided to call his uncle Seth to thank him for submitting his name to the Pre-Olympic committee.

"Hello uncle."

"Is this Omar?"

"Yes Uncle Seth, it's Omar."

                    James Lloyd

"Well, this is a surprise. Are you alright?"

Seth knew that any sarcasm from him was pointless, even though he felt like heaping hefty doses of it on top of Omar's head at this point. He was strong, but not impervious to the misery Omar had caused him through the years.

Omar responded, "I'm fine; much better now actually."

He paused for a moment, cleared his throat, then said, "First of all I wanted to let you know I opened the letter from the Olympic committee and—I just wanted to say thanks for your recommendation. It would be an honor to serve on the committee."

Seth was quiet; feeling Omar was finally turning the corner on his conflict.

"Well, I'm glad you feel that way. The committee would be honored to have you. Did you call the chairman yet about your decision?"

"I will, probably later today. The other thing I wanted to say was that I saw Deon Tuesday at the church where he works."

Seth was quiet again from being caught off-guard by that revelation…

He then said, "How in God's name did you know he was there?"

"It's kind of a long story uncle. I was there with my Supervisor, who actually invited me to go with him. We chatted for a while but after speaking with him, and how he had changed his outlook about things, it inspired me to see my own situation a lot differently; to finally be honest with myself about my feelings. I'm really sorry for the grief I've caused you uncle, and I hope you can forgive me."

"I've waited so long to hear you say that nephew, and of course I forgive you. You're my blood and nothing trumps that, no matter what. What else did Deon tell you?"

"I think you know the answer to that one."

"Ok then. I'm sorry I've been keeping the fact that he's my son a secret from you for so long. Me and Agnes, we had this—fling before she got married. It was a stupid mistake because she had gotten engaged to her fiancé, just before finding out she was pregnant. That kind of thing you didn't exactly shout from the rooftop, you know what I mean? She was skittish about her 'soon to be husband' being willing to raise a kid that wasn't his own, so we both approached her aunt about taking him; adopting him actually. We felt it was the best move for each of us, but for Deon not so much."

Omar actually became sympathetic toward Deon then, understanding where his rage may have come from. He also knew why Seth and Deon were at Breeland's house after the funeral. When Seth tells him about his grandsons, Omar remembers the little boys at the track and tells him about meeting Blake, but not the other son.

"His name's Nathaniel. We call him 'Nate', and they couldn't be more different even though they shared their mother's womb. Nate has a special condition that makes it not so comfortable to talk about, or deal with."

"How's that?"

"He has special needs that require constant monitoring. Don't get me wrong; we love him just as much as Blake, but they're just different, so let's just leave it at that, alright?"

Omar didn't press him for more information, and dismissed any new animosity toward Seth, and his mom, who must have known about Deon being Seth's son. He thought about his own secret of being bullied by Deon to save himself from embarrassment, so no one was aware he even knew Deon then except Breeland, and even he never knew Deon was his half-brother. Omar did have trouble reconciling how Seth could keep quiet about the incident between him and Deon at Dillon. Seth then makes it clear about how difficult it was for him to keep his feelings under wraps.

"It was hard for me to keep quiet about my feelings after that incident because I loved you both and convicting one to spare the other was no solution in my mind."

Omar realizes at that moment just how deep his uncle's affection for him really is.

He then says, "I think I'll have pretty big shoes to fill by taking your place on that committee Uncle Seth."

"It's good to hear you say that nephew; it really is."

Nelson Bean, from Omar's AA group, is a rascal, but he does seem committed to trying to make attending the AA meetings a priority, even though his real motives could always be called into question. He decides to call his friend, and fellow officer Ronnie Bristol, about needing to miss the beginning of their poker night because of his AA Meeting.

"Hey Ron; just wanted to remind you about me getting to the game late tonight; got my AA meeting you know."

Officer Bristol said, "I didn't forget. I'll let the guys know. We won't mind waiting a little while to take your money."

"Yeah, well you might be eating those words afterward my friend. By the way, I spoke with your nephew, Nate, during the last meeting; told him about this bozo, Duncan, who's a part of this AA group. He practically admitted he was the guy that attacked your brother. I could not believe what I was hearing. It was like a gift being handed to me. I know how you guys have felt about not really knowing who this guy was, so I just thought I'd help the cause, you know?"

The Deputy responded sharply, "I wish you hadn't done that!"

"Why not? What's the big deal? I thought you'd want to know."

"Not my nephew, you understand? Not him. We've all been bitter about what happened to Deon, but we've been keeping it in check, but Nate—Nate is different. Because his bipolar disorder is so aggressive, he's become fixated on avenging his father's attack, for real. I've acted out scenes over and over in my mind of what I would do to him if we were ever face to face, but it never really went any further than that. The truth is, Deon's made his peace with it. I even found out today that he and this guy Duncan actually met and buried the hatchet, but Nate knows nothing about that. Even if he did, I'm not sure it would change his mind about wanting revenge. You've made it much easier for him now Bean, and this could get really messy. You'd better hope this thing doesn't blow up, cause nobody else needs to get hurt or put away over this; especially my nephew. Look, I've got to make a call. I'll see you later."

Chapter 15

O MAR'S DAY SEEMED TO move at a snail's pace once his preoccupation with his stalker took control. He missed both his morning and afternoon breaks, and even took a shorter lunch break to try and keep his mind off of it. The information he had gotten from Micki, then Blake's story about his brother, sent him teetering on the edge of paranoia again. He felt he was no closer to identifying his stalker than when he first surfaced. His frustration however was short lived when the bell tolled at 4:00pm, and he made it to the bus stop on time. His ride home was without Rupert again, but Micki did get a chance to show him what she had in mind for a radio spot. They also discussed Rupert again, since Omar was understandably even more curious about his absence now. Micki gave him the 'skinny' on what she had found out so far.

"I called him about you agreeing to do my radio spot for me but could only leave him a voice message. I even called his sister, who still has his car; said she hasn't spoken to him recently either. She said she even tried reaching out to a few of his friends at the cable T.V. Company he was an independent contractor with; Flexitt Cable I believe is who she said it was, but they have not heard from him either."

Omar knows 'Flexitt Cable Co.' is the same one that handles service for his complex so right away his imagination went into hyper-drive. The possibility that Rupert may have gained access to his place pretending to be a service technician was too outrageous to be believed. He checked out for a minute, as Micki kept calling to him.

She finally shook him and said, "You ok?"

"Oh, yeah, I'll be alright; just a little tired I guess."

After about ten minutes of trying to engage him in conversation, she finally gave up and let him alone. Micki was intuitive enough to know that there was no love lost between him and Rupert, but wouldn't expect it to trouble him so. She knew it must be something deeper for two people who hardly saw each other. It really bothered her not knowing, because she was one person he could relax with. They took shots at each other, but it was playful and one of the endearing things about their relationship. It seemed to insulate them from any real turbulence, but she felt the only way she would find out is if Omar happened to volunteer the information.

She shook him again and said, "Well, I'm getting off, but let me know if you happen to get a brainstorm about the spot and want to call me to talk about it, ok?"

"Alright. I'll do that."

She then said, "And Omar, whatever you want to talk about, no matter what it is, you can call me, ok?"

He gave her a curious look, then said, "Alright Mick. I'll keep that in mind."

His first stop was to the office once he got to his complex. He could at least find out from Fred if the cable company tech fit Rupert's description. He had to know.

"Hey Fred, how is it?"

"Hey man. No mail today, but you should have your new lock for your box by tomorrow anyway."

"Good, but that's not why I'm here actually. Do you recall what that cable company tech. looked like that was here the other day?"

"Yeah; black guy, about 6 feet or so; average build I guess. It was kind of hard to tell how old he might be with his cap on; course I'm not gonna be looking at any 'hardhead' that close anyway, you know? Why'd you ask?"

"Just curious; thought he might be somebody I know. Thanks man." Fred's description still wasn't enough to eliminate Rupert as an imposter. He could still check all the boxes for a positive I.D. of Rupert based on Fred's description; then again, lots of other guys could fit that description too without having more information that might distinguish the technician's features. When he opened the door to his apartment and checked the rooms, he noticed nothing had been disturbed; Plus the fact that Fred did say he was inside the apartment with the guy the entire time he was there, let him relax about it; at least for the moment. Omar placed his phone on the kitchen counter while he took a shower before getting ready for his AA meeting, but forgets to let it charge in the meantime. The battery is at 12 per cent, but he gets a call from Clarence while he's in the shower, who leaves an urgent message.—'Omar, it's Clarence. I just got a call from Deputy Ronnie Bristol, who is Deon's brother. He said it might not be that safe for you right now. There's a guy named Nelson Bean who is part of your AA group that you should steer clear of. This guy Bean apparently told Bristol's nephew about you being Deon's attacker and he may want revenge for the attack; and Omar, the nephew is Deon's son. Call me as soon as you get this message, and watch your back.' When Omar collects his snack for the bus ride to his AA meeting, he picked up his phone but the battery power was already too weak for him to even pull up his voice messages, and he typically experienced dead spots for phone service within a few square miles of the Center where the meetings are held. He was 'flying blind', and was completely unaware of it. During the meeting he noticed Bean's coolness toward him, as if he had suffered the indignity of the beat-down himself that Deon received. Bean does nothing to try and warn him, even after the discussion with Officer Bristol, but instead parades around the room wearing a menacing scowl directed at Omar. Omar notices it, and is made to feel like a new enemy may have him in his cross hairs. He knows he's done nothing to cross Bean. He hardly knows him, except what may have been revealed in front of the group at one of the meetings, which makes his apparent indifference toward him even more mysterious.

Omar had forgotten to turn on his porch light before leaving for his meeting, which provided perfect cover for the figure that entered his apartment around 7:00pm that same night. Only the light from one end of the hallway provided subdued lighting to reveal the silhouette of a tall figure gaining access presumably with a key. Rob, Omar's neighbor, happened to be outside his front door and noticed the man and realized he's too tall to be Omar. Rob immediately called the office to see if Fred answers; he did, but Rob then felt it could be someone Omar had given a key to for access when he's not there; a relative or close friend maybe, and he just hung up. He still didn't feel good about it and called Omar who was about to end his AA meeting, but he gets his voice mail instead. Omar and Noggin are already in traffic and on their way to Omar's place. Omar is already fond of Noggin, and feels they could become good friends.

"Nice ride Noggin. This must have set you back a bit, huh?"

"Not really; found it on an on-line auction site for seized property; got it for pennies on the dollar. It runs like a top, but I can't be sure some drug lord didn't have it before me though." They both laughed about it. Omar checked his phone and noticed his low battery reading.

"Mind if I use your charger? My battery is really low."

"Sure, no problem. Will it work with that phone?"

Omar noticed the shape of the plug, plugged it in and said, "Fits like a glove."

When they reached his apartment complex he unplugged the phone and noticed it was only at 68 per cent, but enough to handle normal traffic without blacking out.

"Thanks for the ride man. See you next time."

Omar noticed messages in cue and pulled up his voicemail. As he got ready to climb the first flight of stairs while waiting for the first message to cue up, he got an incoming call. It was Rob and he decides to answer it.

"Hey Rob, what's up?"

"Hey man, look, I saw someone enter your apartment earlier while you were probably at your meeting. It looked like he got in using a key, and it wasn't Fred."

Omar stopped at the first landing to the stairs while they talked.

"Does anyone else have a key to your place?"

Omar said, "No; No one should have." Omar is immediately put on alert; not quite sure what, or who, might be waiting for him inside.

"Look, you might have an intruder, so why don't you stop by my place before you go up. I have an idea."

"Ok, on my way." When he got to Rob's apartment he was visibly shaken. Rob tells him he'll walk over to his apartment with him, and will be behind him all the way. He then handed him a .22 caliber handgun. He let him feel the weight of it, then showed him how to remove the safety…

"Keep it in your belt against your back, just in case. No need to call out the cavalry just yet, since we don't really know what we're dealing with."

Omar takes a deep breath and says, "I don't think I'll need the gun."

Rob remembers what he told him concerning his attitude about guns, but still feels he should reconsider, since his life could be in jeopardy. He gives Omar a curious look, but knew it was useless to try and force his hand.

Omar then said, "Look, if it comes to that I'll just trust you to react in time."

Seth is really high on the fact that Omar agreed to take his spot on the Olympic committee. The 'passing of the baton' to him is a big deal, and he wants to reach out to each member of the committee individually to discuss what they can expect from his nephew. He's on the phone with one of them when he gets a call from Deputy Bristol.

"I've got to take this other call Jeff, but we'll talk some more later." He picks up Ronnie's Call—"Hey son, how is it?"

"It could be better. I wanted to know if you've been in contact with Nate lately, because no one can reach him. Not Priscilla, not Deon, or his brother. I even called his doctor, but no luck."

"I told Blake the other day I did speak with him by phone some days prior. Blake said he would go by his place if he didn't hear from one of us at the end of his shift that day. I guess he wasn't home then if he did make it there."

"Looks that way. I'm gonna place a call to somebody who might have heard from him. I'll call you if I find out anything."

"Alright son."

Deputy Bristol chooses not to tell Seth about Nelson Bean's call to Nate, and how he already knows about Omar being Deon's attacker. He didn't want to alarm him unnecessarily since he didn't have any real indication of Nate's intent. He decides to call Nelson Bean again instead after he hung up with Seth.

"Hey, it's Ronnie; you still at your meeting?"

"No. I'm on my way to the poker game? Did you bums start without me anyway?"

"I'm not at the game Bean. I'm trying to find my nephew. Nobody's been in contact with him for some days and he hasn't been at work either; thought you may have talked with him again."

"Not since that day I told you I called him." Bean paused, but his tone indicated he really did regret the possibility that Nate might be in serious trouble. "I'm sorry Ronnie—I am."

The Officer opened up to Bean about his nephew's condition since he was at the center of what could prove to be his meltdown…

"I spoke with his doctor earlier who said he was due to have one of his prescriptions refilled but didn't, and it's long overdue; without it, he's like a ticking time bomb."

Bean was really quiet and the Deputy began to breathe heavily.

He then said, "I believe you may have helped set something in motion that could end badly Bean. I really hope I'm wrong about it though."

Seth's motivation to continue lobbying for Omar seemed to tank after speaking with Ronnie. He suddenly had a premonition that Omar's safety might be in jeopardy. Knowing how vocal Nate had been about his father's attack, and his desire to get even loomed larger now than it ever had. He knew there was a lot at stake, and wasted no time calling Ronnie back.

"Hey son, it's me again. Look, I've just got this feeling in my gut about something. Can you meet me at Deon's as soon as you can? I want to get to Omar's apartment to check on him; to make sure he's ok. I know he usually has his AA meeting on Thursdays, but maybe he won't be home yet by the time we get there. I believe it's gonna need to be 'all hands on deck' to rectify this thing that's gnawing at me right now concerning Nate."

Deputy Bristol said, "In that case, I might as well tell you this. One of my friends, Nelson Bean, is part of Omar's AA group and he heard Omar describe an incident that happened involving him at Dillon that was too similar to not be one in the same as Deon's. The only thing missing was the name of the victim. Bean then decided to call Nate to tell him about it, naming Omar as his attacker."

"What!"

"Yeah; said he thought he was helping him finally find a way to vent his anger."

"I knew my instincts were right about this."

"To be honest, I feel the same. Does Deon know you're coming?"

"Not yet, but I'll give him a heads up after we hang up."

"Alright. I'll see you there in a little bit."

Seth tried several times to reach Omar, but kept getting his voice mail. He was afraid the treachery may have already begun to unfold. When Seth reached Deon's place, the Deputy was already there. Deon opened the door before Seth had a chance to even knock…

"Dad, come on in." He turned toward the hallway and yelled, "Ronnie, dad's here!"

Seth tugged on Deon's shoulder then said, "How are you son?"

"I'm worried about my boy, pop." His tone was not unlike someone who might have been mourning the death of a loved one. "I just felt deep down he would have trouble leaving well enough alone. I really hope this is a false alarm pop."

"I guess we'll know soon enough."

Ronnie emerged from the other room and said, "Why don't we take the SUV?"

They wasted no time trying to get to Omar's place before their worst fears were realized.

Rob walked quietly behind Omar as he unlocked the door to his apartment. Rob seemed to have an itchy trigger finger for someone who kept his gun out of sight most of the time. The policeman in him said he should fire his weapon at the slightest provocation; but the friend in him was really hoping it wouldn't be necessary. They both looked around the big area quietly, then toward the bedroom. Rob accidentally bumped the shade to the lamp on a table nearby. Soon after, Omar's bag knocked against a tall figurine filled with lots of multi-colored stems that sat on the floor a few feet from the entrance to his bedroom. The noise from both was hardly unnoticed, proving stealth was not a strong suit for either of them in this case. To say that they were uneasy about not having any idea what peril might be waiting for them would be an understatement. Rob stood against the wall next to the doorway with his hand on the stock of his nine millimeter but still in its holster. Omar walked inside, but then his spirit was suddenly overwhelmed with a sense of calm. It was a peace that caused him to pin his hopes on the final chapter of a painful saga maybe coming to a dramatic end that very hour. He scanned the room with particular care before tossing his bag on the bed. Just as he was about to really relax feeling the coast was clear, the intruder raised up from behind the tall dresser where he had been crouched, patiently awaiting the arrival of his victim. The hood was still over his head, as it was in those times he was spotted by Omar from a distance, except for that one time in the elevator. Omar gasped and became rigid when he saw him. He was speechless as the man slowly removed the hood to reveal boyish features. Neither of them uttered a single word for about a minute. Both of them seemed frozen in time. Rob was becoming more anxious, trying to assess what may be going on inside the silence, but decided to be patient. The man stepped from around the edge of the dresser, as the inward bend of his feet became really obvious, as well as a slight hobble. Omar suddenly recalled those scenes at the track, and the two little boys who would always show up; especially the one who just sat on the bleachers, wagging his legs back and forth while watching the athletes that were coached by Seth. The silence is finally broken when the man speaks…

"You're nothing like I expected."

He looked Omar up and down with obvious contempt.

Omar then asked calmly, "How did you get in here?"

Rob stayed put, but listened intently to their exchange.

The man said, "Why, with a key of course."

Omar stared with a quizzical look, as if he wanted to ask how he was able to accomplish that when he didn't have access to any of the apartment manager's keys. The young man sensed it and decided to oblige him with an explanation.

"I pretended to be a Cable Co. technician and got your property manager to let me in the other day."

"What?"

"Oh, don't hold it against him. He didn't know any better, especially after he saw me in uniform and saw the cable truck outside at the pole."

He moved a little closer to Omar and stood erect, then continued…"I sprayed this plastic resin inside your lock while he wasn't looking. It gave me enough of an impression when it got stiff to just pull it out; almost like a plastic mold. It's not one hundred percent reliable, but I guess in this case, it was."

He smiled menacingly at Omar, moving even closer again. Omar took a few steps back in a defensive posture this time. The intruder continued speaking.

"You've got to have access to the dark web to even get the stuff." He almost boasted about his shrewdness as if it was something to be celebrated.

Omar then said, "I don't keep any money inside the apartment."

"Money? I don't want your money Mr. Duncan." There was no mistaking the violence he was committed to, based on the frown that had suddenly replaced an otherwise passive expression…

"What I want is for you to feel the pain my father felt that day; the pain we've all been living with for years."

Omar's posture stiffened again when the man pulled a Billy club from his back. Omar raised both his hands; posturing for the pelting of his body from the Billy club.

He then said, "You don't have to do this young man."

Rob's adrenaline started racing and he began to breathe heavily hoping he wouldn't be forced to discharge his weapon. Just when he decided it was time to intervene, he waited; once he heard what Omar said calmly to the intruder..

"I know who you are and why you might feel that way. I've been living with my own pain for years too over that incident, and have regretted it every day since." Omar lowered his hands slowly then said, "I used to watch you and your brother as kids at the track with your dad, Deon, and your grandad, Seth."

The young man interrupted, with a surprised look on his face—"How do you know about my grandad?" Omar hoped the man would take his mind off of his plan for retribution and respond to his attempt to diffuse the situation when he continued speaking to him.

"I know what you're feeling. I really do. I had my own bout with needing acceptance when I was faced with my own limitations as a kid, even from birth. What I found out was that, it didn't mean the end of the world for me, even if I didn't eventually outgrow my physical problem. It's taken a while for me to get through the rejection and just not feeling a sense of belonging, but with the help of good friends, and especially family, I've been able to get through it."

The young man's aggression suddenly deflated and he relaxed both arms at his side. He then stared off into the distance; his eyes becoming glassy with tears. It seemed his motivation for being there had suddenly vacated his spirit.

Omar then told him, "Seth is my uncle. My mother, Elizabeth, is his sister; so you see, that makes us, family." The young man seemed almost relieved by the news; his anger being turned inside out with the discovery of his kinship with Omar. He dropped the Billy club and Omar embraced him while he sobbed openly. Rob stepped from behind the wall and secured his weapon. There was also knocking at Omar's front door suddenly; then pounding, and loud voices calling for him.

"Omar are you in there? Omar!"

Omar asked Rob calmly, "You mind answering that for me Rob?"

When Rob opened the door, it was Seth, Deon and Deputy Bristol.

"Hey. Is Omar here? I'm his uncle Seth, and these are my sons, Deon and Ronnie."

"Hi, I'm his neighbor, Rob, and yeah he's here."

Seth then said, "We were concerned about him and decided to drop by since he wasn't answering his phone. Is he ok?"

"Come on in and see for yourselves." When they stepped inside his bedroom, they saw Omar still hugging him. Nate clung to him tightly as Omar spoke to him in his ear; helping him to buffet years of pain over his dad's predicament, but appreciating also how Nate must have wrestled with the pangs of self-pity over his own. The Billy club was on the floor next to them. It had now become a symbol of surrender. The three of them stopped suddenly; a bit petrified by what they were witnessing between Omar and Nate.

Rob then asked the three of them, "What just happened here?"

Appearing noticeably relieved, Deon then said, "A break-through happened."

Omar heard Seth's voice and turned to shake his hand, then a stout hug. Ronnie also shook Omar's hand, knowing it opened the door to reconciling his own feelings.

Deon gripped Omar's forearm and said, "Glad that you're ok." Seth, Deon, and Ronnie seemed to huddle around Nate; hugging him and telling him how everything would be o.k. now. Omar had stepped away when he was approached by Rob.

"Do you want to press charges, because I do have the authority to arrest him you know?"

"No. Never mind that. He's suffered enough. We all have." Rob was at a loss, as he watched Seth, Deon, and Ronnie's behavior with Nate; the three of them picking up where Omar had left off. He didn't know much, if anything, about their story, or Omar's. It was obviously a big mystery to him, but he did feel after that night, whatever ruptures their relationships may have suffered, they were well on their way to being healed. Omar offered them coffee and hot tea while they all sat at his dining room table for a while after the drama had died down. He also invited Rob to stay but he declined, feeling it would have been an intrusion on their much needed family time.

After walking him to the door, Omar said, "Hey, good looking out my friend. Thanks; I won't forget it."

Rob high-fived him and said, "No problem. See you soon, and you guys, look out for one another."

When Omar rejoined them, they felt the need to open up about all that had happened over the years. The conversation was filled with regrets, having dealt a blow to the malice each of them gave birth to at a point in their own lives. It had been nursed to 'full bloom', until truth intervened, wilting their stubborn vows of contempt. It was, in fact, a new beginning.

Trying to escape to some quiet time had always been a chal-lenge for Omar, until now. Being hounded by memories that only stirred his guilt and shame into a frenzy, and at the cost of forsaking his friends and family appeared to be behind him now. Seth, Deon, and Ronnie left with Nate and escorted him back home making sure he arrived without incident since he had been without his medication. Ronnie drove his car home for him, and the three of them pledged before they left that they would always keep him close, as well as each other, no matter the challenges that lie ahead of them. It really was their testament, to always esteem family, and its welfare, above all else. Omar sat on his couch for a while, wondering how things could have turned out; how Rob being in place at that point in time; then Seth, Deon, and Ronnie showing up when they did. It was more evidence that he had never been alone in his struggles. He pitied Nate, feeling his trip inside purgatory may have been hastened had he executed his plan, but he finally understood it had to be the hand of grace that covered them all. He remembered to check the messages he missed when Rob called him earlier once he had made it back from his AA meeting. He picked up Clarence's message warning him about Nelson Bean from his AA group. He decided to call Clarence back right away.

"Omar, you must have gotten my message. Are you alright?"

"Yeah, I'm fine now. A lots happened since you called me though."

"Oh, like what?"

"It's really too amazing to go into detail. I'm still trying to process it all myself."

"Now you're making me uncomfortable. You need anything?"

"No, I'm good. I did want to say I know now I'm a blessed man for having such good friends, and family around me. You being one of them."

"Hey, just glad to be of service. You'll always be my friend first, no matter what's going on between us."

"I know. The guy with the great instincts." He laughed a little. "Hey, speaking of which, whatever happened to that girlfriend of yours way back when you were in high school that you were telling me about, when this thing about your instincts first surfaced? You never got around to telling me the end of that story you know. I know there's another inspirational message in there somewhere."

"Oh yeah, that. Well, turns out I married her. We've been sweethearts ever since. She became even more incredible as we grew older and spent more time together."

Omar cleared his throat, "I thought your wife's name was Melanie?"

"Deloris is her middle name."

Omar then said, "Oh, I see. A little misdirection thrown my way, huh?"

"Well, it wasn't a lie."

Omar then said, "Well, I never would have guessed she was considered a—you know, 'duckling' at one time."

"Believe it or not, it wasn't her appearance that was the problem, but her own self- image that got in the way. It wasn't easy, but she finally trusted me enough to realize I was her friend first, and I cared about what was important to her. The rest just fell into place. It was my good fortune I guess; and like I told you, my instincts weren't wrong about her, and I knew they wouldn't be wrong about you either."

"Amen to that. You know the actual shoot for the video is tomorrow. It's not exactly what you would call a 'closed set', except for the area we asked security to keep spectators out of. You think you might want to come and critique the live performance?"

"Thanks for the offer, but I've got a full plate tomorrow; gotta help wrap up final details for opening day, but thanks for the offer anyway."

"I'll see you tomorrow then. Goodnight boss." After eating a light dinner, he decided to record his narration for the video so he could get it to Richie the next day. When he had finished, he decided to shower and get to bed early. Just before he collected his pajamas, he stepped in front of that full length mirror on an impulse, as if something had driven him there. He stepped close to it and stared; close enough to reach out and touch the glass, then his eyes closed momentarily and the lights dimmed. A bright light within the mirror flashed suddenly like before. He placed his palms on the mirror, then the 'orphan' spoke to him once again; Its likeness of him almost crystal clear this time, and the pitch of its voice was jubilant.

"I'm proud of you Omar. The outcome of your trial was as I had hoped. You've done well. Not far to go now, and remember, never look back." (Its voice eventually faded until it disappeared Again)…

OMAR PUSHED BACK FROM the mirror with a sketchy recollection of what happened. It was, to him, a brief hiccup in time that he couldn't explain; as if he just nodded off briefly, but to the 'orphan' it meant the end of its quest was approaching.

Omar's Saturday morning routine was as typical as ever, including getting chores out of the way, then the usual call to his mom. Friday's filming of the video went off without a hitch, so he could really exhale a little concerning the video production until Richie completed his editing that would include his narration. He did feel somehow, the stars were beginning to align in his favor, and expectations were high over Richie's final product. Expectations were even higher over the relationship he wanted to now have with his extended family. He took a break from his chores and decided to call his mom a little earlier than usual for a dose of inspiration.

"Omar, how are you? I was just getting ready to call you. Are you ok?"

"I'm fine mom."

"Seth called me this morning; told me what happened Thursday night with his grandson. I was so mad. Your father too; not knowing about it until two days later. What if he had injured you?; or worse?"

"No harm was done mom, and that's probably why he didn't

call. It's the same reason I decided not to; just didn't want to alarm you guys unnecessarily. Believe me, had it been a different result you would have been the first to know about it. You didn't beat him up about it too much did you?"

"No, of course I didn't; just a little miffed. The thought of—" She began to choke up a little as she spoke. "If anything had happened to you—well it shook me up that's all."

"It actually turned out much better than any of us would have expected, especially for me. So much came full circle that night, after so many years of groping for answers. It was a miracle."

"Well, your father and I are glad things turned out the way they did. Seth confided in us and said Nate really agonized over Deon's injuries. He said the kid sort of felt his life had been dealt a double-whammy when he considered his own problem. I backed off of my anger a bit, when I realized he needed to just talk about it some."

"Nate's got some things to overcome, but we all agreed to rally around him, to try and help him get there."

"Seth also said Deon had researched what orthopedic specialists might be able to help correct the problem with his feet, but no procedures exist yet that any insurance company would be willing to cover. Oh, he also told me you decided to accept the invitation from the Pre-Olympic committee about the judge's position. He said you have an interview with them soon. It's good you're getting involved again son."

"Yeah, it'll be good to be back in the game. You know, they even pay me a stipend, and I've decided I'm gonna set up a fund for Nate with part of it so maybe he can get that corrective surgery he'll need. I'll do some research of my own too. There's got to be a plan out there that can help someone like him."

"That's great Omar. So when did you decide this?"

"Just now actually."

"Ahh—you're such a good son."

"I'd better get back to it mom. You know it's always good talking to you. Tell dad hello for me, ok?"

"I will; Love you son."

Omar had gotten Clarence's blessing for sponsoring lunch at 'Bottoms Up' for the cast on the video that Monday. He was also Omar's point man for getting the ok from the Supervisors of the cast to even participate. Needless to say, it wasn't exactly a tough sell. It was an opportunity the cast took to bond outside of work. Even Omar decided not to waste the chance, but let them see a side of himself that was hidden from view for years until then. Nadine's inquisitive nature wasn't about to let her hold her tongue for long, so she had to ask.

"So Omar, where has this version of you been hiding all this time?" Then she started to laugh, and so did he along with everyone else. He hadn't suddenly become a 'social animal', but the change in his behavior was certainly a pleasant surprise for everybody. They began to surround him like some new celebrity; thankful for the gratitude he had shown them for their good work. The chatter directed at him alone was pitched like the hum of an engine; voices within the chorus, but each wanting to be heard. Because of the emotional rush it gave him, he appreciated more than ever how much he had been missing. Before the work day ended, he told Evelyn about the confirmation for the presentation at Dillon during that upcoming week, and that he would expect Richie's call later that day about screening the final product which included his narration. "Not far to go now Evelyn." He had no idea how meaningful that phrase really was, considering what was in store for him, and the 'orphan.

That Wednesday morning Evelyn and Omar drove to Dilllon to meet with Priscilla and her team for their presentation. They were punctual, and so was Priscilla this time when they arrived at the Visitors Center.

"Priscilla, good seeing you again. This is my associate, Evelyn Beacham."

"Pleased to meet you Evelyn."

"Likewise." Evelyn had no idea Priscilla was the one that got away. Omar was cordial, but strictly professional. Whatever doubts she may have had before about his performance were erased in an instant. Richie's work on the video was exceptional. It happened to be the centerpiece of their presentation, except for the set up before by Evelyn, and the Q & A session led by Omar afterward. The video even received applause from the group, then a Q & A session followed that didn't seem to want to end. Omar and Evelyn both had command of the systems features and turned out to be an effective tag-team when they fielded questions. When the session had ended, they conversed informally with an aid and Priscilla for a few minutes.

"That was a solid pitch you two. The video really sold it." Her aid nodded in agreement.

"I think Earth Burst will be awarded our sponsorship, even though no formal announcement has been made to your program coordinator yet. Based on the group's reaction, I don't think you'd get any 'no' votes."

"That's good news. Clarence will be pleased to hear that."

Evelyn then said, "Thank you for your support. It's really appreciated." She also got wind of the body language between Priscilla and Omar that signaled to her, they'd like to have a moment in private, so she excused herself for a restroom break, while they talked.

"I met your other son last week, under less than ideal circumstances."

"I know, and I'm sorry you had to go through that with him. I really am."

"How'd you find out?"

"I called Deon, just to check on him and he told me about it." She looked away in disgust and said, "The perils of bad blood I guess."

"Hopefully that will change now, for all of us." He kissed her on the cheek and gently held both of her hands as Evelyn was coming back into the room. He collected their laptop and printed materials then said, "You have a pleasant day Ms. Eagan. Thank you for the endorsement, and hope to hear from you soon."

"You will. You have my word." As they were walking out, Priscilla's fantasies truly took her to unchartered territory. She actually began to think, maybe Omar really was the one that got away.

On the way back Evelyn felt like basking in their success at Dillon by re-enacting some of the group's responses to the film, and some questions that could best be described as comic relief. Omar was not dialed into it as she had hoped. He instead seemed subdued for the most part which depressed her a little. She was hoping he would be as animated as she was about it, but it was clear his attention was on something else, or someone else. He did at least compliment her for a superb job when the presentation was over. It would have deflated her ego had he not said anything to her before handing her a 'brick wall' to keep her company, so she let him alone. After about half an hour, he seemed to come to life again when he decided to call his mom.

"Hey mom."

"Hi son. Odd for you to be calling again so soon. Everything ok?"

"It's fine. Just wanted to let you guys know I got a letter from the DMV yesterday, letting me know my license suspension is almost up and I needed to contact them next week to find out what fees I needed to pay to get them reinstated. I forgot to call you about it last night. I'll see if I can get someone on this end to get me to the DMV, then I'll plan to maybe catch a bus or something to pick up the car that same week, but I'll give you a heads up."

"I know you'll be glad to be back in the saddle won't you?"

"Yes mam, that's a fact. It will at least start up won't it?"

"Will it start? Your father pampers that thing like it's some priceless antique. Must be one of those 'way past mid-life crisis' things going on with him." They both laughed about it.

"Well, as long as I don't have to tow it home, I'm good with it. Just glad you guys could hold it for me. I'll talk to you this weekend. Maybe, I can speak to dad too for a change."

"He'd like that, especially after what's happened. Take care son."

That afternoon, Clarence met with Omar and Evelyn in his office about the success of the sponsorship. They had exceeded his expectations based on the call he received from Priscilla ahead of her official written endorsement.

"Ms. Eagan was really impressed with the two of you. I got a call from her just before lunch; called you the 'dream team'. Said you had great chemistry, and you should be considered as permanent ambassadors for the company's initiatives."

Omar said, "Are you serious?"

Clarence said, "I'm serious. She was suggesting there should be a newly created exempt position for 'company ambassadors' who would concentrate mainly on developing the company's public relations brand. She said she has a program model for that very thing that they've been experimenting with, that she could show us. She also said the two of you should be considered to lead that effort. How do you feel about that?"

Omar spoke right up without hesitation, "I'm in. How about it Ev?"

"So am I. I've been wanting to do something different, and more challenging anyhow."

Omar said, "So what's next? He and Evelyn had serious expressions on their faces as if they were enticing Clarence to make sure he took steps to make it happen.

Clarence then said, "I'll have to run it by Corporate, and I may have to enlist Priscilla's help in making a case for it but as far as I'm concerned, the two of you may have new job titles in your future soon."

Omar and Evelyn high-fived each other. Omar then said, "Way to go Ms. Beacham."

She responded with, "Back at you Mr. Duncan."

"There's a nice incentive I didn't mention when I recruited you for this, but it's coming soon too."

Omar then said, "Whatever that incentive is, we'd like our

producer, Richie, to be a part of it. His work on the film was special, and he shouldn't be overlooked. Is that alright boss?"

"I can probably do that. Well, I've got a meeting, but I'll keep you posted on details about the ambassador position as they come down the pike."

When they left Clarence's office, Evelyn suddenly hugged him around his neck…

He said, "What was that for?"

"For thinking about Richie when Clarence mentioned the incentive. That was thoughtful of you."

"It's only fair. He poured it all out for us; for me especially when he didn't have to. He deserves no less."

She looked at him sideways with a flirtatious smile then said, "I think I'm gonna like the new you."

The bus ride home had the full complement of riders this trip, including Rupert. Micki was in her usual upbeat mood. She only ran on one speed at least that was the version she felt people would be most comfortable with.

"Hi Mick."

"Mr. Duncan; any ideas for my radio spot yet?"

"Not yet. You know, if you want, we can plan a strategy session maybe on the weekend when we have more time. Why don't you call me and let me know what day?"

"You'll give up your weekend, for little old me?" He laughed, and so did she.

He then said, "Anything for you Mick."

She yelled at Rupert who was three rows back—"You hear that Rupert? I'm holding him to it too." Rupert struggled to smile, then just turned away. Omar got out of his seat, and sat next to him…

"You know, Micki told me about the help you're getting with the mentoring group for your business too. If you want, why don't you join us for the session we're gonna set up to work on her spot. You might find it beneficial too."

Somehow Rupert felt it wasn't just a line of 'B.S.' from Omar but got a vibe that told him he was a changed man.—"Ok, it's a bet."

Omar said, "Make sure you stay in touch with Mickie about the day and time, ok?"

"Alright, man." They fist-bumped just before Rupert and Micki's stop was coming up. Omar said, "Maybe I'll see you guys in the morning then."

Just before Micki and Rupert went their separate ways after getting off the bus, he stopped her and asked, "Look Mick, I know I haven't been on the bus in a while, but he's obviously not the same Omar I've gotten used to. So what's gotten into him?"

Micki replied, "Life got into him that's all, and that's a good thing; so smile!"

Fridays' interview with the Pre-Olympic Committee was one he actually looked forward to. It was literally a second chance to distinguish himself in the sport. Seth was also at his side. From the look of them, the youngest member in the group was probably at least fifteen years older than Omar. He wasn't intimidated though by what seemed, on its face, a wiser and more seasoned panel. He approached the interview like he decided he would with every new thing in his life from then on. It was just one of many new challenges he would face, but was confident he could win. The committee was really impressed with his knowledge and dedication to the sport, especially having been away from it for so long. The chairman asked if he had anything he wanted to say when they were done questioning him. Omar stood slowly before speaking; eager to relieve himself from the weight of his confessional.

"Yes, I would like to say something. When I was competing many years ago in high school, I responded to my impulses first, instead of listening to much wiser men. I had hopes of being selected by this committee back then, but I made foolish choices and squandered my chances of ever competing at the Olympic level. For many years I blamed others for having lost that opportunity. I guess I let my sensibilities escape me, for years actually, but Seth never gave up on me; not only because he's my uncle, but also as my coach and mentor. He saw something bigger in me than I ever saw in myself." He looked away and smiled a little, then continued—"I've come to realize it's important to really listen to those voices of wisdom, in whatever form they choose to enlighten you. It's what's helped me get to this point in my life. That's why I truly believe my experiences give me a unique perspective on how important it is to preserve the gift athletes are given; recognizing the results of disciplined training along with raw talent, and athletes who appreciate the role coaches play in developing that talent. I know Seth's time here will probably be at least one benchmark I'll need to aspire to as a judge, but I can promise you, if you give me the opportunity, it'll be a responsibility I will never take for granted."

His remarks gave the impression, to some of them, there was a deeper spiritual meaning for him based on their body language. He received a unanimous endorsement once the vote was taken. When the interview was over and he had a chance to mingle with some of the other judges, he and Seth stayed not long afterward before getting on the road to head back to Omar's place.

"Looks like I'd be the baby in that group Uncle Seth."

"You would be, but don't let that discourage you."

"It hasn't. They seem like a really good group."

"They are, and it's not like you only serve for a couple of years or so. You almost have to get booted out, unless you decide to leave voluntarily; and tenure has its perks you know. Oh, and thanks for the sendoff, but they were kind of already aware of our history."

"Oh really?"

"Not as detailed as you laid it out, but you came across as more credible because of your honesty about it."

"I can live with that. That stipend's not so bad either."

"Exactly; pays to have some years under your belt in this thing."

"I told mom I already decided I want to put some of that aside, to try and help Nate get that surgical procedure to try and straighten his feet. There's got to be a medical plan that can help him foot the bill, at least some. I also wanted to talk to Deon about what I'd like to do for him."

"That's mighty noble of you nephew. That's one of the reasons I wanted you to take my place on that committee. I always knew your true heart was somewhere inside that tangled mess of a disposition all those years; So, I just waited for you to show up again, and here you are, finally." Seth smiled broadly, and so did Omar. Seth then said, "You know, we could always use you on the coaching staff at the 'Combine'; got a few guys rotating out and it's another paid gig. You won't have to quit your day job either."

"Ok, let me think about it. I guess this is what it looks like when the heavens begin to open up for you, huh?"

"Something like that, but you've always been blessed. You just needed to say no to that thing that kept you pressed down by the dead weight of lies, because there's really no substitute for real life that truth can bring. Believe me I know about it, because I had to deal with that same conflict concerning my son." There was silence as they both just looked straight ahead to reflect again on the 'inconvenient truth' about themselves they both seemed to have survived.

Omar looked at his uncle and said, "You're a good man Uncle."

Seth responded like his coach and said, "Just make me proud when you take my place on that Committee."

"Yes sir. You know, our festival opens next week. Why don't you, Deon, and Ronnie come up on opening day? We're gonna be showcasing the company's new technology. You can come with mom and pop. I'll tell Blake and Nate about it when I see them at work. Maybe, we can all, 'hang out' later."

"If we can go bowling, I'm game. I've got to try and get even with your father, you know."

"Yeah, mom told me about you two. I'll look forward to seeing you two titans go at it myself."

They both laughed a little. Seth said, "I'll let the boys know about it."

"Alright, sounds like a plan." When Seth dropped him off at his apartment complex, they fist-bumped like they always used to do in parting, then said their goodbyes. Once Omar was inside his apartment, he placed his mail on the counter and headed for the bedroom. The imprint of the Billy club left lying on the floor that night seemed just as vivid. It was an ominous casting of shadows suddenly, over his new found serenity; but just as quickly it was gone. The sorrows that justified his bondage for so long, had finally come to an end. He instinctively turned and stepped in front of the full length mirror. As he stood there, a bright but momentary glint was noticeable in his eyes. He stared for only a moment, but realized what had just taken place. The light pulsed in sort bursts, then gradually disappeared signaling the success of their reunion. He studied his features carefully, realizing the distortion between them had finally disappeared. He casually stroked his beard with a look of contentment on his face, then said aloud, "Hello Orphan, and welcome home."

THE END

About the Author

James Lloyd is a fiction writer whose passion for writing began 50 years ago as an Airman in the U.S. Air Force. His enlistment was at the height of the Vietnam War, when he was trained as a Communications Specialist. During his four year term in the military, and because of his career specialty, he worked continuous shift rotations for three years. Even though his attitudes about a number of things was accompanied with some bitterness, the time during lulls on the night shift made room for his writing. It became the perfect vehicle to express his views about government, relationships, and mixed reviews about the military. Fortunately, along the way he had good friends and mentors, besides a close knit family, that allowed him to gain much needed perspective. His return to civilian life was as he had hoped; with a more purposeful pursuit of a college degree, and ultimately earning his B.A.A. Degree. His passion for writing though never diminished after getting married and starting a family. He even volunteered to become a 'special reporter' for his employer's newsletter, New Horizons; which included a segment he created called Poet's Corner. As a husband and father, his writing became more personal and reflective. He began to pin written portraits as tributes to those personalities that had, or were having, an endearing impact on his life. As the dynamic of his life changed he learned to adapt to numerous challenges along the way, and appreciated even more the strong spiritual foundation that was provided by his family through the exercise of faith, as well as the reliance on grace to impact his circumstances in a powerful way.

His first book, 'Keys, Portraits of Trials & Truth', published in 2019, is available through Amazon Kindle, Ingram Spark, and Barnes & Nobles. It is a testament to the value of embracing our spiritual gifts (as depicted through the lives of the three protagonists featured in the stories), and the real dividends that follow when we become committed to using those gifts in service to others. He fully expects his exploration into fiction writing will allow him to showcase this theme, as well as stories about resiliency of the human spirit, for years to come.

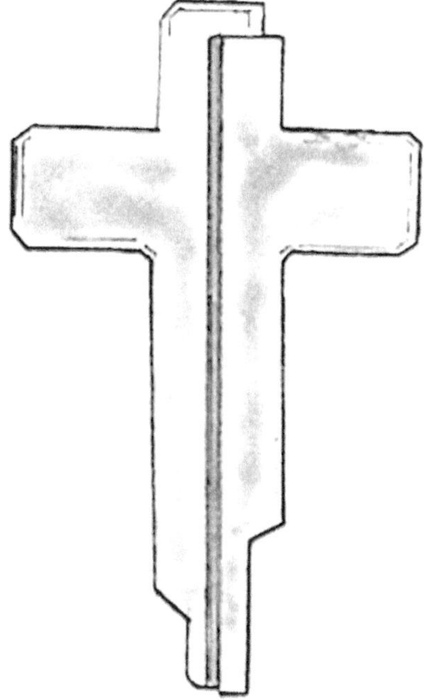

Romans 8: 28

'And we know that all things work together for good, to
them that love God, to them who are the called
according to his purpose'